Marvin Plotnik
and the
Sandy Rivers Hilltop Ranch
for
Wayward Youth,
Juveniles, and Young Adults

A Novel*

*(Or Something Very Much Like One)

WRITTEN AND ILLUSTRATED BY

D. S. Thornton

MONKEYPOD
monkeypodpubs.com

KEA'AU, HI

MARVIN PLOTNIK AND THE SANDY RIVERS HILLTOP RANCH
FOR WAYWARD TEENS, JUVENILES, AND YOUNG ADULTS

For Donald.
Patience beyond words.

*If you can accept the universe as
matter expanding into nothing that is something,
wearing stripes with plaid comes easy.*

—ALBERT EINSTEIN

A Completely Avoidable Introduction...

...in Which We Thumb Our Noses
at Literary Convention,
Tell More Than Show,
Delve Into Our Young Hero's Formative Years,
and Have a Nice Piece of Cake

MARVIN PLOTNIK was one smart-ass kid. If his mother were to ask, "Has anyone seen the peanut butter?" Marvin might look up from his bowl of Nut Crunchies and answer something along the lines of, "If you must know, I'm holding it between my buttocks," or, "Perhaps it was purloined by a band of toast fiends," or simply, "Have you looked under 'P'?"

His mother would then say something along the lines of, "How in the world did I raise such a smart-ass kid?" or "Sheesh."

If Marvin were to pull this kind of thing on his father, his father would do something very typical of fathers: he would roll his eyes, slowly shake his head, and leave the room.

Now up until the time Marvin was in the ninth grade — when he was carted off in a rickety old bus bound for Something He Never in a Million Years Would Have Imagined (and where we shall join him in the exciting plot-driven world of Chapter One) — he was expected to abide by the conventions of a rather uneventful public education. Key word: *expected.*

If we were to begin with first grade, for instance (as of course young Marvin did), we'd find on the first day of school his teacher taping pictures from a nature magazine on the board. The first picture was of a snow leopard, which is not a leopard made of snow but is a leopard that lives much of its life *in* snow. The second picture was of a blue-footed booby, which is not a booby in the hot-chick-in-a-bikini sense, but is a specific kind of bird found on the Galapagos Islands whose wide webbed feet are a striking shade of blue. (Seriously. Look it up.) The third picture on the board was of a chimpanzee dressed in a dashing red fez, which is a tasseled hat worn by funny old men called "Shriners" who like to ride around in teensy-weensy cars in municipal parades.

Pointing to the board, the teacher asked, "What do these three things have in common?" Almost all the first-graders raised their hands. "They're animals," one boy said. "They all have babies," one girl suggested. "They all have eyes," said another. It was only after Marvin came up with, "They all have tasty caramel centers" — after pointing out there were actually four items on the board, if you included the fez — that this particular teacher knew the boy with the oversized glasses was going to be trouble.

In second grade, during a video called *A Journey Through Time,* Marvin took one look at the rudimentary cave drawings of Early Man and blurted out, "How do we know the animals back then didn't really look like that?"

A lesson on Christopher Columbus in third grade prompted him to straighten his glasses and inquire, "How much would a trip like that cost today, adjusting for inflation?"

Fast-forward to middle school, where Marvin's sixth-grade math teacher posed the question, "What is the circumference of a circle with a diameter of four inches?" Naturally, Marvin had no trouble with the answer. The problem was that not only did he say, "12.56" (by multiplying 4 by 3.14, which as you know is the way to calculate circumference), but he felt compelled to add, "provided you are going clock-wise."

You get the idea. It wasn't that Marvin was *trying* to be contrary — he simply had a hard time controlling himself.

Speaking of which, this is as good a point as any to bring up the fact that Marvin Plotnik and your devoted narrator have much in common. We are made, as they say, of the same stuff. I do not mean this literally, although, if one were to analyze our internal chemistry, the combined components of which could *en toto* be traced all the way back to the Big Bang, one might be able to make that argument. No, what I mean is that your devoted narrator also has a hard time controlling himself. No doubt you've already noticed my somewhat unconventional habit of interjecting tangential (and sometimes parenthetical) remarks. So far you've witnessed only slight asides, but I'm taking this opportunity, from the get-go, to warn you: it gets worse.

Of course, this depends on what one means by "worse," but please assume by this I mean "at the most inopportune moments" — like, for instance, this one. Just when you are riding merrily along, sucking in a refreshing lungful of captivating prose, enjoying the scenery, I just might poke an overly digressive nose in the door with a tidbit of Tremendously Impressive Information and, on occasion, How it Fits Within the Fabric of the Universe. I'll even throw in the initial caps.

You'll be glad to know that most of the time my nose-poking (that's nose *poking*, not nose *picking*) will be confined to the bottom of the page, but sometimes, I concede, it won't.[1]

1> Allow me to point out that on the planet Glorfyndrak — some 22.23 light-years away — books not only have footnotes, but footnotes serve as the primary text. So when I say "unconventional habit," I mean of course "by Earth standards." Not that I'm from the planet Glorfyndrak; God forbid. But if a book on Glorfyndrak were to include anecdotal notations about one-armed acrobats, President Richard Nixon's *faux pas* on the island of Mua'ago Pago, Serubian Bog Oil, Space-time Connibulators, heroic Bhutanese monks, the Great Wall of China, Shakespeare, Spanish Conquistadors, and the true makeup of the rings of Saturn — as this one does — such a book would be the norm. On Earth, not so much.

Why, you may ask, is that? I, I might answer, have absolutely no idea.

It's *your* planet — you tell me.

These asides are known in the trade as "experto crede" [*ex-PARE-toe CRAY-duh*] which is Latin for "trust in the expert," or "believe one who has had experience," or, more to the point, "your devoted narrator knows what he is talking about so please do not write his publisher disapproving letters. They hate that." Which means, dear reader: I am not, as a Great Literary Figure once said, making this stuff up.

I do not do this to cause you trouble. I do this because, like our illustrious hero Marvin Plotnik, it is in my nature. (You've heard of recessive genes? Think of these as *digressive* genes.) Because where I come from — *not* Glorfyndrak — not only do we interrupt ourselves, we interrupt our interruptions. Sometimes we even interrupt our interruptions of our interruptions. Sometimes we do it because we must, and sometimes we do it just to "pass the time" (which, you will discover some two-hundred-plus pages hence, is a very amusing phrase).

Mostly, though, we do it because where I come from, we understand the Nature of the Universe, and by this I mean the Interconnectness of All Things, and by this I mean, "If you don't pay attention, you're going to be missing something," i.e., even the tiniest fact might come in handy later on. (I know, because I personally wrote down what happens later on.) Meaning I did not go to this effort without fully intending each word count, including that one on page 215 that gave my editor such a hissy fit. I mean, *really.*

Anyway, I do apologize. I know you people aren't used to this sort of thing.[2]

2> Look, if it's just too much trouble to move your eyes south a few measly lines — or tap a lousy little number on a screen — go ahead, close the book, crack open some Cheese Doodles, boot up an RPG and pretend you're lost in Medieval Japan. Argue online with a complete stranger about who's the bigger dick-wad. Spend all your Swordcraft gold on virtual loot. Update your MyFace page. Post some videos of your dog's rear-end and how it looks like it's talking when the poor thing has hiccups (the dog, not the rear-end). See how many marshmallows you can cram in your mouth. Watch "Spongedude." Whatever.

For the rest of you, I suggest you do what you've already done, evidenced by the fact you're

Now. Where was I? Ah yes, Marvin Plotnik …

As much as young Marvin liked to think his imaginative wit enamored him to his classmates (after all, they did giggle from time to time), in truth, it did not. In fact, at one particular point, i.e., third grade, the other kids in Marvin's class at Harmony Hills Elementary School were so *un*-enamored, they started to call him names. Specifically, "Martian Sputnik" — which certainly wasn't a very clever play on "Marvin Plotnik," but they were third-graders and that was the best they could do. They didn't care if it meant anything. They just thought it was goofy-sounding, like "smidgen" or "rural" or "Sheboygan."

It's a wonder, when you think about it, that Marvin's fellow third-graders even knew the word "Sputnik" — let alone "smidgen" or "rural" or "Sheboygan" — but apparently they did, because in no time there wasn't a third-grader at Harmony Hills Elementary School who didn't use the name, sometimes accompanied by a well-flung Cheese Doodle. (Those of you who took the time to read the chapter on space exploration in your Social Studies textbook like you were supposed to instead of fighting the Gorgons in level four of *Dragon King III: The Crusade,* will recognize *Sputnik* as the first satellite in space, launched by the Soviet Union long before Marvin or any of his fellow third-graders were born … and even longer before the Soviet Union went the way of the dinosaur, and *way* before satellites were used for beaming pay-per-view pro-wrestling matches and monster truck rallies and scantily-clad cheerleaders bouncing about on trampolines.)

Luckily, nicknames grow as people grow. A good nickname by, say, sixth grade might be "The Nickster" for Nick, or "Jack-o" for Jack, or "Goober McMuncherbrain" for Sam Raczkowski. By college you might

---

reading this sentence, which is to join me in my tiny-type digressions and celebrate the Magic of the Literary Footnote. Then later we can all meet at Denny's, make fun of the chowder-heads who bailed, and have a nice piece of cake.

Oh, one more thing: There will be — and I'm not kidding about this — a test at the end. Spelling counts.

run across classmates with names like "The Brewmeister" or "Captain Love Muffin" or "The Patron Saint of Bore," depending on what dorm you land in and/or who your friends might be and/or whether or not you're a liberal arts major. Later, in the real world, depending on what end of the economic spectrum you find yourself, you're either going to hear names like "That Weird Guy Down in Accounting" or "He Knifed His Cousin Joey." The good news is that by the time you're paying off a 30-year mortgage and ruing the day you skipped grad school, you will have all but forgotten whatever nickname your fellow third-graders came up with or the heartbreak it created.

Sidenote: Pity one Harry Butz, a young man who was fortunate enough to attend the fine public schools of Montgomery County, Maryland, from 1982 to 1994, but unfortunate enough to be named Harry Butz. Clearly a lifelong cross to bear. It's no wonder, saddled with such a woefully dreadful curse, by high school Harry started going by "Iceweasel," the unpropitious eventual outcome of which resulted in an ugly after-hours altercation at Tommy's Tats tattoo parlor in East St. Louis and a term of ten-to-twenty-five. During which Harry was known as "Sweetcakes" more than anything else.

Anyway, the name "Martian Sputnik" followed young Marvin all the way to the sixth grade when he began to attend Sunrise Valley Middle School. Here, when no one had bothered to come up with anything better, he began to call *himself* Martian Sputnik. He even signed his papers "Martian Sputnik." He was so proud of the name, in fact, that should a teacher call on him in class — "Yes, Marvin?" — he would feel it necessary to point the error of her ways. *"Martian,"* he would say in a slightly corrective tone, after which (more often than not), the teacher would roll her eyes and slowly shake her head and wonder why she hadn't gone into a nice safe field like commercial real estate.

Why would Marvin Plotnik embrace a name that was clearly meant to ridicule? If he were ever asked (and he never was), Marvin would be happy to point out that taking the name *Martian* as his own was akin to the American Colonists adopting the name "Yankees" during the Revolutionary

War, which really was a word the British used to make fun of them. ("Yankee," not "Revolutionary.")[3]

Marvin, you see, considered his nickname a badge of pride. After all, no one had come up with one for Suzie-Jean Fritz, or ShiVelle Lewis, or even Niancé Flogmartin — which you'd think would be *naturals* — so in Marvin's mind the mere fact that he had a nickname at all meant he'd been singled out as someone special. Which he was ... just not in the sense he imagined.

It was in the seventh grade, then, that Marvin — or, rather *Martian* — having just turned 13, decided it was high time he made the name legal and announced as much to his mother.

"Fine," she said, resting a dish-soap-laden hand on her hip. "You just take the R bus downtown, march into the courthouse and fill out the necessary papers." Which is what Marvin did, even though his mother was being facetious, which means she was being a smart-ass herself, but for some reason after you turn 21 they have special words for that kind of thing.

But a funny thing happened as Marvin waited in line at the local County Clerk's office in Portland Cement City, Illinois (which was where Marvin and his parents lived). As he began to fill out the form entitled PETITION FOR NAME CHANGE, he had an idea:

Even though "Martian Sputnik" had a nice ring to it, this idea went, it wasn't the most practical of names. As long as he was taking the steps, he

---

3> Apparently in 1773 "Yankee" was a pretty funny word. They laughed about a lot of different things back then, like posing in comical "tableaus" or carving molars out of Douglas fir. Then there was that whole dressing up like Indians thing and tossing perfectly good foodstuffs into the harbor. You probably had to be there to get that one. Today, we might not laugh about that sort of thing (today, tea-throwing is Serious Business), but we might get a good chuckle over grown men prancing about in powdered wigs and buckles the size of wombats — on their shoes no less — which evidently in 1773 no one thought remotely out of place.

Ergo, humor changes.

Which explains, you know, Jim Carrey.

might as well take more useful, i.e., profitable, steps (an act which, you will come to find, is very much appreciated on my planet, and, you will also come to find, is the very kind of thing that brought Marvin Plotnik to our attention in the first place).

So, as Marvin filled out the petition papers, in the space where one is to enter the name one wishes to be called, Marvin wrote: *"E Pluribus Unum,"* which needless to say is a phrase that appears on U.S. currency, and, for all I know, other forms of currency I've yet to encounter. In the space at the bottom of the form, where one is to write one's reasons for one's desire to change one's name, Marvin wrote: "So that legal tender in these United States shall, from this day forward, being in my name, be the property of same, *ergo, ipso facto, esto perpetua,* yours truly," under which he signed *"E Pluribus Unum"* with a grand flourish, as though the Great State of Illinois had already granted him its right of use. Here the phrase *"ergo, ipso facto, esto perpetua"* can be translated as, "therefore, by the fact itself, let it be forever," which is impressive as all get-out, but frankly a bit of overkill. The fact that Marvin included it anyway is noted here to illustrate that at 13 years of age, the boy still had not learned when to keep his mouth shut (or in this case, pen).

Of course, *"E Pluribus Unum"* is itself a Latin phrase, which is why it is printed in italic. It means "from many comes one," which the Founding Fathers intended as, "from many people we have united into one," but which Marvin, filling out his name-change form, intended as, "What used to be your money really should be my money." (Why some people choose to use Latin is anyone's guess. In all likelihood the user doesn't speak it with any degree of fluency. And the vast majority of people who *do* are by and large pretty much *deceased* and aren't doing much of anything these days, let alone speaking. Which is why Latin is considered a "dead language," i.e., if you understand it, you are probably dead yourself, or working in the bowels of the foreign language department. Which is basically the same thing.)

Anyway, Marvin's PETITION FOR NAME CHANGE was subsequently and emphatically stamped DENIED by a Duly-Certified Officer of the

Court, and, as if to make a point, was stamped DENIED not only a second
time, but a third time as well. In giant, blaring ALL CAPS. It was also
returned postage-due, which shows just how kindly the State of Illinois
takes to frivolous requests. You can ask a certain ex-governor about that
one.

It should be clear by now that Marvin Plotnik acted as though the
world were his oyster, a decidedly weird phrase I might point out,
considering the planet doesn't even resemble an oyster. I'd go into how the
Earth (which is big and green and blue and particularly sparkly after a
good April shower) compares with an oyster (which is small and hard and
craggy and particularly smooshy inside), and how oysters are for eating,
whereas the Earth is not (unless one were to have tremendously large
teeth, intestines and all that) but it would take up too much narrative real
estate, so I'll leave it at that.

What I mean by "Marvin acted as though the world were his oyster,"
or at least what resulted from it, was that Marvin's teachers, quickly
learning that a raised hand from young Marvin would prove to be time-
consuming at the very least, called upon him less and less as the days of
the school year progressed; and every year, inevitably, his teacher would
reach the point of thinking no job was worth putting up with this
nonsense.

Let us go back third grade, shall we, where it happened in "Science
Corner." The class was asked to bring in three different samples of flowers.
When it was Marvin's turn to stand in front of the room with his three
small paper sacks, he proudly emptied each sack onto the teacher's desk
and announced, "This one is whole wheat. This one is one is rye. And this
one is stone-ground." Mrs. Hammerstein, Marvin's third-grade teacher,
was sitting at her desk at the time, so you can imagine how put out she was
as the contents of each bag reached said desk in increasingly copious
proportions while clouds of flour dust filled the air. If Mrs. Hammerstein's
hair wasn't already white, it certainly would have been. She was so angry,
anyone in the room could have told you, it actually looked like steam was
coming out of her ears. Out the door Marvin went, ear firmly ensnared in

Mrs. Hammerstein's iron-and-flour grip, white clouds poofing from the folds of her skirt. "You know perfectly well I said *flower*, not *flour*," Mrs. Hammerstein squealed. "It's off to the principal you go."

And just so you get the point that Marvin's mouth had no concept of when to stop, at the principal's office, when he was asked what he intended to accomplish with such a stunt, Marvin replied: "Ratings."

Yet, despite having a keen grasp of every subject, Marvin was considered a bad student. Which, if you asked him, was totally unfair. Because unlike Suzie-Jean Fritz, who couldn't stay awake in class, or ShiVelle Lewis, who never paid attention, or Niancé Flogmartin who lost her assignments to all manner of household calamities (like the time her diorama of The Alamo was taken over by her brother's mean-spirited pet iguana), Marvin was awake and paying attention and *definitely* participating, and he never once lost a diorama to an iguana.

Not surprisingly, it wasn't uncommon, after a few days of having his raised hand ignored, Marvin would show up for class to find his seat had been moved to the front of the room, where the teacher could keep an eye on him. At which point, ironically but also not surprisingly, his raised hand was still ignored. (Marvin's fourth-grade teacher, Mrs. Hankersmithy, actually took to requiring that Marvin *sit* on his hands so he would not be tempted to raise them. If Marvin did not follow Mrs. Hankersmithy's instructions, to wit: "Sit on those hands, young man, or I will sit on them for you," Mrs. Hankersmithy would do just that, i.e., plop her satin-sheened derriere upon said appendages, which was not only embarrassing but way beyond gross. Thanks to said derriere — the mere mention of which still brings creep-bumps to Marvin's skin — fourth grade was no fun at all.)

Sitting at the front of the class under the teacher's watchful eye wouldn't last for long. The seat he next would be given was usually out in the hall, where he would have nothing to do but entertain himself.[4]

4> My associate, Jean-Claude, who has the unbearable habit of looking over my shoulder as I write, insists I tell the reader to get their minds out of the gutter. It's not that kind of book, he says, and he will not be party to the Rampant Dissemination of Smut to Minors (his caps). Furthermore, he

But here is the thing: For Marvin, being sent out into the hall was a good thing. It meant he was free to do what he most liked to do.

Marvin, you see, liked to draw.

He also was quite good at it. From intricate renderings of whatever lay before him — his hands, shoes, books, watch; the lockers, the smoke alarm, whoever happened by (he had a knack for remembering what someone wore, the look on their face, what they were carrying, etc.) — to whatever popped into his head (intergalactic battles, intestine-sucking undead insurance salesmen, mutant ice monsters, underground cities of mechanical men … and so on). In short, Marvin was happy as long as he had a sketch pad and a pencil, preferably a 3B.

It was during these sessions, out in the hall, that the most fantastic ideas would come to him. I'm not referring to the ideas that came to his pencil (or, sometimes, pen) — the mutant ice monsters and all that — but, rather, the ideas that came to his brain. Which of course is where ideas usually come, but specifically I'm referring here to the notions that would take hold while he was deep in creation — notions completely unrelated to whatever he was working on.

One such notion, for instance, came to him in the ninth grade, not three months before our adventure begins — soon, I promise (a point, I might add, where we shall start showing rather than telling in a more or less chronological order just to get the editors off our backs). When the

---

says, if I don't point out that this book has no room for rampant dissemination of any sort, *right this very instant,* he is going to point it out himself.

That would mean, unfortunately, he'd be pointing it out in that pretentious French accent of his, and I'm afraid he'd just get on your nerves.

He is adamant I rectify the situation. I tell him I cannot rectify a pretentious French accent, but he is frowning rather rudely at me and impatiently tapping his finger on the monitor.

I, in turn, am giving him a look that says it is no wonder Mr. Hemingway did himself in.

He is starting to open that annoyingly French mouth of his. As per usual, I give in. I am typing the note. This is not so much to satisfy Jean-Claude as it is to saving me the cost of bullets.

Happy, J.C.?

notion hit, Marvin was sitting outside his French class working on his graphic novel, *Winged Avengers of the Apocalypse,* absently listening to Madame LeBlanc's voice drift from the classroom. (*"Je suis un crapaud. Vous êtes un crapaud. Nous sommes tous les crapauds."*)[5]

But rather than wondering why on earth Mme. LeBlanc would be saying she and her class were somehow related to excrement (he *was* listening), Marvin, working on a particularly detailed rendering of the Taj Mahal, had a thought. Wouldn't it be nice, went this thought as he added an ornate finial atop a spire, to learn how to swim?

Now being very good at impersonations, especially of Hollywood celebrities like Arnold Schwarzenegger and Danny Bonaduce, but also of people he knew like Mr. Hadley, his high school principal, and Marion J. Bartholomew, the mayor of Portland Cement City (who was not difficult to mimic because he spoke with not only a pronounced stutter, but a pronounced lisp — the annual "Th-th-thtate of the Th-Th-Thity" address being an annual test of public patience), Marvin took it upon himself to rectify the inability-to-swim situation.

Pretending to be Principal Hadley, Marvin telephoned three swimming pool contractors, requesting their bids on the installation of an Olympic-

---

5> Jean-Claude wants it known this does not translate to anything related to the word "crap." Which is what I'd told him it meant. Again, he is adamant. So, in the spirit of keeping the peace, let me say here that *"Je suis un crapaud, vous êtes un crapaud, nous sommes tous les crapauds,"* translates to, "I am a toad. You are a toad. We are all toads." (This should give you some idea just how far apart English and French really are. I mean, c'mon, c-r-a-p is clearly the word "crap," is it not? Do not come complaining to me if your language is outright confusing. I honestly think the French do it on purpose.)

Alas, that is not the point of this footnote. The point of this footnote, just in case you already knew the toad thing, is that Madame LeBlanc was a bit of a kook. She clearly took immense pleasure in making her students say things that would be embarrassing were they actually to repeat them on the streets of Paris: "Your nose looks like that of a squid," "Your sister smells of baboon," "I wish to lick your shoes," and so on. Given this, I'm sure you'll agree that the words being repeated at this moment — "I am a toad, you are a toad," etc. — were tame by comparison.

sized swimming pool on the grounds of Zadok Magruder High School there in Portland Cement City which of course was Marvin's own school, not some school he'd randomly picked out of the telephone directory. The pool, he told each contractor in his best Principal Hadley voice, would replace the football field, "which has become, we are sorry to say, decidedly tiresome."

The jig was up for young Marvin when Principal Hadley happened to look out his office window one afternoon only to witness one such contractor meandering about the football field. The man was making long and calculated strides, clipboard in hand, pacing off the field — i.e., walking the field in measured steps. Perhaps this contractor was merely assuring himself that an Olympic-sized swimming pool would actually fit on the site. Usually that would not be an unreasonable thing to do in terms of coming up with an accurate estimate, but given the fact that football fields are the same size from Maine to California (which is why they call them a "gridiron," meaning, "the size of the playing field, measuring 120 x 53.3 yards and so encompassing a 100-yard grid marked in ten-yard incremental intervals, is pretty much set in iron, so don't mess with it"), it was pretty much a wasted effort.

Principal Hadley, thinking there was a crazed lunatic loping about school grounds, was just about to call the authorities when he thought better of it, walked out to the field himself and asked the man his business.

It took but forty-five seconds to realize that it was Marvin Plotnik who was the responsible party, not Principal Hadley (who pointed out their football field was fine, thank you very much), and the man was sent on his way.

Thanks to Principal Hadley's well-timed look out the window, a perfectly nice, unsuspecting pool contractor was saved even more wasted effort, that of putting even a single figure to paper.[6]

6> FYI, coming up with estimates is not a slam-dunk easy thing to do. You don't just show up with a number scribbled on a piece of paper. A swimming pool contractor, for instance, would have

The upshot of which was that Marvin never did learn how to swim. But he did learn how to impersonate Principal Hadley, and later that same year it came in handy: One day, while dissecting a frog in biology class, a new idea occurred to him. Rather than poking around the insides of Defenseless Little Creatures Who Unwittingly Gave Their Lives To Science, the idea and accompanying initial caps went, maybe Marvin and his fellow students ought to be studying animals that don't smell like the inside of a coroner's office.

So, when he got home, Marvin let his fingers do the walking, which is an old slogan meaning he looked in the Yellow Pages, which, when that

---

to figure how much concrete and glazed ceramic tile he'd need to purchase, what kinds of permits would be called for, whether the property required environmental-impact studies, how much piping would have to be laid, and what he was going to have for lunch, the corned beef or the turkey — all of which costs *cold, hard cash*. He'd have to know how many workers would be needed over how long, and how many Port-o-Johns would be sufficient and how many feet of cyclone fencing it would take to surround the project and what the square root of 144 is, which might come in handy when he least expects it.

These things are considered "overhead" (except the square root thing, but it's math, too, so best you learn it while you have the chance instead of when someone is waiting for you to come up with a Fair and Reasonable Price by the end of the week). Plus, after all these costs are figured in, the contractor would have to remember to add on a tidy twenty percent, which is called "profit margin," just for dredging up the agony of long division.

Coming up with a bona fide and accurate estimate not only relies heavily on one's abilities in arithmetic, but might, in some instances (for example, coming up with plans and figures for a pool in an unusual shape), require a working knowledge of calculus. Calculus is a fancy-schmancy kind of mathematics wherein one can figure the area and circumference of an irregular shapes like trapezoids, or, say, an armadillo.

So, someday, when you need an estimate for something, like restoring a 1965 Pontiac GTO 389 Tri-Power Coupe or getting 10,000 four-color brochures printed about your new religion, or having your *own* armadillo-shaped swimming pool installed, please keep this in mind.

Ergo, ipso facto, estimates are not easy. They don't just emerge fully formed from between one's buttocks.

line was written like six thousand years ago, was a humongous phone book containing every business under the sun — from Aardvark Appliances to Zweibel's Zemporium of Toys, Crafts, Hobbies and Trains — and was printed on *actual yellow pages,* which was darn clever in those days. Marvin, however, let his fingers do the walking online, where the Yellow Pages logo includes two stylized fingers "walking" with absolutely no explanation of it. I guess you are supposed to type with just these two fingers.

Anyway, in no time at all Marvin was able to order enough live-animal replacements to keep the Zadok Magruder High School biology department busy, and it took but a single call.

"Fifty chickens?" the man on the other end of the line confirmed, who, evidenced by the sound of a 10-key calculator, then figured his price right then and there. (Coming up with a price for live chickens is far easier than armadillo-shaped swimming pools.) Marvin, masquerading as Principal Hadley, asked that the chickens be delivered directly to his office (meaning Principal Hadley's office, not Marvin's office; Marvin didn't have an office), and paid for them with the convenience of his father's credit card (meaning Marvin's father's credit card, not Principal Hadley's father's credit card), the one that gives you Cash in Your Pocket, Each and Every Time You Use It.™ Marvin's instructions were that the chickens be delivered to the school at precisely twelve noon the following day, which, he was well aware, just happened to be a Saturday. (It also just happened to be the Saturday of Memorial Day weekend, which Marvin had quite honestly forgotten about, and which turned out to be the hottest Memorial Day weekend in Portland Cement City's recorded history, a fact that Marvin would not be aware of until it was too late.)

So. Saturday came, and so did the chicken delivery man, and so did the fifty chickens.

Now the chicken delivery man, upon finding no one around (remember, it was Saturday), and thinking he had better things to do than wait around for this "Horace Hadley" whose name was on the delivery ticket, instead opted to go enjoy a nice cold beer at The Concrete Block, a bar down on Seventh Street with $2 refills from 3-5 p.m., which was a much more appealing prospect than spending the weekend with fifty live chickens in anybody's book. So, miraculously finding an unlocked door at the school (thanks in part to the forward thinking of young Marvin Plotnik), the chicken delivery man left the chickens in the cafeteria.

Let me say here that as a testament to the forward thinking of a person at least partially dedicated to customer service, he did leave a note. He left it attached to the largest of the chickens by securing it with a piece of string. The note, attached to the chicken's leg, read:

H. HADLEY

Needless to say, when school reconvened the following Tuesday (after, as I say, the hottest weekend on record), there was horrible unpleasantness to be found. Fifty chickens can make quite a mess, especially if they've been left alone over a long hot weekend with no food or water and even more so if they somehow make their way to a ten-pound sack of chocolate pudding mix.

Chickens, if you are not aware, do not take well to chocolate pudding mix. Or, rather, their insides do not take well to chocolate pudding mix. Chocolate pudding mix, I might add, has a way, when combined with liquids in a warm environment, i.e., the intestines of most forms of fowl — notably, in this case, chickens — of becoming chocolate pudding. And, regrettably, chocolate pudding has a way, especially in creatures accustomed to a diet of poultry feed and insects (i.e. *not* dairy) — again, in this case, chickens — of being barely digestible, which means it is more likely than not to make its way back out from said intestines with much expedience.

Therefore, by the time it reached its destination — aka the floor and walls and counters and chairs and tables and stainless steel carts of the cafeteria at Zadok Magruder High School — it had grown in tremendous volume vis-à-vis its original ten-pound net weight, which, if you had a working knowledge of calculus, avian biology and the metric system, you could calculate in liters. Which was what Marvin and his fellow students and the cafeteria workers and Principal Hadley and, most regrettably, the janitorial staff found upon entering the cafeteria when they returned to school on Tuesday morning. On top of the sheer volume of it, apparently post-pullet-pudding combines rather disgustingly with everything it comes into contact with: a left-behind hoodie, the contents of an overturned industrial-sized trash bin, a 12-page book report on *Wuthering Heights*, countless chicken feathers, unconsumed chocolate pudding mix, the contents of the janitor's bucket, the janitor's mop, and a 16-foot banner advertising the upcoming Spring Into Spring talent show on which the letters were formed with toilet paper rosettes. (Don't let anyone tell you a chicken can't fly.) Add to this 142 wads of chewing gum, 104 plastic cafeteria trays, an old gym sock, poor Suzie-Jean Fritz's "Hang Six" backpack with the appliqué of a surfing ladybug on it — which Suzie-Jean had absentmindedly left in the corner when she was chatting with her friends — six cafeteria staff no-longer-white aprons and matching (but now crushed) paper chef hats, and an opened box of *"Go Zadok!"* PTA-approved Zadok-orange sweatshirts. Which was gross. (Not the sweatshirts, the other stuff. Wait … the sweatshirts, too.)

Aside from the ungodly mess, the only other outcome of the Chicken Delivery Incident was that the note the delivery man had left reading H. HADLEY (meant to be instructions as to whom the chickens belonged, not as a means of identifying that particular chicken), from then on became the basis for a long-term running gag at the school, actually outlasting Marvin's own attendance there. Schoolyard behavior, of course, is rarely funny (ha ha funny, not peculiar funny), so the fact that a lot of the kids would cluck rudely behind Principal Hadley's back every time he ventured into the halls must be taken with a grain of salt. After all, they were just kids. And kids think a lot of stuff is funny that isn't, like pulling down other kids' pants or pretending lima beans are boogers or smooshing their noses into windows so they look like demented pugs (the kids, not the windows).

By the way, Marvin, in a remarkable feat of self-control, never once participated in the clucking. It seemed so unnecessary.

• • •

AND SO IT WAS, in the ninth grade, in the middle of Fifth Period Calculus — the very day Marvin had gotten in trouble in science class for what he felt was an extraordinarily instructive demonstration on displacement (involving a tub of maple syrup and a particularly displacement-inducing bowling ball, a demonstration that Suzie-Jean Fritz later referred to in her usual whiny way as "mean mean mean") — Marvin was told to report to the principal's office.

There he found his parents, along with his science teacher (still carrying the pungent aroma of maple syrup), and Principal Hadley, all with Very Serious Looks on their faces.

Let us all heave a sigh of relief, shall we, for this is where our story begins...

*The only reason for time
is so everything doesn't happen at once.*

—ALBERT EINSTEIN

Chapter ONE...

MARVIN PLOTNIK sat in the principal's office, waiting it out. "It" being his parents, science teacher and Principal Hadley as they all took turns wagging authoritative fingers his way (meaning "in Marvin's direction," not "in the manner Marvin preferred"). They'd had it with his shenanigans, they told him (Ms. Steinmetz pulling at her syrup-laden hair: "It's not funny, young man; not funny in the least"), and in two days' time he was to board a bus bound for the Sandy Rivers Hilltop Ranch for Wayward Youth, Juveniles, and Young Adults in Jasper County, Wyoming, which, if you just joined us, is a perfectly acceptable and timely sentence, but if you've read the introduction — and why wouldn't you — I'll bet you thought we'd never get to. [*See: "Digressive Genes."*]

Marvin pushed his glasses up the bridge of his nose. "You're sending me ... to a boarding school ... a redundantly-named boarding school?"

"It's not quite a boarding school," his mother replied. "It's..." She looked to her husband for help.

"What your mother means," his father said after a bit of lip biting, "is that this camp, er, this ranch, is just the place for someone who's so ... er, so ..." He looked to Marvin's science teacher for help.

Ms. Steinmetz, arms crossed, the scowl on her face perhaps held there by maple syrup (the right side of her hair stiff enough to stand on end), replied, "Busy."

Marvin's mother nodded. "Yes, busy," she said. "Busy."

"Yes," Marvin's father repeated, rather unnecessarily. "Busy."

Up to this point, Principal Hadley had not uttered a word, but apparently deciding he would not only utter a word but a whole slew of them (starting with an erroneous misstatement about his relationship with the boy), looked Marvin in the eye. "Son," — that's the erroneous misstatement — "it's unfortunate we have to resort to such tactics, but considering the ill-advised, uh, *unpleasantries* associated with your, er, *behavior* over the years, I think you will agree … this is the best avenue of action."[7]

"Wholly agreed," Ms. Steinmetz said, wholly agreeing.

It was here that Marvin noticed a large man with a comparatively large handlebar moustache standing in Principal Hadley's doorway. The man, seemingly as wide as he was tall, took a step forward. How Marvin could have missed him earlier is hard to say as it was almost impossible to differentiate the fellow, given his size, from an *odobenus rosmarus rosmarus,* which is yet more Latin and literally means something along the order of "big-nose huge huge," or, less repetitively, your basic iceberg-lounging-tub-of-blubber-and-tusks, the walrus. Which, according to the *Encyclopedia Gargantua,* weigh something on the order of 1,814 kilograms, or, for those of you who have not yet joined the rest of the universe, 4,000 pounds. Meaning massive. Meaning the large man with the similarly large handlebar moustache who had just taken a step in Marvin's direction … was massive. So massive, it so happens, his shadow alone took up the entirety of the room.

Marvin wondered how the man could possibly fit into a chair, let alone through a doorway, but he clearly had, for now he stood before our young hero, humongous shadow and all.

7> These were not onomatopoeic interjections. He actually said, "uh" and "er" and "tactics."

Marvin's parents put their hands in their laps and looked to the Walrus
Man with what appeared to be great admiration. And perhaps, if Marvin
was reading their faces correctly, a bit of hope as well.

The towering man's forehead crinkled as he paced back and forth, his
tusk-like moustache hanging over formidable jowls. He twirled the
moustache in a grand demonstration of the import of the moment. Finally,
he stopped, towering above the boy, and crossed his arms (his own arms,
not the boy's arms).

And in the time it took for a condescending, judgmental and altogether
false smile to come across his face, the authoritative air he was trying so
hard to evoke — and this is a comment that speaks volumes to Marvin's
observational skills — had all but disappeared. Because with that smile
came a particle of nondescript … something — a glutinous gooey glob of
grossness or some other snip of alliteration — lodged between the Walrus
Man's freakishly-large front two teeth. The gooey thing hung there and
sort of … jiggled.

"As I understand it," the man said in a deep walrus-like voice (the little
piece of something *right there* jiggling with every word), "you have been
causing your school and family something of a problem." He put his thumb
to his chin in a sort of exaggerated gesture as if to show he was now
thinking quite hard. His thumb nearly disappeared into his saggy jowls.
Unfortunately, it missed the gooey glob by six centimeters,[8] and so the
glob remained. "Is that correct, young man?"

Marvin could not look at the gooey glob another second. His eyes
darted to the man's shoes. Resting solitarily on the scruffy brown leather
of a loafer was a tassel, but not the kind of tassel that adorns the dashing
red fezzes of Shriners or chimpanzees. This tassel was a little bent, and
somewhat melted, fused into a glob not unlike the glob that now had made
its way to the man's lower lip. As such, it looked less like a tassel than like
a dried-up slug (the glob on his shoe, not the glob on his lip. No, wait, that
looked like a slug, too, come to think of it). In case you are thinking it

---

8> Approx. 2.36 inches.

might actually have *been* a slug, there was no doubt it was a tassel, as was obvious by two perfectly presentable ones on his other shoe.

Marvin eyed the Walrus Man's tie. There were stains on it, pale yellow stains, from perhaps a sandwich at lunch. Tartar sauce, Marvin presumed from the look of it. There was definitely a tartar-saucey air about the man, a distinct tartar-saucey … fishy-ness. Maybe even a whole *bucket* of fishy-ness.

Under the tartar sauce, the tie. It was bright blue with colorful pictures of Mr. Peeps, the dopey cartoon dog that laughs like a deranged hyena when he steals the neighbor's food or knocks down their laundry or jumps in their bathtub while they are taking a bath — a thinly-veiled attempt to make youngsters feel at ease (the tie, not the bathtub-jumping thing).

Marvin wondered why his parents and Ms. Steinmetz and Principal Hadley couldn't see what a big fat blubbery tartar sauce-stained *tool* this guy was. Couldn't they see the man was probably living in the men's room at the bus station? But being a firm believer in what Marvin called Universal Life Lesson No. 42 — "People see what they want to see" — it did not surprise him. And frankly he couldn't possibly care less. *Let* them see what they want to see.

The Walrus Man rocked on his heels, the little fused tassel jiggling and the little piece of goo undoubtedly jiggling, too. (Marvin was at the point he couldn't make himself look at it.) "Well?" the man pressed.

Marvin shrugged. "I was sorta wondering where the sun went," he replied. "It got, like, dark in here." He stretched his neck as if trying to see around a very large diesel truck. "I'm thinking we might be having some kind of eclipse or something."

"Ah," the Walrus Man ahed, rubbing his chin with stubby fish-filet fingers. "I see where you have earned your reputation. I will repeat for you the question at hand: Is it not correct that you have been a problem for your family? For your peers? For your school?"

Marvin thought for a moment. He was thinking about his family, peers and school, yes — I mean how couldn't he when they'd just been mentioned like four seconds ago — but mostly he was thinking about how he'd save Yolando Plumadore, his protagonist in *Winged Avengers of the Apocalypse.* Marvin had left Yolando hanging over a large vat of boiling cream of wheat in the middle of the Himalayas, and he wasn't sure what should happen next. He was also thinking about the look on Suzie-Jean Fritz's face when her shoe came off in the maple syrup — which was *awesome* — and he was thinking a little bit about animal husbandry, because it had just occurred to him what a weird word "husbandry" was. And he only thought of *that* because he had just thought of the word "wifery" and how it wasn't one.

"Me?" he asked. "I've been a problem? I wasn't aware of that, no. I suppose it all depends on your definition of 'problem.'"

The Walrus Man looked at the others in the room as if he saw what they'd been up against, raised an eyebrow, then turned back to the boy.

"Take the 'problem,'" Marvin said as he pushed his glasses up the bridge of his nose, "of high gasoline prices."

The Walrus Man raised another eyebrow. "And?"

"And," Marvin was happy to explain, "high gasoline prices wouldn't be a *problem* if we weren't overly dependent upon, you know, *gasoline,* would it?" [No response.] "Well if we weren't so embarrassingly addicted to a machine that hasn't improved its fuel efficiency since like, what, *1923?* That's like a century of no progress, people. 'Course they did get in those drink cups. That's always good, drink cups. And, you know, automatic windows." Sitting up straight: "*C'mon* now *really.* While everything else has been updated like *six-thousand*-fold, we sit here stupidly reliant on a product that's basically *prehistoric?* How stupid is that?[9]

9> I find young Mr. Plotnik's use of the word "prehistoric" an interesting choice. After all, gasoline ultimately comes from the gurgling black remains of long-dead prehistoric reptiles, does it not? I find this most intriguing. Not that oil comes from dead dinosaurs, which, let's face it, is way cool, but the choice of words thing. Young Marvin's mind works in interesting ways.

By the way, did you know that the dinosaurs, thought long-extinct, in point of fact, aren't? Sure, there are plenty of their oozy remains to keep the global economy going (and a few non-oozy ones for the archeologists to play around with) but mostly, *mostly,* the dinosaurs no longer roam the Earth

"Relying on gasoline," Marvin added, "is like lighting the streets of New York with a single candle, isn't it? Like hand-writing thousands of

---

because — and I'm sure you've heard this one before, but trust me when I say you haven't been privy to the whole shocking truth — they went home.

This is not to say these guys were capable of flying off into the galaxy. I mean, c'mon, they had brains the size of chickpeas. And no opposable thumbs. Try operating an intergalactic vessel with no opposable thumbs. The best a dinosaur could come up with, inventiveness-wise, was that stepping over other dinosaurs was a good way to keep your feet dry.

So obviously they didn't leave on their own. But, having been brought here by the M'iBraxtians (pronounced "MIH-brack-see-uns" with a click in the throat after the M) to graze upon Earth's abundant greenery, and having subsequently eaten the planet dry (thanks for *that*), the M'iBraxtians simply relocated them to their home planet of M'iBraxt ("MIH-bracks"), in the Andromeda Galaxy, where grazing land suddenly became vast and cheap due to a slump in the real estate market.

This relocation, by the way, predated the meteor shower credited with the dinosaurs' extinction by as much as 750,000 years. Now I don't mean to belittle scientific method — after all, what's a few hundred thousand years — I just thought you should know you can't believe everything you see in print. ("Scientists," as we say on my world, "can be such boneheads.")

Anyway, as a result of moving the livestock *en masse,* the savings in transportation costs alone has meant dinosaur meat has come way down in price. Today you can get a brachioburger for like half of what it cost thousands of years ago, and how many products can you say that about? Maybe those little plastic cocktail swords, but that's about it. Cheap.

Good move, then, by the M'iBraxtians. (I could go into how the cheap availability of brachio-burgers has caused a correspondingly high rise in cholesterol levels across all civilizations in the Grambolian Sector, but you can probably just look that up yourself.)

Let me add that the relocation from Earth wasn't an easy affair. They had a hell of a time capturing many of them, especially those crafty *pteranodons,* who were too quick for them, and the meat-eating theropods like *megalosaurus* and *tyrannosaurus rex,* who were too nasty for them. And of course the sea-dwelling *helicoprions,* who were just too creepy to think about. These were therefore abandoned on the planet without a second thought. (We know them today, of course, by their ancestors — e.g., the *pteranodons* evolving into what today we call "birds," and the *T. rex* evolving into what today we call ... that's right ... all together now ... (ready?) ... "corporate attorneys." {~*Rrrrimshot*~}

copies of the newspaper every day instead of printing them on printing presses. Or, crap, like *printing them on printing presses*. It's like washing a herd of elephants with a toothbrush. It's like—" He stopped, as if that was more than enough explanation, then, realizing it must not be by the looks on the Walrus Man's face, added: "Well it's not very efficient, is it?"

The big man blinked in a most clichéd way. "And your point is?"

"My *point* is," Marvin said as if he were talking to a five-year-old, "to say I've been a *problem* to my family and school is a bit like saying we have a *problem* with gas prices, when the problem isn't with gas prices, or even with *gas*. The problem isn't even with the oil companies, who are just doing what companies *do*. The *problem* is with the internal combustion engine."

"The internal—"

Marvin crossed his legs and began to clean his glasses on his shirt. "It's *folly*, is it not? You can't very well blame the *peg* for a problem with the *hole*, now can you?"

The Walrus Man rolled his eyes. Marvin's mother rolled *her* eyes. Principal Hadley and Ms. Steinmetz rolled *their* eyes. And, just to make the point he always makes, Marvin's father shook his head and left the room.

Chapter TWO…

BEFORE HE KNEW IT, Marvin Plotnik was standing in front of Zadok Magruder High School watching his parents huddle in secrecy with the big mustached sun-blocking jiggly-thing-in-his-jowls Walrus Man. Nearby, a bus idled, a dilapidated rusty old heap that looked as though it were on its last legs (or, rather, wheels), which is another way of saying it was way past old and smelled of something disgusting, possibly rancid cheese … most definitely sweaty socks.[10]

10> Ever wonder where your socks disappear to when you put them in the dryer? Well you probably don't, but whoever does the laundry around your house does. You may have been told that socks never make it to the dryer in the first place, that they go down the drain. Well I am here to tell you this is in fact true. But I am also here to tell you that this is only part of the story.

After it goes down the drain, your errant sock is retrieved by your local sewer authority and mixed with other errant socks. They are then sold to a company out of Hogswallow, Arkansas, who pass them on to another company, and so on, until they have gone through so many companies in so many parts of the world they can no longer be traced. (Which is where the word "laundering" comes from.)

Now you may have known all of that, but what you might not know is that eventually, all these tons of mismatched socks are taken aboard Fomlian star-cruisers, from which, for reasons only the Fomlians understand, the socks are released throughout the galaxy into the Great Nothingness of Space. Take a look at the rings of Saturn. You think that happens all by itself?

Marvin couldn't hear what his parents and the Walrus Man were saying over the sputtering engine, the thing spitting and spewing nasty fumes, so he stood there like an idiot, backpack at his feet, awaiting his fate.

The Walrus Man had traded his tartar sauce shirt and cartoony tie for a large T-shirt, a red one — extra-extra-*extra* large, natch — which made him look more like a billboard for Cola-Cola than someone you should entrust with your offspring. After shaking hands with Marvin's parents, the Cola-Cola billboard strolled over to Marvin, moustache forming an enormous grin, like things of Great Import were afoot. The Walrus Man then gave the moustache a tug and eyed Marvin's backpack. "I trust you stuck to the checklist?"

He was referring, of course, to the one-page checklist provided to Marvin's parents at the conclusion of their first encounter, an action I've spared you in lieu of this sentence. It was printed on Sandy Rivers Hilltop Ranch letterhead and it was a list of items Marvin was to bring. It was also one of the shortest checklists in the history of checklists:

❏ 1. Undergarments.
❏ 2. Pursuits of a personal nature.

Under that was written, in italicized type: *"All other items are considered cultural distractions and are not allowed."* And under *that*, in regular type, meaning it was not as important as the italicized bit: "A change of clothes will be provided."

Then came a second list, the one of stuff they were *not* allowed, these cultural distractions. The items on this list, being strictly forbidden, did not have check boxes next to them because naturally no one was going to check off something they weren't going to account for.

This list was 27 pages long. In nine-point type. Single-spaced. In three columns. It went on and on, specifically naming things like GameKids, ePods, ePads, smart phones, portable DVD players, laptops, routers, digital cameras, MP3 players, electronic readers, GPS systems, portable defibrillators and so on.

It read like the site map at everythingbutthekitchensink.com.

Somewhere in there was a long roster of popular fiction — comic books and graphic novels mostly — some specifically named and others more general, among them: "stories involving superheroes," "stories involving robots," "stories involving time machines," "stories involving ghosts," "stories involving space travel," and "stories involving brain-eating aliens." As if stories involving brain-eating aliens were somehow corrupting the youth of America. Like it was 1957 or something (when stories involving brain-eating aliens really *did* corrupt the youth of America).

Marvin did not care for lists. Lists, he believed, were nothing less than *limiting*. What if you made a grocery list with apples, milk, bread and raisins on it, but what you really could use was a box of chocolate-covered macaroons? What if you made a list of all your favorite movies and some dick-wad like Dennis McCrosky got hold of it and read it over the P.A. system during lunch and everyone laughed when he announced you had four stars next to *Samurai Ninjas of the Ninth Dimension,* which is a *classic,* but since they never heard of it they thought you were some kind of freak? What good was a list *then?*

And Marvin certainly didn't know what "pursuits of a personal nature" meant, since, by definition, everything he did was a pursuit of a personal nature, especially that going-to-the-bathroom thing. So he ignored the list, because it was Capital-L Lame, and filled his backpack with what he felt he was going to need over the course of following days: five packages of 10-count Chee-Zee SpudNuggets, twelve Twinkle Bars, four bags of Cheese Doodles, seven packages of unpopped PoppyCorn Lite (in case there as a microwave handy), his drawing tablet, pencils, manual pencil sharpener, erasers, pen and ink, the unfinished manuscript of *Winged Avengers of the Apocalypse,* and six of his favorite graphic novels (all of which involved, to some extent, superheroes, robots, time machines, ghosts, zombies, space travel, and brain-eating aliens, or, in the case of *The Game's Afoot* by Stephen Scott King, a time-traveling, brain-eating alien robot zombie named Hank).

Oh, and the underwear.[11]

So, in answer to the Walrus Man's query, some ten or eleven paragraphs back, asking whether he'd abided by the checklist, and honestly having at this moment a head devoid of anything other than Yolando Plumadore's cream of wheat predicament and what he'd be looking at in the *following* paragraph, Marvin said the only thing one *could* say when someone asks whether you've done something you haven't done, which was, "Of course."

Which was the point he took a better look at the Walrus Man's humongous T-shirt. It didn't read what Marvin had expected, which was COLA-COLA: DRINK IT FOR LIFE. What it did read, in crisp black letters, was this: SANDY RIVERS HILLTOP RANCH FOR WAYWARD YOUTH, JUVENILES, AND YOUNG ADULTS, below which was a drawing: A cabin nestled in the woods, smoke rising from its chimney, two rocking chairs on the porch. Off to the side two tiny figures could be seen fishing from a footbridge. It was inviting and quaint, and beyond the cabin lay a sprawling ranch with horses and cowboys and an animal that might be a steer, or might be a cow, or might be a very large dog, it was hard to tell because it was too small to make out.

Well this doesn't look so bad, Marvin thought, studying the illustration. It looks peaceful. Pleasant. Pastoral. Other P-words. What's the worst that

---

11> Jean-Claude wants it known that I have yet to bring up the fact that Marvin was slightly overweight. He also says I should mention that Marvin's glasses were squarish, that his hair was on the brown side, relatively straight, usually clean, and hung slightly over the left lens of those glasses (Marvin's left lens, not the viewer's left lens), that he liked to wear T-shirts, but T-shirts with absolutely no images on them because he didn't want to be "the promotional monkey for some dude in a Lexus," and that he was a Capricorn. Jean-Claude says this stuff must be introduced *now*, this very instant, "before the reader has formed an unalterable picture of the protagonist." If he didn't do this with that obnoxious accent of his, I wouldn't mind so much, but there he goes in that look-at-me-I'm-French bullcrap *act* of his, and quite frankly I'm starting to get annoyed.

Again with the monitor poking.

Okay, fine. Done and done. (Try to picture how much I'm shaking my head.)

could happen? Chores? Classes of some kind? He'd figure a way out of them, get his usual seat in the hall, get Yolando out of the cream of wheat, and have a nice nap. (Already ideas were eating at him that he needed to get down on paper.)[12]

So Marvin smiled at the humongous T-shirt and the possibilities it implied, flashed his parents a crisp goodbye salute, and stepped onto the bus.

The bus driver nodded hello. Marvin, slightly taken aback by how thin the man was, nodded hello back. *How* thin was the bus driver? Let's just say that if one were to draw a stick figure of this guy, it would look exactly like him. It was as if he were made of pipe cleaners and cotton swabs. Perhaps in an effort to "bulk up," the driver had wrapped a scarf

---

12> Marvin had toyed with the idea of Yolando dropping into the vat of cream of wheat and eating his way out. But then how would his hero survive, undoubtedly covered in the stuff, especially in the everything-will-freeze-here-even-hot-breakfast-cereal Himalayas? And if the cream of wheat didn't freeze, which would be *impossible*, how long would the man last covered in wholesome steamy goodness when he'd no doubt be surrounded by tigers, wild goats, an occasional hoary marmot and teems of hungry Yeti? Ergo, not long.

Plus, it just wasn't believable. And if there's one thing Marvin had learned in writing now eight graphic novels, if it wasn't believable no one was going to read it. [Besides, the prospect of drawing Yolando — a one-armed acrobat whose back-story included being raised by orangutans in the jungles of Malaysia — slurping his way through hot gooey mush quite frankly wasn't something Marvin was looking forward to. A convincing mountain of goo is hard to pull off. (More on this later.)]

And in the first case of uncanny coincidence to appear so far in this tale, believe it or not Marvin had already written and illustrated the part of Yolando Plumadore's back-story where, once freed of the overpowering control of the orangutans (not to mention the smell of the nasty things) he'd spent the remaining days of his youth as an urchin on the streets of Marrakech, Morocco, where — get this — the hat of choice for men was ... a fez. Quite often a *red* fez. Whoa, right?

This, you will come to find over the course of the next twenty-nine chapters, is just one example of the Interconnectedness of All Things, a subject with which I — and soon, you, dear reader — am most familiar.

about his neck, which was weird considering it was 82° outside. The scarf was striped, yellow and green, and it had been wrapped around his neck many times, which made his neck look all the more scrawny.

Marvin saw now there were a couple of kids already seated. A few rows back sat a girl in a floppy hat. At first Marvin couldn't see her as she was scrunched low with her feet pulled up. Her oversized T-shirt was stretched over her knees. The only way Marvin could tell she was a girl was because two long braids hung from beneath the hat, which doesn't necessarily mean she *was* a girl, but statistically speaking it was a fair assumption.

As he passed, Marvin said, "Hello," to which the girl said, "Hello yourself," without even looking up; and that was that.

At the very back sat a sandy-haired young man about Marvin's age. He had staked his claim to the seat that spanned the width of the bus, his arms and ankles crossed, his legs sprawled into the aisle. He caught Marvin's eye, blew an enormous purple bubble, then sucked the bubble in with a snap. Marvin was hit by the distinct aroma of grape Bubblectible. The seat-hogger followed this with a nod that said, "This is the extent of our conversation." Marvin, in turn, nodded back. Message received.

As he took a seat a couple of rows behind the girl with the floppy hat, the bus curiously listed to the other side. This of course felt physically impossible until Marvin realized the Walrus Man had just come aboard. He watched as the big guy gave the driver's bony shoulder a tap and the three kids a quick once-over, before squeezing himself into the front-most seat. There was a grinding of gears and then the driver's spindly hand reached for the door lever and the door slapped shut. I only mention this play-by-play because it was here Marvin caught the driver's eye in the wide rear-view. For a moment, our young hero thought he saw a flash of something there — for just a brief moment. Recognition? Ancient wisdom? A twinkle of amusement?

Marvin decided he'd been thinking too much about the world of *Winged Avengers of the Apocalypse*, where everything was a plot point, everything had meaning, everything was open to interpretation, everything *mattered*. This guy was simply a bus driver. With an eating disorder. That glint in his eye was probably nothing more than a mental note to get the oil changed. Or gas.

The bus coughed and sputtered and began to pull away from the curb. Marvin stole a glance at his parents who were still standing in front of the school. They were smiling. They both raised a hand. Marvin started to raise his as well, honestly touched by the moment, but surprise surprise, instead of those hands waving goodbye, their one and only son off into the world, they smacked together, silently, masked by the grinding of gears and the sputtering engine and the wake of bus fumes.

Not a *bon voyage*; an honest-to-God high-five.

• • •

IN JUST UNDER AN HOUR, the bus pulled up to another school. It was no shock to find there another young man, standing as Marvin had stood — backpack at his feet, parents soon talking to the Walrus Man, the bus idling in wait, and the rest. This new kid was dressed in tie-dyed pants, a bright yellow T-shirt, pumpkin-orange athletic shoes and a purple vest. And if all that wasn't bad enough, he was cursed with more freckles than Marvin had ever seen on a single human being, more freckle than not if you really got down to it, abundantly curly red hair (to the point of looking like a Halloween wig) and a pointy, unnaturally red-tipped nose. If you were to come across this kid on the street (or waiting for a rickety old bus in front of a school) and were struck with thoughts of sad-eyed circus clowns, you would not be the first.

The bus stopped three more times. Three more kids were picked up and Marvin never struck up a conversation with any of them — not with the seat-hogger, not with the girl with the braids, not with the clown-faced kid in the tie-dyed pants; not with the chubby Asian kid with the blue fauxhawk; and not with the last of the bunch, the smallish black kid a year or two younger than the rest of them, who ended up pulling a New York Mets cap over his eyes and napping the whole way.

This is not to say others had not struck up conversations. They did.

With each other. With Marvin they only tried, most notably the Asian kid with the fauxhawk, who'd taken a seat behind our young protagonist and tried to open lines of communication a total of four-and-a-half times, the half consisting opening his mouth, seeing he'd get no response, then abruptly shutting it.

He'd get no response because Marvin was not in a response-giving mood. He had become preoccupied … preoccupied with a certain ill-timed high-five.

For the next twelve hours Marvin remained thus (preoccupied, that is) with the image of that high-five seared into his cerebral cortex like the painful and permanent branding of an iron, or, for want of a better metaphor, the painful and permanent branding of a high-five. It was with him through small towns and large, past rippling hills and open space, fields of corn and wheat and sugar beets, scores of sheep and cattle and grazing horses. It was with him as they approached the Rockies jutting out of the horizon like ancient granite gods spawned from the core of the earth. It was with him as they rounded mountainous bends and alpine straightaways and it was with him even as he caught a glimpse of something, at least twice, scampering like lightning across the floor-boards (or whatever it is they call the deck of a bus).

In fact, it wasn't until they covered miles of prickly pear and scrub and pulled into a dusty parking lot and the bus driver made of pipe cleaners and cotton swabs opened the door and the six of them lugged their backpacks onto the gravel parking lot that Marvin finally was able to concentrate on something else. Because he couldn't ignore it. None of them could. Because it was big.

"Now there's something you don't see every day," Marvin said, eyeing the six-story twisted monstrosity not fifteen meters away.[13] "It looks like somebody wrapped the Eiffel Tower in aluminum foil."

"*Used* aluminum foil," the kid in the tie-die shirt said.

"Then beat it with a sledgehammer," said the girl with the braids.

13> Approx. 49 feet (and no, Jean-Claude, we are not including metric conversion charts).

"Then tried to straighten it out," added Fauxhawk.

Nods all around as Marvin and the others took in this twisted jumble of steel and aluminum. Four stories high, narrower at the top than at the base, it *did* look like somebody had wrapped the Eiffel Tower in aluminum foil. Dropped from on-high and here it landed, half-buried in the dust, it now leaned precariously to the right. Six heads leaned to the right as well.

"Looks like somebody dropped it," the seat-hogger put in, to which everyone nodded. "Don't tell me this is the Sandy Rivers Hilltop Whateverwhatever," he added. "'Cause if it is, I'm like *so* out of here."

Fauxhawk kid shook his head. "Can't be. Sandy Rivers has, you know, trees and stuff."

"And a cabin," said the kid in the Mets hat.

"And, one would assume, a river," the girl added.

"Rivers," Marvin said, "plural."

It certainly wasn't anything like the drawing on the Walrus Man's T-shirt. Not even close. Where was the quaint little cabin with smoke rising from the chimney? Where was the inviting porch? Where were the fishermen and the sprawling ranch with horses and cowboys and the animal that might or might not be a steer?

And just where, Marvin wanted to know, was the freakin' hilltop? Nope. This place wasn't the Sandy Rivers Hilltop Ranch. Not *this* place. *This* place was a train wreck.[14]

14> In the figurative sense of course. No one would suggest it was actually a wrecked train, but from the description above you can assume it looked close to one. It's also been suggested that this building — if that's the right word for it — looked like "an origami swan gone wrong. A Herculean sore thumb. A discordant incongruity."

Let me say this about that: the sooner my trusted assistant learns this is my book, not his, the sooner we will get along.

Now I have that out of the way, the point of this notation is that the term "train wreck" did not always, as one would assume, allude to a locomotive in some state of ruin. In actuality, the phase harkens to the ninth century A.D., long before locomotives were even conceived. In its original

The Walrus Man made a few marks on his clipboard then said something to the driver. The group watched willowy fingers pull the bus door closed with a clunk. A little grinding of gears, a little creaking and groaning, and the bus was on its way to the rear of the monstrosity, out of sight.

Next, as if on cue, what comes tumbling through the bus fumes and dust but a real-life tumbleweed. Like in a B-movie, which is a term you don't hear much anymore because nobody shows double features and if they did they'd charge you two admissions for it. Six sets of eyes followed the tumbleweed until it came to rest against a sign that looked very much like it had been plunked in the dirt not an hour before:

SANDY RIVERS HILLTOP RANCH
FOR WAYWARD YOUTH, JUVENILES,
AND YOUNG ADULTS

Greenlandic Norse, "trænh roekh," translates to, "bowels in a state of upset." It was a phrase you used if you'd had too much mead and potatoes, or had just met your mother-in-law.

Since Greenlandic Norse died out in the fifteenth century, you have to wonder how the phrase entered the lexicon, c. 1856, to mean "a total unequivocal disastrous mess" and has remained thus, unchanged, for another century and a half. [*Example: "Charlie Sheen! What a train wreck!"*]

Chapter THREE...

NOW WHEN YOU FIND YOURSELF standing in a parking lot hundreds of miles from home staring at a cockeyed eyesore (referring to the building, not the Walrus Man), having just spent hours on a rickety old bus and going through Unbelievably Painful Texting Withdrawal — without any music or games or movies or anything the whole stupid way — it is all but impossible not to say aloud how much the situation bites.

Which was why tie-dyed-pants kid said, "This situation bites."

The girl with the braids nodded. "Big time."

"It *so* doesn't look like the brochure," added the seat-hogger, his lip curled in disgust.

Everybody nodded, Marvin included, even though the question in his mind at this point was more along the lines of, "Brochure? *What* brochure?" He'd never seen a stinkin' brochure. He didn't even know there *was* a brochure. How long had his parents studied some lame-ass brochure about how The Sandy Rivers Hilltop Ranch for Wayward Teens, Juveniles, and Young Adults could turn a troublemaker around in four short months — or whatever it was they promised? What'd they do, hide it under their mattress? Or did Principal Hadley or Ms. Steinmetz — or the guy down at the Minute Mart for all Marvin knew — turn to his parents one day and say, "There's a place in Wyoming that can turn your kid around in short order," and his parents said, "Yep, that sounds like just the thing we need, sign us up," and that was that?

Needless to say, the fact that the Walrus Man's T-shirt mocked the genuine (cabin-less, river-less, ranch-less, steer-less, hilltop-less) article before them was not lost on Marvin Plotnik. Nor, we shall assume, on anyone else. Which makes you wonder why, after a shrill blow of a whistle by the Walrus Man, they all followed him like lambs to the slaughter, backpacks in tow, into the half-buried twisted eye-sore that was the Sandy Rivers Hilltop Ranch for Wayward Youth, Juveniles, and Young Adults.

Once they got inside, they were met with a darkened entry. A lobby if you will. Or better yet, because there was no furniture or artwork or receptionist's desk or benches or chairs or colorful abstract painting or any of the other things you'd associate with a lobby, a foyer. Then again, because there weren't any hat-racks or handy occasional table for your keys or umbrella stand or any of the other things you'd associate with a foyer, perhaps we should just go back to calling it an entry, evidenced by the fact that they'd just entered it.

And, as I say, it was awfully dark. For all they knew it was wallpapered with candy canes and rat skulls, that's how dark it was — so there's really not much to say here other than what's been said. Which is why we're moving on, as the group did, to the rear of the space where the Walrus Man opened a door. From whence came blinding light. Blinding *pink* light.

"Holy crap," Marvin said, shading his eyes.

"Holy crap," everybody else said, shading their eyes.

The light emanated from a corridor. A blindingly-pink corridor. A corridor that stretched as far as they could see, i.e., a *long* blindingly-pink corridor. Lined with ceramic tile — the kind you find in public bathrooms or locker-room showers or institutions for the criminally insane — Marvin couldn't help but think, as they made their way down its pinkness, that the Sandy Rivers Hilltop Ranch looked like the kind of place, should you need to wash away a goodly amount of blood or other bodily fluids, you'd have no trouble going about it. He would not have been surprised, as they made their way down the corridor, to find a floor drain or two along the way.

I must point out that Marvin was far off-base on this one. To me, it looked like the kind of tile you might find in your Great Great Aunt Ida Mae's bathroom, c. 1962, along with the hand-crocheted toilet-paper cozy, which I personally find, if you want to know the truth, endearing. (Although this pink tile, unlike, presumably, the pink tile in your great-great aunt's bathroom, went all the way to the ceiling, and then across the ceiling, where it was met with more pink tile from the opposite wall before making its long trek into the Great Pink Tile Beyond.)[15]

And so they walked along this corridor, single file, with the Walrus Man at the lead, until, somewhere along the way the kid with the fauxhawk (or maybe the kid in the Mets cap; it was hard to tell) no doubt trying to get his bearings while shielding his eyes, actually bumped into the kid in front of him, who, in turn, bumped into the kid in front of *him,* and so on, until Marvin bumped into the Walrus Man. The Walrus Man, not slowing down for any of this bumping nonsense, harrumphed a walrus-like harrumph and soldiered on, his girth so wide his arms nonchalantly brushed the tile walls with each waddled step, as though overly-tiled, long, bright pink corridors were everywhere these days, what's the big deal anyway, you kids are a bunch of wussies, you know that?

The trouble with walking down an extra-long hall you've never seen before, especially if it echoes your every move and is *way* over-lit and you're not sure where you're headed, is that long unfamiliar halls can seem

---

15> Ida Mae Wolcott, of Ann Arbor, Michigan, actually has a bathroom much like this — including the tiles and the crocheted toilet paper cozy. Hers is in the shape of a poodle. (The toilet paper cozy, not the bathroom). Whether Ida Mae Wolcott is someone's great-great aunt I do not know, but I find it interesting that I chose a name at random that, thanks to the diligent and thorough research of my trusted-yet-anal-retentive frog-eyed assistant, Jean-Claude, who apparently has an "in" at the Ann Arbor Senior Food Wagon Program, turned out to be the real thing. Once again, Interconnectness. It never ceases to amaze me.

longer than they really are. And when they're pink, they're even longer than that. It's sort of like gym class — it just goes on and on.

One thing Marvin was sure of: all this pink was going to wreak havoc with his cones and rods, which, if you were paying attention in Biology when you were studying the human eye instead of counting the holes in the acoustic ceiling tiles, you'd know has something to do with color perception. (And let's face it, knowing how many holes there are in any particular acoustic ceiling is only going to come in handy if, by some freak laboratory mishap, you find yourself shrunk to the size of a housefly and have to navigate your way home.)

Anyway, if you had paid attention, you'd know that in the human eye there are cones and rods, specialized cells that are sensitive to certain colors. And they go like totally berserk if you overload them. (According to the *Encyclopedia Gargantua*, there are something on the order of 120 million rods and 6 to 7 million cones in the human eye, except if you're color-blind or a miniature schnauzer, in which case there are about 17, maybe 18 if you're lucky.) Experiment: Look at one color long enough, then look away, and you will see its complementary color. Red will get you cyan, blue will get you yellow, and in the case of this particular great-aunt-Ida-Mae-pink hall, Marvin guessed, the color you'd likely get would be a sickly off-putting green.

You have probably seen this happen after watching a gazillion hours of television or staring into your computer screen for hours on end. Turn out the lights, and you might see the shape of the television set or monitor hovering in the darkness {~*insert creepy theremin-infused "floating ghost-television" music here*~}. I call this phenomenon "electronic phantasmagoria," which is a term I thought I coined myself, but according to my favorite search engine, so did thirteen other people.[16]

16> If you don't know what a theremin is, go to allthosefreakinvideos.com and check it out. I don't mean later. I mean now. It'll only take a minute... You're still here aren't you? Seriously, go to allthosefreakinvideos.com and put "theremin" in the search field and watch any three videos at random, your pick, and then meet me back here when you're done. ... Okay then. Assuming you

Down the hall they trudged, single-file, not a little nauseous from all that pink (Marvin hoping all the while he wouldn't be later sent to *this* hall to work on *Winged Avengers*), until, thankfully, someone had the courtesy to break the proverbial ice. [Where they come up with these sayings is beyond me. Why it would be ice that has to be broken in order to make a situation comfortable? Why not something else? "Drinking glass" perhaps. As in, "Once the drinking glass was broken, everyone relaxed." Or, say, "large Grecian urn." It seems a lot easier to break a drinking glass or a Grecian urn than to break ice, which would require a chisel or ice-pick of some sort, rather than, you know, gravity. Maybe that is the point, that ice is particularly hard to break. Ask the captain of the Titanic. Perhaps, then, it is just a matter of size. (I myself have no problem with the crushed variety, especially if it has been doused in copious amounts of gin.)]

The one to break the ice was the Asian kid, the one with the fauxhawk. "It feels like we're in the bowels of a top-secret government complex," he said, his voice reverberating against the tiles.

---

didn't read anything while you were there, because that would mean like even *more effort,* allow me to point out that the theremin was the first electronic musical instrument ever invented. Ever. Cool, yes? Usually associated with 1950s sci-fi flicks, theremins actually date back to 1928, which was like a hundred million years ago. 1928 was also the same year Mickey Mouse was created, which is why really old people think he's funny. [This is because *nothing else was funny in 1928.* Trust me on this; that's all they had. That, and "accent humor." This was when the "comedian" spoke in a (French, German, Italian, "Jewish") accent. It got big laughs back then. Seriously, that was the *joke.* And if the French/German/Italian/Jewish guy looked drunk, well even funnier, right? I'm telling you, 1928 was a laugh riot.]

Anyway, a theremin looks like a cross between a wire coat hanger and a car antenna and it's "played" by moving one's hands in thin air between two metal thingies (high-frequency oscillators, if you want to get all accurate about it), the effect of which is that the notes appear to be coming magically out of one's dental work. It sounds like a cross between a lovesick whale and an out-of-tune violin and atsy-tartsy people like performance artists eat it up.

Fun fact: You can create your own theremin sound by whistling and humming at the same time. (Hint: start with the whistle, add the hum.)

"More like the bowels of a top secret government *robot*," the seat-hogger said. "It's freakin' creepy." Their footsteps echoed as if the robot weren't just secret, but hollow. "Which means, next…"

The kid in front of him peeked under his Mets cap. "Robot *ass*."

"As a general rule," came the Walrus Man's voice from the front of the line, "comparing our fine institution to the intestinal expulsion of inanimate objects is strictly forbidden." Which made everyone look at one another as though this did not surprise them.

Nothing was said for many more pink-tiled steps. *Many* more pink-tiled steps. Too many pink-tile steps to count.[17]

At last, the hallway finally came to and end and the Walrus Man pushed open another door to reveal a very large room. Divided into a grid of four-foot-high cubicles, perhaps fifty of them, the room stretched 25-meters square. This, they surmised, was the dormitory. And it *was* a sickly green.

• • •

TROUBLE WAS, even after their eyes adjusted, the room *still* was a sickly green. Turned out it was *painted* a sickly green. On *purpose*. Worse, in an attempt to make the place seem appealing to "Youth, Juveniles, and Young Adults," some genius had come up with the idea of polka dots. Big gaudy day-glo yellow-and-orange polka dots. Everyone's noses scrunched up as if they'd just come upon a cache of week-old liver-and-cabbage casserole. Or like they'd just stepped inside the lining of a polyester suit, c.1968. Which is basically the same thing. Let's call it "Post-Modern *Blech*."

In each cubicle was a narrow bunk, under which was a desk, and atop which was a thin and unquestionably lumpy mattress. Folded neatly on each mattress was a blanket, two sheets, and a single bed pillow. Next to each bunk was a metal locker. And that was it. No doors. No privacy short

---

17> **Universal Literary Rule No. 17:** When composing a scene, keep in mind it should take your reader about the same amount of time to read a passage as it takes for the events depicted in that passage to take place. You do understand how freakin' *long* this hall was, yes?

of what a cubicle can afford, which, if you've ever worked in a Mumbai call center, isn't much.

"How *nice* for you guys," the girl with the braids said. "Where's *my* room?"

The Walrus Man motioned for everyone to gather around; then, with a certain air of blubbery satisfaction pronounced, "The more perceptive of you have surmised this is your dormitory. *All* of you." He made a point of looking at the girl with the braids so she knew she was included in the word "all."

"This is where you rest. Rest and sleep, sleep and rest. No games, no food or drink, no singing, no music playing, no books, no comics, no paper and pencil ..." — he shot a look at each one of them — "... no fooling."

Noses had not yet un-squished at this point, so Marvin, surveying the dormitory, and in the spirit of more ice-breaking, posed the question everyone was undoubtedly thinking: "What — no foosball?"

The seat-hogger's eyebrows shot up. "Hey yeah," he said. "You have foosball, right? It's not like a *Amish* ranch or something, is it? No games or nothin'?"

"What makes you think Amish kids don't play games?" the girl with the braids wanted to know.

The seat-hogger gave her a wink. "What about skateboarding? We can skateboard, right?"

"Oh," she said, catching on. "And ice skating. Is there a rink?"

"I like darts," the NY Mets kid said, looking around the dorm as if he fully expected to find a dartboard.

The kid with the tie-dyed pants pulled at his purple vest. "Me, I've got to go snorkeling or I'll go insane."

Fauxhawk jumped to his feat. "Yeah, me too. Only it's horseback riding. I'll go *nuts* if I can't go horseback riding."

All at once, six voices:

"Kite-flying?"

"Badminton?"

"Hop-scotch?"

"Zip line?"

"Shuffleboard?"

"Tennis?"

"Parcheesi?"

Everybody got so giddy asking about stuff they knew full well weren't
going to be there, the Walrus Man finally sat down on the edge of a bunk
and began to scrape some catsup off his pants. When at last they were
down to activities such as panning for gold and tomato rustling (that one
was Marvin's), the Walrus Man took a deep sigh and surveyed the group.
"We done? That it? Nobody want to mention bungee jumping?
Synchronized swimming? Zumba?" He waited. "No? Fine. Let us proceed."
He stood up, laced together his fingers, stretched his arms, opened his
mouth and—

"Wait," Marvin said. "I did have one more question."

The Walrus Man sat back down.

"This 'pursuits of a personal nature' … I'm in the throes of translating
the works of Shakespeare into Pig Latin. That allowed?"

"*Amlet-hay*?" the girl wanted to know.

"*Omeo-ray and Uliet-jay* at the moment," Marvin replied.

And off they went on another round of bogus activities, inspired, in
part, by the Walrus Man's own sarcastic suggestions, none of which, Marvin
was sorry to admit, he had thought of himself.[18]

18> *Some* people, by the way — whether it's because their jobs are boring or they haven't

eaten in six hours, or because they just got back from vacation only to find their in-box full of requests

anybody could have done in their absence, or they just had a tooth extracted and are feeling like

their jaw is about to implode, or any number of other things you have no way of knowing about —

who are otherwise pretty nice people who get just as goofy as the next guy in front of a karaoke

machine, can find themselves, given just the right circumstance (like listening to a litany of silliness

when they've got a dozen better things to do), humorless.

Dental hygienists and substitute teachers and Secretaries of Defense, for instance, often find

themselves in situations where they have lost all patience (which would be a good play on words

Again the Walrus Man sat with a sigh and waited it out, rolling his eyes and stroking his moustache and looking generally put out as people who are having trying days do, and when at last the group had exhausted a long list of random activities and the suggestions died down to nothing, the Walrus Man once again pulled his massive frame to his feet.

"Isn't that nice," he said, "getting along so well." He pulled at the neck of his giant red T-shirt as though it was yet another thing that was interfering with his day. "Now, if you would take a look at the dormitory — *all* of you … regardless of sex, race, national origin or fashion sense — and if you would be so kind, I'd like each of you to choose which particular domicile suits your individual needs and/or fancy."

No one moved.

"That means, ladies and gentlemen … *lady* and gentlemen … let's see,

---

with respect to the dental hygienist, but since "patients" and "patience" are spelled differently, the play on words won't work on paper, so just pretend I didn't mention it). And with patience goes humor, out the window like an escaped parrot. Or, rather, escaped punch line.

All of which means: people's reactions to you just might not have anything to do with YOU *per se,* but have everything to do with the fact that they are having a particularly trying day. A tooth extraction that makes a cheek blow up the size of a grapefruit puts you pretty low on a guy's priority list.

So keep this in mind the next time you are handed a traffic ticket or told to write 500 words on why you shouldn't fall asleep under the bleachers, or are sent to the principal's office when you've carved your name into someone else's laptop. Try to imagine the novocaine just wore off.

Side note: I am sorry to report I have found the most humorless person on the planet. It is Staff Sergeant Gregory Humblecryer, 47, of MCB Camp Pendleton, San Diego, California. Try calling SSgt. Humblecryer up in the middle of the night sometime, and you will see what I mean. Try this: ask for Dr. Fliegish Morgenstern, D.D.S. and tell SSgt. Humblecryer it is a matter of some urgency. When you are told there is no Dr. Morgenstern at this number, tell SSgt. Humblecryer that you have just discovered you are Morgenstern's biological clone and it is extremely important that you get together with him ASAP to compare a few notes. Stress the ASAP bit. If Humblecryer hangs up, try again. I did this myself four times last week and not once did SSgt. Humblecryer think it the least bit funny. See what I mean? No sense of humor. What a jerk, right?

how shall I put this … *now.*"

They hesitated at first, but once they saw he was serious, and realizing it is always better to choose one's own cubicle than have one assigned to you, all six got at it, Marvin picking the cubicle closest to the hall, thinking it would probably be closer to the bathroom. A couple of the guys began to throw pillows at each other, but the Walrus Man would have none of it. A shrill warning came from his whistle, a prop I'm sure you'd already forgotten about.

"Note each semi-private domicile, containing your very own private bunk," he announced, "also contains your very own private locker for your very own personal belongings — *approved* belongings — inside which you will find a change of clothes, and hanging on a lanyard, a name-tag."

Sure enough, inside each locker, next to a brown jumpsuit, hanging from a cord (which is a much less pretentious way of saying "lanyard") was a name-tag.

"Who's *this?*" the kid in the tie-dye pants scoffed, pulling a name-tag from his locker. "The last kids who were here?"

"No," the Walrus Man explained, "it is not the last kids who were here. It is the kids who are here now." He began to strut before the group, complete with moustache stroking and blubbery blubber blubbering. "You see, lady and gentlemen, we don't care about your given names. We don't care what name you'd like to be called. We have already selected names for you, and you, by your choice of cubicle, have chosen which one is yours." (It was pretty clear by now this wasn't the first time the man had made this speech.)

"Please wear these name-tags at all times," he went on. "I trust—"

Marvin raised his hand. "What about if we're in the shower?"

"Yeah," seat hogger said. "What about—"

"Let us not go down that road again, my friends. No, you do not have to wear the name-tags while in the shower or while doing anything else that involves the application of, the submersion into, or the subjection in any other manner to, onto, through or *with* water, or any other suggestion you are most undoubtedly conjuring up at the moment. Let us use a little common sense, shall we?"

No one said anything because (a) it's no fun to try to ruffle the feathers of someone who is unruffle-able, and (b) they were out of ideas.

"Now then," the Walrus Man said realizing both (a) and (b) above, "while I am discussing dinner with Winston, our cook, I trust each of you will don your new attire, become accustomed to your new name, and be prepared to answer to it. I will expect you all in the dining hall in precisely thirty minutes." He produced a stopwatch, clicked it, and turned to leave.

"Seriously," said the kid in the tie-dye pants, still staring at his name-tag. "I'm gonna be 'Flinn Karneb'? What kind of name is *Flinn Karneb?*"

"It's a joke," Fauxhawk said. "It's *gotta* be. I'm supposed to be ..." — he squinted at his name-tag — "... *Bennie Sterlati?* What am I, a mafia hit man? I'm *Chinese,* dude. Whoever heard of a Chinese kid named Sterlati? This is *so* messed up."

"They can call me Bullfrog Magee for all I care," the seat-hogger called from his cubicle. He sucked in a large grape bubble. "Don't matter in the least." This of course before he looked at his own name-tag. "Oh fer cryin'— It *is* a joke. *Kit Warnam.* What the hell's Kit? It's like a *girl's* name, ain't it? Short for Katherine, Kate, Kaitlin — some crap like that?"

"It's not a girl's name," said the girl with the braids. "*This* is a girl's name." She turned her name-tag for them to see.

Marvin pushed up his glasses and squinted at it: "Dara Steifer."

She bit her lip as she listened to the sound of it. Then, throwing her hat onto a bunk, she sat beside it with a plop. "What the heck," she shrugged, dangling her legs. "Dara Steiffer's okay with me. I hate my real name anyway."

"Get this," said the kid in the Mets cap. "Harlen C. Skedics. You ever hear such a lame-ass thing?" He looked at the name-tag like he'd been dealt yet another lame-ass hand in a long line of lame-ass hands. "My name is not Harlen C. Skedics. I've got a perfectly good name, thank you. I'm like *used* to it and everything. So's, you know, my *mother.* If they think I'm going to answer to this, they're—"

"Whadya suppose the 'C' stands for?" Fauxhawk — Bennie — asked.

Kit had joined them. "*Certifiable*? Harlen *Certifiable* Skedics. That's a good one."

"No it isn't," Harlen said, turning his cap bill forward. "It's stupid." He crossed his arms like he'd had it with the lame-ass stuff already. "As far as I'm concerned, the C stands for 'No Way.' Harlen C. Skedics? I don't think so."

"Oh I do," came the Walrus Man's voice. He'd been watching this exchange from the doorway. "That is exactly what — who — you are. You are Harlen, and you are Dara, and you are Kit, and you are Bennie, and you are Flinn. It's a nice set of names I think." He tapped at his walrus moustache, then turned to Marvin. "And you, young man? What name were you fortunate enough to secure?"

Marvin was frowning at his name-tag like it was a horse in the linen closet. He blinked. He blinked again. "How…?"

"Yes?" the Walrus Man pressed. He took a step toward Marvin. "You've found something interesting?"

"There must be some mistake," Marvin mumbled, scratching his head and genuinely at a loss for words, which of course Marvin never was.

The Walrus Man tapped at his moustache again. "Yes?"

Up until now, Marvin had reserved judgment of the place. Up until now, Marvin was just going to take it as it comes, find the proper place and time to work on *Winged Avengers,* and wait it out. Up until now, except for that high-five thing his parents had sprung on him, Marvin was relatively content. The Sandy Rivers Hilltop Ranch for Wayward Youth, Juveniles, and Young Adults was just another place to mess with, like Harmony Hills or Sunrise Valley Middle School or Zadok Magruder High or any other place he happened to be. But now, now he looked around to see whether this indeed was some sort of elaborate joke. Now they were messing with *him.* He looked back at the name-tag. "Marvin Plotnik," he finally answered, pushing back his glasses. "Mine says … *Marvin Plotnik.*"

"Excellent!" exclaimed the Walrus Man. "Excellent indeed. That's a dandy."

How it was Marvin chose a cubicle at random only to be rewarded with his own name was beyond him. It made no sense. He had a sinking suspicion that if he'd picked a cubicle in the back, which was his initial instinct, that name-tag also would have read *Marvin Plotnik*. He was about to make that very point when the Walrus Man said, "Good. Fine. Now we've all been introduced. Oh wait … that's not quite true, is it? *I* have not been introduced. I know your names, but you do not know mine. I, lady and gentlemen, am proctor of this fine facility. It is my job to make sure, after you have are well-acquainted with your surroundings, that your stay here at Sandy Rivers Hilltop Ranch is a productive one." With a stiff back, he scanned the group then gave a slight bow. "My name is Skylar Waddell. Not that any of you have asked. You may call me Mr. Waddell."

Again he looked at his stop watch. "Twenty-two minutes," he announced, and with that, Mr. Waddell, the Walrus Man, the Cola-Cola billboard, left the dormitory.

Chapter FOUR...

S O THEY EACH HAD NAMES. They had names before of course, but we are dealing with the circumstances at the Sandy Rivers Hilltop Ranch for Wayward Youth, Juveniles, and Young Adults — it says so right on the cover in case you hadn't noticed — and, as Mr. Waddell had emphatically pointed out, that's all we care about.

Because it's often difficult to remember a set of names, especially in one fell swoop (now *there's* an interesting phrase), I shall let you in on a little secret: There's a trick to it. It's called a "mnemonic device." That's pronounced *nem-on-ic* and why they put that extra M at the beginning is more proof you could build another whole language by using all the extraneous letters in English alone.[19]

19> Count your blessings if you don't have to learn how to spell in *French*. Now there's a language with more than its share of extraneous letters. *In each and every word.* I'm thinking their ancestors, the Franks, simply found a mess of them strewn about after the Battle of Tours in 732 and just couldn't leave them alone. Or the things self-replicate. Imagine being a French-speaking student and being told to "look it up if you don't know how to spell it." (Well you wouldn't understand because it's in English, and you'd be speaking French, but you get my drift.) Nothing over there is spelled like it sounds. Noth. Ing. Or, as the French say, "rien." Go online and see how you pronounce *that*. (Meet you at the next sentence when you're done.)... See what I mean? *C'est dément.* What the French

Suffice it to say, a mnemonic device is a way of remembering things. You are no doubt familiar with many mnemonic devices. Like "i before e, except after c," and "Thirty days hath September..." and "Do not eat the yellow snow." And of course every school child knows, "My Very Educated Mother Just Served Us Nine Pickles," or at least they did before those flaky astronomers changed their minds.[20]

There are mnemonic devices to help you remember all kinds of things, like history ("In fourteen hundred and ninety-two, Columbus sailed the ocean blue"), or music (the notes on the treble staff, EGBDF = Every Good

---

ought to do is give some of those extra letters to the Hawaiians. The Hawaiians are so in need of letters they just keep using the same ones over and over again. And almost all of them are vowels. Now Spanish, Spanish is a language that makes good use out of every letter and each one is always pronounced in exactly the same way. ¡Viva Español!

20> Allow me to comment on the Pluto issue. Because of its diminutive size, astronomers one day suddenly decided that Pluto no longer rated the term "planet," that it more accurately should be described as "dwarf planet," "dormant comet," "asteroid," or even "hurtling hunk o' rock." It is sort of like botanists suddenly deciding that you can't call cantaloupe a fruit anymore. They did this of course because astronomers like to mess with people. ("Hey, let's get rid of that stupid My Very Educated Mother thing!" "Good one, Professor Snarly!")

Anyway, I'm sure these scientists would be surprised to know that Pluto, in point of fact, is none of these things. What they take for a dormant comet is in truth a rather large commercial cooking range once thrust into space a little over 12,000 glirms ago (approx. 100 Earth years) by a particularly irate Kilgorian starship chef.

They're a short-tempered lot, the Kilgorians. And, having six strong arms (seven if you count the prehensile tail), and a muscle-to-fat ratio of 50:1, a Kilgorian can thrust the largest of objects impressively far with very little effort. That's what Kilgorians do. Especially when asked one too many times to do something they have no intention of doing, in this case, to forego the murmulfish in the stargazy pie. They hate that kind of thing. (Not stargazy pie — that they love. It's leaving out a key ingredient they take issue with.) Given that, I'm certain that if the Kilgorian chef who had this particular hissy fit ever were to learn that light-years away astronomers would one day consider his jettisoned stove a minor planet, that fact would very likely tick him off as well.

Boy Does Fine), or spelling ("There is 'a rat' in 'separate.'"). And let's not forget "Aluminum Barometer Cellophane Diaphanous Elephantine Filibuster Gangrene Heliotrope, etc.," to remember that troublesome alphabet.

I happen to know that one of Marvin's favorite mnemonic devices is called "The Method of Loci," which sounds like a surgical procedure or the title of a fantasy novel, but it's not. Here's how it works: Let us say you need to remember an upcoming speech. Let us say it is a book report on a book entitled *Thomas Edison: So Many Bright Ideas,* which, in fourth grade for Marvin Plotnik, it was. He simply picked a place he knew well — in this case, his house — and then assigned different parts of the speech to each room. Then, when he stood before the totally enthralled (read: "yawning") faces of his fellow fourth-graders, he mentally walked through the house.

When he came upon the lamp on the table in the living room, for instance, he was sure to mention that light bulb thing. Having mentally placed a movie projector in the den (to remember that Kinetoscope thing), a record player in the living room (to remember that phonograph thing), a skeleton in the closet (to remember that x-ray thing), and a dirty magazine in the bathroom (to remember that AC/DC thing), Marvin went through his Thomas Edison speech without a hitch. Everyone still looked bored, but the point of a mnemonic device isn't meant to bring one fame and fortune. (Unless of course you're Tom Cruise, when it's pretty important to remember your lines, or the president of the United States, when it's pretty important to remember where you keep the keys to the nuclear arsenal.)

Some people come up with extremely clever mnemonic devices. Years ago, while on a mission, I met a fellow who was able to rattle off the first 7,420 digits of pi. He did this by assigning words to each digit and writing a 7,420-word story. Unfortunately, the story he came up with was not very good. It had something to do with a lonely cane toad who ruled an island of Panama-hat-making iguanas. Still, pretty clever, I must say, because every time the number 8 came up, it was a preposition.

Anyway, all this would lead one to believe mnemonic devices just give you more things to keep track of. Maybe so, but the human brain is an extra-weird place full of all sorts of extra-weird ways of keeping track of all sorts of extra-weird things, which is why your cousin can remember who won the World Series in 1923 and you can't.

Here is a test. Consider the following list:

CUCUMBER

BALLPOINT PEN

ICE CREAM CONE

COW

TULIP

PARIS

STAPLER

YELLOW

VOLKSWAGEN BEETLE

BRAD PITT

Ok, now close the book and count to twenty. See how many words on the list you can recall. Ready? Go. I'll wait.…

WRITE YOUR ANSWERS HERE:

_____   _____

_____   _____

_____   _____

_____   _____

_____   _____

How many were you able to recall? Four? Six? Eight? Ten? If it was less than ten, try this. It's called The Assignment Method…

Think of a group of people you know. Your family or your classmates perhaps, or the cast of "StarQuest" or the 1923 New York Yankees (who, incidentally, won the World Series that year over the New York Giants). It's your choice. Now, look at each word and assign it to one of those people.

You could assign the stapler to your Uncle Harry, the ice cream cone to your little brother, etc. Picture Uncle Harry stapling something. Picture your little brother eating an ice cream cone. You get the idea. Do that with the rest of the list. Picture each person with their respective item. You can even combine them, for instance picturing your mother sitting in a **yellow Volkswagen Beetle,** licking an **ice cream cone,** while **Brad Pitt** chases her with a **cucumber,** which of course would be *way* open to Freudian analysis, but it's your imagination so don't look at me.

So, ok, try the Assignment Method on the list. Here's the list again so you don't have to strain yourself turning back a page:

CUCUMBER
BALLPOINT PEN
ICE CREAM CONE
COW
TULIP
PARIS
STAPLER
YELLOW
VOLKSWAGEN BEETLE
BRAD PITT

Now close the book, count to twenty again and dazzle me with your new-found memory abilities. Again, I'll wait…

WRITE YOUR ANSWERS HERE:

_____	_____
_____	_____
_____	_____
_____	_____
_____	_____

Whoa. Well done.

Such is the power of the human brain.[21]

Anyway, the reason I've gone on so long about mnemonic devices — besides the fact I like to say "mnemonic device" (and yes, there was a reason) — is because Marvin, being a big believer in them, thought a handy one might be in order so he could remember everyone's assigned names.

In fact, when Mr. Waddell left the dormitory, Marvin immediately got to work thinking up ways to remember everyone's name — Kit (seat-hogger), Flinn (freckles, tie-dyed pants), Bennie (blue fauxhawk), Harlen (Mets cap), and of course, Dara, whose name was a cinch because she was the only girl and Marvin had a cousin named Dara, who coincidentally was also a girl, who lived in New Mexico. Not that the New Mexico thing matters. Bennie was of course the easiest of the boys because "Bennie" and "blue" (the color of his fauxhawk) both start with B. But the others proved a little harder and by the time he realized what's coming up at the end of this paragraph, he'd gone through them all, finishing up with Harlen (which sounds like Harlem, which is in New York, which is where the Mets play). Which was the point he realized something that put the whole mnemonic device thing in a new light and which, if you remembered what was in their lockers, you were one step and one lengthy discourse ahead of the rest of us: They all had name-tags.

Or, as they say where I come from: "Duh."

Let this be a lesson to you. Sometimes you work and work at something, like listing a plethora of mnemonic devices complete with an

---

21> Want a mnemonic device to remember "mnemonic device"? Try using this sentence: "Remembering something is a devil of a thing to do." And devils are demonic, yes? So take the word "demonic," remove the D (for "don't need"), replace it with an N (for "need") and you have "nemonic," which at least is how the word is pronounced. It's adding that M at the start that's the bugaboo. The first thirty people who can send me a good mnemonic device to remember that darn superfluous M will receive a nice shiny Limited Edition *Well-Done!* Certificate from yours truly, personally imprinted with your name in AWE-INSPIRING CAPITAL LETTERS to impress your friends, and signed in authentic imitation gold-looking ink.

inappropriate comment about someone's mother, putting in long hours to get it just right, only to find out in the end it was all for naught; you never had to do it in the first place. Ever have a teacher announce there's going to be a test the following day on, say, the Seven Wonders of the Modern World, so you sit up half the night memorizing this Wonder thing and that Wonder thing, and when you walk into class the next morning, the big dope announces the test is off, ha ha just kidding? And you sit there stewing over the fact you wasted all those hours, hours you could've spent on something more important — sampling the audio portion of your favorite cult TV show and playing it backwards to see if there was a cryptic message in it, or posting something on the GAM3HACK3RS forums, or scaring your little sister by putting firefly butts on your eyelids? (Which, by the way, is a lot cheaper and a lot creepier than any store-bought Halloween mask.)

Well, yes, you'll never get those precious hours back. But in the end, all is not for naught and you'll know your Roman Coliseum from your Great Wall of China, won't you?[22]

22> One of the claims to fame of The Great Wall of China, some 4,000 miles in length and originally built to keep out those pesky Mongol hordes, is that supposedly it is the only man-made structure on the planet Earth visible from the Moon. Or so they would have you believe (not the Mongol hordes, the people who come up with this stuff).

But did you know there once was another structure visible from the Moon? (No, not Jay Leno's chin.) Not only from the Moon, but from a lot farther than that. Don't take my word for it. You can see it for yourself if you just know where to look. And you don't even have to go into outer space to do it. Well, okay, that's not *exactly* true. You can't see *all* of it, as only a mere fraction remains today. Key word: *remains*. As in ruins. Ruins commonly believed to be those of the Maya, Inca and other indigenous peoples of Central and South America. Thanks to archeologists and scores of sweaty men with machetes, today bus-loads of tourists in khaki shorts and over-priced sandals can visit what's left of the ancient cities — Palenque, Tikal, Machu Picchu, etc. — as they poke their way through the jungles of the southern hemisphere (the ruins, not the tourists). What they will not be told by their overly friendly tour guides, however, is just how far back the histories of these ancient cities go.

They are told only that many of these ancient sites succumbed to the elements while others succumbed to abandonment and greed. Spanish conquistadors, for instance, arriving in the 1500s, thought the rugged stones of Palenque would be the perfect complement to the king's royal commode, so they shipped it off piece by piece to Spain so King Charles would see how very clever and resourceful they were. ("Conquistador" being Spanish for "men in pointy hats who take whatever they want.")

But more interesting than the conquistadors' dismissal of indigenous culture and the point to this digression and particularly this paragraph, is that the great pre-Colombian cities of Central America weren't always examples of indigenous culture at all. Not originally. Originally they were examples of *Rogullian* culture. Which isn't indigenous at all. By about 32.17 light years.

That is to say, centuries before there were anything closely resembling human beings on Earth, let alone Mayans, inhabitants of the planet Rogull had visited the planet and saw at once a grand opportunity. A grand *commercial* opportunity.

Take a moment to do an internet search on Tikal. Again, I'll wait …

Done? Did you see the pictures? Did you see the temples with their mile-high stairs? Now think about it. What human is strong enough, and dexterous enough, and energetic enough, to climb all those stairs? Who's going to come home after a hard day at work and hit *all that pavement?* Who's going to do it lugging a gallon of milk?

No, it wasn't until *long* after the Rogullians left that the locals moved in. And all *they* had to do was knock down a few walls, carve some bas-reliefs, perform an occasional human sacrifice and call the place home.

It gets better: Today we see these ruins as separate cities, which indeed they were, but understand that before that — eons before that, when the Rogullians were running the place — these sites were actually *connected*. Palenque was *connected* to Tikal, which was *connected* to Uxmal, along with a slew of other sites as yet uncovered, spanning the whole of Central and South America. What modern man sees as a series of circuitous and unrelated stone walls, pyramids and towers, were in point of fact the foundations of a much larger structure built atop them. Think of these walls and towers as footings, supportive structures, or, perhaps more comparably, the 2x4s behind the Hollywood sign.

Because back in the day, if you were on an intergalactic voyage and happened by this part of the Sol-7 System, you'd see that the whole complicated affair — the whole structure built upon this underlayment — was not willy-nilly. It formed words. Rogullian words. And if you were skilled in Rogullian — and the time who wasn't? — you'd recognize the words as a list of delicacies: everything from sprudnil langburgers to phorleberry custard and farkniklügen pie. And you would rejoice, weary

Marvin's coming up with mnemonic devices for all the kids' names wasn't total wasted time. He did discover, while wandering about, that there was a bathroom at the back of the dormitory. Naturally the cubicle he had chosen turned out to be farthest from the bathroom, not the closest, which is how these things usually work out. Don't get me going on the line at the bank.

---

on your intergalactic voyage, as sprudnil langburgers and phorleberry custard and farkniklügen pie were all but impossible to come by — remember this was eons ago — this far from Alpha Centauri. Sort of like finding a good Reuben sandwich in Butte, Montana.

And, if you were familiar with Rogullian anatomy — and at the time who wasn't, if you get my drift — it would be obvious why a very entrepreneurial Rogullian chose the planet in the first place:

Half the graphics were already done!

As you no doubt have noticed if you have taken the time to look at any map of the world, Italy resembles a boot, Florida resembles a you-know-what and Alaska resembles Martha Washington. But what you might not have noticed is that the Western Hemisphere looks amazingly like a hungry Rogullian, with the Gulf of Mexico serving as a humorously drawn Rogullian "nutriment orifice" (they don't have mouths) and the Peruvian coastline something even funnier. [*See: "Florida."*] I tell you, when the first Rogullians came across the galaxy and caught sight of the Gulf of Mexico, it was hard to keep one's mog-milk from coming out of one's phlegmal tube.

And across the great hungry Rogullian face, flashing its welcome? "E-A-T-S." (Translation.) In Rogullian it requires 72 letterforms, which was why, in order to be seen clear to the asteroid belt, it required a whole continent to pull it off. That's right, the Rogullians built a continent-sized planetary billboard, leading the weary space traveler to The Great Rogullian Way-Station of Earth and a heaping helping of phorleberry custard.

By way of comparison, it took the Chinese 4,000 miles to get out one squiggly Letter I.

If this is true, you may ask, what happened to the structure? Why has it not been unearthed by our esteemed archeologists? Why is there no evidence of it? Might I suggest, if you really want to know what happened to the archeological record of The Great Rogullian Way-Station of Earth, you direct your questions, preferably in writing, to the British Museum.

Chapter FIVE...

I T WAS IN SAID BATHROOM that Marvin and Flinn and Kit were taking care of some P.B.E.N. (Personal Business of an Expulsive Nature) when they heard someone yelling. Masked by all the flushing and whatnot, but not so masked post-flush-and-hand-wash when they returned to the dormitory, where it was loud as could be.

It turned out to be Bennie, he of blue fauxhawk and, now, of super-lung-capacity. As a matter of fact, Bennie's yell sounded, in another example of the Interconnectedness of All Things and completely unbeknownst to Bennie or his fashionably upturned hair, remarkably like the war cry of an honest-to-goodness Mohawk Indian, whose haircut the fauxhawk was meant to mimic. The Mohawk were (and are) a tribe of Iroquois who once lived (and live) along the Mohawk and Hudson Rivers in what was to become (and became) New York State. Long before Burger King got there. The Mohawk were fierce warriors, so being able to imitate so convincingly a sound that Bennie himself had never heard, especially without even being aware he was doing it, was something else indeed.[23]

23> There are people who say that if a butterfly flaps its wings in New York, it rains in San Francisco. Mathematicians call this theory the "Butterfly Effect," a very catchy catch-phrase in a very sexy field of mathematics called "chaos theory." While mathematicians in not-so-sexy fields think the

Butterfly Effect is completely horse-rubbish, they don't often challenge it in public for fear of Crazed Mathematician Retaliation, an actual, clinical medical condition, but also because when the chaos theory folks start jotting down a lot of numbers and cosines and brackets and wiggly thingies on blackboards, the next thing you know it's raining in San Francisco.

But that is not the point here. The point here is that, butterflies aside, a person can do something extraordinary and not even be aware of it. Take, for instance, the case of Bartholomew J. Finkensack, M.D., a Philadelphia surgeon who, in the course of removing a pancreas in the summer of 2003 (not from the fridge or anything, from an actual person), in point of fact killed a man in another state ("another state" not being that of consciousness but being that of geography).

Here is how it happened: In the course of surgery, Dr. Finkensack, going merrily about this surgery business, turned on the Kraff-Whiley LaserX3000, a high-powered operating room device that enables surgeons to perform some rather disgusting but often life-saving procedures on completely unconscious patients when they are most vulnerable (the patients, not the surgeons). Unfortunately, it uses significant amounts of electricity in doing it. Which is why hospitals can charge you $27 for a Q-tip.

Turning on the device would be inconsequential under normal circumstances, but because this was an extraordinarily hot August afternoon, the LaserX3000 proved just enough a draw on electric power that across town at Mid-Atlantic Electric, lights and buzzers in the Master Control Room started flashing a warning. Usage levels had reached their maximum and someone ought to do something about it, the lights and buzzers warned, right then and there, or a great portion of Philadelphia could suffer a loss of electric power, causing unforeseen catastrophes, the least of which would be a run on blueberry smoothies.

Unfortunately again, that someone happened to be kneeling on the floor so as to retrieve a toppled can of Cola-Cola, and, upon hearing the warning, reached up to his keyboard to rectify the situation.

Unfortunately thrice, from that precarious angle and in the throes of the moment, the rattled technician confused the configuration of the numeric keypad with that of a telephone — which, through one of Mankind's most bone-headed decisions, is mysteriously upside down vis-à-vis a computer keypad — and so hit a series of nines instead of zeros. Meaning he moved a lot more electricity from one sector to another than he had intended — a *lot* more — the result of which was the loss of power to some 102,000 good citizens of North Tewksbury, Massachusetts, some 318 miles and four states away. [*See: "Another State," above.*] So, during the blackout, which lasted just under nine minutes, the North Tewksbury Sunshine Retirement Village, fearing its elderly residents

"They're gone!" Bennie was yelping, Mohawk-like, his red face set against the blue of his hair. "They're frickin' *gone!*"

Five heads appeared over the top of his cubicle, watching him have what one might call a conniption fit (From the Latin, *conniptio abdomino*, "ready to kick someone in the groin"). He'd dumped the contents of his backpack onto his bed and was rummaging through it as if he'd lost something important. Over and over he'd lift the backpack as if it had been sitting on top of his quarry, and over and over his quarry wasn't there.

"What's gone?" everyone wanted to know, thinking Bennie had gone over the proverbial edge.

"My Crunch Munchies. I had a box of Crunch Munchies in my backpack and now they're gone. So's my SpudNuggets. Gone!" He continued rummaging through underwear and socks. "I'm starving to death. So I figured … Crap! My Bunch-o-Nuts bar's gone, too. This is insane! The fat dude said we wouldn't eat for 20 minutes! I can't *wait* 20 minutes. I can't even wait *two* minutes! A person's property is … is … *a person's property, isn't it?*" He didn't bother to hide what occurred to him next. His eyes darted to the others as if he'd find a crumb of Crunch Munchie on someone's lip.

"Don't look at *me*," Kit told him. "I didn't eat your frickin' Crunch Munchies."

---

would panic in the dark, opted to go on backup power supplied by generator. Now when the generator kicked in, as generators do, it produced tremendous noise. Deafening noise. So when a Mr. Frank Lukenbill, 87, in an attempt at small talk with Mr. Seymour Redding, 93, a new resident of the North Tewksbury Sunshine Retirement Village and, at the moment, his chess partner, exclaimed, "I repped all my life" (meaning he'd been a shoe salesman), Mr. Redding, already lacking in the hearing department but definitely even more impaired by the sound of the infernal generator, thought Mr. Lukenbill had said, "I slept with your wife." So he took out a .38 and shot Mr. Lukenbill quite dead.

Which means Dr. Finkensack's use of the LaserX3000 in Philadelphia, unbeknownst to Dr. Finkensack, killed a man in Massachusetts, making my point that people can do extraordinary things, although not necessarily positive things, without even knowing it. Or, more succinctly, if it's pouring where you are, somewhere else the butterflies are going nuts.

"Neither did I," Harlen said, pulling at his Mets cap. "They're gross."

Everyone else put on their best don't-look-at-me expression until Flinn shrugged, "So you ate 'em. No biggie. Forget about it."

"I did not eat them," Bennie replied, his face turning red. "I'd *know* it if I ate 'em. I wouldn't feel all queasy right about now if I *ate* 'em. I wouldn't—" He pulled at his fauxhawk. "I've got blood-sugar problems, dude. I need a boost every now and then or I get all barfy."

Dara's hands went to her hips like she'd assumed the role of den mother. "You're not going to get it from Crunch Munchies," she said. "It's junk. You need to eat fruit and vegetables and nuts."

Bennie faced her. "Excuse me? I think I know what food does and does not affect my blood sugar. Crunch Munchies, for your information, are caramel-coated popcorn, *with* clusters of almonds, so it's *just* the thing. Boom! Like that. Levels back."

Dara, obviously not being able to help herself, began addressing the evils of processed sugar. Everybody was no doubt beginning to reminisce fondly of the time when Dara was on the bus in her floppy hat and minding her own stretched-out-T-shirt business.

While this all-too-fascinating exchange was taking place, Marvin had gone back to his cubicle and found that his own stash of contraband — the Cheese Doodles, the Twinkle Bars, the unpopped PoppyCorn Lite — was missing from his backpack. And he knew darn well he hadn't eaten it, either, especially the unpopped PoppyCorn Lite, which, without the benefit of a microwave would be hard on the teeth. Which was basically what he told the group when he rejoined them (the part about his stuff being gone, not the part about unpopped popcorn being hard on his teeth).

Everyone ran to their cubicles. Same thing all around. Anything edible secreted among their possessions, gone. Then the second discovery. All their GameKids and ePods and portable DVD players were gone, too. After all, who in their right mind was going to abide by a ridiculously unjust list of forbidden "cultural distractions"? So naturally they'd all brought at least eight of them. That they'd all kept their contraband hidden on the bus ride to Sandy Rivers was the miracle here. And for what? It was all gone anyway.

It looked like the only things they'd been left with were along the lines of underwear and toothpaste, which, unless you're some kind of freak, do not make for a very good time. But then Dara discovered a book she'd brought was in her locker, which made everyone return to their cubicles to the discover the same. Marvin's paperbacks (including his favorite dog-eared sci-fi spoofs, *The Idiot's Guide to Time Travel* and *Not on My Planet You Don't*) were neatly stacked on the top shelf inside his locker, and next to it, his GameKid and all of his GameKid games.

All the truly missing items were edible.

"Maybe there's some reason for this," Flinn Karneb was saying, his nose redder than ever. "Maybe it's some kind of fat farm or something."

"Better not be," Bennie said. "The idea of not having food …"

Flinn, sounding hopeful: "Maybe they'll have a nice big lunch."

Kit slammed his locker door. "I don't care if they have prime rib and mashed potatoes and all-you-can-eat Boston cream pie, you can't drive me across two-and-a-half states and steal my crap. It's *my* crap. *Mine.*"

"I don't get it," said Bennie. "What difference would it make if we brought a little junk food? So what? We'd eat it and then it'd be gone. Problem over."

Marvin agreed. It made no sense. His brain flashed for a second on what he'd seen scamper across the bus floor. Mice? Rats? Then again, mice and rats can't stack MP3 players and GameKids neatly onto a locker shelf. And where was the evidence — the gnawed-up pieces of packaging? Where's the poo? All he knew was that never before had anyone of authority outright taken something that belonged to him. Unless, of course, you count Ms. Steinmetz snapping the maple syrup right out of his hand smack in the middle of an Important Demonstration. But even she didn't keep it. It was right there on Principal Hadley's desk when Marvin was being reprimanded by that tusk-faced tartar-saucey-blubber-ball, Skylar Waddell.

It was here a bell rang. You might imagine the sort of bell you're likely to hear at school to designate the end of class. But you'd be wrong. This bell was nothing like that. This bell was more along the lines of what you might hear if you were suspended from Liberty Bell itself, which, according to the *Encyclopedia Gargantua,* is some twelve feet in circumference and weighs over two tons. Meaning the bell that was currently shaking the dormitory into the depths of hell rang with such an overpowering and unnerving *GONG ... GONG ... GONG,* its reverberations went so far down into one's body that one's kidneys momentarily shut down. It was so loud and jarring, none of the six would have been surprised to learn that any other one of the six had soiled their checklist-approved underwear.

Slowly ... slowly ... *slow-ly* ... as their ears returned to normal, Marvin could just make out the question being posed by Bennie Sterlati, he now of extremely low blood sugar and desperate expression on his face: "How're we supposed to *find* the dining hall?"

Marvin shrugged. "Look under D, I guess."

Chapter SIX...

THROUGHOUT HUMAN HISTORY, all great societies have shared a common list of attributes. Let us call them the Top Ten Hallmarks of Civilization: clear-cut divisions of labor, a stratified social hierarchy, organized religion, recognition of the arts, complex administrative bureaucracies, systems of commerce, organized secret societies, pervasive discrimination against anyone who is different, a certain number of people who insist on being called "Skip," and good signage.

Good signage means that out-of-towners are able to find their way around. Good signage means you can locate the correct platform in a subway station and board the correct train. Good signage means you won't have to wonder why the movie you just walked into is about cute little bunnies having a picnic rather than Jason Statham blowing up a bus. Good signage means you can change lanes on the freeway in plenty of time for your exit without causing the nearest semi to jack-knife and end up in a fiery inferno of diesel fuel and polyethylene.

Good signage, then, might just be the most important hallmark of all.

Not to belabor the point (invariably used when belaboring a point), good signage can mean the difference between applying for a job on the forty-second floor of the Transamerica Pyramid in San Francisco, which has a particularly nice view of San Francisco Bay, and walking into the wrong interview in a different building altogether and landing a job that will mean a lifetime of dismal and dreary data doctoring until you're 67 (or 62 if you opt for early retirement). Which may not sound like a very big deal now, but it will someday, when you come to realize that a view of sailboats gliding carelessly toward the sunset and the Golden Gate Bridge is a whole lot nicer than looking out on a dumpster-filled alleyway, which gets old before you've even had your first lunch break.

If you want to tell which society will find itself buried under the sands of time, look for swarms of people who can't find the bathroom.

So when Marvin and his friends encountered a sign in the pink-tiled corridor that read DINING HALL, under which was an old-fashioned illustration of one of those pointing fingers that one might see on the door of a 19th-century undertaker, it made finding the dining hall a snap. The finger pointed to the right. Which was where Marvin and his five compatriots went, until they got to the end of the hall. At which point they came to another sign, on which was another finger, this one pointing to the left, which was the direction Marvin and his compatriots went, coming upon, what else, another pink-tiled hall and another finger. To make a long story short — which could be a play on words, but in this case isn't — there were two more pink-tiled halls and a couple of flights of pink-tiled stairs (see how "long story short" would be a play on words?), all of which finally led to: a pink-tiled hall. Only in this case I use the word "hall" not in the sense of a long and narrow passageway but in the sense of a spacious room of tables and chairs and napkins and silverware and all that.

And standing inside the hall, making a show of standing inside the hall, was Mr. Skylar Waddell. "Well done," he said, clicking his stopwatch as the group arrived. "Well done indeed." He then took a stance as though he was about to embark on speech he'd most certainly given dozens of times: "Without further ado, I'd like you all to welcome the administrator of Sandy Rivers Hilltop Ranch for Wayward Youth, Juveniles, and Young Adults …" — he thrust out an expectant arm — "… Mr. Reginald T. Foggbottom."

At which point no one appeared.

His arm came down. He cleared his throat. "As I say," he projected in a voice one would use on stage, "Mr. Reginald T. Foggbottom!" Again, a welcoming arm to the rear doorway.

{~*Hollow chirp of lone cricket.~*}

A worried look came upon Skylar Waddell's face. "Mr. Reginald—"

"Oh *my!*" came a voice behind them, "Oh my *goodness!*" The group turned to see a man come charging through the same doorway they themselves had entered only moments before. He had to duck as he passed through the doorway because he was perched atop a TransWay One-Man Vehicle — a device not at all like the Segway® Personal Transporter, which is a highly-trademarked entirely different piece of machinery and isn't the same thing at all even though they both have two wheels and handlebars and no apparent means of acceleration. Traveling at a good clip, he rushed by much like a monkey might rush by while trying to hold onto an irate bull, a monkey-on-a-bull blur going, "Whoa!" and "Oh my!" and "I'll get this baby under control in just … a … my goodness *me*." Which made it clear this was most probably the man's first effort at operating the thing.

Well *this* couldn't be the administrator. This was probably some ranch-hand or whatever-it-is-they-have-here who'd made a wrong pink-halled turn. As the man and his TransWay careened about like some joker hopped up on N-R-G Juice™, the thought passed through Marvin's head that Sandy Rivers just might *be* an institution for the criminally insane. He waited for Mr. Waddell to kick the interloper out, perhaps by means of a large net, posthaste.

Instead, Mr. Waddell clasped his hands together, gave his full attention to the careening TransWay, and waited with a patience the group had not yet witnessed. (Either that, or he was falling asleep; it was hard to tell.)

Meanwhile, the man on the TransWay continued to blaze a circuitous path around the room — zigging one way then overcompensating by zagging the other — bumping into tables, knocking over chairs, flashing the group a smile or a wobbly wave here and there, and generally going amok. He was like that cartoon kangaroo who can't stop "bouncety-bounce-bounce-bouncing" and if you are unfamiliar with the kangaroo who can't stop "bouncety-bounce-bounce-bouncing," count your blessings because he is real-real-really annoying.

When at last he was able to stop the infernal machine, and, miraculously, turn to face the group, he settled alongside Mr. Waddell (albeit a little wobbly) as if that were his intention from the very start.

"Lady and Gentlemen," Mr. Waddell finally sighed, having long ago given up on expecting anyone to appear from what turned out to be the kitchen, "Reginald T. Foggbottom."

Everyone looked to the man on the TransWay (still of course not to be confused with a Segway® Personal Transporter, an entirely different machine altogether). White haired, he appeared to be in his sixties. He wore a wrinkled, powder-blue seersucker suit and thin black tie, and topping off the look, the aforementioned white hair was wild, going helter-skelter, higgledy-piggledy and other hyphenated ways to say "totally messed up."

Combine Colonel Sanders, Mark Twain and a touch of mad scientist and that should give you a good picture of the man, who had spent much of the last paragraph nervously attempting to search his pockets as if for something important, very nearly upsetting the TransWay with each pat of a pocket. He would retrieve an item, such as a folded-up newspaper, from one pocket, put it between his teeth so as to get it out of the way, retrieve another item, such as a pencil, replace the newspaper with the pencil, retrieve another item, such as one of those wooden paddles with a red ball attached by a piece of elastic, and so on, all the while barely keeping his balance. The man in the seersucker suit continued in this manner for a good two minutes, which is a surprisingly long time if you actually sat down and timed it.

This was Reginald T. Foggbottom, Marvin marveled, *the head of the school — er — ranch? THIS?*

Now if you've ever had the misfortune of attending a class on etiquette — and why would you when it's become perfectly acceptable to carry on a phone conversation about what a dumbass Jermaine was in class today, instead of paying attention to the guy at The Pizza Wheel who's tapping his fingers on the counter waiting for your order — it's possible you sat through a session on the proper way to greet a new acquaintance. "How do you do?" is an acceptable greeting, for instance, or "My, what a grand and eloquently gilded ballroom you have." Conventions of etiquette, you would be told, are meant to make those around us feel at home, or short of that, spare their feelings. We all know many of these conventions were dispensed with years ago when it became passé for young ladies to don white gloves or young men to polish their knickers. Not to mention all that bowing and curtseying nonsense.[24]

No matter what your friends tell you, most of the conventions of etiquette are still in force. Being polite when you meet someone pretty much remains the right thing to do, no matter who is before you making a fool of himself on an infernal contraption they clearly are far from mastering. Mr. Waddell, it seemed, was well aware of this. He didn't expect the new arrivals to bow or curtsey or anything, but he did look at them expectantly. To, not unexpectedly, no avail. All Marvin and his compatriots were capable of at the moment was standing there speechless while Mr. Reginald T. Foggbottom, balanced precariously on his TransWay, repeatedly tried to right himself, once even turning a complete (and wobbly) three-sixty. Then the six newcomers all ended up doing the same thing. By this I do not mean they did a three-sixty; I mean they did the

---

24> I am well aware that one does not polish one's knickers. Consider this an example of "creative license." Creative license allows the creator — in this case, me — to muss about with actual facts for the purpose of a Higher Good, e.g., in this case, a joke. Not a very good joke, but still.

Creative license is a wondrous thing. It not only allows us to make things sound better, it allows us to play with bits of reality without being sued in court for being a big fat liar. And it's not just for writers, either. It's for everyone!

Take, for instance, a painter. When a painter paints a still-life of a flower arrangement, she may decide to add a daisy even though a daisy is not in the arrangement that sits before her. Or, conversely, she may choose to ignore an actual daisy and only paint the mums. Then again, she may decide to forego the mums and the daisies and paint a vase full of severed limbs skewered on bloodied sticks.

It's all a matter of degree.

Creative license, therefore, is a reliable excuse to fall back on when the need arises. The next time your math teacher asks why you didn't show all your work on an exam, tell him, "creative license."

same thing as one another: they burst out laughing. Kit Warnam even managed to say, "What a *goof*."

On their behalf, Waddell turned a bright blubbery red, not unlike the red of a Cola-Cola billboard, or, perhaps, the red one sees in the construct of a dashing red fez during a Shriner convention. Which was pretty darn red.

Marvin and the others had failed miserably in the courtesy department.

Reginald T. Foggbottom, however, didn't seem to mind. In fact, he let out a roar of laughter himself — as though he had just heard the greatest joke of his life. "That was some entrance, eh? Not exactly what you expected, I'm afraid, but my goodness, Waddell, who in blue blazes would you have them expect, the Prince of Wales? All that arm waving and such." He looked over a pair of wire-rimmed glasses at the group. "The trouble with big entrances," he told them, "is the only one who gets anything out of it is the fellow who's making the entrance."

Then, as if somewhere in there he'd said the second best thing he'd ever heard, he squealed a squeal of joy. An actual five-year-old squeal of joy (not meaning the squeal was five years old, but that it was a squeal one would expect from a five-year-old). "Aah!" he squealed. "That's a good one! '*Blue blazes*'!" He took out a small notebook from his jacket and began to write with the remains of a stubby pencil (managing, quite amazingly, to balance the TransWay with competence).

"Curious phrase, isn't it, 'Blue blazes'? I'm collecting them, curious phrases. I'm going to call it *Reginald T. Foggbottom's Dictionary of Peculiar Expressions, Adages, Idioms and Other Figures of Speech* and it's going to be all the rage back home … mark my words." His eyebrows shot up. "Ha! Another good one!" His pencil moved. "Mark my words."

• • •

"SO," REGINALD T. FOGGBOTTOM soed, smacking his lips as though it was time to get this thing under way, "welcome to Sandy Rivers Hilltop Ranch, the institution at which each and every one of you will find your place in the world, your mastery of self-control, and your true calling —

not to mention all sorts of other nifty things that begin with 'your.' I trust you all had a pleasant trip?"

Rhetorical question to be sure, so no one actually replied. They merely stood in a semi-circle, waiting. But soon it became apparent Reginald T. Foggbottom did not believe in rhetorical questions. A moment became a pause, which became an interminably long pause. Evidently, he wasn't going to continue until he received an answer from each and every person in the room, including Mr. Skylar Waddell. So everyone nodded. Yes, indeed, they nodded, they'd had a pleasant trip.

"Hmmm ... that's interesting," Mr. Foggbottom said, zipping across the room so he could toss his jacket aside (achieved with considerable aplomb I must say, considering the man couldn't even move the TransWay two feet not so very long ago), "because I watched you all as you came off the bus." He parked again in front of them, started to hook a thumb in his vest, thought better of it when the device jittered, and said, "You did not have looks on your faces that I would associate with pleasantness. You looked, rather ... Is 'pleasantness' a word? It seems to me there must be a better way of saying it. Pleasantism? Pleasantdom? Pleasant- ... um ... -icity? Waddell, look that one up for me, will you please? Now, where was I?"

Waddell: "Their faces, sir. When they got off the bus."

"Yes, right. You in particular, young man," Foggbottom nodded to Marvin. "You looked rather ... *hmmm* ... what's the phrase?" This last part to Waddell.

Waddell complied. "Put out."

"Yes, so. Put out. You looked put out." And, clearly being not the kind of fellow who conducted one-way conversations, he stared at Marvin, fully expecting an answer.

"Me?" Marvin asked. "I wasn't put out. Except in the sense of being 'put out' of the bus, if that's what you mean."

Foggbottom gave Waddell a knowing smile. "Actually, no, that's not what I mean. I mean 'put out' in the sense of being inconvenienced. Have we inconvenienced you?"

Now Marvin had seen enough movies about boarding schools and
military academies and chain gangs to know that if you get on the wrong
side of the Person of Authority from the start, you're going to spend many
a night in a box or other dark isolated place eating a lot of creepy crawlies.
And, eventually, when you are once again allowed to see the light of day,
you will pretty much do anything for a bowl of colorless slop rather than
gag down another spider or cockroach. Marvin just couldn't figure out if
this guy was like the warden in *Lockdown on Cell Block Nine* or the teacher
in *School's Out for Murder* — one of whom seemed like a pretty nice guy
when you met him but turned into sadistic a son-of-a-bitch by the end of
Act I, and the other who seemed like a son-of-a-bitch but turned into a
pretty nice guy by the end of Act II. Which meant you had to deal with
them differently.

There was only one way to find out: "I'm afraid I'll have to answer that
in the affirmative," Marvin said. "I was, indeed, inconvenienced."

"Oh?" Foggbottom pressed, TransWay and seersucker rolling forward.
"In what way?" He'd come a hand's-length from Marvin, stopping,
surprisingly, on a dime.[25]

25> There are two things I'd like to discuss here. The first is the phrase "stop on a dime." It
makes little sense to me, evidenced by the following exchange that took place earlier this week:

Yours truly: "Why do you suppose they chose a dime?"

Jean-Claude: "Pardon?"

YT: "A dime. Why do you suppose, whoever came up with that saying, chose a dime? To turn
on. Why not a quarter or a half-dollar or a folded-up dollar bill?"

JC: "I suppose it is because zeh dime is the smallest of zeh lot."

YT: "Hmmm. I suppose. But why currency? Couldn't one turn on, oh, I don't know … a mote
of dust? A mote of dust would be smaller still."

JC: "Indeed it would, monsieur. I shall send a letter at once to zeh proper authorities."

[If you look up "Stop on a Dime" in *Reginald T. Foggbottom's Dictionary of Peculiar Expressions,
Adages, Idioms and Other Figures of Speech (English)*, you'll find it somewhere between "Shake a
Leg" and "Take a Powder." —*Ed.*]

The second thing I'd like to discuss, or in this case, revisit — or at least Jean-Claude does as

"Well, to begin with," Marvin replied, "I felt inconvenienced in that I don't usually spend fourteen hours on a bus in one sitting, and secondly…" — he thumbed toward the corridor — "you realize it's like way-*pink* back there, right? That's sort of inconvenient, in a cones-and-rods sort of way."

"Plus," Harlen said as he pulled on his Mets cap, "the place is, like, way-weird. Who's your, you know, decorator, dude?"

Flinn: "It's a frickin' maze, man. Left, right, up, down. I keep expecting *cheese* around the corner."

---

he feels I have not made myself clear — is this TransWay business. Jean-Claude says he is getting a bit tired of being asked just how this device differs from the highly trademarked Segway® Personal Transporter, as, I have to admit, am I. He has received countless emails from the editors that are clogging up his spam folder, as, I have to admit, have I. In deference to Jean-Claude, then, please take note, as I do not want to go over this even one more time:

The highly trademarked Segway® Personal Transporter, for one, comes in silver/black with a choice of a "gloss white, anodized black or metallic sage" steering frame. The device Mr. Foggbottom uses does not. The highly trademarked Segway® Personal Transporter, for another, makes use of two large wheels between which is a matted platform upon which the operator stands. This device … might; I'm not saying. The highly trademarked Segway® Personal Transporter, meant to revolutionize transportation but succeeding in not much more than making the San Diego police force look like dweebs, costs, on the retail market, upwards of $5,000 USD, whereas the retail price of the TransWay costs closer to four times that amount and is only available through Authorized TransWay Distributors who may sell the device only through TransWay International-hosted events, held periodically throughout the United States and Canada in the homes of wealthy industrialists and highly-trained underground government operatives. Which makes the TransWay (the descriptive details of which, you may have noticed, I have purposefully neglected to spell out so as to protect myself from the litigious likes of said wealthy industrialists and/or the water-boarding likes of said government operatives) highly coveted and extremely hard to come by, unlike the highly trademarked Segway® Personal Transporter, which can be procured with relative ease at a Segway® dealer near you, i.e., cheap.

That then should put this TransWay issue to rest. Further discussion will be met with derisive glares and other social humiliations, and I assure you neither Jean-Claude nor I will reply to your incessant and antagonistic haranguing on the matter. Give it a rest.

"And what's with the *bell*?" Kit wanted to know. "I got, like, *brain* comin' outta my *ears*, dude. *That's* like pretty inconvenient."

"*Somebody*," Bennie said, stepping forward. "*Somebody* ... took ... our ... *stuff*." He avoided looking anyone in the eye. "Somebody took it and I've got—"

Foggbottom lifted a hand. "Whoa," he said. "Whoa. One thing at a time! First of all, I apologize profusely about the bell. We should have tested it before your arrival. It is far too loud. It was an inexcusable error on our part that I can only attribute to miscalculation. I assure you the problem has been rectified. You shall not be subjected to it ... ever again." After giving Mr. Waddell a glare that said, "See to it," his face took on a look of heartfelt concern. "Second: The pink halls. Yes, they are pink. I agree. Third: *I* am the decorator dude. Fourth: There will be no cheese found around any of our corners. No brains will be coming out of anyone's ears. And D: There are missing possessions?"

Everyone piped in: "My Crunch Munchies ..." "... my energy bars ..." "... six bags of PoppyCorn Lite ..."

The administrator turned to Mr. Waddell. "Is this correct? These, er, fine young people, are missing personal belongings?"

Waddell's jowls jiggled as he blubbered, "I'm not aware of that, sir. As far as I know—"

"Well we are," Kit said. "Aware of it, that is. And Bennie here needed his Crunch Munchies. He's hypo— hypo-*whatever*. Look, he's like all white and pasty."

"My goodness," Mr. Foggbottom exclaimed, seeing that Bennie was not only white and pasty, but seemed a little off-balance as well. "Well I promise you there will be an investigation. An investigation, I say!" The last part he barked whilst pointing an accusatory finger at Waddell, who was looking more and more like a deer caught in the headlights, or, in this case, a walrus caught in the headlights. "Here, son," the administrator said as he tossed Bennie an apple, "that ought to hold you. It may be a few minutes before we can delve into the delicious repast Winston has prepared. In the meantime, we have some preliminaries to which we must attend."

Bennie took to the apple like a starved hyena, devouring it in three, maybe four, bites, while Foggbottom dove into his speech:

"Ahem," he ahemed, "I would like to welcome each and every one of you to the Sandy Hillside Ranch for Wayward Teens—"

"I thought it was the Sandy *Rivers* Hill*top* Ranch," Marvin whispered to Flinn.

Foggbottom looked confused. "What was that? What did he say?" He listened a moment as Waddell spoke softly into his ear, during which Foggbottom muttered things along the lines of "That so?" and "I did?" and "Are you sure?" He then turned to the group. "My apologies. I must have gotten some wires crossed. I've never been very good at names. So then …" — he cleared his throat — "… Welcome to the Sandy *Rivers* Hill*top* Ranch for Wayward … oh, skip the rest, it's just asking too much and, as was recently pointed out, it's needlessly redundant. I assure you, *something shall be done about it.*"

He started to clap his hands, then, afraid it would upset the TransWay (although one must wonder how he pulled off the apple thing) and seeing the group had at least been *somewhat* placated, continued: "So. Why are we here? Why in the world have your parents — and/or teacher or guidance counselor or neighborhood watch group or military tribunal or principal or sheriff or therapist or next door neighbor or whoever else might seek credit — refer you to us?" He fluttered a hand. "Don't answer that; I will tell you. It's simple really: They don't like you."

The administrator then looked over the faces before him. "They want you gone. It's as straightforward as that." He began to move the TransWay to the left, and then to the right, as if he were a general inspecting his troops. "We have here in our presence, in no particular order and without going into details, some rather clever young people. We have among us: a liar, a cheat, an impersonator, a thief, a con artist, a forger, and an overly irritating *pest.* No doubt a certain number of you are more than one of these. One of you, in point of fact, can be classified as 'all of the above.'" (Here he looked directly at Marvin.) "Now of course there are times when lying and cheating and impersonating and stealing is all well and good and can land you a respected position in the U.S. banking industry, but most of the time it's just not nice. *Most* of the time, it puts people ill at ease."

He stopped the TransWay. "We won't go into who did what or when or even why, and we won't even characterize actions in the past as anywhere near felonious. We shall simply state that mistakes have been made and let it go at that. Now it is because of these actions — let us call them 'eccentricities' — you are now under my care. More than wanting *you* gone, the people who have sent you here want your *eccentricities* gone. You and your eccentricities interfere with the smooth proceedings of their day. So — I am sure you will not be surprised to learn — they have asked us to rid you of them. As I say, it's simple really."

There were a lot of murmurs and eye-rolls among the six. Bennie Sterlati, now feeling a lot better having gotten his blood-sugar level fixed thanks to the apple, even went so far as to say, "Wait a minute. I'm not any of those things. I never cheated or lied or—"

Mr. Foggbottom raised a hand as if to say, "No, no, please spare us your sorry details." What he actually said was, "You've been sent to the Sandy Rivers Hilltop Ranch for Wayward Youth, Juveniles, and Young Adults, therefore you are one of these things, and that is the end of it."

"But—"

"Let us move on, shall we? Now. Over the course of the next few weeks, you will be attending classes." (Eye-rolls all around.) "Your day will be divided into three sessions: Morning Calisthenics, Mid-morning Mechanics, and Afternoon Social Studies. After the evening meal, you will each retire to your dormitory cubicle and work at your desk or bunk at Pursuits of a Personal Nature, and the next morning, you shall do it all over again, and so on, until, at the end of eight weeks, many of you will be chosen to participate in a larger endeavor, the rewards of which will become apparent, and others will be sent home."

Marvin raised his hand.

Foggbottom: "Yes, young man?"

Marvin pushed up his glasses. "What makes you think you can rid us of these 'eccentricities' in eight weeks?"

Foggbottom looked at Marvin as if he had just been asked the most perplexing question in the universe, something on the order of "Whence the rings of Saturn?" or "What's up with *lobsters?* Are they, like, giant sea bugs or what?" Foggbottom in turn shot Mr. Waddell a look of complete and utter bafflement, then addressed our young protagonist. "Wherever did you get such an idea?"

"You said you were asked to rid us of—"

"Ah yes! Oh I see!" Foggbottom said, the wrinkles about his eyes showing grand amusement. He paused for a second, as if thinking how best to approach this. "Allow me to clarify." He cleared his throat. "Just today I added a very interesting phrase to my lexicon: 'My bad.' … Isn't it a dandy? I understand it means, 'My apologies, I've made a mistake.' So to you I say: *My bad. My apologies, I've made a mistake.* I had not explained our intentions here at Sandy Rivers well enough." He pulled on a lapel of his jacket and, amazingly, did not upset the TransWay one centimeter. "I said we have been asked to rid you of your eccentricities, that is true … I didn't say we had any intention of doing so."

Oh if you could have seen the look on their faces. If a fly were to come along just then, it would have no trouble whatsoever flitting into Bennie Sterlati's mouth.

"So. I invite you now to enjoy your meal. If I'm not mistaken, I believe we have a request for prime rib and mashed potatoes. Winston has been kind enough to prepare just that." After he exchanged glances with Mr. Waddell, he added, "But don't expect this kind of thing every night. Winston is being most accommodating at the moment. *Most* accommodating. He is quite pleased his new ovens have arrived and is anxious to test them out."

Reginald T. Foggbottom then aimed his TransWay to the corridor. "Feel free to serve yourselves at the back of the dining hall," he called just before passing into The Great Pink Beyond. "And enjoy the all-you-can-eat cream pie."

Chapter SEVEN…

DINNER WAS SO MIND-NUMBINGLY DELICIOUS (the prime rib! the mashed potatoes! the melon balls!), Marvin forgot all about his Cheese Doodles and Twinkle Bars and his packages of unpopped PoppyCorn Lite. Everyone must have forgotten about their missing Crunch Munchies and Chee-Zee SpudNuggets and Bunch-o-Nuts bars, too, because no one ever mentioned them again, which makes me wonder right now why I ever brought it up in the first place.

It's amazing what all-you-can-eat cream pie can do.

The group retired to the dormitory where they didn't even discuss what they'd seen so far at the Sandy Rivers Hilltop Ranch for Wayward Youth, Juveniles, and Young Adults. They were too exhausted. All anyone wanted to do was sleep, which came to them like getting run over by a stampede of wildebeests. Wait… make that a rickety old bus.

No one made their bed, let alone took off their jumpsuits, let alone pursued "pursuits of a personal nature," or even tried to figure out what the heck that meant. They just fell off into a wonderful, satiated, tranquil deep slumber, the kind pharmaceutical companies would love to take credit for.

It must have been early morning when Marvin let out the sleepiest of yawns and plodded his way to the bathroom, his legs leaden with sleep. On the way, he was vaguely aware of snoring figures in the low light of the dormitory. If it's possible to be thankful for heavy eyelids, he was. Last thing he needed after sleeping like a sloth on tranquilizers was to look at those obnoxious polka dots. He was soon joined by Kit and Bennie, and it wasn't until the three of them returned to the dormitory, eyes still half-mast, that the bell went off (thankfully, not nearly to its previous Liberty Bell level), and that was when they stopped in their tracks.

"Whoa," Bennie let out.

To which Kit added: "Whoa."

And Marvin added: "Whoa."

You may recall, if you haven't been distracted by reruns of "That's So Hannah & Cody" or whatever it is that distracts you young people these days, that when Marvin and the others were first introduced to the dormitory, they had their choice of probably fifty or more beds. Now, as the bell rang in the grey morning light, they were looking upon an entirely different scene: Each and every bed, save their own because they'd already gotten out of it, was occupied.

Kit frowned. "This ain't right," he said, as a dormful of kids stretched and yawned and looked around with virtually the same perplexed look on their faces — i.e., with the overall air of a tour group who'd found themselves at the wrong airport.

"Where'd all these—"

"Can you *believe* this?" Dara cried, running up to them. "There's like *fifty* of them!"

There were, in point of fact, forty-six. You'd have to add Marvin and Dara and Bennie and Kit to get to fifty. Flinn and Harlen soon shuffled their way, Flinn bringing up the rear. Whether he was rubbing his eyes to get the sleep from them or the absurdity of the situation I can't say, but as he scratched at his red curly locks and joined the others in a chorus of variations on "What the—" "Did I miss something?" and "Oh for crap's sake, there's gonna be lines for the bathroom," he asked the obvious: "When did *they* all get here?"[26]

26> Ever notice how often people scratch at things when they are out of their element? Well they do. A famous case was that of Buford T. Willicocks of Elvira, Texas. In October, 1947, when

"*When's* the operative word," Dara said. "When *did* they all get here?" Apparently not being one to wait for an answer, she went off into the crowd promising she'd get to the bottom of it. Soon they could see her talking with a blonde-haired girl, whose hair was in braids and was dressed in Pretty Kitty pink pajamas. They could see now the girl had a nose-ring, and she shrugged her shoulders before Dara went off to others, who, each in turn, though not having nose-rings of their own, shrugged their shoulders in similar I'm-just-as-lost-as-the-next-guy ways.

"Looks like everybody remembers coming here on that stupid bus," Dara reported when she got back to the group. "Then they had a big dinner, then came up to bed. Just like us."

A whistle blew, accompanied by the *odobenus rosmarus*-like silhouette of Skylar Waddell, which is a phrase extremely difficult to read aloud, which is why I'd never attempt it. Clearly, Skylar Waddell had a habit of appearing in doorways.

"Let's get a move-on," he announced with another blow of the whistle. "We have much to do in little time. Breakfast is in ten minutes. After breakfast you must report to Morning Calisthenics at 9 a.m. *Sharp.* That is approximately one hour from now." He checked his watch. "And please, ladies and gentlemen, report to your assigned room." This last part he said as if he'd had enough of people showing up in the wrong place.

"Assigned room?" someone called out. "What assigned room?"

---

accompanying his cousin Odell to a local farm auction, being unfamiliar with the protocol of the proceedings, and in an act featured on so many situation comedies it is considered cliché, Mr. Willicocks mistakenly scratched his ear at the wrong moment. As a result, he came away with fifty-two head of Texas longhorn cattle. Which, as dumb luck would have it, turned out to be a good move. If you live anywhere near Texas you're sure to be familiar with Buford T's, the highly popular chain of some fifty-two Texas barbeque eating establishments peppered throughout the state. (One outlet for each steer originally purchased.) Until the day he died (May 7, 1978), Mr. Willicocks was convinced his good fortune was borne nothing short of divine providence and not at all the result of a near-sighted auctioneer and his own itchy ear lobe. And for three decades, even his cousin Odell, who'd witnessed the event, could not convince him otherwise.

Mr. Waddell sighed a very large sigh and nodded to the back of the dormitory. "As is *clearly* posted…" (there did seem to be a piece of paper tacked to the far wall) "…if your name begins with A through L, please report to Room A." Then, as though he had tired of it before he'd even said it, "If your name begins with M through Z, please report to Room B."

A pause. "First name or last name?" Bennie yelled.

Waddell had not quite made it to the hallway. He blew out another walrus-sized blast of air. "Last name, child. *Last* name. Who in the world would alphabetize by first name?"

Bennie shrugged. "My third-grade teacher did."

"We are not in third grade, young man," Waddell said as he exited.

Bennie looked at his name-tag and scratched at his fauxhawk. "Our real last name or this bogus last name?"

Mr. Waddell paused for a beat then passed through the doorway to the hall. His faint voice trailed into nothing from somewhere pink and distant: "We are in no way interested in…"

"Bogus name," Marvin said, patting Bennie on the shoulder. "Go with the bogus name."

Then, from all corners of the dormitory came a mixture of laughing and smirking and eye-rolling and other dismissive stuff at the lameness of it all. Using someone else's name, waking up with tons more people there than when you went to sleep, brown jumpsuits … c'mon, it's stupid. But the laughs and smirks and eye-rolls didn't last long, because all at once everyone found themselves so amazingly uncompromisingly *hungry* — especially Bennie, he yet again of low-blood sugar — that they would do anything at the moment for a food fix, even go by another name.

So, hastily, they took to the showers and donned their checklist-approved underwear and oh-so-fashionable brown jumpsuits and ridiculously Orwellian name-tags, and headed for the cafeteria.

• • •

BREAKFAST CONSISTED of eggs and ham and biscuits and fruit and cereal and milk and tea, and Marvin noticed Kit ate and drank it all. In

fact, everyone did. They even had seconds. Marvin partook only of the
milk and cereal. And it wasn't because the cereal was Nut Crunchies,
which was his favorite, it was because he had this funny feeling — not
ha-ha funny, I-do-not-trust-this-place funny.[27]

In between bites, Marvin and the others were still trying to figure out
when everybody got there. Dara pointed to the nose-ring girl. "See her?
She's from Wisconsin. And that kid's from Idaho and that kid's from Los
Angeles. So it's not like they're local or anything. I mean it had to take
them just as long to get here as we did. Which, in my case, was from
Indiana. Bennie and Marvin got on the bus in Illinois, and Kit, you were
on the bus before me. Where did you get on?"

Kit pretended he didn't hear the question by busily picking raisins out

---

27> Sometimes, when you get a funny feeling about something, you might get a twinge in
your stomach, which is where the term "gut feeling" comes from. (It's also where the term, "I shouldn't
have eaten all that dried fruit," comes from, but that's something different.) A "funny feeling" or "gut
feeling" is also called "intuition" and believe it or not, it's actually a biological function, like hunger
pangs or nodding off to sleep in front of the television at 3 a.m. instead of staying awake through
another episode of the "Space Rangers" marathon. As a survival instinct, it's built into your DNA as
much as the color of your eyes or your propensity for bumping into things or liking peanut-butter-and-
mayonnaise sandwiches.

Ever walk into a darkened room and get a chill up your spine like someone's behind you? That
funny feeling is your intuition telling you there's a big fat ugly hairy monster not ten inches behind you
who's going to slobber all over your neck and then eat your brains. This is not just some contrivance
implanted in you by The Creator of the Universe to screw around with your nervous system. This
actually comes from the days when big fat ugly hairy saber-toothed tigers and other large now-
extinct-but-equally-as-dangerous beasts snuck up behind your ancestors, slobbered all over their
necks and then ate their brains for real.

Meaning you're wired for it. And just like a deer in the woods who's wired to stand up straight
when he hears the slightest snap of a twig, it would be to your advantage to pay attention when a
funny feeling kicks in, because, even though saber-toothed tigers and a lot of other nasty beasts
have been wiped out, the warning system still works. You don't want that funny feeling when you
step off a curb in the middle of traffic to be the last spark of intuition you ever have now, do you?

of a piece of raisin bread and flicking them across the table.

"Well anyway," Dara said, "it looks like buses of six to ten kids came from all directions. We came from the east, and those guys over there came from the southwest, and those guys over there from the northwest."

Bennie was working out the math: "Fifty kids, that's like at least five bus-loads."

"Weird," Flinn said. "I heard Waddell tell my folks that crappy old bus was the only one they had."

The conversation went on like this until Marvin began to notice that the more ham and eggs his compatriots ate, the more distracted they got. The conversation moved from logistical impossibilities to how yummy the jam was and what to expect from a calisthenics class. In the time it takes to read this paragraph, no one was asking how so many kids had gotten there overnight from so many directions, let alone on a single dilapidated old bus. No one was pointing out that either such a feat would have had to take place over a number of days, or that there had to be more than one dilapidated old bus, or that some kids must have already been at Sandy Rivers, or any other scenario.

Bennie was saying that classes were going to make the place feel too much like school.

"What did you expect?" asked Dara. "They're not going to take us out of school and send us to *summer camp*."

"No?" Kit said, flinging another raisin. "I thought they were."

Chapter EIGHT...

S O IT WAS OFF TO Morning Calisthenics, which gave Marvin more funny feelings, mostly because he hadn't participated in gym since like fifth grade — when Mr. Dolenz, the jerk-wad-gym-Nazi, pushed him so hard on climbing that lame-ass rope and touching that lame-ass ceiling, it almost made him cry. (Marvin, not Mr. Dolenz). When it was clear Marvin couldn't do it, Dolenz made him try again and again until his fingers got so raw and sore he couldn't bend them for a week (Marvin's fingers, not Mr. Dolenz's fingers). Marvin never could climb the rope and he hoped Mr. Dolenz died a long and painful death. Not really, but he did hope Mr. Dolenz would be made to do something beyond his capabilities in front of his peers, hopefully in his underwear, and everyone would stare at what a big joke he was and laugh at his bony knees and post it online and it would go viral and everyone in the world would know what a jerk-wad he was and the word "Dolenz" would become synonymous with "jerk-wad." Which was why Marvin always looked for him on the news and TV reality shows, hoping to see him get his comeuppance.

All of which meant that when Marvin and the M-Z group walked into Room B, Marvin was expecting another gym Nazi with a whistle — oh God, please don't let it be Waddell — who'd have him jumping around a gymnasium like a spastic sock monkey. He was all prepared for coming up with an extraordinarily clever excuse for sitting this one out. Indigestion maybe. Extraordinarily clever indigestion.[28]

As it turned out, Room B wasn't a gymnasium at all. It was a regular classroom not unlike the ones Marvin had left behind when he first stepped on the bus. Twenty-five chairs, a blackboard and a desk for the instructor. Behind which sat the slightest of fellows.

Advanced in years, to be sure, the diminutive fellow was slouched over his work, busily scribbling notes with a shaky hand. But it was his half-glasses balanced on the tip of a needle-like nose, gangly eyebrows that went every which way, errant tufts of hair that stuck out about his ears (some of it might have even been coming from *in* his ears) and neat red-plaid bow tie that made him look like he came out of Central Casting. And, as if that all weren't enough physical characteristics to set the old

---

28> Other sure-fire excuses for sitting out gym …

• Profess exemption on religious grounds. Declare you are a member of Puumanji, a remote Sumatran sect that believes in keeping perfectly still from, say 9:00 a.m. to 10:00 a.m. (or whenever your particular gym class meets), which is "Puumanji Sacred Hour."

• Claim an acute medical condition such as personal injury. While holding the appropriate body part, say, "It hurts when I move my arm/neck/leg/groin/spleen." (Warning: this can backfire if your gym teacher feels a need to call the paramedics or, worse, your mother.)

• Claim a *chronic* medical condition such as an allergy. Make sure you tell them you're allergic to something involved in the workout (leather, sneakers, gym mats, or, as Marvin did in the seventh grade — in a stroke of genius — his own sweat).

• Assert future plans. "No thanks, I'm training for a sedentary career in computer science."

• Cry out, "For the love of God, not the rope!"

Note: These same excuses can be used once you have entered the workforce and are required to attend endless meetings about endless uninteresting subjects, and team-building retreats where they make you wear matching T-shirts designed by the receptionist and climb rock walls and fall backward into your awaiting co-workers' arms. Simply rephrase as, "Paintball gives me hives," or, "My therapist says I can't be around human pyramids," or, should you already have a career in computer science, try, "Sorry, I'm in the middle of a quad-core modification test and if I walk away now, you'll all lose your hard drives."

gent apart from anyone else in the room, the top of his all-but-bald head
was crowned with a cluster of age spots that formed, unbeknownst to
Marvin and the M-Z group, a remarkably accurate topographical map of
the nation of Bhutan.

In case you are unfamiliar with it, according to the *Encyclopedia
Gargantua* the elevation of Bhutan, a country in Asia that officially
measures its Gross National Happiness (look it up), ranges from jungle
lowlands of 150-feet (which is not very far above sea level) to over 24,000-
feet when it reaches into the Himalayas, which is a pretty big differential.
(In yet another example of the Interconnectedness of All Things, please
recall that the Himalayas are the very locale where Marvin last left his hero
Yolando Plumadore hanging over a vat of boiling cream of wheat.) Not to
say the age spots on the top the instructor's head reached over 24,000 feet,
which wouldn't even fit in the room let alone on the little man's noggin,
I only mention it to point out that when a topographical map is rendered
onto a human skull, it can be rather repulsive.[29]

29> Truth be told, the human body, though often alluring when you see it in ads for beauty

cream or low-riding jeans, by and large is not the most attractive thing in the universe. Worse — as

you no doubt have noticed if you've ever been able to look at anyone over 40 for more than like thirty

seconds — as one ages, it starts to fall apart. Ears get bigger, toenails get curlier, hair gets coarser,

elbows get wrinklier, senses of humor get cornier, and so on.

Until such time you have to worry about wrinkled elbows and curly toenails, as humans you can

take consolation in the fact that there are far less attractive beings in the Great Beyond. *Lots* of them.

The people of the planet Parabulus, in the Norbetin Galaxy, for instance, from the day they are

born routinely grow finger-like protrusions called "gariphyns" all over their bodies. Gariphyns fall to

the wayside as new ones take their places (sort of like teen idols, Hollywood action heroes, and my

ex-wife's "yoga" instructors).

Which is to say a Parabulusian can't walk ten meters without stepping on someone else's gariphyn,

which is why the Parabulusian footwear industry is one of the most successful commercial enterprises

in the known universe. If you should ever have the chance to invest in the manufacturing of Parabulusian

shoes, you would be wise to take advantage of the opportunity. I myself have 5,500 shares of ParaFlux

Shoes, Ltd., which I would not part with for all the gont in Glavia. And that's a lot of gont.

At the front of the room, the little man, emblazoned with his personal map of Bhutan (which of course he could never see accurately unless he was looking at a photo of himself) announced in a quivering voice: "Velcome to Morning Calisthenics. Please to have a seat."

As Bennie and Marvin shuffled their way to the back, Bennie said in a whisper, "Isn't calis— calis-whatever, like, jumping around and stuff?"

"Indeed," the man agreed, his sense of hearing far better than one would expect. "It *is* zeh jumping about. But novun hass said it is to be zeh *physically* jumping about." He emerged from behind the desk.

They could see now the aged fellow was sitting in a wheelchair. Not a modern-day wheelchair, but one that one might find c. 1932, with a caned back and (presumably) seat. A woolen blanket covered his legs and bony fingers trembled as he deftly operated a steering mechanism mounted on the wooden armrest. All the chalkboards in Room B were set low so he could reach them, which is what he now did. A palsied hand selected a piece of chalk, then, one slow and shaky letter at a time, painstakingly formed the letters of his name: FELIX W. FLÖCKENHEIMER. It was a long and arduous process as Felix W. Flöckenheimer's ancient hands, gnarled and spotted with age, formed each letter with chalk-squeaking difficulty. Finally, his X crossed, his I's dotted, his O umlauted, with a click of chalk he wheeled about, ever so slowly, to face the class.

"You vill find on your desk a piece uff paper und a pen," he told them, his thick German accent hard to ignore. "On zeh left side of zeh paper, I vant for you to draw a dot."

"How big of a dot?" someone asked.

"Zis does not matter. You may choose a dot of your preference."

Which was what they did. (They also rolled their eyes and sighed jaded sighs and said things like, "Whatever," and "*Pffeuh.*")

"On zeh right side of zeh paper," Mr. Flöckenheimer said, "I vant you to draw und-other dot." Which, again, was what they did.

The old man peered over his glasses at Kit Warnam's name-tag. "Now, Herr Varnam," he said, "I vant you to come to zeh front of zeh room, with your piece uff paper, und, for zeh class to see, please to connect zeh dots."

At first Kit didn't respond. He wasn't used to the new name they'd given him, let alone in a strong German accent. Finally realizing everyone was staring at him, he looked around the room like it must be some kind of joke. "You're kidding," he said.

The little man looked surprised. "I do not see zeh reason to be *kidding.*"

Kit gave the room a shrug that said he thought it was a pretty lame idea, but did as he was told, trying to look as nonchalant as possible as he stood and went to the front. Here Mr. Flöckenheimer handed Kit a pen and nodded for him to begin. Kit uncapped the pen, and, placing the paper on Mr. Flöckenheimer's desk, drew a line from one dot to the other. He then gave Dara, who was sitting in the front row, a lopsided smile and presented paper and pen — with a gentlemanly bow — to the little German man.

"Good," Mr. Flöckenheimer said. "You may return to your seat." Mr. Flöckenheimer then held up the paper for the group to see. Kit had drawn a thin blue line from one dot to the other.

Mr. Flöckenheimer then eyed Bennie's name-tag. "Herr Sterlati," he said as he extended the pen, "if you vould be so kind? Please to connect zeh dots on your piece uff paper?"

Bennie walked to the front of the room, put his piece of paper on Mr. Flöckenheimer's desk, and repeated the drawing of a line, from one dot to the other, before handing over the paper.

Mr. Flöckenheimer adjusted his glasses, glanced at Bennie's work, then turned the paper to the room. Bennie's paper looked much like Kit's.

Three more kids were called upon. They did likewise, connecting the dots, handing their paper to Mr. Flöckenheimer, who, again, squinted at their work, revealed it to the room, and called upon the next person.

When the blonde-haired girl with the nose-ring — the same one Dara had talked to in the dorm — approached the desk, she drew for a minute, then, as the others had done, handed Mr. Flöckenheimer the sheet. "Ah," the little man announced, replacing his squint with a smile, "now vee are *gettink* someveres." He turned her paper to the room. She had, indeed, connected the dots, but she had done it with a circuitous squiggle that looped its way across the page from one dot to the other.

Mr. Flöckenheimer peered over his glasses, regarding the group. "Who said zeh line must to be a straight line?"

Some of them shrugged as though that was pretty clever. Some even smiled.

Mr. Flöckenheimer offered the pen to Dara Steifer. Bringing her paper to the front of the room, she followed the other girl's lead, but instead of a squiggle, she wrote a sentence, in cursive, from one dot to the other, without taking the pen from the surface. She had a little trouble with the T's and didn't dot the I's, but you could see what it said:

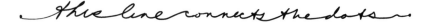

"Good," Mr. Flöckenheimer said. "Yes." Once again, he peered over his glasses at the group. "Who said zeh line must haff only zeh one function? She has got a whole sentence there."

Next came a kid in the second row. She had, in fact, already connected her dots. She'd drawn a string of stick men from one dot to the other.

Mr. Flöckenheimer applauded. "Vell done! Zeh instructions were to connect zeh dots. Nobody has said it must be a line, yah? No one has said zeh pen is not to leave zeh paper. All that has been said is to connect zeh dots."

Up shot Harlen's hand. He wanted a turn. Mr. Flöckenheimer nodded for him to come to the front. But instead of taking the pen, Harlen reached for a piece of chalk. He held the paper to the chalkboard for everyone to see, then, instead of applying the chalk on its end, he laid the chalk on its side and dragged it across the chalkboard — right over the paper and the two dots — in a four-inch (10.16 cm.) swath. He didn't bother starting and ending at the dots. He didn't even bother keeping it on the paper.

Everyone nodded their approval and Mr. Flöckenheimer seemed especially pleased. "Vell done!" he said. "Three in vun. Who said zeh dots must be connected vith zeh pen? Who said it must to be a *thin* line? Who said zeh line must start at one dot und end at zeh other?"

It was here he turned to Marvin. "Und have you a connect-zeh-dot solution, *mein freund*?"

Marvin took a second before taking his piece of paper to the front of the room. He, too, refused the pen when Mr. Flöckenheimer offered it to him, but instead of using a piece of chalk, he simply took the paper and folded it in half so the dots were touching each other. He opened the sheet to demonstrate that they were indeed touching, then, having made his point, he wrinkled the paper into a wad and tossed it in the trash bin. "No one said they had to be connected *by* anything," he said, making his way back to his seat.

Mr. Flöckenheimer applauded. "Excellent! Vell done!" he cried. "This has been most illuminating. Such advancement in little time. But I must admit I haff a slight case of zeh disappointment. Herr Plotnik has stolen much of my thunder." Wheeling to the trash bin, he retrieved Marvin's wad of wrinkled paper. He took the wad, pressed it between his bony fingers, then popped the thing matter-of-factly into his mouth. "Who zed," Mr. Flöckenheimer managed as he chewed, "zeh dots must to remain dots?"

• • •

MR. FLÖCKENHEIMER wheeled to the desk, and, resting his elbows there, brought his fingertips together. His old eyes scanned the room.

"Excellent," he said, satisfied. "Exercise Two. Our final exercise of zeh day. You haff before you more sheets uff paper."

He then instructed the group to divide a sheet of paper into fourths, making each quarter the same shape and size. "Inside your desk, you vill find a pair uff scissors. Please to take your time. Please to use what you haff learned from zeh past exercise." Producing a pocket watch from his vest pocket, he said, "You may start."

Dutifully, everyone complied. But rather than going ahead and folding the paper, then folding it crosswise into four equal quadrants, which would be the first thing anyone would do given a sheet of paper to divide into fourths, they hesitated. They stared at their piece of paper.

Bennie put his finger up as though he had an idea. He folded his paper in half, then folded it in half again, but instead of the second fold being perpendicular to the first, he folded it parallel to the first:

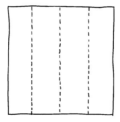

Dara chose to fold and cut the paper diagonally:

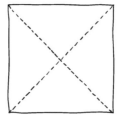

For the next few minutes, the hum of Mr. Flöckenheimer's wheelchair as he made his way up and down the aisles of Room B was interrupted only by the occasional, "Oh!" and "Ah ha!" and similar Eureka!-like phrases from the M-Z group. At one point, when she saw how clever everyone else was being, Dara wrinkled up her paper and began again. Suffice it to say that in a few short minutes, the rudimentary paper divisions shown above had evolved into solutions more along the lines of:

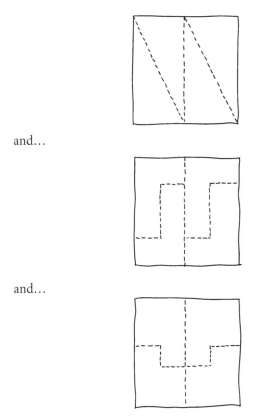

and...

and...

Everyone was looking at everyone else's work, then taking it a step further. Just the realization that each solution seemed to lead to the next somehow became, for want of a better word, fun.

Mr. Flöckenheimer wheeled forward and back, the hum of chair's motor engaging and disengaging as he stopped a minute here and a minute there to watch each student's progress. A lot of them weren't satisfied with one solution; they were coming up with three or four. Mr. Flöckenheimer seemed to be impressed.

Then someone had the bright idea of going back to Dara's diagonals, but adjusting the "arms" that came out from the center point.

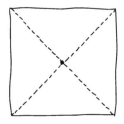 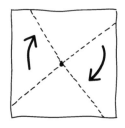 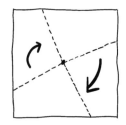

As long as you hit the same point around the square, your four pieces would always be equal! Evidently Harlen was the one who figured out the next step. He pulled at his Mets cap and yelled, "Holy crap! Who says the cuts have to be straight?" He took the center-point solution one more step and got something that looked like a camera's lens, and that took off until one kid came up with a totally crazy thing with a squiggle that went from the center to the corners. As long as each squiggle was identical to the others, this one solution alone had infinite possibilities:

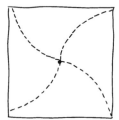 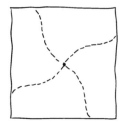 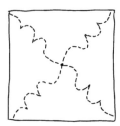

Mr. Flöckenheimer asked Marvin how he had solved the problem. Marvin showed him he'd come up two solutions. In the first, he'd cut his paper like this:

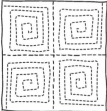

He then pulled the pieces from the centers of the spirals and made them 3-D, like little cones. "Vell done!" Mr. Flöckenheimer said. "You haff broken zeh two-dimensional barrier! Und vut is this one?" He pointed to another sheet of paper on Marvin's desk. Here the paper was divided into a grid of forty equal-sized squares — five squares by eight squares. Marvin had filled ten random squares with a symbol. A square here, a square there, etc. Ten more random squares were filled with another symbol and so on, until he had used four symbols. This is what it looked like:

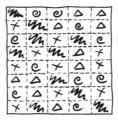

Mr. Flöckenheimer was impressed. "Ah, I see," he said, giving his Bhutan-map of a head a rub. "This we vill call zeh Patchwork Quilt Solution. No von hass said zeh scissors must be used, yah? I only said zeh scissors were in zeh desks. You were told zeh page must be divided into quarters; no von hass said zeh quarters must each be in one unit or piece. You haff divided your page into four types of equal-sized rectangles. Vell Done."[30]

Mr. Flöckenheimer took up Marvin's paper and seemed to linger a little more than was necessary while he studied it some more. "This is

---

30> This is one of those rare instances where I have played with the facts. Having a supply of art materials at his disposal, Marvin had actually filled each rectangle with a different color — red, green, blue and yellow. But since my publisher has the budget of a roadside rutabaga stand (i.e., there will be no color beyond the cover art, and only time will tell on *that*), I used some creative license to convey the same, albeit black-and-white, concept. Of course the rectangles could have been filled with stripes and solids, polka-dots and plaids, but after lengthy conversations and seemingly endless meetings, squigglies won out. Take *that*, Mr. "That's-IT-I've-Had-Enough-Of-This-I-Don't-Care-What-You-Put-In-There-As-Long-As-It's-Black-and-White." (You know who you are.)

most remarkable," he said, his gaze periodically going over the top of the sheet. He did this a grand total of three times, which gave Marvin a weird feeling … like the old fart wasn't studying the *paper* as much as he was studying *him.*

"I zink now," the little man suddenly announced, "you vill all enjoy a solution vat vas vunce submitted in zis exercise by a much astute young fellow. You vill agree zis solution is much fun." He wheeled to the desk, from behind which he produced an ordinary kitchen blender, previously filled with water. Into the blender a piece of paper went, then, with a flick of a switch, the blender was on. "As vith our previous example," Mr. Flöckenheimer called above the grinding of the blades, "who said zeh paper must to remain paper?"

As an aside here, I know what you're thinking. You're wondering why Marvin Plotnik, described herein as the sort of guy who would raise his hand in class at every opportune moment, who normally asked as many questions as was humanly possible, who reveled in rattling the cage of whomever stood in authority before him, somehow decided, in the presence of Mr. Felix Flöckenheimer, instructor of Morning Calisthenics, not even so much as to raise a disruptive pinky. It doesn't readily seem in character now, does it? Ah, but it is. And do you know why? I will tell you: It was because, for the first time in Marvin's young life … he actually didn't want to end up sitting out in the hall.

Unfortunately, this feeling, as is true with so many good things in life such as a good back scratching … this feeling that he'd finally found a place he liked, far away from eye-rolling high-fiving parents and impatient teachers and kids who made up brainless nicknames for anyone who was different … turned out to be short-lived. It lasted about as long as the previous paragraph and faded the minute Felix Flöckenheimer sat at the front of the room and poured pulp-infused water into four identical lab flasks. Because right at that moment, something about this guy made its way into Marvin's cursedly-curious head:

That dude's accent has got to have the *fakest* German accent Marvin had ever heard.

Chapter NINE...

THE NEXT SESSION was to be in the gymnasium. It was called Mid-morning Mechanics, you may recall, and it would include everyone, both the A-L group and the M-Z group. To get to the gymnasium, it turned out, was a bit of a trek. After the A-L group and the M-Z group convened in the hallway outside of Rooms A and B, they had to make their way through a labyrinth of pink hallways, stairways and the like which criss-crossed each other in an equally pink labyrinth of criss-crossiness (all nicely marked with good signage).

It was along one of these circuitous corridors that Bennie, having acquired a particularly bouncy gait since the morning session, asked chirpily, "What did you think?" referring, one would assume, to Mr. Flöckenheimer's morning session. I say "chirpily" because when someone with a blue fauxhawk springs giddily down the corridor, gaily flitting about his compatriots, they look remarkably like a five-foot-four blue jay of happiness. It wasn't just the fauxhawk; it was the body language.[31]

31> Did you know there are people out there who actually *study* body language? For a *living?* It's a field of study called *kinesics* [from the Greek meaning "did that guy just do what I think he did?"] and these people have made whole careers of it. Most of us, of course, can generally read body language without even thinking about it let alone going to the bother of getting a college degree in it. Then again, some people can't. Which is why that girl who keeps hanging around your locker and waiting for you at the bus stop *is not getting the message*.

For most of you, though, when we see someone crossing their arms or putting their head in their hands in an exasperating manner or jumping when you ask them what the hell they're doing rummaging through your backpack, I'm guessing you have little trouble reading them. Combine body language, words and facial expressions and there is little wool that can be pulled over most people's eyes ... which is another odd saying now that I think about it. If you would be so kind as to wait for a moment, I do need to write that one down ...

Now, where was I? Ah yes ... body language. Much of it is involuntary, and it can tell us what a person is feeling or who they are or what they are fond of or whether they like cauliflower or not or if they have recently stumbled into a wasp nest. It can also tell us whether they are lying.

If we were not able to read one another's body language, we might miss out on much-needed bits of information. Say a hoodlum is coming up behind your friend in a menacing manner — weapon held high, snarl on his face, and the like (the hoodlum, not your friend). Wouldn't you feel a lot better knowing that if you gave your friend a quick jerk of your head, he would grasp the significance of the moment and know it was time to — in a phrase I've just recently learned — get the eff out of there? If the situation were reversed, I'm sure you'd appreciate it if your friend were doing the head jerking for you. A well-placed head jerk can mean the difference between the two of you deftly hotfooting it out of there until you could safely stop somewhere and have a nice hamburger ... and *being* hamburger.

Keep in mind that over time, body language — like verbal language — can change. What your grandmother takes to mean one thing might mean something else entirely to you and your classmates. During World War II, for instance, Winston Churchill fancied forming a V with his fingers to stand for Victory. Twenty-five years later, during another war, demonstrators flashed the V-sign to mean Peace. Which not only means two different things, perhaps even opposite things, but that Ps are especially difficult to make with your fingers, whereas Vs are pretty much a cinch. Which explains why uncles like to make "rabbit ears" in family photos.

Needless to say, lifting one finger can mean one thing and lifting a different finger can mean something else entirely, depending on where you are, so knowing when and where to lift what — this finger hails a cab, this one gets you beat to a pulp — is key to your survival.

Consider the following anecdote: In the summer of 1972, while visiting the island-nation of Mua'ago Pago in the South Pacific, President Richard M. Nixon gave a group of brightly-clad

Bennie's body language was soon joined by his *language* language, i.e., as they made their way down the very last corridor to the gym, he said, "Who'da thought something called Morning Calisthenics was going to be so cool?"

"This place might turn out to be okay after all," added Harlen, clearly stoked.

Kit popped a grape Bubblectible bubble. "Aah," he said, jabbing a thumb back to Room B, "he was just tryin' to see which of us was dummies and which of us wasn't."

"So that puts you where?" Harlen wanted to know.

"I ain't no dummy if that's what you mean."

---

villagers the "okay" sign after a rather impressive dance performed in his honor. His "okay" sign was meant to convey his approval. Instead, the villagers took Mr. Nixon's gesture, combined with an awkwardly-executed smile (a showing of teeth), to mean, "I am hungering for your chickens." (Note how the "okay" sign looks much like a chicken. Do this in front of a mirror and you can make it look like the chicken is giving you a big smooch on the cheek. Go ahead, try it. Cute, no?)

Anyway, since chickens are to Mua'ago Pago what oil fields are to Texas, spears were raised, guns were drawn, international treaties were thrown by the wayside and all-out war ensued. Which, in case you haven't been to the South Pacific of late, is amazingly still dragging on today. And, since wars have a terrible habit of wreaking havoc on commerce, the Mua'ago Pagoans soon found themselves in dire need of a natural resource available only from the United States, with whom, as you recall from the preceding sentence, the Mua'ago Pagoans had found themselves at war.

This resource, molybdenum disulfide, was a crucial component in the manufacture of plastic kewpie dolls, the export of which was the lifeblood of Mua'ago Pago — until 1972 that is, when their chickens were rudely coveted in broad daylight, spears were raised, and the rest. This explains why the Mua'ago Pagoan economy subsequently collapsed. Today, because they have nothing else to export, the hapless inhabitants of Mua'ago Pago live on a diet of dirt, rocks and sea snails, having long ago actually consumed, in a National Act of Desperation, each and every one of their sacred chickens.

Side note: Interestingly, President Nixon was particularly fond of making the V-sign himself (with both hands no less), the irony of which was apparently lost on him because, you see, he was the very person the peace demonstrators were making the V-sign against.

Harlen patted him on the back. "I would never imply otherwise."

Flinn Karneb, the only one of the six assigned to the A-L group, gave the others a look. "Are you *serious*? Morning Calisthenics was a *joke*. Some fat oaf in a monkey suit scowled at us for like an hour, making us do one lame-ass thing after another. Drawing circles and crap. Then he told us we all drew crappy circles. Had a stupid name ... Higgenjubber ... Mockenheimer ... something like that.[32]

So. Morning Calisthenics may not have been in a gymnasium like you'd expect, but Mid-morning Mechanics was, like you wouldn't expect. But unlike the gymnasiums at Sunrise Valley Middle School or Zadok Magruder High School, the gym in which they held Mid-morning Mechanics had no wretched rope and it didn't smell like sweaty socks or stinky pits or self-doubt, either. In all other ways it was the same — highly-polished maple floors, bleachers, basketball hoops folded up and out of reach, blah blah blah. Make that all other ways except one:

This gymnasium was full of *stuff*. Tables and tables of stuff. It looked like a recycling center or the remnants of a church rummage sale. Everything from bed frames to brooms, books to bicycles, empty boxes to aluminum cans, neatly laid out, stacked and organized by type. Ten metal carts laden with saws and nails and hammers and such could be found lined up on one side of the gym, which made Marvin assume they were looking at a staging area of some sort. But for what? A construction project? Spring cleaning? Inventory?

Fifty kids filed into the room, sneakers squeaking on the maple floors, voices bouncing off the floors and walls. Marvin, Bennie, Dara and the

---

32> This, you will come to find, was Col. Higgenmeyer-Matheson. Flinn couldn't remember Col. Higgenmeyer-Matheson's name because he didn't have a good mnemonic device for remembering it.

Have *your* mnemonic devices for remembering the names of Marvin's cohorts come in handy by the way? Did you remember that Flinn was the freckled-faced kid in the bandana and tie-dye pants who looked like a clown? Did you remember that Harlen wore a Mets cap? Did you remember that Kit had been the seat hogger? Did you remember that Dara was a girl? If not, thank you for coming and please turn in your reader's permit to the gentleman at the door.

others meandered about, eyeing the piles and shrugging their shoulders as meandering people do. Just as Dara picked up a hammer and asked if anyone thought it had something to do with Mid-morning Mechanics, a voice came over the P.A.

"Welcome to Mid-morning Mechanics," the voice said, which conveniently answered the question but also made everyone wonder what kind of voice it was (as in male or female). "This is Ms. Geraldine Fitzsimmons speaking." (Answered.) "I will be joining you shortly. In the meantime" — she cleared her throat — "please direct your attention to the rear of the gymnasium. You will find there ten wire baskets. In each of these baskets you will find ten ping-pong balls. Your assignment is to transfer these ping-pong balls to the opposite side of the gymnasium, placing them in their corresponding receiving basket, which, you will see, are presently empty. The baskets are numbered accordingly."

Fifty heads looked to the rear of the gymnasium. Ten wire baskets, numbered 1 through 10; each filled with ping-pong balls. Check. Fifty heads turned to the other side of the gymnasium. Ten *empty* wire baskets, numbered 1 through 10; each devoid of ping-pong balls. Check.

The P.A. system chirped and Geraldine Fitzsimmons again cleared her throat. "There are only two rules to this exercise. One: You may not touch the ping-pong balls. Two: The ping-pong balls may not touch the floor.

"Now. You have at your disposal the items before you. You may divide into groups. You have two hours to accomplish this task." The public address system then made another chirp as Geraldine Fitzsimmons switched off her microphone. Then it chirped again. "Ahem," she ahemed in a maybe-I-have-not-made-myself-clear manner. "Go." The P.A. system chirped off.

Marvin felt like a sudden participant in a television reality show. And Marvin *hated* television reality shows.[33]

33> Hopefully you are reading this long after the demise of such soul-sucking rubbish. Suffice it to say that at the turn of the twenty-first century the Great Minds of Network Television decided the world needed to see people make fools of themselves at the drop of a hat. Why they felt the viewing public wanted to be privy to the bathroom habits of has-been celebrities or watch airheads eat worms on desert islands or sing thirty-year-old songs or be locked in a closet with a family of wolverines is somewhat of a mystery, but if the Nielsen ratings are any indication, people watched this stuff by the gajillions. Perhaps it was to remind themselves that if they, too, ever were to find themselves as desperate for attention as the contestants on these shows, salvation was only an audition away.

There are people, by the way, who believe the Nielsen ratings — the television industry's way of gauging how many people are tuning in — are themselves so much baloney. One of these people, Leonard R. Pipswaddle, Ph.D., a renowned statistician at Miskatonic University, has even written a book about it. Not specifically on the Nielsen ratings *per se,* but in his book, *Messin' With Da Man* (Miskatonic University Press, 1996), Professor Pipswaddle postulates that not only are the Nielsen ratings pure poppycock (read: fixed), they are in point of fact no less than the work of chaos-loving anarchists hell-bent on the destruction of Western Civilization.

These devices, connected to thousands of television sets across the United States, are manufactured by a company, Pipswaddle claims, that is thinly-veiled front for a group of subversives in Berkeley, California. This group goes by the name the Cage Rattlers, aka the Wrench Throwers, aka the Soldiers of Confusion, aka the Wrabble Wrousers, aka Smokin' Stu and the Aristocrats — a deliberately sarcastic *nom de guerre.* [It was under the guise of the Aristocrats — a five-piece combo that played '60s rock and roll — that the Cage Rattlers were able to pay the bills (giving the phrase "cover band" a whole different meaning).] And of course, aka The Black Box Manufacturing Group.

Of course, as any student of politics knows, the Cage Rattlers' true-to-its-word slogan, "Wreaking Havoc Since 1968," earned the group a slot on the FBI's Most Wanted list thirty-seven years in a row. This was due to the Cage Rattlers' hand in countless acts — from the kidnapping of dog food heiress Pammy Splern to the infamous "costume malfunction" of WrestleMania XXIV.

Further, and perhaps more importantly, Pipswaddle contends the Cage Rattlers were instrumental in the establishment of a certain ubiquitous coffee-drinking establishment found on virtually every corner, which is basically what the word "ubiquitous" means.

One could argue, therefore (and Pipswaddle does), that everyone in America, being a stone's throw from overpriced coffee, has financial ties to the group, which means the Nielsen folks hold no special place vis-à-vis havoc-wreaking than anyone else. Which, if true, makes Prof. Pipswaddle a bit of an alarmist, don't you think?

That said, I think we will all agree that Americans are not willing to give up their double latte

Bennie, already looking overwhelmed at the prospect of ping-pong transference, pulled Marvin's sleeve. "Did she just say we have two hours? I can't *last* two hours." As much as Marvin wanted to give his friend a much-needed blood sugar boost, the best he could provide at the moment was a sympathetic shrug, the very same kind of shrug you might give someone who'd just managed to drop his keys into a river of molten lava, i.e., you'd like to help but there really wasn't anything you could do about it. Which sent Bennie scrounging the gymnasium for an apple or a candy bar — anything — to prevent a full-on attack. The other forty-eight kids, in turn, went scrounging as well, but in their case they went scrounging for each other.

This is because the natural tendency of people, when put in the same situation, is to pull together — unless you really *are* on a reality show (which, by the way, they weren't), in which case it's every man for himself. In short order, then, as eyes caught other eyes, the room divided itself

---

mocha grandes just because a portion of the proceeds might go to such stunts as flying over the Mormon Tabernacle in a Cessna 150 while skywriting the phrase SURRENDER DOROTHY in August of 1991 or hacking into the arrival and departure boards of LAX on Nov. 8, 2004 (resulting in an estimated 14,000 people showing up at Gate 32A). Or hoisting the Mayor of Oakland's car atop a forty-foot California oak in 2008. I mean, it's damn good coffee.

One more thing: Do not think I'm unaware of the phrase "drop of a hat" at the start of this note. I have often struggled with the question of why it would be a hat one would need to drop rather than something that would undoubtedly and immediately succumb to gravity, like, say, an anvil, which would most definitely drop precipitously if one were to let go of it from any height. As we all know from Mr. Galileo, one thing does not fall faster than another (outside of the stock market, or, say, Cuba Gooding's career) — meaning there would be no advantage in choosing a piece of haberdashery vs. a *sure thing*, would there? A hat (something that could easily be swept away by inclement weather) seems just a tad short-sighted in my book. I wholeheartedly believe whoever came up with the "drop of a hat" phrase was grasping at straws. And, as this note has gone on long enough, I will spare you the whole grasping-at-straws analysis. Rest assured, there is analysis aplenty in *Reginald T. Foggbottom's Dictionary of Peculiar Expressions, Adages, Idioms and Other Figures of Speech (English)*. And yes, you'll even find "in my book" in there.

into teams.

Note I said, "other forty-eight kids." Because one of them, Marvin, accustomed to sitting out a semester in the hallway, had no such natural tendency.

So, one by one, as each of his compatriots approached — Dara, Bennie, Harlen and Flinn (Kit couldn't care less) — asking whether Marvin wanted to be in their group, he begged off, saying so sorry, thank you very much and all that, but he wasn't really interested in the group thing. Instead, he parked himself under wire Basket No. 10 (the one with the ping-pong balls, not the one without the ping-pong balls), removed his drawing paper and pencils from his backpack, and settled himself on the floor against the wall — in effect laying claim to Basket No. 10 and the ping-pong balls within.

Pushing up his glasses, he set to work.

Chapter TEN...

THE GYM WAS SOON alive with activity. Teams of three and five and seven grabbed various items from the piles and scattered off into groups. The girl with the nose-ring had taken charge of one team and within minutes, after a few industrious gestures indicating trajectory and height and the like, they had taken possession of a little red wagon, a set of closet doors, an old rag rug, and a roll of duct tape.

Throughout the gym, it didn't take long before one could hear hammering and sawing and the stacking of things along with the periodic *ZZZIP* of duct tape as it was being unfurled. (This of course without the benefit of Marvin, who remained in his place under Basket No. 10, sketching away.)

The initial problem, the teams found, wasn't so much getting the balls across the room, it was getting them out of their baskets without touching them or having them bounce out of control. ("Ping-pong" being Chinese for "bounces like a mother.") Each basket was equipped with a sort of trap door at the bottom which could be unlatched to release the balls. The receiving end of the exercise proved even more difficult because the receiving basket was three feet off the floor, which meant each team had to come up with a means that would either keep the balls at a three-foot height across the room, or raise them, shoot them, propel them, etc., from floor height to receiving basket height, without, again, them bouncing out of control — not a slam-dunk (so to speak) easy thing to do.

To their credit, the teams came up with a wide range of solutions which I'm going to go out on a limb here to describe as "wide-ranging":

The team at Basket No. 2 went the aqueduct route, or, perhaps, the *dry* aqueduct route if you're one of those people who insist on looking up the word "aqueduct." Their balls would roll along a channel made of folded-up pieces of cardboard, soda cans, PVC tubing and duct tape.

What the team at Basket No. 6 built was another variation of the idea, perhaps more akin to an elevated train track. It made use of scores of books stacked at varying heights and angles. Many of the books lay opened so the ping-pong balls could roll along the open binding; others sat closed so the balls would roll along the channel formed by the pages. Half the group was building the course while the rest were having an animated debate over how to release the balls from the basket of origin, or as Basket No. 5 group called it, "the B.O."

At Basket No. 3, Dara, Flinn and Bennie were working on a catapult. Each ball would fall into a cone fashioned from an old lampshade, land in a small plastic shovel, then be snapped across the room via the use of a piece of stretched inner tube. If all went smoothly, it would land in an outstretched bed sheet, the top of which was presently being stapled by the rest of the team to the wall above their receiving basket. From here each ball would roll effortlessly down the sheet into Receiving Basket No. 3.

Meanwhile, blonde-haired-nose-ring girl and her team had already abandoned their idea due to technical problems. At first their plan was to transport the balls with the little red wagon. They'd open the latch by means of a string (so they wouldn't touch the balls as the latch was released), the balls would fall into the wagon, and they'd simply pull the wagon to the other side of the gym. Easy. But, as it turned out, the distance between the basket and the wagon (.9144m), coupled with the diameter (40mm) and speed of the balls (the Earth's gravitational pull increases an object's velocity 9.8m/sec. for each second of descent), pretty much assured that every time the balls hit the hard metal of the wagon, the darn things bounced out. ("Ping-pong," being Chinese for … oops, previously noted.) Putting an old rag rug in the wagon to soften the landing solved that problem, but when they successfully got their ten balls to the other side of the room, they couldn't think of a way to raise them to the basket.

Plan B: Abandon the wagon. It was too shallow. They decided on connecting the two closet doors with their hinges, forming a nice deep V. The rag rug was then crammed at one end to hold the balls, the string was pulled, the trap door was sprung and the balls dropped into the V. Hooray. Unfortunately, because it took six people to hold the unwieldy thing, every time they tried to scurry across the room, one of the six would trip or sneeze or giggle or cough and at least one of the balls would go flying.[34]

"Not foolproof," then, would be a good description of the Closet Door Transport Solution. So they were working on it — scurrying and pouring, scurrying and pouring.

34> No doubt you've noticed that the moving of large items — couches, televisions, extension-ladders, large inflatable giraffes — can often trigger in people not usually prone to such things, badly timed silliness. Why this is so I cannot say, but although it has been witnessed among the males of the species, it is usually the females who fall prey. Put two girls in a stairwell and ask them to carry a dining room table to the third floor and you will find that before they get to the first-floor landing, they will take one look at each other and let out irrepressible snorts of laughter.

Perhaps it is because moving a dining room table makes one contort oneself into odd angles and the female of the species, far more attuned to these things, knows that odd angles do not make for graceful composure. Or perhaps it is because, when it is the least convenient time, one often finds oneself in need of a bathroom and nothing is funnier than holding something three times your size when you have to pee. (Ok, one thing is, but this is not the place for it.) The Have-to-Pee-While-Moving-a-Couch phenomenon is a chicken-and-egg thing; i.e., if you do not have to pee before you pick up a couch, once you pick up a couch, you will. Let us hope an Institute of Higher Learning will someday study the phenomenon so we might learn the hows and whys of it.

Whatever the reason, kudos to that extra X chromosome. If men were willing to laugh at themselves when they look like spasmodic albatrosses [*See: "Rambo"*], perhaps we could avoid a few whadda-*you*-lookin'-at's.

At the end of an hour, the two swinging doors to the gymnasium swung open. In walked a grotesquely obese woman dressed in an unfortunately tight blue satin dress. ("Unfortunately" referring here not to its blueness or satin-ness, but to its {~choke, heave, gag~} tightness.) As a matter of fact, the woman's blue satin dress was not unlike Mrs. Hankersmithy's blue satin dress, which, you may recall from Marvin's formative years, had creepily parked itself on his hands back in the fourth grade. If this blue satin dress were to do the same, i.e. park itself on Marvin's hands, one could be certain that Marvin's hands would never be heard from again. Which is to say the woman before them was of such unfathomable girth, she made Mrs. Hankersmithy look a svelte size eight.

This, everyone correctly surmised, was Geraldine Fitzsimmons. Who, presently, blew a whistle not unlike Mr. Waddell's whistle, and if that isn't some bit of foreshadowing, I don't know what is. "I am Geraldine Fitzsimmons," the mass of blue satin announced somewhat needlessly, and all the activity in the gymnasium came to a halt, even though much of it already had come to a halt pretty much at the beginning of the last paragraph. Clicking a stop-watch that hung from her neck (not, hint hint, unlike Mr. Waddell's stop-watch), Geraldine Fitzsimmons added, "You now have exactly one hour remaining to complete your task."

She waddled into the gymnasium on puffy porcine ankles, her shoes far too small for her, the clunky heels of which clicked against the highly polished floor like the ominous clicking of a time bomb. A collection of brightly colored bracelets, tight around her chubby wrists, clinked and clattered with every clunky-heel step. She had blue-grey hair pulled tightly into a bun and held there by a collection of hair clips, and balanced on her nose were pointy blue eyeglasses that belonged in a 1962 issue of Life magazine. (Or at least a picture of them because clearly you can't fold a magazine with a pair of glasses in it.) Plus, their thick lenses made her eyes look huge. She reminded Marvin of the invading chameleon-like aliens in Bug Eyed Monsters, Go Home, his all-time favorite graphic novel. Only those guys weren't over-accessorized.

"Please," Geraldine Fitzsimmons told them, holding high (perhaps in
an attempt to conceal it) not a double chin but a triple-quadruple-double-
foldover chin, "do continue."

All activity resumed — the hammering, the sawing, the stacking of
things, the unfurling of duct tape, the scurrying and pouring, etc.

During which time Geraldine Fitzsimmons perused the ping-pong
projects, heels clicking as she went. "Hmmm," she'd say, and "Hmmm,"
and the occasional "*Hmmmmm.*" When she got to Dara and Bennie's
project, she pulled absent-mindedly at the belt digging its way into the
folds of her "hips," adjusted her pointy blue glasses, and said, "This would
be a ... what is it ... a trebuchet?"

"Catapult," Bennie pointed out, adjusting the arm. "Trebuchet's more
complicated." [35]

35> "Trebuchet," French for "hurl stuff over a castle wall," is a form of catapult with gears and
counterweights and the like for getting whatever is being hurled to go way-faster and way-higher
than is possible with a run-of-the-mill catapult. Catapult 2.0 as it were.

They were big in the Middle Ages and heaven help you if you lived anywhere near a castle wall.
Everything from boulders to burning oil to maggot-infested cows would come hurtling by when you least
expected it. It was hard to have a picnic or a yard sale without being rained upon by a plummeting
beehive or a victim of the Black Death. You were forever spending your time looking up for incoming
debris. (This is, by the way, where the phrase "It's raining cats and dogs" comes from; only oftentimes
they were referring to cats and dogs that had been set on fire.) People's necks got so sore in those days
from looking skyward, they had to invent special stiff collars for protection.

Side note: We can credit the Chinese with coming up with the idea of the trebuchet. ("China:
We're Not Just Good at Building Walls, We're Good at Hurling Stuff Over Them.") Of course the
Chinese didn't call it a trebuchet, they called it something in Mandarin or one of those other languages
they use over there, which the French would have none of, so the French made up their own word
for it extra letters and all, and no one else has yet cared enough to come up with something better.

The Chinese pre-date the French by a few hundred years on this one, because, as you will
come to find, the Chinese pre-date everybody in just about everything (pasta, gunpowder, umbrellas,
glasses, fireworks, the toothbrush, ice cream, kites, steel, paper, whiskey, negative integers, swinging around before you kick a guy in the teeth, etc.).

Having inspected the first nine solutions to the ping-pong challenge, Geraldine Fitzsimmons then made her way to Basket No. 10.

Basket No. 10, you may recall, was laid claim by our very own Marvin Plotnik, who was still camped out below, sketching on his sketchpad. Geraldine Fitzsimmons squinted through her pointy blue glasses at Basket No. 10, its ten ping-pong balls still resting fixedly in place. She squinted across the room at Receiving Basket No. 10. She then focused on the space *between* Basket No. 10 and Receiving Basket No. 10 — its contemptible open space, its disgraceful lack of … work. It was a glare really. A big-eyed, grotesquely obese glare. And it was now aimed at Marvin.

It was at this moment Marvin looked up to see the mass that was Geraldine Fitzsimmons, arms crossed over a gelatinous sea of blue satin, chin (or, rather, chins) quivering suppressed rage. Below, at the end of a pudgy ankle, a tapping foot. *Tap tap tap* it went. Then: *Tap tap tap.*

Marvin, pushing up his non-pointy blue glasses, blinked.

Then he set back to work. [36]

• • •

FOR THE NEXT FORTY-FIVE MINUTES, Marvin sketched on his sketchpad, head down, scribbling, erasing, drawing, redrawing, adding arrows and captions and notational references in the margins, and getting his pen to work when it got clogged. Occasionally, he'd lift his head at the sound of someone yelling an order or hitting their thumb with a hammer or squeaking their shoes across the floor or, in the case of Kit Warnam, letting out an outrageously loud burp.

---

[36]> **Assignment:** Using the previous note on body language, compile a list of character types, emotions, tell-tale signs and unconscious messages Geraldine Fitzsimmons conveys. See if you can name at least 20. See how many of them are related to unhappiness, displeasure and/or annoyance. Each correct answer receives one point. Ten extra points for use of the word "curmudgeon." Ten more for using "curmudgeoness," which isn't really a word but it ought to be. I will remind you, as always, spelling counts. (And if you misspell "curmudgeon," you lose all your points since you just read it three times in the same paragraph.) *Don't forget to add your score to the test at the end.*

There were repeated groans from the team at Basket No. 2 when their cardboard-and-soda-can aqueduct, snaking its way across the gym, continued to pose a problem. Invariably, the balls would jam up at a particular juncture, and no amount of duct tape repositioning would fix it. With the deadline quickly approaching, adjustments were hastily being made.

The blonde-haired girl, Marvin noted, was putting her team through a practice run. But every time they'd get to the point where they removed the rag rug to let the balls fall into the basket, somehow — don't ask me how, it's physics — the balls missed the basket. There was much discussion about how such a foolproof thing could go wrong after so many successful runs. "What we need," one boy said, "is a deeper basket."

"What they need," Marvin muttered to himself, "is an anti-gravity device."

When he looked up at the sound of the ping-pong balls' latest escape, he was mildly surprised at the sight of Geraldine Fitzsimmons' still-tapping foot, now not ten feet away ("still" in the sense of "even now" rather than "not moving," which in this sentence would be wrong). Geraldine Fitzsimmons waited until she had his eye, then, at one-hour-and-forty-five minutes since they had begun, she blew a warning whistle. "Fifteen minutes," she announced, not removing her gaze from young Marvin (and the still-untouched Basket No. 10).

And at the end of those fifteen minutes, Geraldine Fitzsimmons surprised them all by announcing it was time for lunch.

Bennie, particularly relieved as the only thing he'd found in the whole damn gymnasium was a stale raisin and a linty gummy bear, let out a "Thank Gawd!" that echoed throughout the gym.

"We will break for an hour," Geraldine Fitzsimmons announced, clicking her way to the door, "then meet back here after we have enjoyed Winston's delicious repast. At that time there shall be rewards for successful completion of Ping-Pong Ball Transference. And … for those who fail?" — she flashed Marvin one last glare — "There shall be repercussions."

Chapter ELEVEN...

LUNCH CONSISTED of a choice of hearty soups, breads, sandwich makings and a full complement of fruits and vegetables, as square a meal as you can get, full of fiber and vitamins and all kinds of good nourishing things, all of which made Geraldine Fitzsimmons' description of a delicious repast highly accurate. Pizza would be better, but you take what you can get.[37]

"I'm famished," Dara told the others at her table. She dipped a hunk of sourdough into a bowl of clam chowder. "Mid-morning Mechanics is tough. I never built anything in my life."

After a few nuts and an apple (inhaled faster than the last one if you can imagine such a thing), Bennie and his blood sugar were doing fine. It had been a close one, too; he'd been feeling woozy long since the linty gummy bear was gone. "I hope the thing works," he said, digging into a tuna sandwich. "I can just see us catapulting a ball right into Geraldine Fitzsimmons' uber-cleavage."

37> The more attentive of you have noticed that Geraldine Fitzsimmons' name has been consistently referred to in full. This is, of course, curious, and I have no explanation as to why this choice was made, even though I was the one to have made it. I suppose it is because "Geraldine Fitzsimmons" has such an engaging tone to it. I cannot imagine calling her "Ms. Fitzsimmons" any more than I can imagine calling her "Annabelle McGilicuddy" who is someone else entirely. Calling her "Ms. Fitzsimmons" — or "Geraldine" for that matter — feels a bit like addressing, say, Vlad the Impaler as "Mr. Impaler" or "Vlad." Doesn't work.

"More like '*heave*-age,' Kit put in.

Everyone scrunched up their noses at the image.

Harlen pulled a tomato off his sandwich, looking at it suspiciously before tossing it aside (the tomato, not the sandwich). "Won't happen," he said at the prospect of a ping-pong ball going into the buxom nether regions of Geraldine Fitzsimmons' chest.

Flinn: "Somebody work up a calculation on the odds … like how many ping-pong balls would it take 'til one got in there? You know, on average."

They sat for a bit presumably running the numbers.

It was Dara who finally got back on track: "I just wonder what the repercussions are if we don't pull it off."

Kit leaned his chair back on two legs and took a bite of his sandwich. "What're they gonna do if it doesn't work? *Fire* us?" (Which sounded more like "Whugg thul gonna do ibid dozzn wok?") He swallowed, tilted forward to reach his soda, then leaned the chair back against the wall again. "It's just *school*, dude. Same old crapola. All that b.s. about not 'ridding us of our eccentricities.' C'mon, dude." He took a gulp of soda, wiped his lips on his shirt, and burped, "You ever been to a place that lets you do what you want? Besides, whadda *you* care if your stupid ping-pong ball thingie works? Who're you in competition with, yourself?"

Kit was right. Why *was* everyone taking this so seriously? It's not like Geraldine Fitzsimmons announced a prize or anything. It's just an assignment, like any other. Marvin was just about to say this when Dara turned to Kit and said, "Who are *you* in competition with?"

"Hey yeah," Flinn put in, "whose team are you *on* anyway?" and everyone looked at Kit as though they'd just realized they hadn't seen him so much as lift a pair of scissors.

"He was hangin' with us a little," Harlen said with a slurp of his soup. (Harlen was on the Basket No. 6's book-track team.) "And I saw him over with the aqueduct squad at one point."

Bennie let out a smirk. "Now *they're* the ones with something to worry about."

A couple of tables away, the aqueduct squad of Basket No. 2 *did* look a little worried. They had to be wondering how one little piece of duct tape could cause so much frickin' trouble.

At least Dara's team had successfully catapulted their ping-pong balls into the sheet with every try. It was just a matter of doing it the same way when they were graded on it. Assuming, come to think of it, they'd *be* graded on it.

Flinn squinted at Kit. "Last time *I* saw you, you were ducking behind the bleachers."

Kit gave him a look that said, "So?" then brought his chair to all four legs. "Look. I connected their stupid dots." He popped a potato chip in his mouth. "What more do they want? I'm not spending like a whole day screwin' around with a bunch of little white balls. I got better things to do."

Flinn: "Like what?"

Kit stopped eating. "Like a little shut-eye for one." He then looked at each of them like the next one to question where he was and what he was doing was going to get a fistful of potato chips up their nose.

Harlen: "Wait a minute. You were *sleeping?* The whole time? You can't do that."

Kit shrugged. "Looks like I can."

"You're as bad as Marvin," Dara said. "He hasn't built anything, either."

Marvin felt everyone's eyes upon him.

"What in the world have you been working so *diligently* on anyway?" Dara wanted to know.

Bennie pulled a piece of lettuce from his sandwich. "Must be a helluva solution. Right, MP?"

Marvin's face twisted into a question mark.

Bennie: "It's a nickname, yo."

"Seriously," Dara said. "What *are* you working on?"

Glad in a way he'd once again been singled out with a nickname, and *infinitely* glad it wasn't "Martian Sputnik," Marvin gave a little shrug. "Just working out some things."

Flinn reached for Marvin's sketchpad and began to turn its pages. "*What* things? You don't have much time left."

Side note: Marvin was used to people grabbing things from him. Because he was considered an oddball. And oddballs get things grabbed from them, or thrown at them, or hidden from them, or any number of other messed-up things, all the stupid time. Get this: In sixth grade they threw pennies. Don't ask him why, but somehow it got started and then everyone was doing it. By the end of the year, he'd accumulated $3.88. Easy math on that one.

Side side note: One of the people who'd grabbed things from Marvin was a kid named Max Carboni. With Max, this was a way of life. In the eighth grade alone, he'd grabbed something from Marvin a total of twenty-seven times, including the times he threw Marvin's jacket into the girl's locker room and his lunch into the formaldehyde bath in biology lab. Max Carboni thought that was a good one.

From the moment Max Carboni came to Sunrise Valley Middle School at the end of Marvin's seventh-grade year, Marvin knew there was going to be trouble. It started the second Max had heard Marvin's nickname. He turned to Marvin and said, "Martian *Sputnik*? What's that make you, a space cadet?" He thought that was a good one, too. He laughed and laughed at it. In fact, he repeated it every time he ran into Marvin in the hall. "Hey, Sputnik!" he'd yell. "What's that make you, a space cadet?"

Marvin took it in stride, pretty much ignoring it. As did all the other kids at Sunrise Valley Middle School because right away they saw that Max Carboni was pretty much a jerk. He'd corner kids in the stairwells and slap their books out of their hands and slam their lockers shut while they were getting out their stuff and block their way in the hall and other un-friend-making stuff. Such was the way of Max Carboni. [38]

38> Consider this a Major Life Lesson: *Some people just don't know how to act.* Sometimes it's because they don't know any better, and sometimes it's because they never *will* know any better. By the tenth grade, for instance, Max Carboni still didn't know how to act. And, like a lot of people

For Marvin, dealing with the Max Carbonis of the world goes with the territory. He'd come up with ways to deal with it as far back as he could remember. There were, in fact, plenty of tools in Marvin's Self-Preservation Tool Kit. The first came in the fourth grade when Rosemary Throckmorton of all people decided, out of the blue, she didn't want to hang with him anymore. "I don't hang with *nerds*," she said one day on the blacktop, and stood there with her hands on her hips until it was so uncomfortably *weird* he walked away.

This act on Rosemary Throckmorton's part, of course, made no sense. After all, Rosemary knew as much about dinosaurs and the solar system and where the treasure was hidden in level ten of *Realm of the Black Caves* as he did, had eaten lunch with him almost every day since second grade, had laughed at all his jokes, had invited him to her birthday parties, etc. She'd even told him she thought he was "way funny." Marvin struggled

---

who don't know how to act, he was arrested for it. Vandalism in Max's case.

He'd let the air out of the tires on the football coach's van with a pen knife, then spray painted — in a very non-clever way — COACH *THIS*, BUTWAD on the back of the van (because Max Carboni didn't know how to spell, either). Apparently, earlier in the day the coach made it clear he didn't think Max was football team material. A couple of months later, a judge made it clear she didn't think Max was good exempt-from-paying-a-hefty-fine material.

Unfortunately for Max Carboni, he never did learn his lesson, especially the it's-not-nice-to-grab-things one. A full decade later, he would find himself at the wrong end of a Japanese katana sword while stumbling upon a thief in the alley behind the Got-2-Sell Auction House in East Forkensport, New Jersey, where he was working as a box un-packer. The proper way to act when you come across a drawn katana sword is to run, in the other direction, like the wind. Max Carboni, unaware of this, decided to relieve the thief of his burden; i.e., rob the robber. "Nice sword," he said, "Give it to me."

And the robber did. Horizontally. Right across Max's belly.

Should this make us feel good? Of course not. In fact, it made Marvin feel terrible when he heard about it.

Fact is, *most* people learn from their mistakes. Just because Max Carboni didn't, doesn't mean the rest of us can't. (I personally learn this lesson at *least* once a month.)

with this rejection for days, then, in the middle of the night, the reason for Rosemary's change of heart came to him: Peer pressure. Ordinary, everyday peer pressure. Just like they show you in a school assembly skit. Rosemary Throckmorton had seen how the *other* kids treated him. And she didn't want to be left out.

To make himself feel better, Marvin decided from that point on, the day Rosemary Throckmorton called him a nerd, whenever he was called a name, he'd pretend it meant something else. [*See:* "*Yankees.*"]

So when Rosemary Throckmorton turned all Benedict Arnold on him, he decided that Rosemary, seeing the other kids were watching, had cleverly sent him a secret message. She had called him something *in code.* An acronym maybe. Yes, that was it. And when he figured out what Rosemary had truly meant, that "Nerd" stood for Nobody Ever Razzes Dummies, he felt even better about it. Meaning nobody would ever make fun of someone who was genuinely dumb, in special ed., etc. This, then, would be he and Rosemary's little secret. They would remain friends, secret friends, and no one would be the wiser.

Of course Marvin knew Nobody Ever Razzes Dummies was stupid. (And not even true. He'd seen, say, Jeremy Brunkman made fun of plenty of times. And Jeremy Brunkman had the mental acuity of pocket lint. Jeremy Brunkman once ate the binding off his English composition book. And swallowed it. *In ninth grade.*) Nevertheless, pretending an insult meant something else did wonders for Marvin's self-image. It helped remind him about rubber and glue, sticks and stones, and other seemingly unrelated things that are mashed together by whoever comes up with these things to make people feel better about themselves.

So at lunch, when Flinn grabbed his sketchpad, Marvin, being used to it, simply resigned himself to the fact that Flinn might take one look at it and turn into Rosemary Throckmorton. Or Max Carboni.

But Flinn didn't turn into Rosemary Throckmorton *or* Max Carboni. Instead, when Flinn got a look at what Marvin had spent the last hour-and-a-half working on, Flinn's freckled face slowly went up and down, up and down. "Cool," he said, his head still nodding. And as he leafed through the pages he *kept* saying it. "Cool … *Cool!*" And even: "This is *so* cool."

Marvin didn't need an acronym for *that*.

Harlen then grabbed the sketchpad and Marvin once again braced himself for the ghost of Max Carboni.

"What is it?" Dara wanted to know, stretching her neck to get a peek.

"I'll tell you what it *isn't*," Harlen said as he turned the sketchpad for everyone to see. "It isn't the ping-pong ball exercise."

• • •

"IT'S A COMIC BOOK!" Harlen marveled, as if that needed to be pointed out. (Which technically it wasn't because it was a graphic novel, a fact which Marvin will shortly set right; but Harlen was on the right track here and that's all that matters.) "There's this one-armed dude, hangin' onto a rope," he told the others, "flyin' over mountains and villages and crap." He flipped through the pages, nodding much as Flinn had along the way. "Dude. This is like … *good*. Those look like real-ass mountains."

"How'd you get it to look so *cold*?" Flinn wanted to know, looking over Harlen's shoulder.

"Cool colors, mostly," Marvin beamed. "Cool-tone, that is. Blues and whites mostly." He cocked his head at the book. "It's the Himalayas. And the rope was made by weaving this raja dude's hair. It's attached to the zeppelin, see? … Turn the page … A *Bhutanese* zeppelin — operated by Bhutanese Buddhist monks. Highly trained in martial arts, particularly Su-tai-fu, which I made up — 'course I made it *all* up — but that's the fun of it." He took a sip of his soda. "And it's a graphic novel. Not a comic book."

Flinn: "Bhutanese monks?"

"From the future. They've come to save him and—"

Dara had taken over the sketchpad, and she, too, didn't turn into Rosemary Throckmorton. "Whoa," she said. "Nice."

Marvin smiled.

Now Kit grabbed the sketchpad, impatiently flipping the pages. "*Who* are these monk dudes saving?"

Marvin took the pad and added a little shading on the cheek of his protagonist. "Yolando Plumadore," he said. "Who else?" [39]

39> Please recall Marvin had no idea the large birthmark on Mr. Flöckenheimer's head was in the shape of Bhutan. That Marvin chose Bhutanese monks over any other kind of monks is yet another example of the Interconnectedness of All Things and makes me exceedingly happy. You're familiar with the term "six degrees of separation," yes? Unless you've been on Neptune, you probably are, but just in case it's new to you, here's the skinny: The phrase refers to the idea that if you took any one person in the world and any other person in the world, and compared who these two people knew and/or who they had interacted with, you'd find these two people were only six connections away from one another. Six degrees.

Let's try it, shall we? Take, say, me, and, oh, you. No, wait, that one's not fair because we are, at this very moment, only one degree apart. We both have read about Marvin Plotnik and the Sandy Rivers Hilltop Ranch for Wayward Youth, and, even more specifically, this very sentence. Let me see … How about me and, oh … as long as we're already talking about Buddhist monks … the Dalai Lama. The Dalai Lama, of course, is the spiritual leader of the Tibetan Buddhist religion. Presently, he lives in exile in a little town in India called Dharamsala. Of course he should be living in Tibet, which is in China, but the Chinese government can be downright mean, so they have kicked him and his people out.

Let us see how we can make the connection. Ah, I have it. Let us start with a small Indian boy, also of Dharamsala. His name was Sunil Misra and many years ago, when he was but six years old, he would often pass the Dalai Lama's residence on his way to his father's cobbler shop down the lane (the boy's father, not the Dalai Lama's father). Each day, if His Holiness could be seen at the window (usually tinkering with his many clocks), the young boy would wave excitedly to him, and the Dalai Lama, being a kind and generous man, would wave back. It got so the young boy looked forward to receiving his very special greeting as he was often told that no one else in the village had such rapport with His Holiness.

Now, years before, Sunil's father, Gopal, originally from Mumbai, was given the chance to travel to Cornwall, England, specifically the town of Saltash, for a week's respite. He was a poor man, but had won this trip by entering a contest by the Saltash Saltine Works, makers of Bartholemew Biscuits, a product Gopal simply adored. On his first day in Cornwall, Gopal came upon a lovely young woman on the Tamar Bridge who was taking in the splendor of a particularly striking sunset. She had beautiful flowing golden hair the likes of which Gopal had never seen, and eyes in which he could lose himself. They took up conversation, spending an hour-and-twenty-seven minutes in one another's company.

Gopal was so taken with her, he could not get her off his mind. For the next week, instead of seeing the sights of Cornwall, he searched for the fetching young woman he had met on the bridge. Finally it was time to return to Mumbai. On his way to the ship, he happened by a small pastry shop in Falmouth called "Sweets for Sweets." There at the till, to the joy of his aching heart, stood the lovely young woman he had met on the bridge.

Gopal did not go to the ship. Nor did he return to Mumbai. For the next three weeks he stopped by the shop every morning to purchase a small sweet roll in the hope the beautiful young woman would once again look into his eyes. In time, he learned her name was Penelope Hastings and, despite his family's pre-arranged marriage plans in which he was to marry a girl he had met only once at the age of three, he swore he would instead make Penelope his bride.

He decided to win her heart by staying in England to pursue a degree.

In order to buy textbooks, Gopal secured a part-time position as a product tester at the Failsafe Research Institute. One day, while testing the efficiency of an industrial laundry-folding machine, he found himself accidentally caught in the device during an unusually violent pleating cycle, resulting, sadly, in the loss of both hands.

Now when Gopal did not come to Sweets for Sweets for his usual pastry, Penelope Hastings inquired about him, and hearing of his misfortune, took it upon herself to visit him in the hospital, bringing each day his usual pastry, which she hand-fed him with great kindness. Witnessing the extent of his bravery and optimism under terrible circumstances, Penelope Hastings fell madly in love with him, and they were wed a mere four weeks later.

When the young couple moved back to India, in order to avoid the disappointment in his parents' eyes (for ignoring their marriage plans for him), Gopal and his bride decided to avoid Mumbai altogether and settled in Dharamsala, where people soon came from far and wide to see the young cobbler who, despite being bereft of hands, could repair shoes with solely (no pun intended) the use of his teeth.

I will speed this up. Penelope's father was a professor of archeology, who, after many years in Central America subsisting on a diet high in seafood, had developed a bad case of gout in his right knee. He sought help at a local clinic where a physician by the name of Carlos Roberto Arturo Mendoza, M.D., only six months into his residency, mistook the professor's gout for a boil and lanced the painful area, which did nothing more than further irritate an already-inflamed joint, along with, understandably, Professor Hastings.

Five years later, Dr. Mendoza was tried and convicted for half a dozen cases of assisted suicide in the state of South Dakota. He was entering his cell in the South Dakota State Correctional Facility for the first day of a sentence of twenty-to-thirty-five, when — and I am sure you'll be relieved I am getting to the final connection — I turned from my cot and introduced myself.

So there you have it. His Holiness the Dalai Lama, Sunil Misra, Gopal Misra, Penelope Hastings, Professor Hastings, Dr. Carlos Mendoza, and yours truly. Six degrees. Frankly, you could cut out everyone in between the Dalai Lama and myself, making it one connection, since I do see him every so often anyway. You know, for tea. I just didn't want to brag.

Chapter TWELVE...

THIRTY-TWO MINUTES after the ping-pong exercise reconvened, Marvin found himself sitting outside a door marked in crisp gold letters: REGINALD T. FOGGBOTTOM, ADMINISTRATOR. Marvin, thinking he might be getting used to the ever-present pink of the Sandy Rivers hallways after all, sat on a wooden bench that looked like it had seen better days ... days probably during the Roosevelt administration. Maybe even Coolidge.[40]

40> If you'd listened to your fourth-grade teacher go over the U.S. Presidents like you were supposed to instead of writing the name of that cute curly-haired girl in the margins of your Social Studies book, *Life on the Plains,* you'd know Calvin Coolidge was president before Franklin Roosevelt (when men were men and women were women and everyone wore hats) and that it was a long time ago. What your fourth-grade teacher probably didn't mention was that Calvin Coolidge was an idiot. Okay, not really, but he talked so infrequently people began to wonder. He was the first U.S. president to have more jokes told at his expense than all of the previous presidents combined, the gist of every one of them being that Coolidge rarely said a word. Which doesn't sound very funny, but at the time it was a veritable laugh riot. Take, for instance, this one: upon hearing that Mr. Coolidge had died, Dorothy Parker, a famous writer and also something of a wit, remarked: "How can they tell?"

BTW, when Coolidge did talk, he tended to say things like, "When more and more people are thrown out of work, unemployment results." Can you think of any other president who has made similar idiotic remarks? I'll bet you can.

A flash of blue satin started out of the door marked REGINALD T. FOGGBOTTOM, ADMINISTRATOR, went back into the room, then reappeared in the hall. "He'll see you now," Geraldine Fitzsimmons huffed with her nose in the air. "Now we shall see what repercussions *mean* around here." She held the door for Marvin and motioned him in with a look of sheer satisfaction. A look that also said *she* would be waiting in the hall.

On the other side of the door marked REGINALD T. FOGGBOTTOM, ADMINISTRATOR, Marvin found something he had not expected. For a minute he thought he'd walked onto the set of a elegantly furnished costume drama. To wit: a warmly-lit library of two-story bookcases (housing not only leather-bound books but antiquities — Italian vases, shiny brass sextants, bronzes and the like), dark mahogany walls, an antique pedestal globe, two leopard-skin throws, a Buddhist prayer-wheel, a coat of arms on red velvet, an entire wall of knives and swords, an exquisitely detailed Persian rug, an ornate limestone fireplace with a blazing fire within, a suit of armor (complete with battle-axe), and so on. Such a room, we can all agree, can only be described as high-class. And blue-ribbon. And high-end. And probably a few other compound adjectives like "fancy-schmancy" and "hoity-toity."

Now when one finds oneself turning in circles in such a room — innocently caught in a thinly-veiled-mood-symbolized-by-setting narrative device — humbled, or at least baffled by its opulence and Old World charm, when one stops to regard the expansive Medieval tapestry on the far wall (a unicorn, penned), one cannot help but feel as that unicorn: dizzyingly out of place. (Unless of course your name is Carnegie or Trump or Baldwin, then you'd be perfectly at home.) As out of place as this inner sanctum felt to the cockeyed pink-tiled monstrosity that contained it. Which was why Marvin, pushing up his glasses, turned one more circle in the middle of that elegant Persian rug.

"As I understand it," came a voice he'd only heard once before, from, you may recall, atop a TransWay (still in no way to be confused with the highly trademarked Segway® Personal Transporter, widely available from a Segway® dealer near you), "you have been sent to see me because of a disruption."

At first Marvin was confused because it sounded like the voice was coming from one of a dozen African masks that adorned the far wall. But then he saw, just below the masks, a lavish Louis XIV desk, and, illumed by the soft amber glow of a desk lamp, an aging hand, and in it a cigar, and from that, a rising curl of cigar smoke. Marvin moved a few inches to the right. There sat the man in the seersucker suit, wild white hair and all, no longer obscured by the lamp.

"I wouldn't call it a disruption," Marvin said. "It was more of a, uh, an unexpected turn of events."

Reginald T. Foggbottom sat in the shadows of the African masks and pressed together his fingertips. "Is that so? Perhaps then you should tell me the circumstances. I must inform you, however, that Ms. Geraldine Fitzsimmons has provided me with a particularly *dark* interpretation of these events."

Marvin took the opportunity to sit in a chair opposite the desk. "Well, it's simple really. We were supposed to move these ping-pong balls from one basket to another. The only rules were we weren't supposed to touch the balls and the balls weren't supposed to touch the floor. Everyone had come up with different ideas. They all worked, even the aqueduct. They'd been having problems with it, see, and—"

"*That is not true.*" It was her. Geraldine Fitzsimmons. Apparently, she could not contain herself and had come back in the room.

Mr. Foggbottom's fingertips patted against each other. "You're saying the aqueduct didn't work."

"That is not what I'm saying," she said, approaching the desk. "I'm saying this young man has intentionally misstated the rules."

Marvin's eyebrows went up as if to say, "I don't think so."

"You most certainly have. You were *supposed* to use the items in the room. We'd given you a gymnasium *filled* with tools and a world of paraphernalia. *Oodles* of paraphernalia! A whole gymnasium! You have gotten the rules all wrong."

"Excuse me," Marvin said, pushing up his glasses before turning to her. "And I quote: 'There are only two rules to this exercise. One: You may not touch the ping-pong balls. Two: The ping-pong balls may not touch the floor.' I believe that was the extent of the rule portion of the exercise."

"No," she said in a corrective tone, "there were items—"

Happy to show his knack for impersonation while counting off her very sentences, Marvin continued: "'You have at your disposal the items in the gymnasium. You may divide into groups. You have two hours to accomplish this task.'" Finished, he turned to the slight figure of Mr. Foggbottom all but overshadowed by the Louis XIV desk. "I'm pretty good at remembering things," he said. "She distinctly said, '*may* divide into groups.' I didn't *want* to be in a group. She distinctly said items were at our disposal, which would imply if you *need* them. I didn't. She distinctly said, 'You have two hours.' I didn't *need* two hours. I had it solved in like thirty seconds and I used the rest of the time to work on something else. I don't see what—"

"This is unacceptable!" Geraldine Fitzsimmons fumed. "He knew perfectly well what he was supposed to do."

Marvin straightened his glasses, thinking that if he had a dollar for every time he'd heard that, he could afford his *own* over-the-top inner sanctum. "I agree," he said. "I did know perfectly well what I was supposed to do. I was to move the balls from one basket to the other without touching them. It's simple. I went to my basket, took off my jumpsuit, wrapped it around my hands, unlatched the door, let the balls fall into the jumpsuit, then walked across the room to my receiving basket and let them go. I didn't touch them. They didn't touch the floor. I played by the rules."

Geraldine Fitzsimmons had turned a deep shade of purple. "I want this young man removed from this facility," she demanded out of the blue. "I can understand why he was sent here, but mark my words, he is nothing but trouble."

Mr. Foggbottom rubbed his chin. "I'm trying to understand this. If the boy followed instructions—"

"He did *not* follow instructions," Geraldine Fitzsimmons said, stomping her foot. "He specifically—"

Marvin to Foggbottom: "I have this effect on people."

"It was chaos!" the woman wailed. "Ping-pong balls flying every which way. Fifty rambunctious teenagers removing their jumpsuits, throwing them about like wild natives. Why, I was hit in the face with one of them." [She means she was hit in the face with a jumpsuit, not a wild native.] "Do you know there is a young man back there at this very moment completely encased in duct tape? The idea!"

Marvin could not suppress a snicker. It was pretty funny, the kid in the duct tape. He couldn't remember whose idea it was, wrapping duct tape around things, sticky side out. He thought it might have started with the sneakers-taped-to-broomsticks lacrosse game. That one was Bennie's. Then the items got bigger and bigger until this one kid asked another kid to wrap him completely with the tape, which naturally led to jumping up onto the wall to see if he could stick.

Marvin could feel them looking at him. "What, it's my fault? Can I help it everyone goes nuts? Can I help it they want to test the catapult, er, trebuchet, on other stuff? What'd *I* do? All I did was—"

Geraldine Fitzsimmons stomped her foot again. "All *you* did was say, 'No one said we had to use this stuff. No one said we couldn't do it this way' — in that *ridiculous* German accent — and the next thing I know, fifty of them are yelling, 'and no one said we couldn't do it *this* way! And this way and *this* way,' and they're running amok. Half-naked, the lot of them. It's obscene I tell you! Obscene! You put the idea into their heads, young man. They were perfectly content at building their contraptions — *with* the items provided, mind you — until you opened your mouth.

"Mr. Foggbottom, if we were to put this boy in a maze, he would climb *up over the walls* rather than make his way through it. Do you know what he said when I asked what he hoped to prove by simply *dropping* his ping-pong balls into the receptacle? Completely circumventing the very intention of the exercise? *Do* you?"

Mr. Foggbottom shook his head.

"*Physics.* That's what he said. *Physics.*"

For a few seconds Geraldine Fitzsimmons stood breathing heavily, the purple in her face very much resembling the rainbow-colored rump of a fully mature mandrill monkey — i.e., *not* attractive. I know that sounds harsh, but it is the gods' honest truth.[41]

The administrator of Sandy Rivers Hilltop Ranch for Wayward Youth, Juveniles, and Young Adults, looking nothing like the rump of a mandrill monkey, now tapped his thumbs together. He looked back and forth between Marvin and a woman who looked as though she might just very shortly explode. Then, checking his wristwatch, Reginald T. Foggbottom made a decision. "Perhaps the boy and I should talk. If you would be so kind as to leave the two of us alone for a while, I would be most grateful." Then, in a highly rewarding (to Marvin) moment of insincerity, Reginald T. Foggbottom flashed Geraldine Fitzsimmons a smile.

Geraldine Fitzsimmons looked as if she had been slapped in the face.

"If I want you," Foggbottom said, "I will call."

And with that, as if her ears were on fire, Geraldine Fitzsimmons stormed out of the room, the heels of her shoes clicking all the way.

41> According to the *Encyclopedia Gargantua,* mandrill monkeys are the largest monkeys on Earth. They're almost too large to be called "monkeys" at that size. They have freaky red-and-blue faces (not unlike their red-and-blue bottoms), a long yellow beard (not unlike General Custer), and enormous fang-like teeth (not unlike Hilary Swank). Mandrill monkeys look as if they'd been designed by committee. Especially if the committee were made up of Salvadore Dali, Lady Gaga and Stan Winston.

Mandrills are not like other monkeys. If you were to put a red fez on a mandrill (not a good idea), I'd hate to see what you'd look like thirty seconds later. Do a search for "mandrill teeth" and see what would be coming at you. ... Not good, right?

That said, all the giant-teeth-baring in the world doesn't seem to be saving the largest monkeys on Earth from jerks in trucks with high-powered rifles (the jerks, not the trucks). Apparently there are people in Cameroon and Equatorial Guinea who will go out of their way for a mandrill monkey burger. Which isn't the most despicable thing in the universe, but it's close.

Chapter THIRTEEN...

REGINALD T. FOGGBOTTOM looked amused. He often looked amused, but in this case he looked amused about sending Geraldine Fitzsimmons from the room. "Methinks the lady doth protest too much," he finally said once she was out of earshot. He was trying on a little Shakespeare for size, which he did from time to time.[42]

42> Did you know that people in Shakespeare's day didn't really talk like that? (I mean, c'mon — "methinks"?) In point of fact, all those goeths and harks and whithers and betwixts were in actuality just the Great Bard — or "GB" as they called him in those days — having a little go at a bit of novelty. [*See: "Creative License."*] Fact is, no matter what they tell you on The Discover Science Channel, people in William Shakespeare's day in reality talked just like you and I, give or take a doth or two.

You'll have to take my word on this one. The truth seems to have been buried along with all the worldly possessions of Mr. Funk and Mr. Wagnall and no amount of letter writing on my part seems to do any good. ("Again with zeh letters!" Jean-Claude tells me. "The people have a right to know," I say. And he gives me that French-steeped eye roll of his again.)

Anyway, here's how what we today know as "the Shakespearean form" came about:

It's 1588, right? Smallpox, the plague, leprosy and any other disgusting disease you can think of is rampant, the Anglo-Spanish war is afoot, and people are regularly throwing garbage out of windows right in front of you when you're trying to get to work. If you could get work. Which you couldn't. Because there wasn't any. And because of that, things weren't going so well in the playwright biz. Mr. Shakespeare's first two plays, *Waiting for Gruel* and *Horatio, Have You Seen My Tights?* had already bombed — or, as "GB" put it, "suffered a horrible eye-gouging death." And let's face it, the man had bills to pay. He had to come up with *something*.

Which, in fact, he did, one night at the local pub …

"It'll be like a code!" he suddenly blurted out after a long series of overly-warm ales. "They'll need footnotes and marginal explanations and cross-referenced dictionaries just to know what the characters are *talking* about! People will eat it up!"

And he was right. Once the public got a taste of all those harks and goeths and whithers and betwixts, they really took to them. Pretty soon everyone was using the words Mr. Shakespeare had pulled out of thin-and-most-probably-pipe-smoke-laden air. In practically no time you could hear it everywhere — anon this, and anon that; methought this and methought that; accursed this's and naked villainous that's. It was all the rage. Even the king was into it. (And, as kings often do, he took credit for it, decreeing thereafter it be called "the King's English." They do that, kings.)

Suffice it to say, it was Shakespeare's idea, that smoke-filled night in 1588 in the neighborhood pub, of simply inventing new words. None of this glacier-paced language evolution. I mean, c'mon — who's got the time? Not with the *plague* around.

He even made up the word for it.

"Slang?" his wife later asked in the parlor. "Isn't that some sort of sludge or something?"

"'Tis true, 'tis true," her husband replied, "but nay, 'tis now much more." (To which for some reason he added, "I am constant as the northern star," and then, "Why then tonight let us assay our plot," which made his wife realize he'd had way too much to drink, so she put him to bed, shaking her head and tsking judgmental 16th-century tsks.)

Let us, then, give credit where credit is due. It was William Shakespeare, and William Shakespeare alone, who can be credited with turning the English language on its ear, making it as varied and ever-changing — and difficult to parse — as it is.

Thanks to Shakespeare, himself responsible for more words than we can count, by the 20th-century there were so many new words invented, every year whole forests succumbed to the paper mills so that the dictionaries could be reprinted. (Someday, when you have a lot of patience, sit down with your grandparents and ask them about words. They will tell you how *legs* became *gams*; *coffee* became *joe*; *swell* became *cool* became *boss* became *groovy* became *cool* again became *bitchin'* became *rad* became *awesome* became *the bomb* became *off da hizzle fo-shizzle,* and Uncle Henry became Aunt Genevieve when he had that operation).

Watch. I'll prove it. *Schmookah*. There, I just made one up. Pulled it right from between the ol'

Reginald T. Foggbottom gave his head a little shake. "Geraldine Fitzsimmons," he explained, "is driving me insane." He produced a fresh cigar from his desk, cut off the end of it (the cigar, not the desk), and lit it with a match (again, the cigar, not the desk). "It is *so* hard these days …" — he puffed a few puffs — "to get …" — he puffed a few more puffs — "What is that phrase I want?"

"Oh …" Marvin ohed, remembering from their first encounter the man was not one to ask a question without actually expecting an answer. "A good cigar?"

---

literary butt-cheeks. That took like a millisecond! That'll mean, from now on … uh, let's see … *house*. How easy was that?

If you really want to change the world — and why wouldn't you — forget about coming up with a cure for cancer and other boring stuff that requires, at the most, advanced degrees, and at the least, a lot of homework you'll forget later anyway. Spend your day making up words. You can even do what many writers do (not, of course, I) and make up people who say them. Or you can go into government and pretend a word — like, hmmm, "torture" — means something else entirely.

Which brings up another concept we can add to the ever-changing language discussion. Why make up a new word when already there were *gobs* of them just sitting around doing nothing? Why not simply change what they mean? That would be even easier, wouldn't it?

See, up until the twentieth century, when the terms "jeepers creepers" and "rock 'n' roll" and "gay Paree" made their way into the lexicon, once a word was created, it stayed that way for eons until, when there was no more use for it, they wrapped it up in newspapers and threw it out the window with old cantaloupe rinds and potato peelings and moldy fruitcake. Which wasn't only disgusting but was wasteful. Why not be ahead of the curve, so the logic went, and save all that unnecessary window-tossing? Why not just *change* a word you never really liked in the first place?

Today, people are so used to a word meaning one thing on a Monday and something else entirely by Friday afternoon, they don't even notice when "Ha!" becomes "LOL" in a record-breaking .32-seconds. (And doesn't even save a keystroke).

Either way, change a word or make one up; you, too, can change how we communicate. Just think: one day, you could crank out new words by the hundreds, live in a big lavish schmookah, and have people argue endlessly over what the hell you meant.

And you can thank Mr. William "GB" Shakespeare for that.

"No, it's something else." Tapping a finger: "It's so hard to get…"

"*Two* good cigars?"

"No, that's not it, either. That would be nice, but that's not what—
These days, it's so hard to get … it's hard to get … ah yes, I have it:
An overbearing sanctimonious blowhard. That's what I was I was looking
for." He glanced at his cigar. "Surprisingly, they're hard to come by."

Marvin turned to the door to make sure the sanctimonious blowhard
in question hadn't snuck up behind him again. Then he looked around the
room for a good ten seconds, pushed up his glasses and asked, "Is it me …
or is she, like, way hostile?"

"She is indeed," Foggbottom said. "And unhappy as well. And irascible.
Definitely irascible. And, as I say, sanctimonious. How I get saddled with
the most unhappy, *irascible*, sanctimonious souls in the universe is beyond
me. It's not like it's in the want-ad. If there *were* a want-ad. Which there
isn't. Which is why I used *were*." He let out a small stream of smoke.
"Which brings up the issue at hand. Not the want-ad, nor the use of the
subjunctive, nor even Ms. Geraldine Fitzsimmons. She may be an unhappy
soul, but it is not she who is sitting before me." Another stream of smoke
and he looked Marvin in the eye. "As I understand it," he finally came out
with, rolling the cigar around in his mouth, "*you're* not happy as well."

Marvin: "I'm not?"

"Indeed." At this point Foggbottom produced a manila folder. Now
manila folders typically contain things like old report cards and bank
statements and cancelled insurance policies, and are not usually something
to get concerned about, but when one is "called upon the carpet" so to
speak (don't get me going), and the carpet-calling Person of Authority
pulls a manila folder from his or her files, you can almost certainly expect
the contents of said folder to be along the lines of decidedly judgmental
records from one's past — dossiers, reports, arrest records, signed affidavits
from the Federal Witness Protection Program, and so forth.

As Marvin Plotnik had never been in the Federal Witness Protection
Program, he looked at the manila folder with something akin to
befuddlement.

The administrator opened the folder and, perusing its contents, cleared his throat. "In the 1800s," he read, "what factor was most important in the growing of cotton?" He paused. Marvin thought for a moment. He didn't know how to answer this one.

"It's a test," Mr. Foggbottom pointed out, "from your fifth-grade Social Studies class." He turned some papers. "Allow me to recite some of the answers suggested by your classmates. The question was, 'What factor was most important in the growing of cotton?' Answers I see here: 'Slave labor.' ... 'Dry summers.' ... 'Access to river transportation.' All good answers," he nodded, clearly impressed. "Your answer?" He turned back to the first sheet. "Cotton."

He made his way through the papers — the folder being disconcertingly thick — before another page caught his eye. "Biology. Seventh grade." He knocked the ashes from his cigar (surprisingly, given the nature of the room, onto the carpet). "'Identify each stage of mitosis in the images below.' I see here you had no trouble with the answer, but I am curious as to the need for *these*." He handed Marvin the sheet. Sure enough, it was Marvin's seventh-grade biology test, where Mr. Tarlofski had written a big fat red A at the top, crossed it out and wrote C– next to it, then scrawled, "30 points off for failed attempt at humor."

Foggbottom wasn't curious about the space where Marvin had correctly identified the stages of mitosis (metaphase, anaphase, etc.), but was referring to the images where Marvin had added two cartoon balloons coming from each cell at the moment of division. One read: "Ow, that's smarts." The other read: "My centrosomes are bigger than your centrosomes."[43]

43> For some reason the picture of a controsome in this particular test looked downright indecent. Go online and see if you can find an X-rated-looking picture of a centrosome. (Hint: don't search for "X-rated centrosome"; who knows what you'll get. Just find a picture of a centrosome.) A quick online search will get you more than you ever wanted to know about them. I'll wait. ...

Back? Hopefully you found pictures that did indeed look dirty and now understand Marvin's joke. If you only found pictures that look dirty, do not fret. People who see sex in everything are

Foggbottom was silent while he made his way through the remaining pages in the manila folder. Every now and then, he'd remove a page and place it on the desk for Marvin to see. Among them:

- A page from Marvin's sixth-grade Social Studies book on Egyptian hieroglyphics, with its angular-shaped figures. In the margins, Marvin had scribbled: "A chiropractor back then would make a *killing.*"

- A multiple-choice test from seventh-grade English. Marvin had selected an answer on every question all right, (A) through (D), but he'd also added a fifth choice, (E), to almost every one of them, including one that said, "(E) Stacey Brillstein is an idiot," and another that said, "(E) Bite me."

- A 12 x 16 piece of construction paper from the third grade entitled "My House" on which students were asked to paste pictures that best represented their home life. (A common yet all-too-transparent attempt by schools to find out how messed up a kid's parents are.) On Marvin's paper, he had cut out a picture of a flower pot, on top of which balanced the following items: a pack of cigarettes, a monkey wearing a diaper, a pair of fuzzy dice, the words "Corn Flakes" with the C made into a B, a pipe-smoking yard-mowing father figure from a birthday card, a hula girl from another birthday card, the word "crackers" from a box of saltines — all topped with a cut-out tube of hemorrhoid cream from a magazine ad. (In the margin, his teacher had written, "Mr. and Mrs. Plotnik, please see me ASAP!!!!");

---

usually male, between the ages of 13 and 24, and have a hard time separating their gonads from — ok, from everything under the sun. Sometimes, literally. (I would insert here the story of Kreelut Ynetsua, a 16-year-old from Nome, Alaska, who in 2010 got himself in a bit of a "bind" with a tackle box, but my editor says no. Actually, my editor says, "You will do no such thing." Then again, my editor says lots of things, none of which seem to be, "Let me buy you lunch." But one must pick their fights, so I graciously let him have his way as often as possible.) Anyway, if you are in this demographic and you only found pictures that looked dirty, you are probably just fine. Suffice it to say, some chromosomes have bulbous protrusions young men find humorous.

and
- A snapshot of the Magruder High School marquee in which Marvin had rearranged the letters from WELCOME STUDENTS to read U CLOWNS TESTED 'EM.

Needless to say, Marvin was beginning to feel like the guy in *Lockdown on Cell Block Nine* where the kind-but-shadowy warden (or was it the "shadowy-but-kind warden"?) reads the jumpsuit dude's record. Manila folder, natch.

"Let's see ..." Foggbottom was saying as he turned pages (long thin fingers looking more suited to removing cotton from medicine bottles) "... fifty live chickens ... pudding over the cafeteria ... dropping of bowling ball into syrup ... rearranging letters ... arguing the follies of the internal combustion engine ... oh, and this ..." — he stopped at what looked like a form — "... a State of Illinois Petition for Name Change."

Marvin, taken aback, blinked. He was about to question what the point was of the Right to Privacy form his parents signed every year for the Portland Cement City Unified School District when out pops the name change form, which shouldn't even be in school records. And who'd cut a page from his Social Studies book, anyway? He certainly hadn't. That's destruction of school property right there. His eye caught the fire in the fireplace, warm and inviting. He wondered where that inviting cabin was of Skylar Waddell's humongous red T-shirt. He wondered why, year after year, he'd been called on the carpet in one administrator's office or another. Why he wasn't allowed to—

He was just about to finish that thought when the following sentence caught his attention: "But here at Sandy Rivers Hilltop Ranch you have not displayed any of this behavior. You have, rather, chosen to 'lie low.' Now how do you account for that?"

Marvin didn't know how to account for that. He watched the yellow flames lick at the logs in the fireplace, he eyed the African masks and suit of armor and the unicorn tapestry, and, wondering how the items in this manila folder came to be in Foggbottom's possession, generally did a lot of

other narrative tricks for breaking up dialog. He shrugged. "Geraldine
Fitzsimmons seemed to think—"

Mr. Foggbottom knocked on the desk to get Marvin's full attention.
"I don't know what your problem is, young man, but if I have to sit down
with you one more time, when I have a *world* of things to attend to, an
actual, literal *world*, I promise you will not be a happy camper. Did you not
hear me only nineteen hours ago announce our job here is *not* to rid you
of these tendencies? Do you not realize these idiosyncrasies of yours are
the very reason you have been sent to us? Had I not made that abundantly
clear? This is not Zadok Magruder High School, my boy. This is not
Portland Cement City, Illinois. This is the Sandy Rivers Hilltop Ranch for
Wayward Youth, Juveniles, and Young Adults, and we have a reputation to
uphold. A reputation, I might add, that goes far beyond the four walls of
this fine institution. Far beyond." He held Marvin's eyes. "So I ask you once
again: how is it you have chosen to lie low?"

Marvin took his time before he ventured a word. He looked again to
the fire, and then back to Mr. Foggbottom. He didn't know what the man
wanted from him. Again, he shrugged. "Physics?"

Foggbottom glared. "I believe you used that one already."

Marvin's eyes searched the room. "Uh … The light's better down
here?"

Foggbottom shook his head.

"I'm anemic."

Foggbottom shook his head.

"I wanted to see time fly. To, uh, to get to the other side. To keep my
pants up. Uh, uh … who let the dogs out."

Foggbottom's head went to the left … and the right … and the left …
and the right.

Marvin held up a finger with his best ok-here-it-is expression. He
hoped the man would be impressed with this one because holding up a
finger in a "this-is-it" manner usually gives a person an air of authority. It
was an old trick. [*See: Body Language, Use of Extended Fingers.*] He cleared
his throat and proclaimed proudly, "There is method to my madness."

Mr. Foggbottom nodded a most satisfied nod. "*Now*, my chicken-ordering friend, we have an *understanding*."[44]

Marvin wasn't sure what they had an understanding about but as "we have an understanding" was accompanied by a dismissive wag of the hand, it meant Marvin was free to go. The tête-à-tête was over. Which was why, without further ado, Reginald T. Foggbottom produced a newspaper, opened it, and gave it a good I-believe-our-time-is-up shake. Behind which, a small stream of cigar smoke inched its way to the ceiling.

Marvin's lips slowly mouthed the expanded form of WTF. "I don't get it," he said as he went to the door. "You *want* me to, uh, what, order some chickens or something? You're short on chickens?"

The fire crackled. The newspaper rattled almost imperceptibly. The smoke rose.

"What…" — Marvin shrugged for the third time in the last five minutes — "…ever." A second out in the hall, he came back. "Yo. Dude. What's with the names? Everyone else gets a new one and I'm stuck with the same old Marvin Plotnik? What's with that?"

From behind the paper: "I believe, Mr. Plotnik, you are late for Afternoon Social Studies, are you not?"

44> Marvin was smart but like many people he was not aware that many phrases we use day in and day out come from one Mr. William Shakespeare, whom we've just touched upon. This phrase in particular is a paraphrase of the line, "Though this be madness, yet there is method in't," which uses an apostrophe in a way you don't see every day. It's something the character Pelonius says in the play *Hamlet*, Act 2, Scene 2, when he sees Hamlet is screwing around with him. And guess what? Pelonius says this as an aside, to the audience. Just like a certain narrator does by way of footnotes and parenthetical remarks. Coincidental, in't?

BTW, had Marvin *known* he was quoting Shakespeare, he would have assumed that this was indeed the reason Mr. Foggbottom, having quoted Shakespeare himself only minutes before, had been sufficiently satisfied. In truth, Foggbottom was satisfied because of Marvin's raised finger, which greatly impressed him. If Marvin had used the gesture on any of his other answers, Mr. Foggbottom would have been perfectly happy at whatever point it was used. Why? Experience. Or, to put it another way: there was method in *his* madness.

Chapter FOURTEEN...

WHEN MARVIN ARRIVED at Afternoon Social Studies [*See: "Good Signage"*] he thought he'd gone to the wrong place. Because as he approached the double doors to the auditorium, he could see the door windows were darkened. He pushed opened one of the doors only to discover the lights were out. Had he gotten the time wrong? Was the session over already? He backed out to check the piece of paper he'd seen taped to the door:

AFTERNOON SOCIAL STUDIES
PLEASE COME IN

Well it was the right place all right. He cracked open the door and looked again. The lights were definitely out; but now he noticed that the room seemed submerged under water, awash in a faint blue glow ...

"Please have a seat," came a voice from within. "This is a limited-time session." The voice was female, one he hadn't heard before. It sounded, if he were to think about it, vaguely mechanical, though in what way he had no idea. It also sounded vaguely — and he didn't have to think about this — hot. Really really *hot*. As in sultry and sexy and other titillating S-words. "A neat appearance," the voice went on, "is most appreciated."

Marvin's eyes began to adjust. In a manner of seconds, he could make out the size of the place: as big as the gymnasium. But unlike the gymnasium, it was not filled with baskets, or ping-pong balls, or duct tape, or cardboard, or anything else (one would assume) good for ping-pong ball transference. There was, however, around the perimeter, something he had not expected. Not in a hundred million years, which, of course, is an exaggeration, but narrators are allowed to do that sort of thing. There, glowing eerily like the Pods of Angradorra, were fifty consoles.

The Pods of Angradorra, if you have possibly spent the last decade in a hermetically sealed Hideaway Capsule (more on this in a bit), are egg-shaped vessels encountered on the sixth level of *Styzzyx IV.* The Pods of Angradorra emit a pulsating blue glow so appealing, so alluring, no player — not one — out of thousands — out of tens of thousands — has yet been able to sidestep and get on with the game. (Not even Chuck Widmeyer, who was the guy who wrote the thing.)

According to *The Gamer's Guide to Staying Alive Longer Than the Loser Sitting Next to You,* hideaway capsules (not to be confused with the aforementioned Hideaway Capsule) make their debut in the *fourth* level of the same game and are well worth the effort of putting in one's pocket. Immersing a tiny aspirin-sized hideaway capsule into only a trace amount of water — spit will do — will produce, in the blink of an eye, a life-sized hermetically sealed Hideaway Capsule into which you can climb like the small prey-like animal of your choice, for hours of Safe, Shielded, Personal Protection — which should be a slogan for some sort of personal hygiene product but it's not — much like the safe personal protection of the bean-bag chair in your parent's basement.

To the untrained eye, the words 'hideaway capsule' and "Hideaway Capsule" look almost identical. They are, in fact, not — that fact being that one term starts with capital letters and the other doesn't. Implying, of course, that the terms serve two purposes. (Compare, for instance, "That Dick Cheney, he sure does go on," and "That dick Cheney, he sure does go on.") Lower-case *hideaway* as in "fits in one's pocket"; upper-case *Hideaway* as in "you can hide in it." Lower-case *capsule* as in "looks like a pill"; upper-

case *Capsule* as in "space capsule." One's big and one's small, see? (Hey, no
one said the people who write video games are any more clever than the
rest of us. I'm just reporting the purpose behind the terms. They actually
had focus groups on this, and staff meetings in the conference rooms of
Mind Games, Ltd. With colorful explanatory charts and everything.
Which, btw, I will happily pay top dollar for if they happen to be sitting
at the back of your closet.)

As anyone knows who has tried to blast a Pod of Angradorra with a
Mendelevium Beam (Level 2, under the Blob Master's floorboards), the
pod will immediately expel a nasty-bad yellow-green ooze — from which
it is all but impossible to extricate oneself, no matter what scary-ass-
looking avatar you happen to have picked out. The gist of which is that
before you even *think* about blasting a Pod of Angradorra with a
Mendelevium Beam (again, not a good idea), you better have a hideaway
capsule on you or you are going to find yourself becoming very yellow-
green and very *very* incapacitatingly stuck; game over and all that.

Which meant, to Marvin — who was still staring at the blue-glow of
fifty consoles while I digressed into the intricacies of a popular video game
you probably already knew about — these consoles around the perimeter
of the Afternoon Social Studies room, were, in a word, alluring. They
clearly had been alluring to everyone else, too, for Marvin now saw, as his
eyes fully adjusted, that all forty-nine of the other kids had already claimed
one.

Which meant, to Marvin — who had finally learned the don't-blast-a-
glowy-blue-pod thing after falling for it a grand total of seven times before
abandoning *Styzzyx IV* for games that didn't have it in for him — the blue-
glow of the consoles around the perimeter of the auditorium was somewhat,
in another word, spooky.

Which meant, to Marvin, he'd have to check them out. Besides, in
some entirely different words, they were frickin' awesome looking.

These pods made the video game consoles in arcades — where, at the
wheel of a motorcycle or race car you try to impress the extra-cute girls
with your razor-sharp agility, ability to dodge whatever it is you're dodging

and still hold onto a 32-ounce Mega Gulp — look like tricycles. It was the streamlined acrylic shells that did it. Picture the cockpit of a fighter jet or one of those souped-up land-speed vehicles rich white guys in rich white jumpsuits race on the Bonneville Speedway, then multiply that coolness by 416, and you'll get an idea of just how enticing these babies were.

"Nice," he said, extremely grateful for the Sandy Rivers Hilltop Ranch for Wayward Youth, Juveniles, and Young Adults' budgetary choices (i.e., better they spend the bucks on this than that crappy old bus).

That sex-filled voice came again: "Please have a seat," it repeated. "This is a limited-time session."

There was only one console remaining, the fourth on the left, and as Marvin made his way to it, he saw the neighboring consoles were occupied by familiar faces. Kit, then the blonde-haired girl, then Dara — all basking in the eerie blue light of video-screens, which was what gave the consoles that Pod of Angradorra-like glow.

Marvin lifted the acrylic shell to his console, climbed in, and shot a glance to the console next to his, where Dara's head, seemingly disembodied, floated within her acrylic shell. He couldn't see what was on her screen — he couldn't see what was on any of them — but from the look on her face, she was completely engaged in it.

On his other side, Bennie's fauxhawk caught his eye. Bennie was motioning him, which, frankly, Marvin first took as an oddly-timed come-on (Bennie seemed to be pointing to his crotch). "Ah," Marvin nodded, finally understanding, "strap myself in." He pulled the acrylic shell into place and mouthed: "Why?"

Bennie's eyebrows did push-ups. He grinned. Big. Then, with a jolt, Bennie's attention was back on his screen as his console began to shake and pitch. It pitched to the left, to the right, then forward in small staccato jolts, and Bennie, grin on his face, let out a yelp, not unlike the Mohawk yelp he'd let out in the dorm, only this time in a good way. Pitch, shake, pivot, *yelp*; pivot, pitch, dip, *yelp*. (Terribly sorry, but I cannot accurately convey this yelp. It was something along the lines of: *"Yeeagawgh!* — with an extra A in there — but that seemed to overwhelm my spell-checker and

I kept having to relaunch the word processor.)

Marvin turned to Dara, so involved with her video screen she hadn't noticed him. Unlike Bennie's console, shaking and pivoting, her console was steady. They must be at different stages of the game, Marvin thought, wanting desperately to see what the game was.

With the click of his seatbelt, Marvin's screen came alive. Yellow letters on a black background hummed into view:

> WHAT DO YOU WANT TO DO? <

Marvin frowned. "Whadya mean, what do I want to do?" he asked aloud, looking for a way to interact with the thing — keyboard, joystick, anything. "What do *you* want to do?"

The words changed:

> PLAY <
> EXPLORE <
> QUERY <
>>> YOUR CHOICE <<<

"I'd pick *explore*," Marvin said, trying two levers he'd discovered at his hips, "but I can't figure out—" The word EXPLORE went large and larger until it burst, the black screen replaced … with a field of wheat.

Marvin smiled. "Speech recognition. *Nice.*"

The field of wheat waved in the breeze. The image was so clear, so crisp, down to the smallest grain (clearer, crisper than anything he'd ever seen on television, even in hi-def), for a moment Marvin swore he felt a cool breeze at his neck.

Words superimposed on the screen:

> WHERE TO? <

Marvin looked for a microphone, didn't see anything that resembled one, then said, "Forward." Nothing happened. Maybe the speech recognition didn't recognize movement commands. He experimented with the levers. Just to be clear: these weren't joysticks; that is, they couldn't move in any direction but forward and back. Then he remembered the controls on the air-foil bumper cars at GreatTown Adventure Park. Back in sixth grade his cousin Lenny made him ride the stupid thing like fifteen times in a row until Marvin finally made the point that he wasn't interested in the damn thing by pushing Lenny's bumper car into the corner and holding it there with his own, immobile, until the time was up. Three rides in a row. Hadn't seen Lenny since.

Now Marvin pushed the right-hand lever forward. His view of the field moved counter-clockwise. He pushed the left lever forward. The view moved clockwise. He pushed both levers forward. The scene pressed ahead, shafts of wheat bending as he plowed through the field. To come to a stop, he simply let go. He pushed both of the levers back. The scene moved backward. Just like the air-foil ride. Easy.

He searched for a way to turn his view skyward, just in case he needed to look up at something. Then he found it, or rather, them: a button on each of the levers a pinky stretch away. Right-hand pinky lifted the view skyward until, as his seat reclined more and more, Marvin was looking at a sunny, partly-cloudy crisp blue sky. Left-hand pinky returned the view to its original eye-level position; continue pushing the left-hand button and he was looking at the ground beneath his pod.

Leveling out the pod, he wandered around the field in this manner for a minute or two, getting the feel of the controls — pleasingly surprised at their sensitivity, as the slightest movement moved the image — until the words on the screen began to flash:

> WHERE TO? <

~

> WHERE TO? <

~

> WHERE TO? <

Then he saw it. On the horizon. A farmhouse? No, a cabin. A small cabin, smoke rising from its chimney. Naturally his reaction was that this was the ranch they'd been expecting when they got off the bus, the cabin on Skylar Waddell's humongous T-shirt.

Marvin headed there, full-tilt.

As he approached, he saw he was right. It *was* The Sandy Rivers Hilltop Ranch of Waddell's red T-shirt. Rockers on the porch, the horse, the cowboys, the animal that might or might not be a steer (nope, cow), the smoke rising from the chimney, all of it. And it looked nice, and it looked welcoming and it looked serene.

Marvin turned to Dara, who, still glued to her screen, was biting her lower lip as though she was deciding something. Beyond Dara, at the next console, he could see the blonde-haired girl, her pretty face basked in blue. She was laughing. She was laughing uproariously.

Marvin turned to Bennie, who was gleefully riding his console like a whirl-a-tilt, maneuvering up and down and right and left, a bumpy ride of jolts and dives.

"Either this is one helluva game or we're not all seeing the same thing," Marvin said, almost under his breath.

Words superimposed on the screen:

> \> UNDERSTATEMENT. <

To which Marvin replied: "Whoa."
The words transformed:

> \> WHOA INDEED. <

Marvin sat up a little straighter. "What the hell?"

> \> I'M SURE I DON'T KNOW. <

Then:

> CONTINUE EXPLORE? <

Marvin pushed up his glasses. "If you think I'm buying this is anything other than someone totally messing with me, you've — Wait a minute. What's this?" *This* was a button. On the floor. A red button. It was between his feet and, like many buttons and levers and thingamabobs, it called out "push me" in a squeaky little button-like voice — not literally, it was a *button.* [*See: "Creative License."*] So, feeling as amenable as the next guy to follow squeaky pleading voices from utterly irresistible buttons, Marvin pushed it with his foot.

It clicked.

And before you could say "blink of an eye," a rocket, seemingly launching from below his console, blew the nice and welcoming and serene cabin to smithereens.

Roofing, flooring, rocking chair and all — reduced to airborne splinters and animal-that-turned-out-to-be-a-cow blobs raining in all directions. Sky high.

Marvin: "Oops."

To which the screen replied:

> WAS THAT NECESSARY? <

"I thought it was going to turn up the pod lights or something," Marvin answered, yanking his foot clear of the thing, "not take out a perfectly good cabin. And probably a perfectly good cow."

~ NO, I MEAN THE OOPS. ~

And that's when everything began to shake.

• • •

IT IS DIFFICULT TO TELL, when your teeth are clattering and your brain is sloshing against your skull and your eyeballs are shaking like pebbles in a maraca, whether you are the only one vibrating or whether everything around you is vibrating. Marvin could not tell whether it was just his own skull or his own pod or all of the Sandy Rivers Hilltop Ranch. Or maybe even the entire universe.

This thought came to him as his upper teeth became his bottom teeth and vice versa, as his dashboard morphed into a double exposure of a double exposure, as his cheeks joined his ears. And in case you ever find yourself shaking like a bag of gelatin, every molecule mixing with every other molecule, you'll find that the reason your cheeks have joined your ears and pinned your head against your seat — the G-force — makes it hard to turn your head. But Marvin managed it, was able to see his friends, was able to see the look on their faces, the way they were all holding onto their consoles for dear life ... pitching, jumping, whipping ... and was able to surmise one undeniable fact: it *was* the whole universe.

With great effort, he forced a look back at his screen. The field of wheat, the flying cabin fragments, all of it, had been replaced with something else, something he knew. Something he knew very well.

It was The Tornado — a roller coaster unlike any other — specifically, the 80-degree plummet of Dead Man's Drop, which, having made that drop at least eighty-seven times, Marvin knew the feel of from every seat. There was little doubt, at this particular plummeting moment, that he was seated in the front car. The drop came and went, his stomach turning over as he careened into the first turn, a 70-degree bank to the left, his right hip jammed against the side of the pod, then the quick rise and drop of the build-up and up into the loop, and if he could trust what he saw on his screen and the cheek-to-ear thrust of 4.9 G's, he was now screaming into Tornado Alley, the double-corkscrew before the alternating banked turns, the horseshoe roll, the quick blip of a hump, and then the end.

Mid-horseshoe, he forced another look at Dara and Bennie and the others — cheeks to ears, every one of them. And through the vibrations, through the swaying and the clacking and the pitching and the grinding, as everyone hung onto their levers or their dashboards or whatever they could grab, each and every face had the same look on it:

They were having the rides of their lives.

Three jolts and a bump and it was over. Just like that. On Marvin's screen, the steel track of The Tornado gave way to the platform, where three pimply-faced kids in white jersey shirts and MarvinTown Adventure Park name-tags waited as the train came into the station. Because The Tornado wasn't a real-world roller coaster; The Tornado was a roller coaster Marvin had created himself, some two months prior, in VirtuCoaster. (A companion to VirtuLife™, VirtuCity™, VirtuMall™, and VirtuLasciviousOldMen™.) Only Marvin hadn't finished his design. *This* version was complete.

Let me be clear about this: it was one thing to "ride" The Tornado on your own home computer, and quite another to ride it for real. Although, c'mon this wasn't real. Was it?

The video screen went black.

> SESSION OVER. <

It was eerily quiet for a moment, the consoles still, the auditorium dark. That oh-so-intriguing voice came over the loud speaker: "Please do not exit your pod until all lights are on and your console has opened. Upon exit, please watch your step." The voice then added, "Good posture is the key to good circulation."

The lights came on, fifty acrylic shells sprung open, and from within Bennie's console came a whoop of delight. "Holy freakin' *crap*," he yelled, smacking his dash with both fists. "That was freakin' *awesome!* That's the freakin'est most *awesomest* most best ride I've *ever freakin' had.*" His eyes lit up like the opening credits to *VisionQuest* — filled with nothing short of adrenaline-charged bliss.

And then the room erupted with other whoops of delight, and whistles and whoas and Oh-my-God-did-you-see-thats.

Someone off to the side yelled, "Afternoon Social Studies *rocks!*" which made everyone cheer in agreement, high-fives and fist bumps all around — even between kids who hadn't yet met.

Kit stepped out of his console, hardly trying to hide a wobbly-legged landing. "Social Studies my *ass*," he trumpeted. He jabbed a thumb at his console. "We get *that* every day, I ain't *never* goin' home."

Flinn backed into the center of the room to join them, keeping his eyes on his console like it was the glow from the Holy Grail. He swallowed. "That thing … makes *DinoTours* look like a pony ride."

The blonde-haired girl slapped him a high-five.

Marvin, however, wasn't celebrating. He remained seated, in his console.

High-fives were still going around when the sultry voice came again over the P.A. "Afternoon Social Studies is now complete," the voice purred. "We will expect you tomorrow at the same time. Please exit the auditorium. Dinner is served at 6 p.m." Everyone looked exceedingly pleased that this would happen again the next day. Then, almost as an afterthought it seemed, the voice came again: "The unibrow is associated with the species Neanderthal. Unibrows are unsightly."

Marvin looked at his screen, lifeless and dark. He looked at his friends, high-fiving and fist-bumping and back-slapping as they headed for the hallway. He looked at the acrylic-shelled pods, one after another, now still, shorn of their eerie blue glow.

For a second there, Marvin actually wondered whether he himself had installed the Tornado into his pod. To paraphrase his thoughts: "What the *eff*" — pardon my French — "just happened here?"[45]

45> "Pardon my French" is an expression with an interesting etymology. I'd intended to skip this, but Jean-Claude, my ever-worried assistant, tells me it is imperative to point it out because, as he says, "it is most unfair to think zeh French are zeh cursers of zeh world."

Therefore, FYI, a history:

It was in the fishing port of Byblos, c. 1320 B.C., that the phrase first appeared. A Sumerian officer had just discovered that his slave, a near-sighted Phoenician, had mistaken an Akkadian fishing boat for a hammock. The Sumerian officer, finding his slave fast asleep sprawled out among a full day's catch of mackerel, humbly apologized to the fisherman by saying, "Pardon my Phoenician," meaning "Pardon my slave, who is as blind as a bat and an imbecile to boot, for he seems to have

---

lain with your fishes." This of course was in Aramaic, but it's a fair translation.

Over the centuries, the phrase went through a series of iterations including, "Pardon my Athenian," "Pardon my Mongol," "Pardon my Ottoman," "Pardon my Prussian," and somewhere in there the short-lived, "Pardon the loin of my rabbit" which took place in the 8th century BC, and clearly was coined by someone short on the concept. It is easy to see how the phrases' meaning shifted from person to language ("French" as in "from France," could clearly be confused with "French" as in "the language of France.") The rest of course is history.

Side note: Jean-Claude thinks the expression should be "Pardon my Esperanto" because, for one thing, nobody blames Esperanto on anything and it's really due some grief, and for another, "all of zeh Esperanto sounds like zeh dirty talk."

Chapter FIFTEEN...

A
S MARVIN MADE HIS WAY across the dining hall, two ProPower Energy Bars, a bag of NutriSnax Trail Mix, and a can of Cola-Cola on his tray, the room was abuzz. Groups who had sat alone earlier had joined other groups, and everybody but everybody had something to say about Afternoon Social Studies, the pods, the shaking ...

"Whadya mean you didn't notice? Dude! It was like obvious!" ... "Are you nuts? What ghost planet?" ... "Couldn't shoot the dungeon master. He had the key to the Ferrari." ... "It even *smelled* like salt water." ... "*Who* did you say you saw?" ... "You could totally *be* a Gorgon, yo." ... "No, *Jupiter's* moon."[46]

46> In English text, the use of ellipses can be used to imply snippets of overheard conversation. You might be interested to know that the Darvinians on the planet Farnus-7 use a character called a dididah for this kind of thing. It looks something like this:

To me, a *dididah* looks more like a pair of googly eyes or perhaps a pair of something else. Interestingly, on Farnus-7, each dididah further communicates that the speakers of the snippets are of questionable intelligence (note how the English word, "duh" seems to be derivative). Luckily, this is not the case with the ellipse. Ellipses in English can be used for any speaker regardless of race, creed, sexual orientation, national origin, religion and/or brain capacity. English is an equal-opportunity language.

"I'm tellin' you," Kit was saying when Marvin got to the table, "I never seen *nothin'* like that."

"You can say that again," Bennie said. "I'm balancing an AtomBall from *Thunder* and I turn around and see a Gatlin Blade from *Z-Lax2*. Next thing I know it's Sclitherns and Sclavins and those hot whadyacallem, Blorin babes — from *Creed of Twi-Night?* What's that, like six games in one? And they're not even by the same game maker? That's like ... frickin' *nuts!*"

Kit pulled back his head like this was all news to him. "What the effin *crap* are you talkin' about? I didn't have no freakin' AtomBalls or Blorin babes or Sclavins or none of that. I got *MotorSpeed Raceway* start to finish. With that, like, crazy thing at the end. They must've programmed—"

Harlen laughed. "You stayed in *MotorSpeed,* you got ripped off, man. I went from like *MotorSpeed Raceway* to *GI Rocket Tanks* to *Gear 4*. It was *awesome*. Racing one car on another game's course, driving *up a frickin' building,* hoppin' roofs and crap. Pretty freakin' cool. It's the freakin' *dinosaur* that blew me away. Not the cool-ass dinos from *Jurassic Island* — it was that lame-ass kiddie dino *Bernie*. Purple dude comes out of *nowhere,* starts eatin' *everything*.."

Bennie: "How'd they *do* all that? Even dudes on GAM3HACK3RS can't do it. They've been tryin' crossovers for *years*."

"Yeah, but *Bernie?* That was more than a cross-over, dude. I'll never look at that freak the same again. Do you know he's got *teeth* in that purple pie hole? *Rows* of them. He's even eatin' the *cars*. Droolin' and shit. Picks up this truck I'm in and shakes it like a dog got a rat It was downright scary. ... Cool, but scary. I could totally *smell* his Bernie breath. *Disgusting*."

Listening to all this, Marvin's face had contorted into a question mark. So had Dara's. The two looked at each other like they were the only ones who saw something wasn't right here.

"This is *so* not what I saw," Flinn was saying, his face so red his freckles had disappeared. "*Twi-Night, Thunder, Z-Lax2?* Not in *my* pod."

Dara: "What *did* you see?"

"You know, like a nature show. Or maybe like that — what's that ride where you fly over orange trees and stuff?" He scratched a reddened cheek.

"Hang Glider," Marvin said.

"Yeah, like Hang Glider. Only I'm flying over Mount Everest and the pyramids — then like all over Europe and Africa and shit at like a million miles an hour. You can swoop in on the Eiffel Tower and crap like that. Even down into a volcano. A frickin' volcano! It was like Hang Glider mixed with Google Earth — *way* better'n either one of 'em — it's like the two of them on … you know … what is it? That sports stuff."

"Steroids."

"Yeah, steroids. You could feel and smell and hear like *everything.*"

Marvin asked Flinn what he had picked.

"You mean like pick the oranges? There weren't oranges, dude. I'm saying it was *like* that ride where you fly over oranges." He turned to the others. "You know, though, it was so freakin' *good,* I totally think I *could've* picked oranges if I'd come in on some orange trees. Everything felt so—"

"No," Marvin said, "I mean what choice did you make, you know, in the beginning?"

"For the Hang Glider thing? I didn't make any choices. I just flew."

Bennie agreed. "I didn't pick anything, either. I just like, *went,* like Flinn's saying. You couldn't *pick* anything."

"No, I mean in the beginning, you were given three choices, right? 'Play,' 'Explore,' 'Query'?"

Bennie thought a second. "Oh yeah, that. I forgot. But not three." He shut an eye and scrunched up his face, trying to picture it. "Nope. It was two, wasn't it? 'Play' and 'Explore'? I picked 'Play.'"

Marvin let out a lungful of air. He was trying to figure this out. "Flinn? You pick anything?"

"I dunno, 'Explore,' I guess. I don't remember picking anything."

"Okay. At the beginning. When it first booted up. You *say* anything? It's speech recognition."

Flinn shrugged, scratched his cheek again. "I guess I said, 'Explore what?' But I don't think—"

"Kit?"

"'Play,' he said, giving Dara a flirtatious wink. "Definitely 'Play.'"

"Well I picked 'Explore,'" Marvin said, "and I found myself in a field. Then I blew up a cabin, then—"

Dara: "Wait. What happened when everything shook? What was going on … on your screen?"

"That's what I was about to say. I blow up this cabin and the next second comes the shaking and I'm on a *roller coaster*. Only the thing about *this* roller coaster—"

Kit: "When everything's shakin'? I just missed this bad-ass wreck, right? Spins me around like crazy. I come outta the spin and there's smoke and—"

Harlen: "I was coming into IceWorld 9. There was a squadron of Sclavins—"

Flinn: "I was splashing down into the Trunda Trench, off the coast of Bali. Not that I know where the hell the Trunda Trench is. It was labeled and all."

Harlen: "That purple maniac was *shaking* me, dude. In the truck. Like thirty feet up. And I'm hangin' on for dear life. Dude, it was *whacked*. I am *so* never lookin' at that dude the same."

Everyone looked at each other like they didn't know what to make of this. The rest of the room was still comparing notes. Then Marvin stood up on their table and shouted across the dining hall. "Hey! Guys! Hold up a minute!" which, coincidentally, took exactly that — sixty seconds on the nose — for the room to quiet down. Marvin looked over forty-nine faces: "Did anyone here pick 'Query'?"

{~Crickets.~}

Marvin tried again. "What? Nobody here pick 'Query'? Out of the six of *us*, half picked 'Explore,' and half picked 'Play.'"

Flinn pulled at Marvin's pants leg. "Dude. What's this 'Query' crap? There wasn't any 'Query.' It was 'Play' and 'Explore.'"

"That's what *I* told him," Bennie said. "Sorry, dude. It's just two. 'Play' and 'Explore.'"

Agreements all around. Marvin seemed to be the only one with the third choice. Still standing on the table, he looked down at Dara. Had he seen her start to raise her hand back there? Now her face was saying, "Don't look at me," to which her mouth added, "Maybe you dreamt the third one."

Marvin got down from the table feeling pretty stupid. Which didn't happen to Marvin very often.

The room broke out into murmurs repeating what they'd experienced in their pods — one kid had gone to Saturn and Jupiter's moons, another had turned into a parasite inside a human body, another had ridden a pterosaur. There were more scenarios like that as well as similar cross-game experiences like Bennie's and Harlen's.

No two alike.

And not one saw a rollercoaster — or any other world he'd created himself. Not one.

One thing they all agreed on was that at the same exact point in time, they'd been put through some serious G-force and shaking, they'd all had similar—

Marvin looked at the group: Kit, Flinn, Bennie, Harlen and Dara. It wasn't half and half. He replayed in his mind each of their experiences. Kit, Harlen and Bennie were in video games; they'd picked "Play." Flinn was in some kind of real-world simulation; he'd picked "Explore." Marvin had picked "Explore," too, and got a simulation, but it was anything but real. So that's only five.

He flashed back to when he thought Dara was about to raise her hand. He looked at her, point-blank, until she looked a little uncomfortable:

"You picked 'Query,' didn't you?"

Dara shrugged, almost apologetically. "Nope," she said. "I picked 'Explore.' Underground caves. Pretty cool."

And Marvin, attuned to body language without the benefit of a degree, knew she was lying.

Chapter SIXTEEN...

EVENING HAD COME and it was time for Pursuits of a Personal Nature. Everyone had settled down remarkably well, the occasional reading light the only illumination in the otherwise dark and quiet dormitory. Marvin didn't know what the others were going to do with their allotted time, but he knew what he'd do with his. He'd work out some details to Yolando Plumadore's predicament.[47]

47> This is as good a place as any to put in a word about something I'd meant to mention earlier had I only had a moment to think about it: *Time management.* As anyone knows — student, office worker, miniature-railway enthusiast — time management is the key to a full, happy and productive life. That and a good thin-crust pizza, but that is not the point of this note.

If, for instance, instead of working on your calculus homework you were to spend your evenings mixing episodes of "Two Guys, a Girl and An Annoying Neighbor" with, say, "Lost in Space," so you could post it on ViewTube, you'd soon watch that easy B+ slide right down the alphabet into slingin'-fries range. Of course, if you end up transferred to Remedial Math you'd have more time to devote to such things, but let's face it, you'd be sore at yourself for giving the boneheads on the math team something to tease you about.

Fun Fact: On the planet Merssenthurlia in what you know as the Andromeda Galaxy, the notion of time management is nonexistent. There, because of the massive gravitational pull of the planet, time and space have so folded upon themselves, school kids often finish their homework before it's even assigned. Then again, all that space folding means most Merssenthurlians are twenty-inches high and fifty inches wide; so there's that.

One is not so lucky in this corner of the Milky Way. On Earth, students must start and finish their work assignments in that order, with all that middle-work stuff in between. Here, one must rely on good time management skills so one does not end up wide awake at 4 a.m. forcing oneself to read *Pride and Prejudice*. ("Elizabeth laughed heartily at this picture of herself and said to Colonel Fitzwilliam..." Aaaaah!)

Here, then, are some things you can do to make sure your time is well spent:

• **Never make your own meals.** That's what parents, and friends' parents, and the good folks down at Burger Barn are for. If you must make a meal, make it in a microwave and always *always* stick to a single digit on the keypad. This will avoid wasting valuable time while moving from one digit to another. One minute, of course, can be entered as 1-0-0 or as 6-0 — how a microwave knows you mean a single minute is a subject to be taken up by minds far more studied than mine — but how about 6-6? How about 5-5? Better yet, if your parents had splurged on the 1100-watt model, "Add a minute" is much quicker than any of them, and no one's going to come arrest you if you open the microwave door at 57 seconds.

• **Schedule your tasks.** Since that itself takes minutes away from your day, consider *scheduling* scheduling your tasks. This way, you will be sure to fit it in.

• **Multi-task.** Combining two tasks into one time-frame can shave hours off a typical day. These hours can be spent infiltrating chat-rooms, trolling a scrapbooking forum ("Are those your children in the camping photo? And you decided *not* to leave them in the woods?"), or putting your mother's underwear under your little brother's pillow. So you won't miss out on quality time like this, combine tasks that are easy to do together, such as walking to the bus stop with brushing your teeth. Or sleep in, miss the bus and the teeth brushing, let your mother get good and teed off and she'll drive you in half the time. Warning: Do this too often and you'll be walking all the way to school for a year, and that is a big time sucker. Which brings me to ...

• **Do away with time-sucking tasks.** Shower? Why?

• **Break down tasks into mini-tasks.** Large tasks do not have to become overwhelming. For example, this morning I happened upon the following to-do list in the men's room. Under the heading, "Take Over Planet," could be found the following bulleted items: "Secure local air space," "Control the media," "Instill fear," "Enslave populace," etc. The writer of this note clearly has a good faculty for time management.

The dormitory quiet, Marvin retrieved his drawing pad and took up where he left off: Somewhere beneath the forbidding peaks of the Himalayas, Yolando, last seen hanging upside down above a steamy cauldron of boiling cream of wheat, was pulling himself up in such a way as to untie his ankles. Which on one hand wasn't hard because this hanging-from-the-ankles thing happened to be Yolando Plumadore's daily abdominal muscle strengthening exercise; but on the other hand, it was no walk in the park. Yolando had only the one arm, you may recall, at the end of which was his one-and-only hand. Which, Marvin had so far worked out, was not only tied, but was covered with a substance that Count Marmaduke, head minion of the evil Lord Balderon, had called "plastiloid."

Marvin had already finished the panel where Count Marmaduke had said this with a nasty sort of knowing smirk just before he slammed shut the mammoth iron door at the top of the torture chamber stairs. To wit: "Have fun, my friend, freeing yourself from the unyielding grip of plastiloid!" After which he broke into the wild cackles of evil minion laughter.

Marvin, it so happens, had come upon the plastiloid idea while the

---

• **Set realistic goals.** For example, on the above-mentioned list, the final item, "By Friday, January 12, the Earth will be ours!" the author has set an achievable goal within a reasonable time frame.

• **Never touch the same item twice** (girlfriend parts exempted).

• **Eschew cutlery.** Saves on needless dishwashing time.

• **Remove unnecessary distractions from your work area.** Television, MP3 players, buxom blondes, etc., have no place cluttering up your surroundings when you are trying to work. Wait ... the blonde can stay.

• **Cut out unnecessary steps.** Know how Xiaochang Bicycle Works outsells its top U.S. competitor 2:1? Streamlining, that's how! Less parts in box: less overhead; poorly tooled parts: future parts sales; untightened bolts: replacement bike! And skipping all those extra words like "Insert Rod A into Slot C" saves paper *and* ink! C'mon! Is *every* step necessary? Streamlining *your* process just might be your key to success.

• **Skip using the letter D.** It's a crutch.

others were engaged in the ping-pong ball exercise, which explains why, if I hadn't mentioned it earlier, he was a little irked at Geraldine Fitzsimmons' implication he was lazy. Plastiloid, he had worked out, was a form-fitting plasticene made by chemically combining the excretions of the Indo-Sumatran Mollusk (the stickiest substance on Earth) with iron-aluminum alloys, acrylic polymers and reduced-fat oleo margarine. Marvin had also worked out that plastiloid was something the likes of which Yolando Plumadore had never before encountered, let alone while hanging upside down over a steamy cauldron of boiling cream of wheat.

Unfortunately, plastiloid was also something *Marvin* had never before encountered, which meant that at this particular Pursuit of a Personal Nature moment he was struggling with how it should be depicted. Should it be outlined in dotted lines to imply invisibility, à la Kirby Lightman's Invisible Mutant Biker Chick and her invisible Harley Davidson V-Rod? And if so, should the dotted lines be black, or white? Or should plastiloid be transparent, a faint blue or gray perhaps, so the underlying hand showed through? That would make it appear more ghost-like, à la the great Stan Woodhall's work on *Infinite Ghost,* which was a lot cooler, but way harder to pull off.

Marvin made some sketches. They sucked. He made some more sketches. *They* sucked. Yolando's one hand kept coming out looking like a inking mistake.

And for the third time this week, Marvin wanted to smack himself in the forehead for writing himself into a corner.

This, by the way, was Marvin's private hell. I'm guessing you have your own.[48] Perhaps more concisely, Marvin's private hell was that he continually came up with ideas that were almost impossible to draw. He did it time and time again and he wanted to shoot himself in the foot for it. It had taken him sixteen tries to get Count Marmaduke's smirk right, and here he was, a full week later, still hammering out the same scene, stuck (so to

---

48> Mine involves a certain editorial assistant who loves to use the phrase, "pure unadulterated bull-twaddle" in an increasingly annoying accent. Good God, it's irritating.

speak) on plastiloid, a sticky substance. This is the kind of thing that Sigmund Freud would have a field day with (i.e., a writer stuck on a plot device that's sticky; only Herr Freud would get a penis image in there somewhere).

Marvin looked skyward. Why must *Winged Avengers of the Apocalypse* be so frickin' *perfect* anyway? Couldn't it just be fun? Did *every* scene have to fight him tooth and nail?[49]

Invariably Marvin steered the story toward something that would cost him valuable production time. Water, for instance. A plot involving water would be just so much time-sucking extra work. Liquid, solid, vapor — didn't matter, water always always *always* caused him grief. Other people cannot draw hands. Marvin cannot draw water, which under other circumstances would be a play on words but under this circumstance isn't.

Or fire. Ever notice how fire, in the comics, always looks — what's the word? — cartoony? Marvin never could think of a way to draw it convincingly. Or umpteen other things: cellophane … gooey gelatinous globs … Cleveland. Now smoke — smoke he could handle. You wouldn't think so, but he could. Smoke was just clouds with a little more gray in it. And smoke from a cigarette, easy peasy, which is a phrase I promise I will never, ever, use again.

So it didn't necessarily have to do with things that were transparent. Or things that were "conceptual." Or things that were subjective. (He had no problem with loneliness, for instance, or jealousy, or things that smell

---

49> When I first came across the phrase "tooth and nail," I thought it was a play on the Klaztonian phrase "shooth and knayell" before I remembered that Earthlings don't speak Klaztonian. But after some investigation (and not much), I learned the phrase was literal. As in saber tooth tiger literal. As in saber tooth tigers had big teeth and big nails, so fighting one was dangerous in the extreme, and, I'm sure, frustrating to boot. BTW, "Tooth and nail" can be found somewhere between "Take a Powder" and "Whoa, Nelly" in *Reginald T. Foggbottom's Dictionary of Peculiar Expressions, Adages, Idioms and Other Figures of Speech (English),* coming soon to a bookstore or handy ebook site near you.

like baloney.)

And of course he had no problem with solids, like concrete or iron or wood. Or marble or glass. Or leather or brick or sweaty brows or moldy bread or rat-infested sewers or just about anything else short of watery gelatinous goo wrapped in cellophane. Which just wasn't his thing.

So Marvin sat on his bunk thinking over this plastiloid business and the corner it had gotten him into. He thought about it long and hard. Now as you may have noticed when you are three weeks into a science project that's due, like, *tomorrow,* the more you struggle with making something work that isn't working, the less you know you are headed down a dead-end. You end up so immersed in the details — *that aren't working* — you cannot see the forest for the trees. Ask the Defense Department. They won't tell you, even with a Congressional subpoena, but it's true. They get so mired in the details and in the assumption they are headed down the right path, they forget to question the path. But unlike the Defense Department, every now and then Marvin was lucky enough to sit back and recognize a dead-end when he saw it. It might take him fifty sheets of drawing paper, but hey, it's only paper.[50]

And just like that, plastiloid — be it invisible, transparent, sticky or whatever — sounded lame in the extreme. Which is why Marvin decided he'd scrap the whole idea. Who needs the aggravation?

He'd just give Yolando some sort of fancy-schmancy mechanical handcuff, a hand-restricting device of some sort, and be done with it. Iron he could do. He'd just make up a contraption that could shackle not only Yolando's wrist, but immobilize his fingers as well. Marvin's hero wouldn't

---

50> I'm sure there are geniuses out there who could come up with a mathematical equation that would prove how many pieces of paper (or Photoshop files) it would take to come up with a valid, marketable, graphic novel. It might look something like this:

$$P = \left[\frac{I_1\,(Ink) \times I_2\,(Ideas)}{S\,(Snacks) \times B\,(Breaks)} \right] + \left[\frac{S_1\,(Self\text{-}Image) \times S_2\,(Self\text{-}Doubt)}{A_1\,(Artistic\ Ability) \times A_2\,(Ambition)} \right] \times \left[T\,(Time) \right] - \pi$$

Note: You can transpose most of these variables and still get the same result.

be able to pick his nose much less pick a lock. Again Marvin began to sketch. It could look like a cross between Roggie the Robot's mechanical hands, say, and something else. A mitten. A pair of pliers. A nutcracker. No, a lobster claw. Roggie the Robot's hands and a lobster claw. But mechanical.

And it could require a special key. A key without which, if the contraption were opened by force, would blow the special reinforced underground lair of the evil Lord Balderon and the entire Core Brigade — not to mention Yolando Plumadore and half the Himalayas — sky high. A key that wouldn't look like a key. Perhaps a key that had once appeared somewhere else, or *in* something else, that *looked* like something else, that the reader already had seen. Something in plain sight.

Marvin looked around his cubicle to see if anything could work as an appropriate model. Too dark. He angled his reading lamp to use as a spotlight. Not much to work with. He made a few rough sketches of the items at hand. The reading lamp itself, the light bulb, a pencil, an eraser, his zipper pull, his glasses. Nothing looked like a key. No matter, it would come to him. He'd just keep his eye out for the right thing.

Okay, that was it then. Not only would it be *tons* easier to draw, but it was already opening up plot possibilities. All he had to do was go back and weave in the new prop, the special key that doesn't look like a key and so on, so that now, as Yolando pulled himself upright, he simply had to regurgitate the thing with his well-toned intestinal fortitude (literally, not figuratively) and reveal to the reader that two scenes ago, when they saw Count Marmaduke throw Yolando at the feet of the evil Lord Balderon, what they had taken as some sort of odd behavior on Yolando's part — a faint, a cough, a nod into the distance ("Look, a goat!") — was really the point Yolando had palmed the key. What was once a mish-mash of *set design* would now be key (so to speak) to the plot.

For the reader, it'd be an "aha moment." And Marvin liked aha moments. What he didn't like was the phrase, "aha moment." It had become as overused as "game changer" and "You made it your own, dawg," and "24/7" and "under the bus" and "on the same page" and "yo *mamma*" and it drove him insane. But he *did* like aha moments themselves. I mean, who doesn't? Civilization is *built* on aha moments. [51]

51> **World-changing Aha Moments, a timeline:**

265 BC: Archimedes yells "Eureka!" while in bath, upsets rubber ducky, comes up with idea of displacement, gets wrinkly toes.

105 AD: Cai Lun in China smooshes up wood pulp and says, "Hey, let's write on it. Quick, somebody invent writing." (Only he says it in Chinese.)

1492: First-mate of Christopher Columbus: "I don't think this is India." (Only he says it in Italian.)

1513: Ponce de León discovers Florida, builds first retirement village.

1543: Copernicus realizes sun is true center of solar system, not mother-in-law.

1666: Isaac Newton watches apple fall from tree, posits "Theory of Apples"; i.e., "apples hurt."

1752: Benjamin Franklin flies kite, posits "Theory of Electricity"; i.e. "theories hurt."

1821: Michael Faraday creates current by moving wire though magnetic field, opens way for electric mixers, light bulbs, and rock 'n' roll.

1849: Safety pin is invented, Falling Knicker Syndrome plummets to 3% incidence rate, textile stocks rise comparably.

1859: Charles Darwin purposefully trips hairy-knuckled opponent in foot race, is first to cross finish line.

1876: Alexander Graham Bell, tired of yelling into next room, reluctantly uses "that talkie-listenie do-hickey thing."

1896: Henri Becquerel and the Curies discover uranium is way *way* creepy-ass stuff.

1905: Albert Einstein suddenly realizes E does not stand for "egg salad."

1928: Alexander Fleming mixes spit and mold to make penicillin. Mrs. Fleming says, "Gross."

1953: While playing Chutes and Ladders, Watson and Crick come upon structure of DNA.

1970: 3M Labs research assistant: "Man, this glue sucks." Marketing Dept: "Let's pretend we did it on purpose." Products dismissed before deciding on PostIt Notes™: SuckyGlue™, JustWon'tStick™, Gee Your Paste Isn't Terrific™

1986: Computer programmers at Apple, Inc., decide WYSIWYG ("What You See Is What You Get") makes more sense than WABORG ("What A Bunch Of Random Gibberish").

2004: Archimedes turns over in grave at coinage of term "Aha moment."

2012: Archimedes vows to continue turning in grave until people *stop saying the thing already.*

To tell the truth, the more Marvin thought about this, the more he was having an aha moment of his own. He could feel the perfect solution to the key-but-not-a-key problem slowly creeping into his head. Finally, like a gift from the Cartoonist Gods themselves, the answer was there. Yolando would find the key to the mechanical bracelet in a place that looks exactly like … wait for it … Foggbottom's office. The Louis XIV desk, the tapestries, the Italian vases, the battle-axe, and, lo and behold right there like Marvin had conjured them up himself: African ceremonial masks. What better place to hide a key than inside the mouth — or eye-socket, or whatever — of an African antelope or gazelle, the very symbols of freedom? And, revelation of revelations (it is always a mystery how these things work out), what better symbol than masks, meant to hide the identity of the wearer, to symbolize the fact that the evil Lord Balderon was not what he seemed? Bingo. Done. Over and out.

Marvin made a few quick notes that Balderon's digs would look *exactly* the same as Foggbottom's office, that the key to the mechanical handcuff would be hidden in Balderon's collection of African ceremonial masks, which would look exactly the same as Foggbottom's, and that Balderon was hiding his true identity, the details of which at this point Marvin hadn't quite worked out.

Not bad for a half hour's work.

Of course to get the mask right, Marvin would have to go online when he got home (he didn't want some hotshot anthropology professor writing him to say he'd used some mask that represented the "female mystique" or a fertility god or some crap like that). He (Marvin, not the professor) might even sneak into Foggbottom's office at some point to make some sketches of the masks. In the meantime, there was no reason he couldn't start the preliminary layout using masks as the hiding place for the key.

So, turning over a new page in his sketchbook, he eyed it with confidence. He sharpened his pencil in his little plastic pencil sharpener. He blocked out the panels. He added some very light pencil sketches for "camera" angles, pacing and the like. He got hit in the face with a pair of underwear.

"Dude!" Bennie, owner of said underwear whisper-yelled. "I'm jonesin' for some grub, yo."

Marvin did not look up. "Eat something," he shot back, tossing aside the (hopefully unused) briefs with a thumb and finger. He was trying to *draw,* fer cryin' out loud.

"Seriously. My blood sugar's like in China. If I don't eat something like pronto, I'm kissing the linoleum. C'mon, dude. Midnight snack. S'go."

Midnight? Marvin looked at his watch. A half hour's work it wasn't. It just seemed like a half hour's work. No wonder Bennie was hungry. It'd been six hours since dinner. Four since Waddell blew the Pursuits of a Personal Nature whistle.

Bennie kicked him on the foot then headed toward the kitchen. "There's a jar of peanut butter with my name on it down there, I just know it."

Come to think of it, Marvin's stomach did seem a little on the empty side … and drawing *is* a lot easier when you have a sandwich or a bowl of popcorn nearby … and after all, the hardest part *was* taken care of … he *had* forwarded the plot … and he sure didn't want Bennie slipping into a diabetic coma or anything. He looked up just in time to see a reflection of ambient light on the tip of Bennie's blue fauxhawk. Marvin made a note so he wouldn't forget:

**✳ BEAMS OF MOONLIGHT
REFLECT ON MASKS**

"Wait up," he whisper-called, tossing his sketchbook aside. "Peanut butter sounds downright delectable."

Filing past the other cubicles, Bennie put a finger to his lips and quietly hummed the opening bar of "Rock-a-Bye Baby." Marvin nodded. The only Pursuit of a Personal Nature going on at the Sandy Rivers Hilltop Ranch dormitory involved Rapid Eye Movement.

Chapter SEVENTEEN...

WHAT LITTLE LIGHT there was in the dining hall came from the back, seeping its way from under the kitchen door, exactly where Marvin and Bennie were headed. (The kitchen, that is, not under the door.) Bennie announced that if that chef dude Winston was in there, he was going to talk him into a sandwich. Something more substantial than peanut butter that's for sure. Something with a little heft to it. "Something bigger than my head."

Marvin, now past peanut butter territory and picturing all kinds of goodies like a fat juicy cheeseburger, agreed. Based on what they'd been served so far, if this Winston was anything, he was accommodating. I mean all-you-can-eat cream pie for crying out loud.

Now for those of you who are reading this in short increments (i.e., trips to the john), you may recall that somewhere back there, way before ping-pong balls and hybrid video games and lousy German accents, I used the word "prehensile." (If you don't recall the passage, it is perhaps because you have neglected to read the footnotes. See? I'd warned you they'd come in handy.) Specifically, and I quote: "They're a short-tempered lot, the Kilgorians. And, having six strong arms (seven if you count the prehensile tail), and a muscle-to-fat ratio of 50:1, a Kilgorian can thrust the largest of

objects impressively far with very little effort. That's what Kilgorians *do*."
Then I went on to say that one such thrust involved a particular industrial
cooking range, for years mistook by Earth's scientists as the planet Pluto.

Did you know, when you first came across that passage, what
"prehensile" meant? If not, did you look it up? Probably not, because who
looks up things these days, but if you had, you'd have found it means
"capable of grasping." As in the prehensile tail of a spider monkey or a
Jackson's chameleon or a seahorse or a kinkajou, which I suggest you look
up as well because it's the cutest darn thing you ever have seen.

All of which means that a Kilgorian has a tail capable of grasping,
much like that of the North American opossum, which is a word with an
extra letter at the beginning that people are expected to pronounce but
very few people actually do. Only, unlike an opossum who uses his tail for
balancing on small branches, a Kilgorian — some eight feet in height and,
as I say, in possession of a short fuse — could not balance on a small
branch even if he wanted to, and would most likely use *his* prehensile tail
for such things as, as I say, hurling large appliances, and, unfortunately,
grabbing unsuspecting young men by the ball sacks.

So when Marvin pushed open the door to the kitchen and caught
sight of a prehensile tail as big around as his own adolescent thigh, he
understandably was no longer thinking about cheeseburgers or peanut
butter or anything other than humongous prehensile tails. This particular
unsightly thing was not hurling an industrial cooking range (although
there was one present because after all it was a kitchen), but was holding,
in a rather non-hurling way, a salt shaker.

And if you were to follow this prehensile tail to its point of origin, you
would see it was connected to the derriere of a hulking figure, who, thank
goodness, was presently facing the other way.

Marvin and Bennie stood slack-jawed as they peered through what
was now just a crack in the door. Not only were they surprised to see a
prehensile tail busily shake salt, but they were equally surprised to see six
arms — from the same beastly creature, you understand — each in the
throes of one activity or another. Two of the brute's hands were busily

rolling out dough, while another busily diced a vegetable of unknown variety and still another was busily operating a decidedly alien-looking cooking utensil the likes of which, to my knowledge, even Mr. Popeil never imagined.[52]

Another of the creature's hands was holding a perfectly ordinary wooden spoon, though Marvin and Bennie were not privy to it because at the moment it was being dipped into a king-sized pot of steaming something-or-other the wafting aroma of which smelled very much like the inside of a dirty Port-o-John. If I haven't completely covered all six hands, I believe the last was busying itself by cleaning out one the creature's large and unsightly left nostrils.

The prehensile tail, having dispensed with the salt shaking bit and seeming to have a mind of its own, now wrapped itself around a leg of a stainless steel kitchen stool, upon which sat owner of said tail, dressed in chef's hat, chef's smock, and the rest, whose six arms were, as I've made redundantly clear, busy. It was not difficult to see, given the size of the beast, that the owner of said prehensile tail was also in possession of remarkably pig-like knuckles, skin somewhat akin to that of an African elephant crossed with a crocodile, and, once the creature turned to an obliging angle, a forehead the size of Kentucky.

This thing made the billboard-like countenance of Skylar Waddell look like that of a scrawny schoolboy.

At this point, Marvin and Bennie noticed something you don't see in a kitchen every day (besides a six-armed elephantine chef): there, at the

---

52> Ronald "Take Advantage of This Amazing TV Offer" Popeil is the American inventor of such essential devices as the Veg-o-matic, the Dial-o-matic ("Slice a tomato so thin it only has one side!"), and the Pocket Fisherman. You can thank Mr. Popeil for today's late-night infomercials with obnoxious British shills pushing the likes of The Tummy Tucking AbCrunchBuster, Little-Brother-B-Gone and Appendectomy-in-a-Can. $49.95? Guess again. $39.95? Not even! Still only $19.95! Call in the next 15 minutes and we'll double your order! We'll even throw in this automatic heel scaler! Operators are standing by. Batteries not included. Shipping and handling extra. Offer not valid in the State of Minnesota. May cause rash, accelerated heart rate and/or diarrhea. Sorry, no C.O.D.'s.

end of the stainless steel counter, was a cage. And sniffing rather innocently in the cage was a number of smallish furry animals. Ferrets? Weasels? Something along those lines. (In truth they were Favarian ring-tailed skerlish, and seeing as how skerlish are found only on the island of Favara in the eastern hemisphere of Pog, neither Marvin nor Bennie had the means — nor the wherewithal at this point — to look it up.)

They (the skerlish, not the boys) had pointy ears and noses, tiny pinkish eyes with amazingly long and curly lashes, a round body the size of a good-sized avocado and soft-and-furry black-and-white coats in varying mixtures of soft-and-furry black-and-whiteness. If there were feet under that fur, you couldn't see them.

Maybe seven of them in all, these pointy-nosed little fur-balls were going about their business — rubbing up against the side of the cage, skittering along on their little exercise wheel, sniffing each other's rear-ends, eating scrumptious leafy greens, lying on top of one another like kittens, and looking altogether cuddly and fuzzy and adorable as all get-out. Which meant if there *were* feet under there, they were most undoubtedly tiny and pink and cute.

The hulking chef continued his chopping, stirring and the like, but then, in an instant that would stick with our two heroes for some time, in one quick motion his sixth hand — or was it his third? — moved from nostril to cage, plucked one of the poor darlings from his cage-mates ... and popped the thing into his repulsive gaping-hollow of a corpulent, revolting, slobbery and overly-adjectived mouth. Like a bon-bon. Fur and all.

At this, the other fur-balls in the cage let out screeches the likes of which I cannot do justice, the sort you might hear in the jungle in the middle of the night and wonder what the heck type of animal *that* was. Monkey? Macaw? Man-eating marsupial? Some other animal that starts with an M? "Ack ack — AAAACK!!" the little darlings went, in ear-shattering unison, sending chills up Marvin's spine that quickly bore themselves into in his middle ear like termites into a two-by-four.

For a moment Marvin and Bennie could not look at one another. All they could hear was those horrible screeches reverberate on the stainless steel counters and pink-tiled (natch) kitchen walls. All they could see was the six-armed ferret/weasel-eating monster, who was, in a word — as you have no doubt already surmised, clever reader that you are — Winston. He was also, in some other words, *most likely not very accommodating.* And, in case you have missed something here, Winston the chef was also wholly, unquestionably, unapologetically, in yet another word, Kilgorian.

And as I have said, possibly more than once, the Kilgorians are a short-tempered lot. Remember that image of the mandrill monkey teeth? Double that. And double *that.*

Naturally, Bennie Sterlati, like Marvin, was unaware of this fact. The ferret/weasel-eating beast should give Bennie a clue but as anyone who's had their extended family over for Thanksgiving dinner knows, some people will eat anything. Unlike Marvin, who as I say had forgotten about peanut butter let alone anything more substantial, Bennie had not. His blood sugar level wouldn't let him.

Now low blood sugar has been known to cause rational people to act out of sorts, fly off the handle, do irrational things and the like, which, one could argue, explains a lot (the overcrowded penal system, the 2000 election, the popularity of "Cats," etc.). Napoleon Bonaparte, for instance, was a great sufferer of low blood sugar, and most likely would not have invaded Waterloo had he not been desperate for a good *crème brûlée,* which, of course, is French for "yummy custard with blow-torched sugar on top."[53]

53> Those French. As Comedian Steve Martin has said, "The French have a word for everything." [*See: "Trebuchet."*] Mr. Martin is a very nice fellow and all and I'm sure he'd be extremely amusing as a dinner guest, but to declare the phrase as his own would be misleading at best. In point of fact, Mr. Martin — in his defense, perhaps unknowingly — quite possibly hijacked the phrase from writer Raymond Chandler — who, for all I know, hijacked it from some other fellow, the attorneys for whom are probably long dead — to wit: "The French have a word for it. The bastards have a phrase for everything." (*The Long Goodbye, 1953.*)

Notable here is that in 1953 the use of the word "bastards" was rather risqué, vulgar even.

Marvin, staring into the kitchen at this six-armed monster like it was just that, was starting to ease back on the kitchen door with every intention of high-tailing it out of there when the door moved out of his hand and in the other direction — i.e., forward, not the direction it was supposed to move at all, which was ever-so-slowly backward until it was closed without so much as a creak. And through the door went Bennie. "Through it" meaning "into the kitchen." The kitchen with the pot-stirring, scaly-tailed, many-nostrilled goon.

Marvin tried to grab Bennie by the jumpsuit as he went past, but it slipped through his fingers. He debated, for a split second, going in after him. But after seeing that ferret-popping incident, he wasn't about to move. It was all he could do to keep his mouth shut. He didn't want to risk a single "*pssst,*" let alone, "Are you effing insane?!?" He was forced to stand there with the door open only the width of an eyeball, watching helplessly as Bennie tip-toed past stainless steel blenders and pots and mixers and other items prevalent in the industrial cooking oeuvre, keeping low, creeping around to the other side of the counter, the tip of his fauxhawk looking like a small blue shark making its way through a stainless steel sea.

Winston continued his chopping-rolling-stirring, oblivious to the fact he had a young intruder.

Suddenly there was a squeak. If one is able to freeze after one is already frozen, that's what Marvin did. As did our yellow-skinned disgustingly

---

Back in 1953, nice people didn't use words like that. Not in mixed company anyway. Nice people wore suits and ties and stockings and gloves, and washed behind their ears and said things like "gee whillikers" and "hokey smokes" and "mares eat oats and does eat oats and little lambs eat ivy."

Today, what was risqué in 1953 isn't risqué by a long shot. Ever notice how, over time, words that once offended lose their shock value? Someday when you're old and feeble and cannot help but drool down your fashionably futuristic shirt, you can tell your grandchildren that when you were a kid you couldn't say [insert four-letter word of your choice] on television. Then, when they look at you like you're a fossilized drooling old coot, which you no doubt will be, you can tell them what television was.

wrinkled and scaly chef. All six arms and prehensile tail stopped mid-task. The squeak came again. The monster's head shot in its direction. It came once more. Then again and again, which was the point both Marvin and Winston — and one would presume, Bennie, who had somehow vanished from sight — saw that one of the fur-balls, probably realizing a cage-mate was inexplicably missing, had jumped onto the tiny exercise wheel in a futile attempt to flee, eyes wide, running/squeaking his way, full throttle, nowhere fast.

Winston, snorting a "*hmmph … skerlish*" sort of snort, once again took up his chopping-stirring-rolling and Marvin, relieved Bennie had not been the source of the squeak, let out a lungful of air. His eyes then darted desperately around the kitchen.

Where the *hell* was Bennie?

The sound of the chef's stool scraping the floor came next as Winston stood, his massive form plodding across the kitchen in heavy footfalls, his tail swinging left and right, knocking into the occasional ladle, bowl or measuring cup, like a bull in a china shop, or as they say in Thelrinese, "a Kilgorian in a kitchen."

The massive Winston rounded the counter, his foot claws clicking against the tile. Marvin cringed. He was sure Bennie had had it. Panic-stricken, he patted his pockets for something to throw to distract the brute. He was all but ready to swing open the door and yell, "Last one home's a rotten egg!" or some other dumb-ass thing, when the Kilgorian opened the refrigerator door, removed a bowl of eggs, and returned to his stool.

Again, chopping-stirring-rolling, and now, beating.

When Winston's hand reached for something out of sight, Marvin fully expected it to return with a gasping Bennie, who would be popped into the waiting Kilgorian maw and smacked down without so much as a glass of milk.

Instead, the kitchen was filled with music. Loud music. And Winston, evidently pleased with what he had last left in the player, began to whistle along.

Kilgorians, apparently, like to whistle while they work. (Who knew, right?) And what is it they like to whistle *to* while they work? I will tell you. You're not going to believe me, but as I say, I do not make this stuff up. Here it is: Gary Vaniloe. I kid you not. *"Candy girl, you make me cry / Today I caught you in a lie..."* and all that. Which was exactly the song being whistled by Winston at this very moment.

And so, as the massive beast whistled along with outdated saccharine drivel, Marvin watched as the refrigerator door began to open. Evidently by Bennie. Ever so slowly.

As much as you'd think this would keep Marvin's attention, for surely the chef would see it and in a millisecond Bennie would be swallowed up like a Cheese Doodle, you'd be wrong. Because it was the *reflection* in the stainless steel refrigerator door that caught Marvin's attention. And he was sorry it did.

Because what he saw turned his stomach: Winston, having put all his potatoes and alien-looking vegetables into a thick industrial pie pan, was now throwing five, count them five, innocent little skerlish into the pan, ladling the hot something-or-other from the king-size pot over the poor little things, and, with the efficiency of a well-seasoned multi-armed pro, topped it off with a thick slab of gooey-soft dough. Five furry parboiled heads poked through, eyes wide with fear and pain as the little darlings flailed about like flies caught in fly paper, screeching terrible ear-shattering screeches all the way up to the terrible moment the Vaniloe-loving brute popped them smartly into the oven ... and closed the door.

"Dude."

Marvin's eyes were on the oven door. Marvin's eyes were then back at the cage, watching the last terrified fur-ball go into a frenzy, rearing up against the back of the cage, clamoring for the cover of darkness, shrieking in terrible—

"Dude!" Bennie hissed again, pulling Marvin back back *back* away from the kitchen door. [54]

54> Winston's concoction, of course, is a variation on a recipe for stargazy pie. If you are not familiar with stargazy pie, here is the recipe in a nutshell, er, pie-shell:

Arrange 6 to 8 small fish into a shallow pie dish in an artful fashion. Add 2 sliced hard-boiled eggs, 2 chopped onions, 10 oz. heavy cream, bacon bits, the juice of one lemon, parsley, salt and tarragon to taste. Top with pie dough. Carefully pull each fish's head through the dough, also in an artful fashion. Bake at 425° until crust is a golden brown and fish look appropriately (and crisply) mortified.

The point here is that the fish are arranged so their little heads poke through the crust as if "star gazing," which is not only gross but amazingly *apropos* due to the fact that it's a favorite on starships.

But here is something very interesting, and, as you will soon come to appreciate, more proof of the uncanny Interconnectedness of All Things: According to the *Encyclopedia Gargantua,* stargazy pie is not only a Kilgorian delicacy, where the fish of choice is the murmulfish (given they thrive only in the Fandolöckin Straits on the planet Kilgore), but stargazy pie is a dish for which the county of Cornwall, England, is famous. The very same Cornwall, you may recall, where young Gopal Misra met his love, Penelope Hastings, on the Tamar Bridge. Stargazy pie is big in Cornwall. The fish of choice in Cornwall of course is pilchard, which is basically a sardine by another name. (Any small fish will do — mackerel, anchovy, herring and the like — as long as they have teensy tiny bones for added crunch.) Want to know something else? Gopal Misra once had a pet hamster named ... Winston. Cross my heart.

Anyway, that Winston (the chef, not the hamster) chose to use in his recipe the adorable skerlish (which you'd think, *not even being fish* would be a culinary *faux pas*) — that's the surprising thing here. Let's not forget it was a request to forego the murmulfish in the very same recipe that had set another Kilgorian chef into appliance rage. Surely Winston was aware of the incident. This I suppose is proof that cooking as an art is as open as any other to creative license, even to Kilgorians. And though I am tempted to say the choice of the adorable skerlish was meant as a culinary play on the term "cutie pie," I'm afraid Winston was not that clever.

Chapter EIGHTEEN...

MARVIN AND BENNIE tore across the dining hall in 1.7 seconds, down a pink-tiled corridor in 3.5 seconds, and, in another 17 seconds, flew down the stairs, down another corridor, across the dormitory and into the boys' bathroom. It took then a full 22 seconds of serious panting and breath-catching, and 18 more seconds of serious panting and breath-catching, until Bennie was able to manage something along the lines of, "It ... it ... it ... it ... it ..." by which he meant, "Holy crap, that thing had six arms and a frickin' ginormous 'possum tail and it frickin' *baked* those innocent little furry dudes!"

To which Marvin replied (between pants), "This ... is no ordinary ... ranch."

To which Bennie, nodding a concurring nod, retrieved an apple from his pocket and bit into it. At least the fridge raid had paid off. He took a deep apple-laden breath, clear sweet juice rolling down his chin. He didn't bother to wipe it away. Half out of breath, he chewed. No matter what was going on here, at least he wasn't going to faint from low blood sugar.

Marvin and Bennie looked at each other much like two people who had just run for their lives look at each other. What were they to do now? Luckily for them, as Mr. Poe once said, suddenly there came a tapping.

Without embedded audio, I cannot reproduce it accurately here, but suffice it to say it sounded more like the tapping of a telegraph line than a limited-vocabularied raven. Which is why the brains of Marvin and Bennie were both immediately struck by the notion that what they were hearing was Morse Code, that someone was trying to send them a message. But since Marvin and Bennie had never been exposed to Morse Code, they had no way of knowing it was *not* Morse Code.

It went something like this: *Tuh-tap tuh-tap tuh-t-t-t-tap. Tuh-tap tuh-tap tuh-t-t-t-tap.*

Bennie stopped chewing. They listened. They followed the sound out into the dormitory, where it (the sound, not the dormitory) stopped for a couple of seconds then took up again. *Tuh-tap tuh-tap tuh-t-t-t-tap. Tuh-tap tuh-tap tuh-t-t-t-tap. T-tuh-t-t-tuh-t-t-tuh-t-t-TAP.*

It was coming from the girl's bathroom.

Slowly … *slowly* … because they now weren't too keen on what they'd find on the other side of any door … they pushed it open. Just an inch at first, then, as they saw what and who it was, they pushed it open all the way. There, by the far sink, was Dara. She was in her nightgown — in this case a long T-shirt that went to her knees. Her pigtails were swinging left and right, right and left, and she was tapping. As in dancing. As in tap dancing. The water was on in the sink, presumably to mask the sound of the taps. Obviously, it didn't.[55]

The taps echoed against the tile of the bathroom like a submarine

---

55> Please do not write me letters about how I am promoting the waste of precious natural resources among easily influenced young minds. I'm sure your fellow readers realize that running water to camouflage any sound is a wasteful act and wouldn't in a million years consider it. So give them a little credit. Besides, everyone knows it would take at least two faucets running full force to provide enough sound to cover the sound of anything that needs covering, and even then, anyone on the other side of the door would recognize the ruse for what it is because no one really runs two faucets full force unless they are running a scuba-diving school, and therefore will imagine the faucet-turner doing far worse things in there than they are actually doing, and please do not write me letters about how I'm promoting *that.*

communications room, which is another reason it sounded like Morse
Code. Of course, Marvin and Bennie had never been in a submarine
communications room, but I have, so you have to trust me on that.

Dara was practicing the same syncopated steps over and over again.
*Tuh-tap tuh-tap tuh-t-t-t-tap. Tuh-tap tuh-tap tuh-t-t-t-tap. T-tuh-t-t-tuh-
t-t-tuh-t-t-TAP.* Again and again. Loudly. Please understand: you can't get
that sound with ordinary shoes. You can only get that sound if you are
wearing tap shoes. Which she was. Patent leather tap shoes, with big black
bows on them and cute white ruffled socks in them. Dara was exercising
her Pursuit of a Personal Nature. *Tuh-tap tuh-tap tuh-t-t-t-tap. Tuh-tap
tuh-tap tuh—*

"For God's sake!" she wailed, holding her chest. "You scared the
bejeezus out of me!"

Under normal circumstances, i.e. circumstances that didn't involve
happening upon a ferretcidal Kilgorian chef in the kitchen, Marvin would
have said something along the lines of, "My, what pretty black bows you
have," and Bennie would have done one of those fall-into-the-other-guy-
laughing bits, wishing he'd caught this display on his cell phone for
ijustmadeafoolofmyself.com. But they didn't. Instead, Bennie went head-
long into how he was having this blood-sugar attack and everybody was
asleep except Marvin and how they headed down to the kitchen for some
peanut butter or something more substantial, anything that would help,
and he didn't get any peanut butter but he did get an apple and you-know-
the-rest because you just read it in the last chapter.

The echo of the taps, still hanging in the air of the restroom, subsided
as Dara turned off the water. She looked at Marvin, then Bennie. But
instead of saying, "Holy crap!" (meaning she couldn't believe what she was
hearing) or even "Yeah, right," (meaning she *didn't* believe what she was
hearing) or any number of other things you'd expect someone to say when
they've just been told the chef is a leathery goon the size of a small tank,
she said, "I was afraid of that."

Marvin: "'I was afraid of that' as in you knew we'd catch you tap
dancing or 'I was afraid of that' as in you knew there was a freakoid six-

armed rat-tailed dude in the kitchen who cooks up cute little ferrets like they were SpudNuggets?"

Bennie, swallowing a piece of apple: "Weasels, yo."

Marvin: "SpudNuggets are not weasels, my friend."

"Not the SpudNuggets. The weasels. He cooked up weasels, not—"

"I think I know a ferret when I see one. They were ferrets."

Bennie shook his head. "Weasels. Seen 'em on TV. No, wait — not weasels. What're those things…? Warthogs."

Marvin: "You mean *hedgehogs*? Warthogs are big-ass things, like boars—"

Dara cleared her throat. "I'd *like* to say 'I was afraid of that' meant I was afraid two geeks were going to dream up some bogus don't-separate-or-the-monster-will-get-you bullcrap so they could come in here to scare the bejeezus out of me," she said, proceeding to sit on the floor to untie her shoes, "but what I really meant was that second thing."

Marvin and Bennie looked at each other like two people look at each other when a) they're picturing five shrieking ferret/weasels being popped into an oven; (b) they suspect they were probably *this close* to getting eaten themselves; (c) they'd just caught someone tap dancing in their pajamas, and (d) they couldn't remember what the second thing was.

"I was afraid," Dara said, reminding them what the second thing was, "that there really *was* a freakoid six-armed giant rat-tailed dude in the kitchen." Then, surprisingly, she stood up, brushed herself off and said, "It's Winston. He's a Kilgorian starship chef. And I'm afraid the Sandy Rivers Hilltop Ranch for Wayward Youth, Juveniles, and Young Adults is his starship."

• • •

IN THE TIME it would take to get to the chicken and dumplings line of "She'll Be Comin' 'Round the Mountain," Dara had managed to change into her jumpsuit, sneak down to the dining hall, peer into the kitchen, and run to the stairwell where Marvin and Bennie were waiting, shaking their heads at how she'd come up with this Kilgorian starship stuff.

"Okay," she said in a low tone, looking back over her shoulder, "so you weren't screwing with me. I mean, it's possible you saw the same thing I did in the pod. It's possible, later, you decide it'd be funny to—"

"Wait a minute," Marvin said. "You saw that rat-tailed dude in the pod?"

Dara: "I just said that. Although I think it's more of a 'possum tail if you want to get picky about it."

Bennie: "You saw that rat-tailed dude in the pod?"

Dara looked back and forth between Marvin and Bennie like they were on something. "I … just … said … that."

Marvin thought for a moment then looked her in the eye. "You picked 'Query,' didn't you? Man, I wish I picked 'Query.'"

And the next thing they knew they were following her into the heart of Afternoon Social Studies, feeling their way through the darkened auditorium until they were standing before her lifeless pod.

"Rat-tailed dude in the kitchen?" she asked. "Same dude I saw in here." She pulled open the acrylic shell. "Hop in." Which is what they did, and which, if you really wanted to know, was what Marvin wanted to do from the moment he saw Dara on that bus, some 16 chapters ago. Sit next to her, that is. With no room, not even a millimeter, between them. The fact that Bennie was just as close, millimeter-wise, on Marvin's other side hadn't really hit him yet, but given Bennie's distaste for personal hygiene, once that acrylic shell closed, it would.

It was nice in there, all things considered. And until Bennie's lack of deodorant and/or soap and/or deodorant soap kicked in, it even smelled good. Dara's hair touched Marvin's cheek. It was soft. (Her hair, not his cheek, although, if truth be told, his cheek was soft, too, but that in time would change and doesn't add anything to the point I'm trying to make here.)

The acrylic shell came down. The screen came to life.

> WHAT DO YOU WANT TO DO <

"Start," Dara ordered. The screen changed.

> PLAY <

> EXPLORE <

> QUERY <

>>> YOUR CHOICE <<<

Marvin pointed to QUERY in a distinct "I told you so" sort of way.

"So there's three," Bennie said. "Doesn't mean *I* saw three."

"Maybe it does. Maybe you just—"

Dara shushed them. "Query," she instructed. The screen went black. Then:

> PLEASE STATE YOUR QUESTION. <

"Inga," Dara said as if they were on a first-name basis. "Tell us where we are."

Marvin, finding it hard to believe Dara knew these things: "How do you *know* these things?"

Then came the same sultry voice he'd heard in Afternoon Social Studies. Only this time the voice didn't say it was a closed session. This time it said, "I know everything."

"No, I mean, *Dara,* how do you know these things?" (Whispered out of hte side of his mouth.) "How'd you know its — her — name is Inga? How'd you know about that *thing* in the kitchen? What's this *starship* business? How'd—"

"Shhh!" Dara shhhed. "Inga, tell them where we are."

The voice responded. "We are currently .117 light years from destination." With this, the screen displayed colorful graphics detailing, with arrows and rotational 3-D rendering, each spatial point. (And when I say "spatial point," I mean "*spatial* point.") "Current inter-ether speed is alpha-zeta: 77.4; omega-omega: 5.33. X-axis: 774.15; Y-axis: 97.73; Z-axis: 999.004. Trajectory quotient: 0-7-0-2. We should reach destination in

approximately…" — pause — "… 1.32 glirms. Dara knows my name
because she has queried. Dara knows many things because she has queried.
All you need do is query. That is why I am here. Please," the voice added,
"remember to brush your teeth after every meal." With this, the screen
displayed a very nice animation of a man brushing his teeth.

"She's always doing that stuff," Dara said with an eye-roll. "Inga, how
far are we from Earth? And what's the Earth time for 1.32 — uh, whatever-
it-was — glirms?"

"And most importantly," Marvin wanted to know, "what if we skipped
this teeth brushing thing?"

Dara elbowed him in the ribs.

The voice answered: "Point-one-one-seven light years from destination
is approximately 39.4 light years from Earth, Sol-7(3). We are no longer
within the Sol-7 system. We have ether-jumped to Zeta Reticuli, Sol-1143,
destination star system. The ether jump has transmuted 39.4 light years
into approximately 375,600 kilometers, roughly the distance from Earth,
Sol-7(3) to its moon; 1.32 glirms is approximately three days, Earth time,
Sol-7(3). Teeth brushing is important because good dental hygiene pre-
vents gingivitis and other periodontal diseases." (The graphics here were
revolting.) "If you do not have teeth, it is highly recommended to take care
of all components of your mouth, or similar intake organ such as proboscis,
bill or beak. Since we are speaking English, which is spoken solely by
humans on the planet Earth, Sol-7(3), I assume, unless you have had some
manner of hapless accident and/or genetic disorder, you are equipped
with teeth. The brushing of teeth also gives you fresh breath to aid in the
acquisition of friends and so as not to offend those around you. When
traveling, always bring a pair of spare underwear."

Let me restate that the voice in the pod had a certain sultriness to it. If
you were to ask Marvin and Bennie what they thought of it, they might
even tell you that sultriness ranked high on the sultry scale, say a 9. Which
was why, when the voice asked whether they had any more questions,
Bennie nervously ran his fingers through his blue mane, leaned into the
screen and inquired, "Inga, is it? What're you, like, *wearing*?"

Dara smacked him upside the head.

"I am not wearing anything," the voice said as the video screen came to life.

"Now that," Bennie said, straightening his collar, "is one hot computer babe."

"I assure you," the voice said with accompanying expository graphics, "all my components are made of re-atomized materials in constant state of re-atomization. Barring an interruption of the re-atomization process, they will not wear down."

"Ah," Marvin nodded, "she's not *wearing* anything. Get it?"

Bennie plopped back into the seat. "Wouldn't you know it? She's a frickin' sci-fi cliché."

The voice came again. *"Would you rather I sound..."* Three octaves lower, like the Spawn of Satan played at half speed: *"...**LIKE THIS?**"*

"Um..." Bennie ummed. "The other one, please. *Way* better."

Marvin, Dara, and Bennie sat in silence, the blue glow from the screen awaiting their next move, the auditorium eerily quiet around them. Their minds raced now, trying to process all they'd been told; after all, they'd never been faced with a situation like this — whisked away on a starship — at least without the ability to hit PAUSE. Nobody looked at anybody. Marvin stared at the screen. "Did she — he, it, whatever — just say what I thought she said? We're three days out from wherever it is we're headed?"

"That's what I got out of it," said Dara. "And wherever we're headed is really far from home. As in Earth. As in really *really* far from Earth. Which was why I was tap dancing. I always tap dance when I'm nervous."

For the first time since Marvin met her, Dara looked a little scared.

Bennie put his feet up on the "dashboard" and scoffed. "It's bogus," he said, trying to wiggle enough room to lean his head back into his palms. (He gave up, crossing his arms instead.) "It's a *game*, bro. It's all, you know, CGI and crap. They're messin' with us."

"And I suppose that freak in the kitchen is part of it?" Dara argued. "That's some mean graphics ... bro."

Bennie's face went blank. "Good point. I still can't get over how he baked those little furry dudes. The *dick*."

"First thing's first," Marvin announced, giving the acrylic shell a push. "We look out a window."

"He's right, Dara said. "You realize in the time we've been here we haven't seen a single window?" Now that they thought about it, there hadn't been windows in the dormitory or the dining hall or the stairwells or the auditorium *or* the gymnasium. Not even in the classrooms. The last time they'd even *seen* outside was when they stepped off the bus into the parking lot, which, considering they hadn't even noticed, says something of the state of modern civilization, not to mention its Vitamin D levels.

Marvin flashed upon the only place he could imagine having a window and in no time the three were standing outside the door marked REGINALD T. FOGGBOTTOM, ADMINISTRATOR.

Chapter NINETEEN...

A TURN OF THE KNOB and they were in.

"Doesn't anyone pay the electric bill around here?" Marvin muttered when he saw it was yet another dark room. He could just make out the shapes and shadows of things he'd seen on his previous visit — the bookcases, the globe, the suit of armor. But Dara and Bennie, never having been there before, were in the dark (so to speak) and were reluctant to move. It was up to Marvin, then, who made his way to Foggbottom's Louis XIV desk. He patted along the desktop until he found the lamp. And flicked it on.

Causing Bennie, now being able to see the room, to turn in circles, much as Marvin had done the day before. Bennie turned a full 720-degrees, his mouth open for 700 of them. "It's a frickin' *museum*," he said, clearly impressed. "I never *saw* so much stuff."

Marvin nodded. He was surprised to find much here he'd missed during his little tête-à-tête with Foggbottom — a hand-carved totem pole from Papua New Guinea, for instance. A full-size statue of a Roman centurion. A thick book upon a wooden pedestal. A leopard-skin rug. There was a set of two Chinese urns, a heavy iron chandelier, a statuette of an angel draped in grief over a jeweled box. Add to this the African masks, tapestry and suit of armor, and Marvin was working hard to make a complete mental inventory, trying to weigh the different ways he could depict these things on the page.

As if he were ever going to get back to *Winged Avengers of the Apocalypse*.[56]

"Reginald T. Foggbottom likes the finer things, that's for sure," Marvin said mid-inventory.

Bennie, taking it all in: "The finer *gay* things."

Marvin ran his fingers along the ornate desk. "Note, however, what you don't see."

Bennie looked around, shrugged.

"A window, dummy. There's no window. Even a hermit takes a look outside every now and then."

Dara had been quietly walking around the room, examining all she could. "I've seen this movie," she said. "Ten-to-one Foggbottom shows up wearing an ascot. He's probably behind that unicorn right now, spying on us."

"No way," Bennie said, eyeing the wall-hanging. "There's no, you know, like, eyes. You gotta have pop-out eyes." He pointed to his eyes, as if that would help them understand the concept. "And it's gotta be a painting, not a rug."

56> **Universal Literary Rule No. 12, "The Writer's Curse":** Many writers find them-selves mentally writing narration in every waking moment. (If they have been at it long enough, they will also write narration in every dreaming moment.) For instance, if you were to find yourself looking down the barrels of a Nicaraguan firing squad, you would probably close your eyes and pray for an Act of God. A writer, cursed with habitual minute-by-minute narration, might find himself immersed in the scene: the cold blue steel of the rifles, the lifeless eyes of the guards, the warm feel of the cracked stucco on which he leans, the humiliation of poor bladder control.

There is, of course, an *Artist Corollary:* Painter, illustrator, sculptor or cartoonist, the artist will mentally draw it. It is not hard to imagine, then, that a graphic novelist such as Marvin, whose pen is burdened with both words and images, finds himself doubly cursed. Which is why, if you've ever met a graphic novelist, they have that crazy eye-tic thing going on.

Dara: "Tapestry."

"Whatev." His eyes began to search the room, as though looking for that painting with removable eyes.

"I've seen this movie, too," Marvin put in, still examining the desk, "or maybe it was an episode of 'Danger Dawg, Private Eye.'"

"All I know," Bennie said, "is that we're stickin' together. I don't wanna see one of you guys disappear into the paneling or ... you know." He pulled his thumb across his neck. "Somebody *always* gets it in the library, yo."

In the meantime, Dara had started to pick up everything she could get her hands on — letter opener, small wooden box, statuette — and was presently running her finger along a glass case that housed six Amazonian shrunken heads when Marvin, still feeling around the desk, made the following announcement:

"What have we here?"

He'd discovered something. Under the lip of the desk.

Now the last button Marvin pushed managed to blow up a perfectly good cabin. So it's no surprise he held his finger over the button he had just found for a second, debating. At a second-twenty, he'd made his decision. He'd pushed it. And the tapestry against the far wall, the one of the unicorn kept in a pen (which, as an item of Great Symbolism, you no doubt recognize as being carefully weaved into the initial description of the room), began to rise. And behind the tapestry, no spying Foggbottom, no ascot, just what they were looking for: A window.

A huge window. *Huge.* And beyond the window's thick glass?

Stars.

• • •

EVER CAMP OUT on a moonless night in the middle of nowhere and be astounded by just how many stars there are out there? When, far away from the filtering shield of street lights and smog and houses and Cola-Cola billboards, the night sky is not pitch black, is not even dotted with the occasional star, but is so blanketed with white pinpoints of otherworldly glow it is difficult to take it all in?

Well triple that.

To say the stars went on forever would be an understatement, though, of course, the stars *did* go on forever, but there they were, millions upon millions of them — above, below and beyond, like … now I don't want to wax poetic or anything, but if one is allowed to wax poetic about anything it is this — an astral blanket of gossamer, and, nestled within, vast arrays of gaseous space dust, filaments of light in reds and browns, yellows and blues. The majestic dome of the firmament. The heavens. Space, the final frontier, and all that.

Neither Marvin nor Dara nor Bennie had ever witnessed anything like it, not even at the planetarium, not even in Circle-Vision-360 or IMAX … not even in their wildest dreams. Bennie, in fact, gasped. Not the sort of gasp you gasp when you discover your cell phone battery went dead or you just stepped in a pile of dog poo, but the sort of gasp you gasp when you look out a window and discover you really *are* drifting millions of miles from the gravitational pull of any celestial object, let alone the one on which you've spent the whole of your Earthly existence.

Marvin remembered reading there were something on the order of 10^{12} stars in the galaxy and that there were something on the order of 10^{12} galaxies in the universe, that for every grain of sand on Earth, there were hundreds (thousands?) of stars in the Milky Way galaxy alone. *For every grain of sand.* Thousands. Of *stars.*

Marvin, Bennie and Dara stood transfixed.

And stood transfixed.

And stood transfixed.

"That right there?" Bennie finally managed, not taking his eyes off of it, even to blink. "That right there is frickin' *ginormous.*"

How long they'd stood there Marvin didn't know, but he found himself feeling — considering the vast expanse of the galaxy (of perhaps the universe) that loomed before them — very small and inconsequential.

Dara must have felt it, too, because she said, "I feel like a pill bug must feel when he looks up to the treetops."

Marvin nodded.

Bennie nodded, too, but he apparently was a little less enchanted. "They're gonna frickin' boil our brains, yo. That chef dude's fattenin' us up for soup. They're gonna liquefy our bones and drink 'em out of our skulls. That frickin' *thing* in the kitchen's gonna make eyeball-soufflé out of us."

Dara touched him on the shoulder. "They're not going to boil our brains."

"I don't know," Marvin said, suddenly feeling like something he had no word for but which, if he were able to look it up, meant their destinies were being decided by someone else. "They might."

Which was when the three of them realized that standing on this side of a door marked REGINALD T. FOGGBOTTOM, ADMINISTRATOR, probably wasn't the smartest thing in the world. Foggbottom could walk in any minute. Or Waddell or Flöckenheimer, or even Winston the opossum-tailed goon. Or worse {~shiver, gag, heave~} Geraldine Fitzsimmons. And so, the smartest thing to do at this point was to quietly close the door marked REGINALD T. FOGGBOTTOM, ADMINISTRATOR, and head down the hall. Which is what they did.

Dara and Bennie did anyway, because it was somewhere down the hall's grating pinkness that they realized Marvin was not with them.

For a second it really did feel like an episode of "Danger Dawg" — when Danger, ever the bumbling bundle of nerves, turns to find his lovely assistant Tammy Truesdale had disappeared into the shadows of the haunted mansion, or warehouse, or Egyptian tomb, or bat-filled cave, or other such dark, dank, and spooky place.

Back to the door marked REGINALD T. FOGGBOTTOM, ADMINISTRATOR. A quick peek over their shoulders and then inside found Marvin running a hand along the wall behind Foggbottom's desk. "Come look at this," he called quietly.

You couldn't see it right away. It was hidden among the mahogany wall panels behind Foggbottom's desk, where earlier Marvin had caught a glimpse of something — something his brain hadn't yet registered. It wasn't until they'd left and he replayed his mental inventory of the room did it pop up — a vague sense of something he couldn't put his finger on.

So he'd gone back to find it. "It" turned out to be a small gap between two wall panels, like a door that hadn't been quite closed.

By the time they stood at the secret mahogany panel, Bennie had decided he didn't care what was behind it. And why should he? He didn't have a blood-sugar problem at the moment. And even if he did have a blood-sugar problem and there *were* an apple on the other side of that panel, which there probably wasn't, no way was he interested. One opossum-tailed goon for the night was enough, thank you very much. He'd just as soon go back up to the dorm and wait this thing out. Maybe even wake up in the morning and find it was all some kind of elaborate joke, ha ha.

"Fine," Dara told him, "you wait here in the dark with the creepy-ass masks and the shrunken heads and the dead knight. We're goin' in." She pushed at the panel. It creaked, Danger Dawg style.

Beyond, another room. And — go on, guess — dark or pink? Dark. Marvin flicked on the light switch. Which made the room — go on, guess again — pink. It wasn't big by any standards, but big enough to hold, in a snug sort of way, the following: a divan, a chair, a wardrobe, a hat-rack, and a small table upon which sat a vase of lilies. Pink lilies. And pink vase, carpet, hat-rack, upholstery on the divan and chair, and of course the satin-striped walls.

"It's Barbie's dressing room," Marvin whispered.

"It's not *all* pink," Dara added in a whisper. She nodded at the sizable wardrobe at the rear. The wardrobe, I am pleased to report, was white.

All of which, Bennie apparently decided, was not in the least bit scary. Which was why he ended up being the first one through the dressing room door. And, deciding in a few short steps he was not going to come 39.4 light years from Earth without opening the only thing in the room that could be opened, reached for said wardrobe and, with a creak of its hinges, looked inside.

Now you may not be personally familiar with a wardrobe other than reading about one in thinly veiled religious allegories posing as children's books or seeing one in the accompanying Hollywood movies. But once upon a time every home had one, before people came up with the good sense to build closets (including the "water-closet," which you no doubt recognize as the turn-of-the-century euphemism for "we've moved the crapper inside").[57]

Not all wardrobes lead to lions and witches. Most wardrobes, by definition ("ward," as in "keep"; "robe," as in "robe") lead to ... robes. And of course other sorts of attire such as suits and ties and jackets and shoes. As did this one. As a matter of fact, this one, at the back of the hidden room behind Foggbottom's desk, was filled with quite a collection. Which Dara proceeded to rifle through like a seasoned clothes horse, which, it goes without saying, she wasn't.

Naturally, a few seersucker suits and smoking jackets were expected in Foggbottom's wardrobe, but a blue satin dress certainly was not. Nevertheless, there it was. Dara held it out on its hanger like she'd found a soggy head of lettuce in the dishwasher, which is why she said, "Ew!"

Marvin was suddenly hit with the sick feeling that Reginald T. Foggbottom and Geraldine Fitzsimmons were {~*choke, heave, gag*~} lovers, something he couldn't fathom on any level. And when Dara tossed aside some ties and belts and pulled open the first wardrobe drawer, this nauseating theory still did not go away. Because it was from this drawer she produced a pair of pointy blue glasses. Not only that: two wigs. One

---

57> We haven't had an aside for a while, so let me point out that a euphemism is a word or phrase that's substituted for another word or phrase that society feels is unpleasant or unsavory. [See: "Effin," "Freakin'," "Frickin'," "Farkin'," etc.] "Euphemism" comes from the Greek, "euph-mismos" meaning "sounding good" and "pheme" meaning "speech," meaning "this sounds a lot better than that other thing that bothers people so much." No doubt you've heard dozens in your lifetime ("passed away" instead of "died"; "collateral damage" instead of "dead civilians"; "Spend more time with my family" instead of "they fired my ass"; "Commander-in-Chief," instead of "George W. Bush," et al.) Interestingly, bodily functions chalk up the most euphemisms ("indisposed," "dropping the kids off at the pool," "draining one's lizard," "blowing chunks," "making gravy," etc.), because, after all, what's more unpleasant and unsavory than human biology? (And don't say "France.")

was that of wild unkempt white hair, the same wild unkempt hair Marvin
had last seen poking its way over Foggbottom's newspaper, and the other
was of the blue-grey variety, the hair pulled back into a bun by a series of
hair clips.

"Holy crap," Dara exclaimed. "They're doin' each other." She had come
to the same {~*gag, heave, choke*~} conclusion Marvin had. She looked like
she'd just taken a swallow of vinegar.

Bennie: "And they're bald!"

"Then what would *this* mean," Marvin asked, holding up an oversized
red T-shirt (still, I might add, with tartar sauce stains on the front). "It's a
three-some?"

Marvin then pulled out of a second drawer a rubber bald cap
(emblazoned with a "birthmark" in the unquestionable shape of Bhutan).
They took a moment to process this (not that the birthmark was in the
shape of Bhutan, because they really weren't familiar with the shape of
Bhutan, the other stuff).

"See?" Bennie said. "Bald."

Their eyes shifted from wig to wig, seersucker suit to blue satin dress,
red T-shirt to bald cap.

Dara held out a glue-on handlebar moustache like it was a dead spider.
"Are you thinking what I'm thinking?"

Marvin: "That Skylar Waddell and Reginald T. Foggbottom—"

"—are *it?*"

"When you think about it," Marvin mused, "it *was* a little weird."

"Whadya mean *it?*" Bennie wanted to know. "*It* what?" He looked
back and forth between them. "Wait! Crap! You guys are saying Foggbottom
and Waddell are, like, the same person, aren't you?"

"No, we're—"

"Good 'cause that's messed up. I've never seen, you know, that Simon
Cowell dude and like the *President* in the same place, but I'm pretty sure
they're not the same — HolyCrapAlmighty look what I just found." Bennie
had pushed the clothes aside and there, pushed to the rear of the wardrobe,
behind the clunky black old-lady shoes of Geraldine Fitzsimmons and the

slug-tasseled loafers of Skylar Waddell … was their contraband. (Not Geraldine Fitzsimmons' and Skylar Waddell's contraband — *their* contraband.) Bags of Chee-Zee SpudNuggets and Crunch Munchies and PoppyCorn Lite, Twinkle Bars and Cheese Doodles and all of it. With which Bennie delightedly began to stuff his pockets.

Dara rolled her eyes. "We're *saying*," she said, "there's just two of them."

"Oh fer crap's sake," Bennie mumbled, his mouth now savoring the sweet goodness of a bite of Bunch-o-Nuts, which, if you've ever been stranded 39.4 light years from home is the perfect thing. "Dudes. Take a reality pill. If this is a starship, there's like a whole crew. Captain, ensign, engine room dudes, red shirts — all that stuff. Somebody's gotta *fly* this thing, you know." He cocked his head at the wardrobe. "This place? It's the staff locker room. It's a *gay* staff locker room" — nodding at the pink striped walls — "but it's a locker room."

Dara opened another drawer. "Oh … my … God."

Marvin, who'd dutifully joined in the pocket stuffing: "More munchies?"

"No," she said, pulling out a long yellow-and-green striped scarf. "The bus driver. I forgot all about the bus driver."

"I rest my case," Bennie said. "Staff locker room." He looked back at the mound of clothes they'd pulled from the wardrobe, took another bite of candy bar. "So Geraldine Fitzsimmons wears a wig. So what?"

"And Foggbottom wears a wig … and Flöckenheimer wears a skull cap … and—"

Bennie, looking like he was trying to convince them as much as he was trying to convince himself (after all, two people cannot operate an Eiffel-Tower-sized starship): "Dudes, it's the staff locker room."

Dara shook her head. "Nope. Waddell and Foggbottom. That's it."

Marvin held the white wig in one hand, the blue-grey wig in the other. "Look," he explained, "Waddell: fat. Foggbottom: skinny. Geraldine Fitzsimmons: fat. Flöckenheimer: skinny. And the bus driver … skinny. I mean *nobody's* in between!"

Dara: "Except the chef. He's, like, fat and then some."

Marvin: "Then some arms."

"And tail."

"And teeth."

Bennie pulled open a Twinkle Bar. "What the *hell* are you guys talking about?"

"Think about it," Marvin said. "We've only seen two people at the same time."

Dara: "Foggbottom and Waddell."

"Waddell and the bus driver."

"Geraldine Fitzsimmons and Foggbottom."

"Always a fat and a skinny. A fat and a skinny."

Dara looked like she thought of something else. "And Flinn said his Morning Calisthenics teacher was fat. We had Flöckenheimer, who's skinny."

Bennie stared into the wardrobe, then closed his eyes to concentrate. He stopped chewing his Twinkle Bar, swallowed. "The fats are all one person and the skinnies are all another person? *Dude.*" He flopped down into the pink upholstered chair, grabbed a tuft of blue fauxhawk. "Wait a minute. You mean *Foggbottom*, the head honcho, *drove* us here?"

Chapter TWENTY...

I'D LIKE TO TAKE this opportunity, while we are on the same page (literally), to go over what has been thus established. This is known in the literary trade as "plot summation" which is a fancy way of saying, "The narrator will now remind you what you already have read in case you have not been paying attention and/or have a very short attention span and/or are reading this at the bus stop," and traditionally it hits just about here.

Don't get me wrong. Sometimes a plot summation becomes necessary because the plot is so convoluted no one can make heads or tails of it and the editor's afraid it will languish on the shelf between *The Verisimilitude of Hyperbole* and *Reflections of an Egotist, Vol. XXVII*. [*See: "Ulysses."*] In which case he tells the author, "You'd better explain this or your reader's going to need a lobotomy." But mostly a plot summation becomes necessary just because That Is The Way Things Are Done Around Here so who am I to mess with it.

A plot summation can be handled in a number of ways, all of which, in capable hands, have one thing in common: it is weaved into the narrative so seamlessly that after it's over the reader doesn't even realize he's been told the same thing twice. A character, for instance, might say something along the lines of, "You mean to tell me that after you found Cryderman's corpse you traipsed across the country with a dwarf, a hooker and a carpet salesman, met up with characters of questionable repute, one of whom shot you in the back, that you then escaped from a warehouse guarded by seven masked ninjas, knocked them out, tied them together with dental floss, blew up a couple of dark-windowed Towncars and a Mercedes ... only to find your girlfriend had been feeding your whereabouts via transmitter to Dr. Farfel, your arch-nemesis, before she ran your boat aground in the Caribbean? Puh-leese."

Which clearly is a cheap literary device.

That is why, dear reader, I prefer the more direct approach, i.e., I'm out-and-out telling you, directly, at this very moment, that you are being plot summarized to.

{~*Ahem.*~}

What we know thus far: (1) We know young Marvin has a penchant for doing whatever he wants; (2) We know "ranch for troubled teens" is an outright ruse; (3) We know fifty kids arrived seemingly overnight from all directions on a single bus; (4) We know that after 90 seconds of serious G-force, in all likelihood the building-that-didn't-look-like-a-building took off from the planet surface and quite possibly rocketed our heroes to the Far Reaches of the Universe; (5) We know the kitchen is manned by a culinary brute possessing more than the requisite two arms and two legs one usually finds among kitchen staff, who treats innocent woodland creatures much as he would a basket of mushrooms; (6) we know the staff of the Sandy Rivers Hilltop Ranch consists of one fat guy and one skinny guy; and finally, possibly of the greatest import ... (7) We know Reginald T. Foggbottom has *impeccable* taste.[58]

58> Jean-Claude seems to believe that this last item should be deleted. His position, that tapestries such as the one that hangs in Mr. Foggbottom's inner-sanctum (depicting the likes of unicorns, knights in battle, damsels in distress, etc.), were, to the Middle Ages, what dogs-playing-poker-on-velvet are to the modern age. To which I say: piffle and tommyrot, J.C. You are being a nuisance.

Which brings us up to date. Which also brings Marvin and Bennie and Dara to a point where they have to make a decision. If they really *were* thousands, millions, of miles/kilometers from Earth, what the hell were they going to do? Bennie voted for a good game of pinochle in the dorm, preferably under someone's bunk where they could wait this thing out, but Dara and Marvin seemed keen on finding a real solution. Once again, they sat in the stairwell, heads in hands, with looks on their faces somewhere between "I can't find the keys to the van," and "We're gonna die, we're gonna die, we're gonna die," but a little, if truth were told, closer to the latter.

So what was it? Instigate an uprising? Take over the helm? Blow open a hatch and jettison, without even the benefit of a map, into the vacuum of nothingness? And go where?

It was, indeed, a sticky predicament. And if there was one thing writing about Yolando Plumadore had taught Marvin about sticky predicaments, it was this: you cannot get out of one unless you have a plan.

Which he didn't.

Which was why they decided they needed help. Off, then, to the dorm, to get Kit, Flinn and Harlen. Out of the six of them, surely they could come up with something.

• • •

FORTY-ODD sleeping souls filled the dormitory. Marvin, Bennie, and Dara bee-lined it to Flinn. But it was no use. He was dead away and no amount of shaking was getting him up. He lay there, still as a corpse, looking like a little circus clown marionette without its strings. They shook and poked him for two full minutes with no discernible effect. On to Harlen, who'd passed out in his Mets cap. His breathing was deep and rhythmic — the kind that happens only in the deepest realms of nod — a tell-tale sign it was no use here, either. Again, the shaking, the poking and the giving up.

To Kit's cubicle, then. Here it was the same. They tried whispering in his ear that they'd found the contraband, all of it, in Foggbottom's closet. Bennie even tried jiggling a bag of Chee-Zee SpudNuggets a few inches from Kit's ear, then opened them and held the bag under his nose (Kit's nose, not Bennie's nose), hoping the irresistible aroma of day-glo cheese might bring him to. No such luck.

Somewhere in there Marvin finally wondered aloud what he had wondered not-aloud earlier: "If they're sleeping *this* soundly, who's to say they how long they could be out like this? Who's to say they couldn't sleep for days on end? Weeks even." He looked over the whole room of sleeping lumps. "New group comes in, knock 'em out, get the next group in and so on. Hibernation. Drugs. Suspended animation. Whatever. You don't *need* a whole starship crew."

The three suddenly felt very much out of control. Marvin, in fact, had almost hit upon the word for having your destinies decided by others, but it was still on the tip of his tongue and therefore out of reach.

"You know what? Screw it," Bennie finally said in a normal voice, then, way louder (yell-at-the-second-baseman louder), right in Kit's ear: "Wake up, dumb ass! We're on a frickin' starship!"

Nothing.

Except…

Unfortunately…

A shrill whistle. A shrill and disturbing *loud* whistle. As in Skylar Waddell's shrill and disturbing loud whistle. Everyone jumped. Everyone, that is, as long as you were talking about Marvin, Bennie and Dara. If you were talking about Kit Warnam or Flinn Karneb or Harlen C. Skedics or any of the other forty-four sleeping souls, you would most definitely be surprised to find that after such a loud and disturbing whistle they did not jump. Nor did they groan nor turn over nor twitch nor moan. They didn't even open their eyes.

They slept.

"I trust, from your Very Touching Attempts at saving your compatriots from a Fate Worse Than Death, as surely their fate must be," came a voice enunciating initial caps quite plainly, "you are most probably quite disappointed." Skylar Waddell looked as though he wasn't sure they were following. "You *did* want to wake them, yes?"

The three looked at each other not just like they were most probably quite disappointed, but like their goose was most probably quite cooked, which is a fascinating phrase I will have to investigate further.

"Actually," Marvin came out with, "Bennie here was hoping for a pinochle tournament." He made a point of scanning the dorm. "But nobody seems interested." He turned to his friends. "Okay, guys, it's just us tonight. Who's got the deck?"

"It seems," Skylar Waddell said, "they're not too interested, either. It appears your friends have had enough for the day." And with that, Bennie keeled over stiff as a board, face first, right into Kit Warnam's bunk, like this was as good a time as any to demonstrate how low blood sugar can lead more or less directly to rigor mortis. "This one's definitely had it," Waddell said, poking a finger the size of a wiener dog into poor stiff Bennie's side.

Dara hit the floor with similar stiffness, and frankly didn't look too comfortable there, wedged between Kit's bunk and his locker like a china doll that had fallen behind the nightstand. Only this china doll snored.

"Oh-kay," Marvin let out. He glanced around quickly in case he should fall and hit his head onto something Sharp and Deadly. He backed away from Skylar Waddell, who stood patiently at ease, waiting for the inevitable. That inevitable, of course, being that Marvin would eventually fall as his friends had fallen. The only good thing to come out of this inevitability was that the second before he did fall, some twenty seconds after he'd said "oh-kay," he finally came up with the word he wanted, the one that meant his destiny was being decided by someone else. He came up with it mid-fall, just as Bennie's words — "We're on a frickin' starship" — replayed in his head. The word came as all other words subsided, as his body went limp, then horizontal. It became the only word left in his soon-comatose brain: "Prisoner."

Chapter TWENTY-ONE...

OUR HERO AWOKE WITH A HEADACHE. This particular headache came not so much from the sounds of the dormitory — the flushing of johns and brushing of teeth, the slamming of locker doors, the zipping-up of jumpsuits — as from the inner workings of his brain.

For several minutes, he lay on his bunk, eyes closed, trying to block out the din. Something important had happened the night before; he was sure of it. He kept his eyes shut, trying to remember what he'd done before he'd gone to bed. He only hoped he hadn't fallen asleep just as he'd come upon a good plot point for *Winged Avengers of the Apocalypse*. If he were to count how many times *that* had happened, he'd come up with a very big number indeed. (Marvin was of the mind he could have produced a dozen more graphic novels solely with the stuff he'd forgotten.)

Allow me to bestow upon you an Unwritten Rule of the Universe: *An idea that comes while one is semi-conscious is only as good as the paper it's written on.* If you come upon an idea while you are drifting in and out of the Land of Nod, succumbing to anesthesia, down for the count, etc., and you don't write it down, especially if you think that because of the sheer perfection of the thing, the *obviousness* of it, there would be no need because *there would be no possible way* you would forget it, not in a million years … you will. Forget it that is. Guaranteed.

So it is with nocturnal revelations. I suppose it happens to scientists and economists and mathematicians and choreographers as well, but since I am a chronicler of events, I know it as a fact for those who deal in the written word. Which includes Marvin and his graphic novel.

Like that perfect dream, the one with the intricate plot or the deep and satisfying emotion that was so dead-on, so important to your whole being, that if, upon waking you moved your head, you opened your eyes, you shifted your weight, it's gone like a wisp of smoke … so it is with things that have yet to be written down. Which is why, when Marvin opened his eyes, he did not move. It is also why he forced his eyes shut again. Tight. If a lost idea is to be regained, it must be seen peripherally, not straight-on. At least that's how Marvin saw it. Or, in this case, wanted to see it.

"Dude!" It was Bennie of course, giving Marvin's carefully-not-moving foot a prod. "You'll sleep through breakfast you don't get your ass up in like thirty seconds. The bell rang *and* Waddell's blown the whistle … *twice* already." Another foot prod. A pause. "Yo. You okay, bro?"

Marvin, not entirely beaten, grunted — this for Bennie's sake, so that Bennie, knowing he was alive, would *Leave Him the Eff Alone.* Eyes still closed, he reached under his bunk for his sketchbook, hoping, if the thing came to him, he'd at least have a chance of getting it down on paper. And if it didn't, well maybe, *maybe*, he'd already written it down the night before. Short of *that*, maybe he could trigger it again once he saw where he'd left off.

Head firmly buried in his pillow, he peeked at the sketchbook with one eye. And was reminded that the last thing he'd played around with was some half-baked idea about "plastiloid," a substance he'd come up with during the ping-pong ball exercise. The last page with anything written on it was filled with failed drawings of the stuff in all its iterations — black dotted outline, blue dotted outline, and so on. Marvin shrugged, once again certain that somewhere among his lost ideas was the one that would have brought him fame and fortune.[59]

So, having checked his sketchbook and having convinced himself that his lost idea was just that, Marvin was off to a quick shower, breakfast (not very notable), and Morning Calisthenics, where the M-Z group was surprised to find, sitting at Mr. Flöckenheimer's desk, not the smallish bald-headed fellow who had yesterday given them an exercise in paper dividing, but a large — let's just say it: uber-massive *behemoth* of a man

---

59> On April 19, 1859, Mr. Theodore Lamsvonkle of Schenectady, New York, was issued Patent No. 23,694 by the U.S. Patent Office for a device he called The Lamsvonkle Thought Reconstitutor. In those days, patents were not issued without the submission of working models, the vast majority of which, over time, have disappeared into private collections, museums, warehouses, and the occasional periodontal office. Not all inventions make it into production, you understand, and the only model of The Lamsvonkle Thought Reconstitutor that was ever produced was the one Lamsvonkle created for the patent office.

Which, as luck would have it, turned up 146 years later, in 2005, when it was discovered wedged between a stuffed moose-head and a box of autographed Pat Boone LPs in the attic of a deceased sugar beet farmer just outside of Saginaw, Michigan. Subsequently bequeathed to the Smithsonian Institution, Lamsvonkle's patent model made its way into the museum's 2007 exhibit "America's Inventors: What a Bunch of Kooks."

As evidenced by its name, The Lamsvonkle Thought Reconstitutor was claimed by Mr. Lamsvonkle to have the ability to retrieve one's lost thoughts. *From his patent application:*

"The nature of my invention consists of a series of Coiled Copper Arrays *(fig. 1)* suspended in a solution of mercury, manganese and basalt contained in a 32-oz. Glass Vessel *(fig. 2)* by which electro-magnetic impulses are sent by means of a Hand-Crank *(fig. 3)* directly into the user's Cerebral Cortex *(fig. 4)* in such manner as to restore Memory, Lost Thoughts, Forgotten Dreams, Disregarded Family Recipes, the whereabouts of Misplaced Items (keys, socks, &c.), and similar particulars consigned by the Human Brain to oblivion. Such arrays are so constructed as to easily attach to the cranium by means of two adjustable Leather Straps *(figs. 5 through 12)*."

Tragically, in 1881 Theodore Lamsvonkle passed away, destitute and forgotten on the streets of Schenectady, his invention forfeited to the annals of time (largely due to the regrettable fact that he could not recall what he had done with it).

Note: The box of autographed Pat Boone LPs sold on eBay in 2006 for $1.19.

— who, wearing a stiff white shirt and tight black waistcoat looked much like an Orca whale had somehow managed to wedge itself between chair and desk. (According to the *Encyclopedia Gargantua,* the Orca, or Killer Whale, is really a misnomer. Actually the largest dolphin on … oh bother … if you would be so kind as to look it up yourself, it would save me a good deal of narrative real estate.)

If you leaned far enough to the side to be able to see it (the man was fat, remember), on the board behind the Orca were the words COL. MARCUS HIGGENMEYER-MATHESON, PH.D., printed in tidy block letters.

Under which was printed in equally tidy block letters: HAVE A SEAT.

It seemed Col. Higgenmeyer-Matheson had no patience for introductions. He also had no patience for explaining that he and Mr. Flöckenheimer would be swapping classes every other session, a fact which, if the M-Z group were the A-L group, they would be hearing at this very moment in another classroom by way of a noticeably sub-par German accent.

So. Col. Higgenmeyer-Matheson — once again not so subtly compared to a dangerous Predator of the Deep[60] — rose from his seat. He did not wear a walrus-sized handlebar moustache, but rather a square "toothbrush moustache" of the Chaplin and/or führer variety, depending on your historical and/or comical reference point. [*For both at once, see: "The Great Dictator,"1940.*] Dark hair, neatly parted, doused in hair tonic and combed flat against his orca-sized head, gave the impression that the man behind the desk was a man out of time, not in the sense of "harried" but in the sense of "living in a time period not his own." Which, from his attire, complete with bow-tie, vest, and the aforementioned shirt and waistcoat, one might guess as somewhere between 1865 and 1911. And, as long as we are toying with historical references, if we were to concentrate solely on American references (which, as a matter of conjecture I imagine a certain percentage of us might) we might come upon a vision of William Howard Taft, under whose countenance the *Encyclopedia Gargantua* reads: "See *Orcinus Orca,* family *Delphinidae (Killer Whale)."*

60> [*See previous discussion re: one fat, one skinny. Hint hint.*]

Col. Higgenmeyer-Matheson, having not yet uttered a word, proceeded to waddle his cetacean way between the desks until he stood not two feet away from Marvin Plotnik. Which, if you were to hold a tape measure to your nose, you'd see was pretty damn close. The man waited until our young protagonist, well-nigh hidden in his shadows, looked up, *déjà vu*-like, much as he had done that first day in the offices of Principal Hadley when Skylar Waddell, the Walrus Man, had stood above him.[61]

61> Again, those French. *"Déjà vu,"* from the Greek, literally meaning, "This again?" is the feeling one gets when events presently being experienced feel as though they had been experienced before. This phenomenon can occur at any moment — while biting into a piece of pizza, while waiting for a bus, while sculpting dryer lint into life-size celebrity busts, etc. This eerie and bizarre feeling of reliving a moment is often accompanied by the phrase, "Holy crap, this happened before. And this. And this. Wait up, guys, I'm serious! It's still going on. This is too weird. It's … crap, never mind, it stopped."

Not to be confused with the all-too-familiar (Seriously? Again?) feeling one gets when asking someone out on a date (just after that ridiculous belly laugh) (which is another thing entirely) (but one that I'm sure we are all familiar), *déjà vu* is experienced by almost everyone, in every culture, throughout the world. Make that "throughout the galaxy." If you haven't experienced *déjà vu,* it is only — as will become clear in the next paragraph — a matter of time.

Now you can take this with a grain of salt, but believe me when I say **This is Going to Matter, So Listen Up:** The feeling of *déjà vu* in truth is nothing more than "temporal transmigration displacement," or, more simply and with a lot fewer letters, time travel. Or, if you want even fewer letters, TTD. Granted, it's time travel on a very small scale, but it is time travel.

Some neuro-physiologists would scoff at such a notion, arguing that TTD is the stuff of science fiction, that *déjà vu* is merely a chemical reaction in the brain, wherein neurons are triggered in such a way as to mimic memory.

I say: Poppycock and pig twaddle. If it quacks like a duck, it *is* a duck. If it feels like memory, it *is* memory.

How, you might ask, does it work?

First, some rudimentary physics: No doubt you have seen graphic depictions of how large objects such as planets and stars, because of their size and mass, bend the three dimensions of space, and with them the fourth dimension of time, referred *en toto* as the "space-time continuum," yes? This is usually depicted as a ball nestled in a grid, like a basketball resting on a trampoline, the trampoline representing space-time, and the ball representing a much bigger ball. Of course you'd have to be an astrophysicist or at least have a good grasp of Euclidian geometry or "Futurama" to get the mathematics of it, but that's it in a nutshell.

But let us imagine for a moment that the space-time continuum is affected not only by massive planet- and star-sized objects, but by all objects, no matter their size. Let us imagine that, just as large objects fold space-time on a large scale, smaller objects fold space-time on a lesser (relative) scale. The smaller the object, the lesser the scale; ergo, the less the space-time bending.

Let us *now* imagine one of those lesser scales is the *human* scale. Naturally vis-à-vis the great expanse of the universe this would seem infinitesimal in comparison, but this is what we mean by "lesser scale" so do me a solid and go with it a minute here.

The next time you experience *déjà vu,* take a look around. Undoubtedly you will be caught up in the fact things seem eerily familiar and you will be tempted to go into your usual "Holy-crap-this-happened-before" spiel, but try to ignore that and take note of the larger things, like that Taco Bell or that Hummer H3X or, say, your lard-butt porko sister. If you don't have a lard-butt porko sister, see if there is some other lard-butt person around the house. If you happen to *be* a lard-butt, stand back, will ya? You're upsetting the balance of the universe! (Sorry, couldn't resist. Won't happen again.)

Seriously, things of greater mass (your lard-butt sister), near something of lesser mass (let's say, your brain), affects, on a teeny-weeny scale, the lesser mass. Thus, your lard-butt sister affects your brain. Which, I'm sure you are saying to yourself, might explain a few things. (If it helps you to picture this better, feel free to replace the item of larger mass with any of the following: "iceberg," "dumpster," "M1 Battle Tank," "mother-in-law," "The Brooklyn Bridge," "Stephen Colbert's ego," or "Greenland.")

So where does this time travel thing come in? Let me explain: One object's mass affects another object's position in space-time, right? Your brain, therefore, or at least portions of it, thus affected by the mass of a larger thing (or things) around you, makes the journey through bent space-time on *an infinitesimal scale* into the not-too-distant future, and, logically, sometimes *on an infinitesimal scale* into the not-too-distant past, which is why you can't resist that second helping of ice cream. This is by nanoseconds mind you — fractions of fractions of a second. In this manner, when TTD causes you to leap into the not-too-distant future, because you are looking back at yourself in time, in nanoseconds, you are *remembering what you just experienced,* which, in truth, *is actually happening in the present.*

And if that's not cool, I don't know what is.

Col. Higgenmeyer-Matheson, standing over Marvin much like a mountain stands over a pup tent, looked down upon the lad with a studied eye. Somehow satisfied with what he saw there, or perhaps didn't see there, he handed Marvin a sheet of paper from those he held in his hand. He then handed each of the other members of the M-Z group a sheet of paper, upon which they read:

LIST BELOW,

IN NUMERICAL SEQUENCE,

THINGS YOU SEE IN THIS ROOM.

Col. Higgenmeyer-Matheson then produced a familiar stopwatch, waited a second, and said, "Go."

Almost immediately, pencils and pens started to move. Dara, head down, was dutifully making her list. Even Kit was jotting down something, and so far Kit hadn't participated in much of anything, which meant even he was seriously intimidated. Bennie, on the other hand, spent the first few minutes looking around the room, pen in teeth, as if he were trying to decide just what the best things were to include. But he, too, soon began filling out his sheet with a numbered inventory of items in the room, and in no time he had not only filled his sheet, but had started to write in tiny print around the edges.

Marvin, as you know, hated lists. Especially lists other people wanted. He therefore struggled with a way to make a list but not make a list. And just as he started to write, "1. A plank of hardwood floor. 2. Another plank of hardwood floor," and so on, he happened to actually look at the hardwood floor. Which was when something caught his eye. Something Marvin was more than familiar with. It was piece of Strathmore 400 80-pound acid-free drawing paper, folded into eighths. It had undoubtedly made its way out of Colonel Orca's corpulent pocket. And it was right in the center of the aisle.

Just so I'm clear about the significance of this piece of paper, please understand that Marvin would never — and I mean *never* — rip a sheet of sketch paper out of a sketchbook. He still had drawings he'd done when he was *nine* for crying out loud. (In case something was usable later on? To remind himself that his skills had, indeed, improved? Because he was just, flat out, anal?) So this particular piece of drawing paper couldn't be his. But it meant that someone else at Sandy Rivers Hilltop Ranch was interested in drawing — which was an infinitely fascinating possibility. He even allowed himself *this* thought: Maybe it was even someone he could bounce ideas off of.

Certain this piece of paper was confiscated property, and with a deftness one learns only after years of Hiding Crap in Class, Marvin reached a foot forward, pulled the paper inconspicuously to his chair, and picked it up. And while others were writing their lists at a frantic pace as if a whistle were about to blow at any second — which of course one *was* — Marvin unfolded the piece of paper.

He frowned.

He frowned some more.

There, in his very own handwriting, in 3B graphite at the top of the sheet, was written:

PLASTILOID = LAME = FORGET IT!

Below which, alongside rough renderings of African ceremonial masks, shrunken heads, a reading lamp, a light bulb, an eraser and most interestingly, a contraption of some sort that looked like a cross between a lobster claw and Roggie the Robot's mechanical hands, was scribbled, again in his very own hand:

☐ FINGERS IMMOBILIZED

☐ REQUIRES SPECIAL KEY

☐ KEY LOOKS LIKE SOMETHING ELSE

And:

✱ BEAMS OF MOONLIGHT REFLECT ON MASKS

It was definitely his writing. It was definitely his sketches. And it was definitely the thing he couldn't remember when he woke up. All at once, just like that, in the blink of an eye, a heartbeat, a flash, an instant and other thesaurus-found moments of realization, Marvin remembered everything he'd blocked out. He remembered how the moonlight shone off Bennie's blue hair, he remembered the fauxhawk making its shark-like way through the kitchen and the freakishly monstrous prehensile tail and the ferret/weasel pie and Dara's tap dancing and the tapestry rising and the wardrobe full of disguises. And most of all, most of all, he remembered stars. Billions and billions of stars.

Marvin looked over at Bennie. Surely Bennie remembered. And Dara, too. Surely—

"Stop," Higgenmeyer-Matheson announced. For a second Marvin took this to mean he was to stop remembering, but then realized it meant to stop making lists. Which was easy since he hadn't even started one.

The big man pulled two chairs together at the front of the classroom and set about sitting on both, one cheek (presumably) on each chair. "Now," he said as he straightened his tie, "let us share our lists, shall we?"

A slight and nervous boy who Marvin hadn't yet noticed, up to this point hiding behind Kit Warnam, was singled out. Col. Higgenmeyer-Matheson motioned for the boy to rise, and with a quivering sheet of paper in hand, the boy nervously began: "Twenty-five kids, twelve girls and—"

"Numbered, please," Col. Higgenmeyer-Matheson said.

"What? Oh yeah, um—"

Higgenmeyer-Matheson cleared his throat. "Is 'what' one of your items? If so, please number it accordingly."

The boy's paper stopped quivering and began to shake. "What? No, it's— um—" Beads of sweat began to form across his brow. Awkwardly, still standing, he crossed his legs. You could actually see his kneecaps wriggle up and down. "My list is, um, okay here it is. One. Twenty-five kids, twelve of which—"

"You have two items there already, young man. I believe the twelve should be item Number Two."

"Pardon?" asked the boy, looking lost. He took a moment to think about it. "Oh. Okay. Um, One: twenty-five kids. Two: twelve of which are—"

"Whom," Col. Higgenmeyer-Matheson said in a corrective tone. He looked intently at his fingernails. (His own fingernails, not the boy's fingernails.) "Twelve of *whom*."

"What?"

"Again, is 'what' an item? You have not made that clear. I'm beginning to find myself discombobulated."

Everyone was getting nervous for the poor kid, who cowered at the intimidating hulk like he was facing a bear, or in this case, a killer whale. "What?" the boy barely stammered, his list shaking even more than before. His eyes darted about the classroom, searching for what he was supposed to do.

The big man spread his fingers low, further admiring his manicure. "I tell you what ... when you have decided whether 'what' is an item on your list, feel free to speak up. In the meantime, we shall go on to someone else. You: young lady in the pigtails. Pray tell. What's on your list?"

Ever so slightly, Dara's brow furrowed. "My list has 232 items on it," she announced, scanning her list quickly in case she'd made the same mistakes the boy had made. She cleared her throat. "One: A wooden desk. Two: A pair of athletic shoes. Three: A stapler. Four: A ballpoint—"

"I think it would be best if you were to dispense with the indefinite articles."

Dara looked bewildered. "Articles?"

"Indefinite articles. Yes. You may dispense with them. Please point out

which ballpoint pen you are singling out. I suspect there are a number of
ballpoint pens, tennis shoes, *et cetera,* in the room."

Dara looked even more bewildered until Marvin whispered to her
that 'a' was an "indefinite article" and "the" was a "definite article." He gave
her a thumbs-up. "Be specific. "

"Oh," she said, again clearing her throat. "One: *the* wooden desk —
there." She pointed to Higgenmeyer-Matheson's desk. "Two: the pair of
athletic shoes ... um, Nikes, those, right there, that Kit's wearing. Three:
the stapler ... um, on the desk? Four: the ballpoint pen that — um, the
ballpoint pen ... okay, the one in my hand. Five: The piece of paper I'm
writing on. Um, I mean, I *was* writing on." She went on like this for a good
four minutes. Really. Four minutes. Watch a clock and see how long four
minutes is. It's frickin' *long.* Every now and then someone would groan
when Dara mentioned something they had on their list, too. By the time
she got to "One hundred twenty-seven: The piece of white chalk on the left
of the board thingie" and Col. Higgenmeyer-Matheson seemed to have
dozed off, he came alert, waving his hand as if that were quite enough.

"Next please."

It is here I fully intended to describe the rest of the proceedings, but it
would have gone on for twenty-odd pages with thousands of items named,
from the mole on Harlen's cheek to the blotch on the wall in the shape of
a lizard. A good five pages would have been devoted to Kit's list alone,
which named each of the hairs on his left forearm. Separately. With a
description of each one. I had even written the whole thing out. But I'm
afraid it would have interfered with the pacing of the story and frankly,
given the sameness of each of Kit's arm hairs, it read more like an autopsy
report than anything else. Halfway through, when even I found myself
falling asleep, I tore up the manuscript and swore it would never again see
the light of day. (Letters of appreciation are most welcome.)

At one point, however, Col. Higgenmeyer-Matheson finally did call
on Marvin Plotnik. Marvin had been sitting there most patiently all this
time, and when the moment finally came upon him, he rose with great
resolve. He lifted his paper — the sketchbook paper you understand — as

if to read from it. Not unsurprisingly, there was no list on that paper, not of items in the room — the big man surely knew this as well as Marvin did the second he saw just what paper was in the boy's hand.

But that didn't stop Marvin from pretending there was a list. "I spy with my little eye," he announced, "something black and white." The room, of course, gasped at this, or at least the people in it did, and Marvin looked to the colonel, expecting to be called on it. But the colonel did not rise to the bait. In fact, he closed his eyes. At first Marvin thought the man had dozed off, but it became clear he was listening, as every few items he would gesture for Marvin to go on.

Which Marvin did: "I spy with my little eye … a head the size of a watermelon. I spy with my little eye … a nose the size of a slightly smaller watermelon." He went on this way for some time, describing nothing beyond what sat upon Col. Higgenmeyer-Matheson's own two chairs, which of course was nothing other than Col. Higgenmeyer-Matheson and all of his visible bodily parts, garments and the like.

"I spy with my little eye," Marvin continued, "a pair of shoes that each seem to be as large as the box they came in. I spy with my little eye a pair of shoelaces on that pair of shoes. I spy with my little eye a pair of aglets on the pair of shoelaces on that pair of shoes."

"Stop."

Marvin looked at Higgenmeyer-Matheson as though he was not finished.

"What, pray tell, is an aglet?"

Marvin looked at him as if he were dim-witted. "An aglet? An aglet is that little do-hickey on the end of a shoelace. Are you not familiar with the word 'aglet'?"

Once more, Col. Higgenmeyer-Matheson waved Marvin to go on and stop wasting valuable time.

"I spy with my little eye a man sitting on two chairs when most people sit only on one chair. I spy with my little eye … ten fingers that look like breakfast sausages." At this point, Marvin noticed that the colonel's face had turned a color that resembled not a sausage but a slab of fresh raw

meat. "You know what?" Marvin said in the best tone he could come up
with to address a rump roast, "I'm thinking it might be better to dispense
with the 'I spy' bit. It didn't get a reaction at all and it seems like a valuable
time waster." He did not wait for a reply. "I'm thinking it might be better,
too, to dispense with what I'm *seeing* in the room and describe what I'm
not seeing. Among which are the following" — here he looked directly at
the colonel with a surprisingly steely gaze, foregoing the paper or the
pretense of looking at it — "I do not see a handlebar moustache. I do not
see a pair of tasseled shoes, one of which is missing its tassels. I do not see
a big red T-shirt emblazoned with an outright deceptive misrepresentation
of a ranch that probably doesn't exist in the first place. I do not see a blue
satin dress. I do not see a pair of pointy blue eyeglasses. I do not see anyone
who wears seersucker suits or striped scarves or goes around in a
wheelchair or on a TransWay or sits at a fancy desk in a room that looks
like it belongs in a frickin' *castle*, and I don't see a secret room or hidden
disguises, and I *certainly* don't see a cook the size of a small tank *or* his
ginormous creepy-ass tail."

By this time Col. Higgenmeyer-Matheson, in a rare burst of energy
for a man his size, had bounded toward Marvin like a freight train.
Proverbial daggers shot from his eyes like sci-fi photon rays, which doesn't
go with the orca or the freight train thing as much as it goes with the
starship thing — but he was clearly too angry for a single metaphor. By the
time he had grabbed Marvin by the collar and rushed him from the room,
Marvin was calling over his shoulder,

"Dara! Bennie! Know what else I don't see? I don't see a window!
I don't see stars!"

Chapter TWENTY-TWO...

THE UNIVERSE is full of coincidence. Just as you mention to your buddy that you haven't heard from a mutual friend in ages, the phone rings and it's the mutual friend; for a couple of weeks, every time you look at a clock it's 11:11; you have the same birthday as two other kids at school, and all three of you have the same initials; you walk into a store, pick out a DVD, and when you get to the check-out, you run into your ex-girlfriend who you haven't seen in a whole year, and she's buying the same DVD; you look up something and happen to see, on the facing page (or on an online link you just happen to click by mistake), an answer that is more perfect than the one you were originally looking for; just as you hear the word "syzygy" on television, you look down and see "syzygy" in the book you're reading; for the next week, you see "syzygy" four more times.

We've all experienced it. And if you *haven't* experienced it, you are not paying attention.

Allow me to suggest that perhaps there is more to this than meets the eye. Take, for instance, the following:

- A full 7,842 planets in the Milky Way galaxy are remarkably like Earth (146-152 million km from their respective sun; 12,750 km in diameter, 22- to 25-hour axis rotation, 350- to 370-day orbit, and host to a thriving cosmetics industry).

- The laugh track used in entertainment broadcasts of over 72 million cultures annoys exactly 98.5% of their respective viewing audiences. The other 1.5% are either deaf or possess no ears.

- This same 98.5%, to the person, do not like the taste of cauliflower.

- The length of the lunar cycle on Jupiter's Titan is the exact length of the gestation period for the three-toed slither sloth of Sklee.

- "Three-toed slither sloth of Sklee" is as much fun to say in Mörflaxian (phonetically, "krilel-cronk al-klurken klaad à Kree") as it is in English. Plus, it rhymes.

- 88% of all cultures have a single word for "what're *you* lookin' at?"

- In Glormish, on the planet Firla-8, that word is "butthole."

- There are 11,450 convicted felons incarcerated in the Butte County Correctional Facility in Orosville, Texas, the exact number, according to Rev. Franklin Burmeister III (*The Universe and God*, Bookman House, 1997) of angels on the head of a pin.

- "All the live-long day" means exactly the same thing in six languages on five planets. This is not to say there are phrases on each of these planets that translate to "all the live-long day," but that all six languages actually use the very same words to convey the very same notion. That's out of over 887 billion (with a B) languages throughout the galaxy. There is even a language, Farfuten, on the planet Lymel-7 that uses the variant, "day long the all live," to mean the very same thing. [Then again, the people of Lymel-7 do an inordinate amount of things out of sequence. If you speak Farfuten, you can read about the history of this phenomenon in the book, *Nutty Lymellians Those* (Galactic Press, G©14732.3TB).]

- Every culture of every civilization in the universe, without exception, prepares some form of pancakes.

- In 1.5% of these cultures (coincidentally the same percentage who *do* like the taste of cauliflower), pancakes are used as currency.

• • •

NOW THERE ARE plenty of people — some of whom have degrees from Places of Higher Learning — who argue these sorts of things are not coincidence at all but are merely examples of "factorial probability," "serendipity," or "anomalies of statistical analysis." To which the coincidence folks say, "Oh yeah? Bite me."

Why I even mention this coincidence thing is because right about now, as Marvin was once again sitting in a chair waiting to see Reginald T. Foggbottom, unbeknownst to him (Marvin, not Foggbottom), as of course most things are — again, statistically — another person of notable importance was sitting in a chair waiting to see someone at precisely the same moment. That person, you might be surprised to learn, was none other than Mr. Albert Einstein.

Now you might say, as any reasonable person would, that Albert Einstein, as evidenced by the historical record and about seventeen PBS miniseries, is deceased. That he is, to use a classic sci-fi title, "Not of this Earth." (Still not available on DVD; curse the DVD gods!) I agree, Albert Einstein is "Not of this Earth." I will not argue the fact. He is, however, as of this writing, also not deceased. Or, more accurately, he's deceased *and* he's not deceased. Or, even more accurately, if you were to follow a timeline, you would say he is deceased, but if you were to follow the circuitous nature of that timeline, in which Mr. Einstein has traveled to a point in Marvin's future, he is not *yet* deceased.

It's all to do with this folding of space-time business, a subject with which Mr. Einstein is well acquainted.

Rest assured, we'll join Mr. Einstein at the appropriate time and place — the very place I might add to which Marvin and his friends were headed, and which, I might also add, so was I — a destination, as INGA so kindly pointed out, not three Earth days away. I'm certain you're now wondering just where the heck Mr. Einstein is, what he's been up to, whether he foresaw microprocessors, the internet or fiber optics, cell phone technology or tongue piercings, whether he still smokes a pipe and rides a bicycle, his preference for boxers or briefs, and so on. And of course why in the world INGA is capitalized. Patience, dear reader. *Experto* — need

I remind you — *crede.*[62]

So Marvin — completely unaware of this Einstein business — having been pushed by the shoulders in a most unpleasant way into the chair opposite Foggbottom's Louis XIV desk by the cetacean likes of Col. Higgenmeyer-Matheson, pursed his lips together (Marvin's lips, not Higgenmeyer-Matheson's lips), put his feet up on the desk, crossed his arms in a "Whatever," sort of way, and watched as Higgenmeyer-Matheson closed the door behind him.

After some time, he heard voices just outside that door, which of course was the one marked REGINALD T. FOGGBOTTOM, ADMINISTRA-TOR.

"I did not," one of the voices was saying.

"You most certainly did," the other voice replied.

"And how is it that I'm the one who's supposed to clean up all the messes around here?"

"Because, my good fellow, that is your job."

The door then opened. In came Col. Higgenmeyer-Matheson (wad-dling in his orca-out-of-water-like way; looking none too happy) and Felix W. Flöckenheimer (wheeling in his guy-in-an-ancient-wheelchair-like way; also looking none too happy). The colonel rushed by Marvin and pushed the secret panel behind the desk. He was purposefully letting our young hero know he didn't mind one lick if Marvin saw him enter the hidden anteroom.

The slight Mr. Flöckenheimer wheeled to Foggbottom's desk, then, pulling at his scalp in a casual, unconcerned sort of way, removed the map

---

62> Please do not assume Mr. Einstein's waiting is a Story Question. I will tell you right now what he was waiting for so you don't go the rest of the book expecting some Big Revelation and then write me chastising letters when it does not come to fruition. He was waiting for his dentist. And dentists are/will be a lot better today than they were in 1953. Not very exciting, is it? The important part is that he was waiting at the very same moment in time Marvin was waiting.

That's Story Question enough if you ask me. "Asked and answered," as my attorney friends are so fond of saying.

of Bhutan and the bald cap it adorned. Under which was more baldness. Only this baldness was covered in short reddish stubble, the kind of stubble one gets from using clippers, not the kind one gets from male pattern baldness. "I suppose," he sighed with an air of resignation, "I don't have to go to the trouble of putting *this* on either, now do I?" He held up the white disheveled wig of Reginald T. Foggbottom, administrator.

Marvin's eyes went to the anteroom door, left wide open, where they caught a glimpse of the colonel as he cast off the subterfuge of black-and-white, removed his Chaplin/führer moustache, and opened the wardrobe. The man made no attempt to hide the blue satin dress as it went over his head, nor any attempt to hide the donning of the tan-toned support hose of Geraldine Fitzsimmons as he inched them up his (her?) jumbo {~*heave, gag, choke*~} calves.

Of course Col. Higgenmeyer-Matheson *was* Geraldine Fitzsimmons. And Skylar Waddell and who-knew-who-else, and Marvin *knew* Col. Higgenmeyer-Matheson was Geraldine Fitzsimmons and Skylar Waddell and who-knew-who-else, and Skylar Waddell knew he knew it, and Marvin knew he knew he knew it, and Reginald T. Foggbottom, now unmasked as his stubble-headed self, knew they all knew what they knew as well. Which is why, as Marvin now sat before him, Reginald T. Foggbottom did not bother with the pretense of disguise.

The bent-over, shaky bearing of "Flöckenheimer" had given way as Foggbottom sat erect, lit a cigar, and scratched at his stubbled scalp. "I must say," he said, "I am none to happy. Our circumstances were not to be announced until we reached final orbit. It's in the rule book and everything. We cannot course correct. Not at *this* point anyway."

• • •

REMEMBER HOW we talked about six degrees of separation? Remember that bit about how Gopal Misra met his love, Penelope Hastings, on the Tamar Bridge in Cornwall, England? And how stargazy pie is a dish for which Cornwall is famous? And that Winston prepared stargazy pie right there on the starship? And remember how those things were previously relegated to the digressive arena of tiny type at the bottom of the page (or, for you e-book readers, relegated to hyperlinks)? Watch now as they migrate from irrelevance to relevance, i.e., into the main text, meaning *you should have read the damn footnotes like I asked you to; I wasn't fooling around.* But also meaning it's time to reveal some pretty uncanny connections:

- The reason **Penelope Hastings' father** spent the good part of a quarter-century in Central America (where he came down with a nasty case of gout, remember?) was because he was working with other archeologists (and aforementioned men with machetes), helping to unearth the great Maya ruins of **Palenque**. [*See: "Great Rogullian Way-Station of Earth."*]

- Professor Hastings, never trusting in doctors again, in 1998 teamed up with none other than Professor **Leonard R. Pipswaddle,** he of Nielsen-bashing fame, to co-author a best-selling and scathing critique of the American healthcare system entitled *Ouch, That Not Only Hurts My Appendix, It Hurts My Wallet.* (Ramshackle Press, 1998).

- The syringe that was mistakenly used to relieve Professor Hastings' gout was manufactured by **Kraff-Whiley,** the same company that made the kilowatt-hungry **LaserX3000**, the failure of which caused the North Tewksbury, Massachusetts, blackout of 2003 (which in turn caused the shooting death of retired shoe salesman **Frank Lukenbill.**) [*See: "Butterfly Effect."*]

- **Frank Lukenbill** once sold a pair of hiking boots to Jeremy Lamsvonkle, great-grandson of **Theodore Lamsvonkle,** inventor of the Lamsvonkle Thought Reconstitutor.

- Twenty years later, armless cobbler (not a pun) **Gopal Misra** repaired those very same hiking boots when Mr. Lamsvonkle III was on a sight-seeing trip to Dharamsala, India.

- **Gopal Misra** was also once asked to sew the likeness of a **walrus** onto a woman's leather bag. The woman, as luck would have it, was the second-cousin, once-removed — remember now, I am not making this up — to Gerard Kesey, the man who delivered the **live chickens** to Marvin's high school. [*See: "Skylar 'The Walrus Man' Waddell"; "Chicken Ordering Scheme"*]

■ Gopal's son, **Sunil Misra,** who as a boy would wave to **the Dalai Lama,** grew up to be the Indian attaché — again, not making this up — to **The Kingdom of Bhutan.** [*See: "Flöckenheimer, Skull Cap"; "'Winged Avengers of the Apocalypse,' Bhutanese Monks"*]

• • •

SEE JUST HOW PERMEATING this connection business is? I'd draw you a chart, but frankly right now I don't have the time. (Perhaps at some point I will post it online.)

So, what do we have here? Let us review, shall we?

We have coincidence. We have six degrees of separation. We have the butterfly effect. And we have a lot of other things I won't go into, things that number in the tens of thousands and have a bunch of security clearance issues, but trust me when I say they get way complicated and require a lot of math. When taken together, these phenomena all add up to one thing, and one thing only…

Allow me to bestow upon you a Great Truth … the Big Kahuna of Unwritten Rules of the Universe. And this one you can take to the bank. Ready?

Everything is connected to everything.

Let me repeat that and put it in bold print and capital letters so you can truly appreciate it:

EVERYTHING IS CONNECTED TO EVERYTHING.

It may be by six degrees or one degree or 752 degrees. Doesn't matter. One, six or 752, the fact is that if you are aware that everything is connected to everything, and if you were to somehow be able to track it and, for want of a better word, to "operate" it, you could make profitable use of it. (Which is why, when I mentioned that "take it to the bank" thing four paragraphs back I wasn't kidding.)

And this is what, in turn, Reginald T. Foggbottom, sitting now stripped of all disguise in all his red-stubble-haired glory, tried to convey to Marvin Plotnik. That is, by way of example: "If I explained this to your great-great-grandparents," he began, "or even your great-grandparents," he went on, "or even, I'm afraid, your grandparents," he added, "they might have had a harder time with it. The advantage you have is that you're quite accustomed to this Internet business, and that, by far, is the best analogy we've found yet. Kudos on that one. We used to rely on The Fishing Net Analogy, but it is far more convoluted and frankly, far more of a stretch. That was followed by the Map of London Analogy, The Human Body Analogy, the Military Industrial Complex Analogy, and so on, until, at last, we have the Internet Analogy, which is the best by far, believe me. I mean, after all, it's called a web, is it not?"

Marvin nodded. "O...kay," he conceded, after which, thinking Foggbottom might be one of those people who need you to repeat what they said or they will not believe you heard them, added, "A web."

"Good," Foggbottom nodded. "Now I need to make this quick because we haven't much time." He looked at his watch then directly at Marvin. "I needn't remind you how every piece of information on the web is connected to another piece of information, and so on, through servers and personal computers and all that."

He waited for a nod from Marvin, got instead a look that said, "duh," and pressed on. "Okay then. Now. Keep that 'web' business in mind while I belabor the point. To wit: If you were to take an item, say this desk lamp, and connect it to another item, say that coat of arms ... *INGA! If you would please demonstrate for Mr. Plotnik...*"

A familiar sultry voice came over the P.A. system. "I would be most happy to," the voice replied. A narrow beam of light — picture the neon-green precision of a laser — shot from the desk lamp to the coat of arms on the far wall. Then: "Hair-care Tip No. 31: When wet, a comb is the proper tool; when dry, the preference is a brush. Be careful not to over-brush or you will damage the follicle."

Marvin crooked a thumb over his shoulder. "You have *got* to tell me what it is she's got about, you know, hygiene."

"Ah," Foggbottom said. "This ship was originally built for the Pyrsnykis. And the Pyrsnykis, as you are well aware, are quite the fastidious breed. You know the old saying, 'Give a Pyrsnyki an inch, and they'll clean it.' Now INGA, if I have this right, is short for Integrated Navigational ... what is it now? ... Guidance Assistant. But when she was built for the Pyrsnykis, INGA was short for Integrated Navigational *Grooming* Assistant. I know it's a bit irritating, but try as we might, we have yet been able to program it out of her. Good thing, if you ask me. Some months ago I almost left the ship completely unaware I was still in my sleeping clothes. INGA saw to it I didn't embarrass myself. She would not unlock the hatch until I had looked down to find I had no pants." He laughed at the thought of it. "It would have been quite the scene—"

"It's in English."

"—in front of the ... I beg your pardon? It's in English?"

"INGA. The acronym. It's in English. They speak English, these Pyrsnykis?"

Foggbottom looked utterly surprised. "Is it? It's in English?" He thought for a second. "Integrated Navigational ... Why it is, isn't it? Hmmm. That *is* peculiar. I hadn't noticed. I have some trouble differentiating languages from time to time." He pointed to his mouth. "Which is this?"

"English!"

"Ah yes. Well done. Anyway, it would have been quite the scene for me to appear before the United Nations in my night shirt, don't you think? I mean, just imagine! They'd have laughed me all the way back to Istanbul. Thank goodness for programming glitches, that's all I can..." — scratching his stubbled scalp — "I suppose it's in English because the Pyrsnykis speak English. That must be the reason for it. Now if you were to ask me why the Pyrsnykis speak English, that I cannot—" He caught himself and tapped the desk in a "Let us keep focused here" sort of way.

"Now. If you were to connect this item to other items in the room..." The beam from the desk lamp to the coat of arms was then joined by other precise neon-green beams emanating from the desk lamp and connecting to more items in the room — the suit of armor, the tapestry, the globe, etc.

"And if you—"

Just as a beam hit the bear-skin rug, something darted out of the bear's open mouth. It bolted across the floor with the speed of a Xerqipi subterranean morphlinbeast, which, according to *The Encyclopedia Gargantua* is the third-fastest animal, galaxy-wide, on record. (The fact was, this thing that darted across the floor was the *fifth*-fastest animal on record, but Marvin would have no way of knowing that. Not for another three paragraphs anyway.)

In its fifth-fastest-animal haste, it brushed the back of Marvin' leg.

"What the—" he yelped, springing out of the chair. "That a rat?"

Foggbottom was busy lighting a cigar. "Ah," he said between puffs. "I believe that's Pookie." He looked at his watch as if his schedule, though now completely compromised, would just have to wait. "Skittish, isn't she? And fast, too. Fifth-fastest animals on record you know, galaxy-wide. But as I say, skittish." (By comparison, the cheetah, considered the fastest land animal on Earth — clocking in at speeds of 120 km/h, (approximately 75 mph) — ranks *thirty-fourth* on the Fastest Animal in the Universe scale, a virtual tie with a creature of your planet: the American female shopaholic at the grand opening of a Nordstrom shoe outlet.)[63]

Had Marvin not seen scampering somethings from the moment he got on that bus, he would have paid it no more notice than a rush of air. The thing was just that fast.

"Come, my little angel," Foggbottom called. "Come on to daddy. It's okay. The scary ol' light won't hurt you. C'mon, baby."

In a flash Pookie was in his arms, clearly not accustomed to beams of green light hitting her hiding place. A furry little round thing not eighteen centimeters in diameter (approximately seven inches), Pookie shook like a chihuahua. Foggbottom held her to his chest, stroking her soft black-and-white fur. "There's my girl," he mewed and cooed. "There's my little Pookie-poo."

63> "*All* the jokes can't be good. You gotta expect that once in a while." — Groucho Marx, *Animal Crackers*, 1930

Marvin's face scrunched into the shape of something that had just heard the gayest name in its life. "Pookie? You named your ferret Pookie?"

Foggbottom corrected him: "Favarian ring-tailed skerlish." He gave Pookie's little ears a rub. "Though it's all but impossible to see her ringed tail. And yes, her name is Pookie. *Yes it is, isn't it, my love?*" (This last part, of course, directed at Pookie, not at Marvin, in exactly the sweet syrupy tone you're imagining.) He patted Pookie's back, whispering names like "baby-cakes" and "fluff muffin" and "honey bunny," and burying his nose deep into her thick soft coat. Clearly he was no longer concerned with time constraints. Nothing, it seemed, would come before Pookie, whose shaking had now calmed to an occasional shudder, although that's probably too long a word for it.

"I can see the resemblance to a hedgehog perhaps," Foggbottom said. "That's the closest thing you might relate to." (Bennie had called that one right.) "She's a bit of a rascal ... *isn't she, my sweetness? Yes she is. Yes she is.*" (Ditto on the syrup.) He held Pookie to his chest. "She does like to run away, this one. And, I'm afraid, to steal things. *Doesn't she like to steal things? Yes she does. Yes she does.*"

Marvin bit his lip at this embarrassing display.

"You've already found her cache of contraband," Foggbottom said. "Thank you, by the way, for taking it all back. Cheese Doodles do not agree with her delicate system, I'm afraid. *Do they, my sweet? No, they don't. No, they don't. We don't want the widdle tummy upset. No, we don't.*"

Little Pookie made a low and curious sound, much like a cross between the coo of a pigeon and the purr of a cat. Then came a clicking noise as she turned and snuggled her nose deeper into Foggbottom's arms, cooing her way into the folds of his clothes before twisting onto her back. Four stubby pink legs wiggled adoringly in the air, her little spotted belly squirmed for pets, and a few belly rubs later she was closing her eyes, cooing and clicking tiny fur-ball grunts of ecstasy. There she stayed, nestled into Foggbottom's lap like it had all the warmth of a feather pillow, and in return, Foggbottom whispered sweet nothings into her pointy little ears.

Marvin had to admit she was pretty darn cute. "What is she again? A smerlish?"

"Skerlish," Foggbottom said as he caressed her tiny ears. "With a K. Favarian ring-tailed skerlish. From the island of Favara. On Pog."

Now if Marvin had just spoken up at that very minute, had mentioned he'd seen her kind before, five of them in fact, just that once, and that they were pretty busy screaming that terrible scream, what with being shoved into a 425° oven at the time, and if Foggbottom had only known about Winston's aspirations in the Sixteenth Annual Greater Kilgorian Festival of Feasts and Starship Exposition, particularly in the Master Pie Baking Competition, and if only he'd known the competition was being held the very next day (Earth time, natch) … the next few hours might have gone differently (and we'd be 97% through our story arc, not 67%).

But Marvin hadn't spoken up, hadn't known he was supposed to, and short of traveling back in time and fixing the oversight — which was, I'm telling you, still possible at this point — they were destined to let the day play out, and I was destined to continue describing what happened next…

Which was this:

Col. Higgenmeyer-Matheson — or should I say Skylar Waddell — now fully transformed into his/her Geraldine Fitzsimmons persona and, struggling like someone who was never going to get used to walking around in women's shoes, came as close to charging out of the anteroom as was possible (given those horrid shoes). And seeing Marvin was still there (and of course Foggbottom, Pookie and the laser-like expository light beams), acknowledged them all with an upturned lip much as one might acknowledge a chronically messy room or a newly found abscess. He/she even made a point of an exaggerated eye roll. After which, just to make sure they saw it, he/she did it again.

Pookie was not so kind. The little skerlish suddenly came to her feet, arched her back, bared her teeth, flattened her ears, and screeched. Having already experienced this in the kitchen, five-fold, Marvin had thought he

was ready for it, but it bore into his spine like giant fingernails on a pro-
portionately giant chalkboard.

Foggbottom tried to soothe his little darling. "There there, pumpkin,"
he murmured, petting her back in long comforting strokes. "It's only our
dear Geraldine Fitzsimmons, who at this moment is *late for Mid-morning
Mechanics*. As soon as she stops ignoring her duties, everything will be
just fine. *Yes it will, my little Pookie-woo. Yes it will.*"

At this, Geraldine Fitzsimmons didn't look bristled in the least. She
didn't even blink. She did, however, make a point of stopping by the door
on her way out and tapping her toe a few times as though, once again, she
was putting up with the most absurd things.

"In case you're interested," she said, not hiding the contempt, "the
anomaly is still in play. As soon as we break for lunch, *I'm* headed down to
fix it." Here she showed Foggbottom a wrench. "Otherwise," she said,
"oh never mind. If you feel a jolt, it's me tinkering with the manifold." She
took another step toward the door, then, looking back at the green lights,
added, "Why you have to waste INGA on these ridiculous presentations
is beyond me."

Foggbottom watched the door until Geraldine Fitzsimmons was good
and gone, counted to ten, made sure Pookie had settled back into a restful
ball, then said, "Now, where were we?" After a moment: "Ah yes, the
connections! I will hurry this along, Mr. Plotnik, so you may return to
session. You don't want to miss out on Mid-morning Mechanics this
morning. I understand they'll be transferring ping-pong balls across
the gymnasium in the most ingenious ways."

"We already—"

Foggbottom held up a finger as though he was getting to that. "What
if," he said, "this desk lamp were also connected to every other item in the
room? In fact, what if *every* item in the room were connected to every
other item in the room? *INGA, if you would be so kind…*" And all at once
the room filled with a vast web of neon green and his "were's" were changed
to "was's." Now there was so much green web, one could hardly see the
items in question.

"Now," said the administrator, "imagine these beams of light are pieces of string."[64]

Then: "Now imagine you are an insect. Pick your species, doesn't matter. And you want to get from the lamp to, say, that strikingly stylish candelabrum over there. You could walk along the string from the lamp to the candelabrum, or you could walk along the string from the lamp to the globe to the candelabrum, or from lamp to vase to globe to candelabrum, or from lamp to chair to dictionary to tapestry to candelabrum, *et cetera.* You have an infinite number of routes."[65]

Marvin: "Why wouldn't you just walk directly from the lamp to the candle thing? Why even bother with the longer routes?"

"Because," Foggbottom explained, "all routes are not available at all times. Construction, traffic and the like. Now let us say you've picked a very slow insect. Or, better yet, a snail. Even the most direct route, from lamp to candelabrum, would take, in snail time, a whole year."

"But a snail isn't an insect. Already you've changed the criteria."

"My boy, this is for the purpose of demonstration. If you'd like to go back to an insect, it makes no—"

"Well anyway, a year, that's a pretty slow snail."

"Okay, a snail with a ... a limp. Whatever it is snails get, slowness-wise, this snail has. An obstructed slime gland. Typhus. *Whatever.* Now, imagine your string ... Let's see if I— ah, yes, I happen to have a piece of

---

64> You can do this yourself at home with real string if you like. Simply run string from one item to another until all items have been connected to all other items. It looks way cool. [*Note: the author, publisher and their assigns will not be held responsible for unforeseen consequences from this act including, but not limited to, broken collar bones, displaced shoulders, swollen ankles, fat lips, internal and/or external bleeding, shattered light bulbs, broken furniture, injured pets, confused and/or enraged third-parties such as household members, civil servants (including public safety personnel such as fire or police services), or similar.—Ed.*]

65> "Candelabrum," from the Latin, meaning "crazy-ass candle holder." [See also: *pianus accessorus liberaccus* and *creepus hauntesium castleus.*]

string right here in my pocket.[66] And if you were to touch one end of the string to the other end of the string … like *so…*" — here, as if it were a magic trick, he held out the string, touching one end to the other — "… much like you proved in our dot-connecting exercise, you would have no distance to travel at all."

"Yeah, but how can a snail get one end of the string to the other? I mean, he's a *snail*. How can he move it?"

"Not move it, bend it." And Foggbottom crumpled the string into a ball and put it in his pocket. Then, with much panache that would have taken at least twenty manuscript pages and would have repeated text you have already enjoyed in much less space, Foggbottom explained that whole déjà vu, bent space-time lard-butt sister business, and if you have been reading the footnotes you are still with me. After twenty minutes of bent-space-time relativity and a virtual plethora of six-degree-like connections I personally chose not to have bored you with, Foggbottom pushed his glasses low on his nose and looked Marvin in the eye.

"See where I'm going with this?"

Marvin got up and crossed the room to the giant tapestry. He gazed upon the tapestry as if it had already risen and the window behind it again took up the whole of the wall and the millions upon millions of stars shone before him. He waited a good 30 seconds, pushed up his glasses and asked, "So, are we the snail … or are we the dude who crumples up the string?"

Foggbottom clapped happily (startling little Pookie). "Now you see," he chortled, "this is what I love about my job. Every mission, there's someone— Take young Albert, for instance. He was twelve when he came to us if I remember correctly…" Foggbottom smiled at the recollection. "He was a pistol, that one. Why, there wasn't anything that young man couldn't grasp … including, eventually, my second wife, a fact still today I am pained to admit. Ah well, what's done is done, water under the bridge

---

66> I know, weird, huh? Other things in Foggbottom's pockets at the time: a melted after-dinner mint, half a piece of grape Bubblectible gum (used), a small pocket watch, a cigar cutter, his notepad and pencil, and an item that will come in very handy later on.

and all that. You remind me of him of course; that's why I mention it.
A keen grasp of every subject. An inquisitive mind. I remember it like it
was yesterday. When Albert saw *this...*" — Foggbottom reached for the
button and watched as the tapestry rose and the heavens were unveiled
— "... he was simply beside himself." [67]

At this, the administrator wheeled from behind the desk and glided
through the web of green like a deer through fog, or, perhaps, a duck
through water, or some other animal through something else. He joined
Marvin at the window, the cosmos spanning without limit before them.

"Technically," he said, looking into the great beyond, "we're both the
snail *and* the string-crumpling fellow.

67> Did you remember that the tapestry was of a penned unicorn? Did you get a chill as it
rose, the image — a rare and mystic animal unable to run free — juxtaposed against the great
expanse of the universe? If not, do you now? How about now?

Chapter TWENTY-THREE...

FOGGBOTTOM STOOD in front of the giant window. "Of course, I don't understand any of it," he explained. "Cesium oscillators and gamma venting and phlebotinum fields and magnetic induction arrays ... C² chambers, micro singularities ... blah blah blah. I don't know what *half* these things are. Don't have to.

"I just know it's all down there in the engine room churning away. Suffice it to say, thanks to 'string-crumpling,' we don't have to seek out gravity-mass conveyance curvatures or any of that. We carry our own, right here with us." He pointed downward, presumably to the engine room below. "We create them I mean. Our own ... now what would you call them? You know, short-cuts. Portals. Wormholes. Whatever."

"Crumpled string."

"Exactly."

Marvin gave him the look of someone who was being sold a load of Togglenian horg droppings, not that he knew what Togglenian horg droppings were. "So what you're saying..." — in a I've-just-been-handed-a-load-of-Togglenian horg droppings way — "is that this ship, INGA, is a time machine."

Foggbottom's head shot backward. "I hadn't made that clear? Although, to be more accurate, a *space-time* machine. To be even more accurate: A space-time *cruiser.* Level 4. And INGA's not the name of the ship; INGA's the navigational assistant. I thought I made that clear, too. The ship is christened *Grace.*" He gave Pookie a gentle stroke.

"And that's, what, Gravitational…?"

"No acronym, just *Grace.* It's the Pyrsnykis, you understand. Still using female names for ships. There's the *Ginger,* the *Brittany,* the *Sister Mary Agnes Margaret…*"

"And you don't need to travel *to* a wormhole to *use* a wormhole," Marvin said, in all honesty trying to hear it out, just in case. "And you don't have to figure the course."

"My very point," Foggbottom assured him. "It's all taken care of. Programmed and calculated and mapped and scheduled and checked and rechecked." He nodded to the web of neon green still connecting every item in the room with every other item in the room. "From any place in the universe to any other place in the universe. It's even our official slogan: 'Any Time. Any Where.' All I have to do, basically, is turn the thing on. The connection I mean. And set the destination. I don't even have to go down to the engine room." He peered over his glasses to make sure Marvin was following. "Of course it's all, you know, physics … and calculus and whatnot. Believe me, if I don't have to account for all that endless turning and careening and orbiting and bent space and *moving* nonsense, it makes the doing a whole lot easier. Leave the math to others if you can, that's what I always say.

"Of course, once you get near the speed of light you have that weight gain issue, but all in all it's a good system. Otherwise, it's smoke and mirrors as far as I'm concerned."

He turned to Marvin. "I ask you," — as if this were a sore point with him — "does the average driver need to know how to build a carburetor? Isn't it enough to know the long skinny thing makes it go, the short stumpy thing makes it stop? A little bit of petrol and a steering wheel and you're on your way, am I right?"

Marvin pushed up his glasses and pressed his lips. Of course he unpressed his lips, too, because a moment later he was able to say, "And it's all built in. And that's why you don't need a crew."

Foggbottom nodded. "Like the man says, 'it's what's under the hood that counts.' Fact is, I don't even need the *ship*."[68]

Looking back on this moment, by the way, where Foggbottom had just finished explaining the Interconnectedness of All Things, Marvin realized that Foggbottom had patted his pocket. At the time he thought this was because Foggbottom was looking for his notepad to write down that "under the hood" thing, or perhaps searching for his cigar lighter, but it wasn't until later that he realized the man was patting his pocket as if the means to space-time navigation were right on his person. The mention of which I am first to admit might have saved our young hero quite some time. Anyway, Foggbottom didn't mention what he had been patting his pocket for, and Marvin didn't ask, and it's just one of those little things that can add a few thousand words to a narrative.

By now Foggbottom's eyes had set themselves far off into the heavens. He had a look on his face Marvin had not yet seen. Pensive, perhaps.

"In case you're interested," the administrator pointed out, "that's where we're going. Right about … there." He aimed his cigar in a more or less easterly — for want of a better term — direction.

Marvin squinted into the void. "So like now you're gonna tell me we're off to Xaxon or Xoltrax or, uh, Xeexix-9. Some planet with a bunch of

---

68> I hardly need point out there are two figures of speech at work here. Since, as you know, figures of speech should not be taken literally, the first, "like the man says," doesn't refer to any one man in particular. It should probably read, "Like some man once said," but doing so would move it from the Figure of Speech column into the Direct Quote column, or at least the Unsubstantiated Rumors column and that would defeat the purpose of using a figure of speech. The second figure of speech here — "It's what's under the hood that counts" — might be used when trying to sell a '66 Dodge Charger with a 426 Hemi, but it also might be used when describing a tricked-out computer system or hoochie skanks on the streets of Berlin. Depends on what you're getting at. Such is the beauty of figures of speech; they're one-size-fits-all!

X's in it."

Foggbottom looked confused. "Xaxon…? I'm sorry, I'm not familiar
with it. Is it in the sector?" (Your narrator is embarrassed to say it took the
normally astute Reginald T. Foggbottom a good eight seconds after he said
this to realize Marvin had been pulling his leg. The administrator wasn't
used to people pulling his leg, especially if the pulling involved the pulling
of planets out of thin air.)[69]

"Ah," Foggbottom said, making a mental note that he owed Marvin a
good leg pulling himself. "No, I'm afraid it's none of those. We're headed
home, my boy. Or, rather, it *was* home. And it doesn't have any X's; at least
not the last time we saw it." Pookie squiggled in his lap so he gave her little
ears a little rub. "Mr. Waddell and I have been off on one mission after
another for so long it's hard to call any place home these days." The pensive
look returned and he stared into the distance, as if he were replaying these
missions of his.

Marvin stared off into the void as well. He was still trying to digest
this concept of a portable wormhole.

Foggbottom, breaking the reverie: "Let me give you a piece of advice."
He caught Marvin's reflection in the thick glass of the window. "If some
day you're sent halfway across the universe to a place with very few things
you hold dear —Major League Marbury, etc. — you would be wise to heed
the following: Make the best of it. Find something worth pursuing while
waiting out your stay. A hobby. An outside interest. For me I have found
three things to occupy my time: my lexicon of phrases, my collections…"
— motioning to the things in the room — "…I'm particularly fond of that
globe by the way. It's a Belladini. *Famous* Italian map maker. Got it a number of missions ago from an ill-tempered antiquities dealer in Barcelona

---

69> Again, figures of speech. Why pulling a leg vs. pulling any other body part would imply
playful deception, and why air would have to be thin for something to be pulled out of it is not wholly
clear. [These phrases of course can be found in *Reginald T. Foggbottom's Dictionary of Peculiar
Expressions, Adages, Idioms and Other Figures of Speech (English)*, available soon at a book
dealer near you.]

who—"

"What was the third thing?"

"Ah, yes, the third thing! Why my chronicle of each mission of course!"[70]

Foggbottom continued: "At least *you* get a warning," he said. "I'm so often plucked from one world and plopped into another I don't know which end is up. One minute I'm in the middle of a Stybergh Procession on Pog and the next, in the blink of an eye ... Hold on. Hold on." He patted his pockets. "I must write that one down." He reached for his notepad and started to scribble. "That phrase would work on so few planets," he pointed out. "All eyes don't blink you know."

Marvin looked out into space. "So this planet of yours ... if it doesn't have any X's, what *does* it have?"

"Well let's see," the administrator mused. "It's got an N and an O and a R and a W and an A and a Y. And a hyphen. I believe you know it as 'HR 7030.' Or some such nonsense. Not you specifically of course."

Marvin laughed out loud. "*Norway?* You named your planet *Norway*? *That's* original."

A wave of his cigar: "Not *Norway*, *Nor-Way*."

"That's what I said, *Norway*."

"My good man. We've used *Nor-Way* long before some 'Earthling' came along and picked it out of a fur-lined hat. We've got you beat by like two *millennia* on that one, my boy. Not to brag, but *mi-len-i-a*. Frankly, we've got you beat by two millennia on most everything, so mind your derision."

Marvin removed his glasses to clean them on his shirt. "Anyway, seems stupid to me. Two places with the same name. And don't think I didn't notice you like totally just put quote-marks around 'Earthling.' Talk about derision."

70> The very words, dear reader, you are now enjoying. I *had* mentioned that Reginald T. Foggbottom and I are one and the same, had I not? I know I hinted at it a number of times. I'm sure, clever reader that you are, you had that one figured out when I first showed up in Chapter Six.

"Oh pooh and balder-bunk. There may be two 'Nor-Ways' in the galaxy — more for all I know — but there are no fewer than *eight hundred and fourteen* 'Earths,' my boy. That's why the quote marks. Wait … make that eight hundred and thirteen. There was that one … *thing.*" (He looked a little embarrassed here.) "Anyway, seems like the whole damn *galaxy's* calling itself 'Earth' these days. It's the 'Justin' of the Milky Way! They're a dime a dozen, my friend. 'Course the others go by 'Earthites' or 'Earthians'. The '–ling' thing's a nice touch, I'll give you that. And by the way, no one's got a lock on originality here. *New* York. *New* England. *New* Jersey. *New*foundland. Like *you* guys ever came up with anything original." (Jotting down "dime a dozen.") "Besides, they're not the same at all, Norway and Nor-Way. Hell-o? *We* have a *hyphen.*"

Suddenly there was a jolt. It only lasted a second, but it was definitely a jolt.

"Ah. Perhaps Geraldine Fitzsimmons has fixed our loop problem. Banged on a few pipes I suppose. Things should go a little more smoothly from here on out. No more ping-pong ball experiments, you'll be glad of—"

"Whoa whoa *whoa,*" Marvin whoaed. "Hold on there, Gramps. *What … loop?*"

[Assume here there was a pause here about as long as a section divider; but not quite as long because they were still in the same room, having the same conversation.]

"Look, it's no big deal, really it isn't," said the administrator. "Every now and then we inadvertently get ourselves into, uh … an anomaly, and we have to … 'Gramps'?" He looked genuinely hurt that Marvin would think he was that old. He was *only* 185. With a bit of a pout, he went on: "Every now and then we have to, you know, *revisit* a spell — which doesn't happen very often, but—"

"Oh fer cryin' … like a *time* loop? Like going in circles? It, like, would've been nice to *know* along the way, don't you think?"

"Not circles. Just circle. Or line segment if you want to picture it that way. Stuck in more than one space-time loop is tremendously unlikely.

Not unheard of, but tremendously unlikely. No, it's just the one. Think of it as a do-over. That's what *I* do." [Popular Nor-Wayan bumper sticker: ANOMALIES HAPPEN.]

Marvin's hands went to his head. "What's the use of a do-over if you don't *know* it's a do-over? Just how many hours have we *been* in this loop?"

"*This* loop?"

"Well yeah this loop!"

"Oh, I'd say ... let's see here ... twenty, twenty-five. And not hours. More like days. Or thereabouts."

Marvin blinked. Then he blinked again. "You're telling me we've lived our first day at the Sandy Rivers Hilltop Ranch — and who the hell came up with *that* one by the way — twenty-five times."

"Or thereabouts. And *I* did."

Marvin had a thought. "We've done the ping-pong ball experiment twenty-five times."

"At least."

Marvin had a worse thought. "And every time I put my balls in my jumpsuit. Uh, so to speak."

Foggbottom: "Every time." He gave Pookie's ear a little rub. "And I *like* 'Sandy Rivers Hilltop Ranch for Wayward Youth, Juveniles, and Young Adults.' It has a nice ring to it. Someday I intend to put it on the cover of a book."

Marvin had to think this through for a minute. Not the nice-ring-to-it thing or the cover-of-a-book thing, the twenty-five-times thing. Now *that's* upsetting — in a I-came-up-with-the-same-frickin'-solution-every-single-time-question-mark sort of way. He was hit by this as one might be hit by discovering he'd written the same sentence a thousand times and didn't realize they were all the same, or discovered he'd worn the same pair of pants for a month, or tasted brussels sprouts again without having to. He felt like a one-trick pony and man, I have got to write that one down.

Pardon a second.

Back.

"What about you guys," Marvin asked, "you and … Waddell. You in
the loop, too? Or have I asked that twenty-five times already?"

Foggbottom smiled. "Listen. If it makes you feel any better, sometimes
you didn't pick basket No. 10. Sometimes you picked basket No. 8. And a
couple of times you teamed up with Mr. Sterlati and Ms. Steifer. So it
wasn't *always* the same."

At this, Marvin had yet another thought. He pulled the sketch page
from his pocket, saw the drawings of the mechanical handcuffs, and
smacked the page with the back of his hand. "Don't tell me I did *this*
twenty-five times." His face curled into a pained grimace as if to say, "This
was the best I could do?"

"You see?" Foggbottom said. "You're upset. This is why each evening
we removed your new sketches. We needed to keep you in the loop, with
the others." (And yes, I'm well aware "in the loop" usually means keeping
someone informed of the situation, whereas here it means the exact
opposite. See what I mean about "one-size-fits-all"?)

Foggbottom went on: "Think about this. If you had discovered your
work and had no recollection of it, why, you would begin to question
everything, even your own sanity. We had to protect you from—"

"So what!" Marvin cried, now not only confused but insulted. "You
told me I was supposed to, you know, rabble-rouse … whatever. That
means *questioning,* doesn't it? *For me it does.* I thought I'd finally found a
place…" Marvin let this thought hang in the air. "Now you say if I question
something too much it's going to, what, screw me up or something? I think
you mean screw *you* guys up, that's what I think."

"I'm simply saying we couldn't risk it. I'm truly sorry. The manual
specifically states that in the event of an anomaly, and I quote, 'All guests
shall be kept blissfully ignorant of the situation.' Regulation M-1774(2)(b),
Section VII."[71]

71> Interestingly (or at least not surprisingly given the nature of the Nor-Wayan Fetch-Haul
program and its propensity toward loops), the very same regulation appears in Regulation G-2117(3)
(a), Section V and Regulation WZ-1447(2)(c), Section IV. Verbatim. This is explained by the fact that

Marvin unfolded the sketch page he'd found on the classroom floor. "But what if I came up with something, like, something … you know … good?"

"I think that solution you have there is *very* good," Foggbottom replied with all honesty.

Marvin stared at the sketch page for a good twenty seconds. He frowned at the words:

$$\textit{PLASTILOID} = \underline{\textit{LAME}} = \textit{FORGET IT!}$$

He frowned, too, at the rough renderings of the African masks and shrunken heads and at the lobster-claw-looking mechanical bracelet. He stared at his notations about a special key and how Yolando's fingers would be immobilized.

Marvin sat down on the stool by the dictionary podium. It took another twenty seconds until he spoke again: "Let me tell you about my Uncle Cliff. Honest-to-God rocket scientist. For NASA. Then he got Alzheimer's. You know, when he got old? No more rocket science. Eventually, he couldn't remember where he lived or the names of his family or how to make toast — let alone, you know, how to calculate … like fuel consumption ratios … and stuff. I wouldn't even know there *were* fuel consumption ratios if it weren't for Uncle Cliff."

The look on Marvin's face was clear. He thought that must be the most terrible thing in the world — not the forgetting-how-to-calculate thing (although that would be pretty upsetting), the forgetting-who-you-were thing.

Marvin continued to stare at the drawings and notations he'd done

---

the manual was proofread during one such anomaly. It is a mystery, however, that during four subsequent revisions, none of which occurred during a time loop, the repetitions remain in place. This can be explained quite easily by Darwin's fourth postulate in his Theory of Evolution (i.e., "If you come from monkeys, odds are you're gonna have some residual effects").

but not done. "It's like Uncle Cliff must have felt, you know, looking at an old photo of himself? He wouldn't have recognized it, even though he was, like, right there, clear as anything, smiling at the camera." He studied the sketches and shook his head. "And for me, this stuff? It's just plain weird."

Foggbottom looked genuinely concerned, because, of course, he *was* very concerned, and I could go into the whole he-reminds-me-of-myself-at-that-age rigmarole, but this story is about Marvin Plotnik, not Reginald T. Foggbottom. Suffice it to say he could see the boy's pain; and so, after thinking it over, he made a decision. "I suppose there's no reason in prolonging it," he came out with. "You would have seen them eventually, once we got to Nor-Way. Now, with things in flux, I suppose you might as well … Over there, my boy, in the desk. Twenty-four attempts. Safe keeping and all that. Just don't tell the others."

In the time you can say, "Of all sad words of tongue or pen," Marvin had bolted through the web of green and was pulling at the drawer of the Louis XIV desk.[72]

"I must say," Foggbottom called from his wheelchair at the window, "I *have* been thoroughly impressed. You've been quite creative on the *Winged Avengers* front. Very few repetitions. Hardly any at all."

Marvin's fingers explored the drawer.

"And to answer your question, whether Mr. Waddell and I have been in the loop… What can I say? We seem to be immune. It seems, through some fluke of genetics, Nor-Wayans—"

"Nor-*Wayans*?" Marvin tittered. "You mean Nor*wegians*."

"Come now. Nor*wegians*? Does *that* make sense?" The Nor-Wayan found his cigar had grown cold, retrieved his lighter and got it going again.

72> "For of all sad words of tongue or pen, / The saddest are these: 'It might have been!'"
—*John Greenleaf Whittier, "Maud Muller," 1856*

Note how your narrator uses a phrase to reflect the moment, i.e., Marvin's deep-felt questions of self-worth. Weaving in an appropriate reference is known in the literary trade as "showing off" and there is an art to it. After all, I could have just as easily used, "There be varmints in my garments," or "Higglety-pigglety poo," but it would not have had the same effect.

"Anyway, what can I say? We seem to be immune. Which is why we were the ones to conceive the map. You can't expect the rest of the universe to come up with wormhole conveyance systems if from the trying they forget what they set out to do. Without that immunity, it's just one anomaly after another ... one after another. Discombobulating is what it is!

"Why, one time Mr. Waddell and I ran into a fleet of Bijoolian exploration vessels, stuck in the Mingholde Belt for forty-eight rotations. That's *Nor-Wayan* rotations, mind you, twice as long as your own. Recrossed the same treacherous asteroid field 622 times." He chuckled. "You should've seen the look on their faces. Couldn't figure out why they were so darn *tired* all the—"

"Aha!" Marvin cried, raising high the confiscated sketchbook pages. If grasping them to his chest wouldn't have made him look like a total *goober*, he would have done it. Instead, he quickly flipped through the papers; his lips curved into a grin; the grin curved into a smile. Page after page of ideas, all solving Yolando Plumadore's predicament. Some the same, or variations thereof, most not. "Ho-ly crap," he oozed, clearly pleased with what he saw: form-fitting latex body mitts, electro-magnetic restraining rings, balloon-shaped suspension shells, telepathic immobilizers, drug-induced paralysis (no device to draw here at all!), and of course the obligatory watchful goon at the door. Marvin's smile doubled. "It's like finding ... the Holy Grail."

"Only this Holy Grail is of your own making," Foggbottom put in. "The Holy Grail of Holy Grails if you ask me."

Marvin heaved a sigh of relief. This time, the thought of doing the same thing over and over was replaced with the comfort of knowing that when it came to doing what he loved, his creativity knew no bounds. Each effort a different outcome. When it came to something he couldn't give a rat's ass about — like moving ping-pong balls from one basket to another — he inserted his head into the proverbial sand.

And so, while Marvin perused his forgotten work, Foggbottom turned his wheelchair to the vast expanse outside the ship's window. He held the cigar just shy of his mouth. "It'll be good to get back home. Sometimes I think—" He drew on the cigar. "Sometimes I think if only I had just a taste, a bite mind you, of a farkniklügen pie" — the flame pulsed at the end of the cigar — "or a nice glass of gont on a lazy afternoon, I'd be set for the next fifty rotations. But," — turning to Marvin, letting out a thin stream of smoke — "you do without. You get used to it. You even begin to appreciate the things your new home has to offer, the ways of your host planet. 'Course you don't want to go native or anything. One of our fetch-haulers landed himself on Pra'ahGa and next thing you know he's leading a rebellion against the local warlord. Had to fetch-haul *him* before he screwed up their whole socio-economic equilibrium. Why, I myself spent twelve rotations on Marrf before I—"

"Mars?" Marvin asked, at last hearing something he recognized. He emerged through the web, confiscated sketchbook pages in hand.

Foggbottom let out another stream of smoke. "Not Mars, Marrf. You wouldn't know it. Not the nicest of planets. R-class. You know, all that methane and xylene? Wreaks havoc with your complexion, not to mention your psyche. And *breath*. Any fetch-hauler worth his salt knows not to get stuck on Marrf. Ah! 'Worth his salt'! I have to get that one down. I'm coming up with them like clockwork today. There's another! 'Like clockwork'! I do wish I'd begun this lexicon missions ago," he marveled. "It's amazing how much you pick up without realizing it. Give me a moment."

And once again, the Nor-Wayan opened his little notebook. "You might be surprised to learn that on the planet Mörflax a person really *is* compared to the worth of salt," he said, his stub of a pencil moving along the notepad. "Well, not salt *per se*, but granulontan, a sort of salty compound. Once a year, every man, woman and child of Mörflax makes the *tremendously* inconvenient pilgrimage to the capital city of Grangronne where they are weighed on an annoyingly accurate public scale, counterweighted with five-kilogram bags of granulontan. They're then each assessed what amounts to a tax. A salt tax, if you will. I understand a salt tax was quite the thing on your own planet, though as I understand it, they were taxing the salt itself, and not using salt as a …" He tucked the notebook in his pocket. "Well, considering no Earthling has ever encountered a Mörflaxian — at least not to my knowledge — it would be highly unlikely, although coincidental in the extreme, that the English phrase 'worth their salt' derives from the rather literal Mörflaxian phrase, 'worth their granulontan.' Don't you think?"

Marvin didn't know what to think.

Truth be told, Foggbottom didn't either, as he'd quickly lost his train of thought. "Now where was I?" he seemed to ask, noticing the cigar had once again gone cold.

"Twelve rotations on Marff."

"Ah yes, I spent twelve rotations on Marrf." He gave Pookie, still sleeping soundly in his lap, a wistful stroke along her back. "I even came to like the place, got teary-eyed right along with the locals over a Piercing Ceremony or glok-ox gutting. Nasty business, that. Of course I wouldn't want to *retire* there or anything."

"Okay now you're just making stuff up," Marvin said as he stashed the sketchbook pages into his jumpsuit. "You must think I'm a total—"

"Now *your* planet took some getting used to. Odd, that bit about hand shaking for instance, never got used to that" — he winced to make it clear he thought it disagreeable — "but I soon learned the ins and outs of the place."

Now Marvin never had much proclivity toward patriotism (or whatever it's called in relation to a planet) but frankly he felt a little dissed. And what he was about to say in defense of his Fellow Man and the hand-shaking habits thereof, which surely would have taken up a good three-hundred words had he said it, we are all spared because, instead, it was interrupted with a thought. Which went something like this: What if this guy really *is* making this stuff up? What if I'm standing here with some nut-job with a really nice hi-def home theater system, whose only goal here, under the guise of Straightening Me Out, is to screw with my head? 'Ooh, look at me! I'm from another planet! We've chosen you specially to Save the Human Race or Galaxy or Some Other Unbelievable Crap.' What a trope; gimme a frickin' break.

Of course there were the sketchbook pages. Foggbottom certainly didn't make *those* up. It was definitely Marvin's own handiwork. And no way Foggbottom could have pulled off those pods or the serious G-force that went with them. And of course there was Winston, and the skerlish. So, instead of defending his Fellow Man and its hand-shaking ways, Marvin let Foggbottom spout his own three-hundred words on the Hellhole that is Marff, and when it seemed like a good place to interrupt, somewhere around the part about Marff's 'utter lack of a decent wastewater collection system,' Marvin looked out into the void and asked: "Where are we headed again?"

"There, to the right," Foggbottom replied, pretty much done with Marff anyway. Again he pointed his cigar into the great beyond. "Two o'clock. The pinkish one."

"I guess that explains all that pink," Marvin said, indicating the rest of the ship.

Foggbottom snickered. "Actually, that's the Pyrsnykis. Pinkaholics, every one of them. Take a Pyrsnyki into the girls' aisle in ToyLandUSA and they go absolutely bananas. It's downright embarrassing. Every time I've suggested changes, INGA goes into another—"

"And what about that … over there?" Marvin wanted to know. "Nine o'clock." He watched it for a moment. "Closely approaching zero o'clock, like the center of the clock, where the hands meet. Like where we are."

Foggbottom's eyes shot to the left.

First he said, "Uh oh."

Then he said, "Kilgorian warship."

Then he said, "That's not good."

Chapter TWENTY-FOUR...

FOGGBOTTOM SPUN his wheelchair to the door. "As ominous as this sounds," he said, "we really need, as I recently noted in my phrase book, to 'get the eff outta here.' Posthaste, I should think. *INGA! Please check on Mr. Waddell's progress in the—*"

"Not necessary," came a voice Marvin had no trouble recognizing. There at the door, slivers of blue satin showing though green webbing, stood the portly countenance of Ms. Geraldine Fitzsimmons. "It's all fixed," she announced, blue wig slightly askew. "The anomaly I mean. Took some" — she cleared her throat — "uh, *doing*, but we're back in business. Had to put in a new, you know, gamma thingamajiggie. Smooth sailing from here on out. If you're done with your little everything's-connected-to-everything business" — she brushed a hand at the green lights — "a hop-skip-jump and we're on our way."

Even through the web Marvin could tell Geraldine Fitzsimmons had undergone some sort of transformation. She — or should I say he, because let's face it, Marvin knew who she was now — she seemed, somehow, different, though he couldn't imagine in what way. Whatever it was, this *new* Geraldine Fitzsimmons, Bizarro Geraldine Fitzsimmons, who used phrases like "not a problem" and "smooth sailing" — seemed downright human. (Give or take a few hundred pounds.)

"You did hear me say 'hop-skip-jump,' yes? That everything's, uh, operational?" She looked from one of them to the other. "Hop-skip-jump?" Then she looked at the other and back to the one. Then, her shoulders sinking when she saw the look on Foggbottom's face: "What?"

The administrator nodded at the quickly approaching Kilgorian ship.

"That's not good," Geraldine Fitzsimmons said, of course recognizing it for what it was — a ship full of nauseating boil-faced space pigs bent on death and destruction.[73]

Foggbottom: "That is exactly what *I* said. It is, indeed, not good."

"Well that's an easy one," Geraldine Fitzsimmons announced, as though it was decided. "We just put the ol' girl in gear ..." She turned, one assumed, to do just that. And got all of one step away.

Because that's when another voice came, this one unfamiliar and new, from just beyond the open door. This one with a disgusting sort of guttural gurgle to it. "No more loop," it gurgled. "No ... more ... *ship!*"

And with that, the giant prehensile tail of Winston, Kilgorian starship chef, came crashing down. And Geraldine Fitzsimmons, aka Skylar Waddell, aka Col. Higgenmeyer-Matheson and who-knew-else, fell into a heap at the creature's colossal clawed feet, suddenly, I'm tempted to say, bearing more than a striking resemblance, given that he was still clad in Geraldine Fitzsimmons' blue satin dress, to yet another giant sea creature, which I swear to you will be the last of my sea-creature comparisons when it comes to Mr. Waddell because I'm just as sick of it as you are: a beached blue whale.

73> My apologies if you happen to be Kilgorian. But since the Kilgorian economy has long held a disdainful and patently discriminatory embargo of all non-Kilgorian goods, I believe we can safely assume, in all likelihood, the chances of a Kilgorian reading this text is close to nil. If a copy of this tome should by chance get through the strictly enforced — and utterly unfair — embargo, please understand, dear Kilgorians, and I say this in all honesty: this is a work of fiction, and any reference to it being true, "every word of it," is just so much, as we say on Nor-Way, "Togglenian horg droppings on toast." [.ti fo drow yreve ,eurt si ti ,haN :uoy fo tser eht oT]

• • •

"GOOD," WINSTON BELCHED, satisfied with his felling of half the Nor-Wayan crew. Then, seeing the quickly approaching Kilgorian ship, belched it again: "Good." (Only this "good" sounding a bit too much like, "Our ride is here," and unfortunately not at all like, "My ride is here.") Tossing aside the blue-satin heap with his tail with no more thought than moving a pile of dirty shorts, Winston approached the view window and abruptly saluted. Three-fold.

As might be expected, the window had opaqued in a most clichéd way — which is why I said "as might be expected" — and had turned into a viewscreen, three-quarters of which was now taken up by the boil-covered mug of a scaly skinned and god-ugly *clearly* Kilgorian pig-faced eye-sore, this one with a foot-long wiry-haired unibrow, four pulsating-with-snot nostrils, and a lump on his head the size of a small child, who quite honestly made Winston look like a freakin' matinee idol. In extreme close-up. And 3D. Which made Marvin and Foggbottom flinch.

"Hail thee Slag Udyedsu, Grand Commander of the Kilgorian Fleet, Just and Honorable Warrior, Master of the Abyss, Seeker of the Second Realm, Overlord of the Underlords, Quasher of the Outer Dominions," Winston gurgled with a click of his heels, holding his three-armed salute. Then, less formally, "It is an honor to see you, your Slagship. You are looking fit."[74]

Slag Udyedsu yawned, half-heartedly saluted (*one* disdainful hand,

---

74> No doubt you are aware that rearranging the letters of words or names often produces humorous and/or telling results called "anagrams" [from the Greek, "gramma" ("letter") and "ana" ("let's make fun of famous people.")] Anagrams such as Britney Spears: *Yep, Brain Rests;* Stephen Colbert: *Belches Portent;* Charlie Sheen: *Inhales Cheer;* and of course Mom: *mom* (this one being a palindrome as well, but we won't get into that), are easily arrived at with nothing more than an old Scrabble set and a dateless Saturday night.

Why I mention this is that the name of the Kilgorian commander, "Slag Udyedsu," spelled here phonetically, coincidentally anagrams in English as "Ugly Ass Dude," which, should you someday come face to face with His Slagship, I recommend you not bring it up.

not three) and leaned into the lens (the 3D effect of which was that his scaly snout seemed to come into Foggbottom's inner sanctum in a most disturbing way). "Please do not take my time with frivolous accolades, Shar Winston. If your hatch-producer and my mate were not co-hatchlings, I would still be blasting Gygaxian Togships in the Mewithe Sector where I belong. Instead, I am to be baby sitter and taxi service to one for whom the word 'beating' pertains to eggs."[75]

Winston started to protest, but Slag Udyedsu held up a scaly hand shortly followed with another scaly hand. "I understand I am to take you … where is it?" — here he produced a clipboard-like device, pushed buttons with curled and thickened yellow claws and belched a contemptuous belch — to the "Sixteenth Annual Greater Kilgorian Festival of Feasts and Starship Exposition." He rolled his bulging snake-like eyes (they rolled vertically, left-to-right) like he had never heard anything more preposterous in all his boil-encrusted days. "Along with …" — here he checked the device — "… some fifty specimens of Sol-7(3)."

Whom, of course, Marvin immediately recognized as himself and his fellow wayward youths.

The warship commander heaved a monstrous sigh as though this errand were the biggest pain in the prehensile tail with which he'd ever been burdened.

"That's correct, your Slagness," Winston said, standing up as straight as he could. "I am to enter my delicious stargazy pie into the Master Pie Baking Competition, the fifty specimens on board being my secret ingredients. And, as a *secret* secret ingredient? Yams. They will *never* expect yams." Chuckling proudly at this fact, he then belched, "*Mon pâté en croûte c'est un chef-d'œuvre, un pièce de résistance … c'est magnifique!*" which is French meaning, "My pie is delectable, it's the

---

75> The Kilgorian term *"Slag,"* an honorific, can be likened to such English addresses as "Mr.," "Ms.," "Sir," "The Honorable," and, in the case of my first wife's divorce attorney, "No Account Swindler, May She Rot for Eternity in the Deepest Pits of Hell That Lying Bitch-Whore." The Kilgorian term *"Shar"* translates roughly to "birdbrain."

best ... yum."[76]

Here, as if to underscore the French chef stereotype, Winston tritely kissed three fingers — *mwah!* — and bowed his head (a bit of drool exuding from his lower lip). "I have taken the liberty of entering your ship into the exposition, your Slagship," he drooled. "Its win is sure to bring *fläng* to the Kilgorian fleet.[77] Surely you have time for *fläng*?"[78]

From the monstrous screen, Slag Udyedsu, twenty times his actual size, looked down upon the chef (in this case, both figuratively and literally). "What would bring *fläng*[79] to the Kilgorian fleet is to blast Gygaxian Togships!" he bellowed. "Which is what I was doing until I was so *rudely interrupted*."

"But your Slagness, there will be awards! Ribbons! Trophy cups!" Seeing he was perhaps making headway with this, Winston teased, "And Slag Perescu will be there."

Slag Udyedsu stopped pushing buttons on his device. "Perescu?"

Teasingly: "I've heard he's planning quite the demonstration."

If one is to equate Kilgorian pleasure with nose picking, and I assure you one is, at the mention of trophies and accolades and definitely at the mention of Slag Perescu (who had once referred to Slag Udyedsu as a "slaxel-sucking slyzx"), the commander shoved a yellow leathery finger up

---

76> Or something along those lines, which, even after replaying the recording over and over took Jean-Claude three whole days to decipher and Jean-Claude speaks French like nobody's business. My apologies if he got it wrong, but by the third day he was done with it and I can't blame him for giving up, and you know it's not easy for me to compliment J.C.

Kilgorian speech has made lesser men vomit after only 30 seconds,

77> *Fläng:* Roughly, "honor." [*GP's Newly Revised Ultimate Guide to the Celebrated Language of Kilgore (Kilgorian-to-English/English-to-Kilgorian),* 23rd ed., Galactic Press, G©14732.3TC]

78> *Ibid.*

79> *Ibid.*

one of his left nostrils (the effect of which, being that his nose appeared
directly above their heads, was unnerving).[80]

"Quite the demonstration?" Slag Udyedsu repeated with a repulsive
smile (most likely picturing at last showing his nemesis who the slaxel
sucker was and who the slaxel sucker wasn't). "Is that so?" Then: "Prepare
for transfer of fifty specimens to our ship." And, with a second scaly finger
up his other left nostril in yet more unbridled pleasure: "Commence
transfer in—" At which point a Kilgorian crew member whispered something in the commander's disgustingly scaly broccoli-like ears.

"What's that?" Slag Udyedsu sighed. "All full?"

The crew member nodded it was so.

Turning to the view-screen, the commander apologized. "I am afraid
all 127 of our holding cells are occupied by Gygaxian scum. You will
therefore retain your 'secret ingredients' on board your vessel." He began
pushing buttons on another device. "We shall rendezvous at the festival in
twelve cycles. Over and—"

"Wait!" Winston cried at the screen. "I'm a chef, not a pilot!"[81]

Slag Udyedsu rolled his snake-like eyes once more and released a long
and deep pain-in-the-prehensile-tail sigh. "Very well then," he snorted.
"We will put you on magbeam and tow your vessel." Another long sigh.
"I suppose you will need security for your 'secret ingredients.' I will send a

---

80> Thank goodness Slag Udyedsu's nemesis, Slag Perescu, had a cleft palate. Had he not,
he might have been able to recite the entire Kilgorian nursery rhyme, which goes like this: *"In
southern Sluthers, scores of slyzxes slither the slippery slopes, skittering side by side whilst supping
scores of squirmy slaxels, sucking upon their snouts."* (In Kilgorian, it rhymes.)

81> Winston's attempt at humor — a take-off on a popular Kilgorian catch-phrase, "I'm a
warrior, not a barber," which comes from an outdated-but-revered Kilgorian GalaxyNet show and
movie franchise — of course not only sounds ridiculous, but makes no sense to anyone but a
Kilgorian. Other catch-phrases from the same franchise: "I'm an aristocrat, not a monkey," "I'm a
freshman, not a cantaloupe," and "I'm a warthog, not a librarian." Ditto on the making sense thing.
(Look, I don't write 'em, I just report 'em.)

squad of troops to assist."

"Oh no," Winston chuckled. "That will not be necessary. The specimens are presently in deep trance, thanks to my unparalleled" —(chuckle, chuckle)— "culinary skills." Here he polished his nails on his chest because they actually do that on Kilgore.

Slag Udyedsu snorted, "Brok Cragmar then. And that is final."[82]

The commander flashed one last salute, again one-handed, did not wait for the same, and the screen went back to window mode — the stars twinkling to eternity.

• • •

THAT THE GRACE had no holding cell for prisoners says something not only of the Pyrsnykis, who'd built her, but of the Nor-Wayans, who didn't. Neither thought it necessary. The Pyrsnykis, because putting someone in a jail cell not only seemed rude but would wreak havoc on the color scheme, and the Nor-Wayans, because they had better things to do than lock people up.

As the Kilgorian commander had pointed out, however, the Kilgorian warship not only had a brig, but had multiple brigs, and, in the case of the KC-1400 (and turbo-charged KC-1400-S, which Slag Udyedsu's particular warship was), 127 of them. All of which, as he also pointed out, presently filled. There was, therefore, just to be clear here, no place on the Kilgorian ship *nor* on the *Grace* for Winston to lead his prisoners, which is why it took a few turnarounds in the pink-tiled halls of the Sandy Rivers Hilltop Ranch, etc., aka the *Grace*, for him to think it over. But not before he gurgled, "Please to follow…?" in the manner one usually reserves for times of handgun pointing, which this most definitely and most effectively was, six times over.

It's amazing, by the way, how your desire to Do What You Want (e.g., "get the eff out of there" as Mr. Foggbottom so eloquently put it) goes by the wayside with six alien-looking weapons pointed your way. Not wanting

---

82> *"Brok"*: roughly, "Lieutenant."

to learn the capabilities of any one of them, Marvin politely did as he was told. Likewise for Foggbottom, who already knew the capabilities. None of which were pretty.

So they made their way down pink-tiled hall after pink-tiled hall — occasionally ducking the Kilgorian's massive tail as it swept and swung, coiled and recoiled — all three knowing perfectly well that Winston's "unparalleled culinary skills ... deep trance" line would preclude any chance of eating anything he'd offer, including, they'd later discover, the delicious strawberry torte that was presently awaiting one final diner.

Naturally, Marvin was thinking about his compatriots. It wasn't just the space-time loop that had kept his friends increasingly uncurious, he now realized, it was the mac and cheese. By now, lunch being over, everyone was no doubt strewn about the cafeteria like bags of potatoes. Which, if Winston's plans for the pie-baking competition came to fruition, they might as well be.

All of which meant it would be really nice to get to the cafeteria — to Dara and Bennie and Kit and Flinn and Harlen — to wake them up. But then what? At the very least keep their sorry Earthly asses far away from pie dough, that was for sure. But, as I say, *then* what?

And what, you might be wondering, became of Foggbottom's cherished skerlish, Pookie? Don't think I have forgotten about her. Considering she was scared youknowwhatless at the mere appearance of a few beams of expository green light, surely upon seeing a weapon-wielding eight-foot Kilgorian she would have bolted into the duct-work. Especially if she knew her fellow skerlish had been downed like bonbons by this very brute only a few hours before. But she hadn't. Somewhere in there, little Pookie had nestled herself deep into the folds of Foggbottom's shirt and stayed there. Which should be just enough foreshadowing to keep you rooting for her.

Back to our heroes. After a number of minutes, Winston's pace had quickened. He'd clearly hit upon an idea which was why they soon found themselves approaching the double-glass doors at the end of a hallway on the second floor. As they approached the doors, Foggbottom let out a low and worried whistle, the kind one might let out when one doesn't like the sound of this idea.

For beyond those doors was the very room Foggbottom had spent months designing and setting up for his last mission, a fetch-haul run to Serubia Minor, the largest of four moons of the planet R'Anton-Wil. (Don't ask me why it's called "Minor" if it's the largest moon; you would have to go back quite a few generations to ask the guy who came up with it.)[83]

Before I tell you about R'Anton-Wil's moon, Serubia Minor, allow me to describe the planet around which it orbits. This will take some time, as I want to spell it out for you and thereby prevent the future overtaxing of my spam filter with unnecessary queries.

If you are not familiar with R'Anton-Wil, it is located in the galaxy referred to as Andromeda (or M31 if you want to get all astrophysical about it) and is classified as a gas giant. Meaning R'Anton-Wil is covered with dust clouds, in this case a mixture of sulfuric acid, helium, sodium hydroxide and ammonia.[84] Needless to say, astronomers believe it impossible to "land" on a gas giant, as most likely beneath this cover of dust and gas there would be no solid ground, much like the talent pool of "America's Got Idols." But I assure you, not only is it possible, it's preferable, as the outer atmosphere will burn your face right off if you do not get through it with some degree of expediency.

83> I am told by our esteemed colleague and self-proclaimed "proofreader extraordinaire," Ms. Eucinda Princip, that there was indeed a larger moon, Serubia Major, that had once circled R'Anton-Wil some 400,000 years ago. As I am not aware of the existence of such a body, and since Ms. Princip cannot provide corroborating evidence, like for instance *anything in writing, anywhere,* I have asked her to "stet" the paragraph, which is Latin for "leave it the eff alone." Ms. Princip has chosen not to talk to me for the duration of the editing process and has taken to eating her lunch in private. She says this "has nothing to do in the world whatsoever" with our personal relationship — though, if that were true, one would think she would have left her toothbrush at my place. I have reinserted this footnote a total of seven times now. Should you see it in the final narrative, you can assume I have won the battle (or Ms. Princip has returned the toothbrush).

84> Coincidentally the same ingredients in "Appendectomy-in-a-Can."

There's a thin line, however, between *preferable* and *desirable*. Because on R'Anton-Wil, below the layer of gaseous cloud is unfortunately another layer of gaseous cloud. And below that, another layer, and so on, each having scary sounding names, until, eventually, under the umpteenth layer of clouds, absolutely nothing. And when I say "nothing," I do not mean still another layer of dust or gas, or even "a barren unforgiving wasteland of sand and rock and fog and death-strewn hopelessness that is the Skeleton Coast of Namibia," or, say, North Dakota. I do not even mean "devoid of substance," like what lies between a certain hotel heiress's ears. I mean *nothing* — no rivers, no mountains, no lakes, no trees, no under-brush, no 7-Elevens, no sand dunes, no *anything*. Not even a good-sized rock to sit on. It's like a close-up of Quentin Tarantino's forehead. And it goes on and on like forever. So though it may be possible (and even preferable) to land *on*, vis-à-vis the gaseous void one would expect of a "gas giant," it's really not very desirable, which is why R'Anton-Wil is not inhabited. And is also why no one ever visits it. Even for vacation.

Now to the aforementioned moon, Serubia Minor. It, too, is covered with cloud layer, but this cloud layer, some twenty meters in depth more or less uniformly covering the globe and hovering some equal number of meters above the surface, does not have the face-eating properties of the clouds engulfing the mother planet. Which is good. This cloud layer, commonly referred to as "Serubian Bog," is far less toxic. Which is also good. But it does contain traces of sulfuric acid, so it is also quite, shall we say, "stinky." Which is not good. Picture being stuck on the subway during a snow storm with a team of geriatric Ukrainian soccer players after two extra-time games and a post-match borscht-eating contest. Meaning you'd probably want to hold your breath a lot. Which is also not good.

And that's why no one ever visits Serubia Minor, either.

But it *is* inhabited. Mention tourism to a Serubian and his eyes will well up in utter despair. This despite the Serubians' thermo-forming the cloud cover to spell "WELCOME VISITORS" in over four thousand languages. And building, underneath said thermo-forming, more landing strips per square meter than any other inhabited world.

And why is that? Because the Serubians — who by the way breathe through their skin and appear quite gaseous themselves (although this is largely due to their diet) — are quite possibly the most optimistic, friendly species in existence. How they are friendly with a gut full of gahl (sharp-toothed krill-like crustaceans) is beyond understanding, but the average Serubian — highly intelligent, eager-to-please, ever-hopeful — welcomes visitors to Serubia Minor like Disneyland welcomes six-year-olds. Hence the landing strips.

Not to imply the Serubians are wallet-sucking capitalists — and certainly not to imply the generous, inventive and well-bankrolled good folks at Disney *are* (hint hint) — far from it. The Serubians are merely accommodating souls who like nothing more than to crack open a case of champagne, serve you a four-course meal and ask about your day. They want nothing in return other than your good conversation and company. Why, I once had a Serubian ambassador offer me his first-born son rather than see me do without a fork at the dinner table.

Unfortunately, that Serubian Bog makes it impossiblefor anyone with an olfactory system to visit, six-year-old or otherwise. Meaning all those airfields sit unused. Then again, they built Las Vegas, so you never know.

So what do the Serubians do besides wait for visitors? They invent, that's what. They've got their hands (or, as we like to call them, "knobbies") in everything you can think of — space travel, medicine, agriculture, mechanical engineering, genetic modification, sub-ether programming … you name it, they've made advancements in it. All of which they will gladly give you, gratis, if only you'd spend a few measly hours with them. And since we Nor-Wayans are seriously lacking in the smelling department due to our mostly vestigial schnozzes (meaning through the course of evolution they have lost their original function, lucky us), this makes the Serubians perfect for the Nor-Wayan Fetch-Haul Program. Which is where Foggbottom comes in; i.e., ergo, me.

What I'm getting at — which our heroes have graciously waited for outside the double doors on the second floor while I worked my way up to it in the narrative — is that in anticipation of his previous mission to

Serubia Minor, and knowing how accommodating his guests would be
were they hosting *him,* Foggbottom had built — and here's my point — a
Serubian Bog Chamber. And if you've ever built a Serubian Bog Chamber,
you know they do not come fully-formed from between one's buttocks.
They do not even come fully-formed from everythingbutthekitchensink.
com. They do not come fully-formed at all. Which means they have to be
built, piece by piece, bolt by bolt, out of thin air.

The sodium hydroxide alone is a bitch.

Plus, once it's constructed, there's all that red carpet, floral
arrangements, white linen tablecloths, formal place-settings (from soup
tureen to finger bowl), various-sized forks, monogrammed napkins, petit
fours and silver tea services to deal with, all of which the Serubians just
adore. Which is why it took months and months and not a little bit of
worry and muscle, plus a shamelessly large budget and a snooty event
planner named Dieter (don't get me going on *that*) to get it all accomplished.
Which is why Foggbottom had not yet disassembled it.

A decision which, as Winston led his prisoners toward the doors,
Foggbottom now knew was going to bite him in his overly accommodating ass.

Because beyond those doors, where fifty young Serubian hopefuls
were housed on their short but well-appointed trip to Nor-Way, were fifty
individual silver-plated vats of Serubian Bog Oil, each three meters wide
and teeming with sharp-toothed, snapping krill-like gahl, nestled in a
noxious cloud of Serubian Bog. All kept at a constant 130°C. Plus all the
aforementioned accoutrements, which is yet another French word, in this
case meaning "fancy-schmancy stuff that cost me six month's pay."

Needless to say, for a Serubian this bog chamber would feel like a
weekend at the Ritz. For the rest of us, not so much. [85]

85> I will not go into the other chambers on the ship (you've already seen the one with large
yellow-and-orange polka-dots); let's just say there were "a bunch."

Chapter TWENTY-FIVE...

LET ME TELL YOU something that might one day prove useful. When you are hanging by your ankles over a large vat of Serubian Bog Oil, you'd do well to keep your wits about you. One false move can plunge you head first into a face-eating cocktail of noxious toxicity and other unpleasant redundancies and you'll be wishing you'd paid attention to that foul stench when you first walked in the door. Of course, if a couple of eight-foot ill-tempered scaly and repulsive multi-armed beasts had shackled you up there (Shar Winston & Brok Cragmar), you wouldn't have much choice in the matter. Still, a word to the wise.

"I'm beginning to think I'm a terrible judge of character," Foggbottom muttered. He wriggled against the heavy chain that bound them.

Marvin followed his gaze to the far side of the chamber where the Kilgorians had just exited. "They're, like, not *nice*, that's for sure," he said, his hair pointing southerly toward the vat below. "You might want to look into your interview process."

"I can only take responsibility for one of them," Foggbottom said as he began to swing to and fro. "The other one's an interloper. You can't blame me for interlopers."

He then caught Marvin worriedly eyeing the vat. Evidently recalling Marvin's dossier, he said, "Swimming is the least of your worries." And by this the Sandy Rivers administrator meant, "If you read the first paragraph of this chapter, drowning would be looking pretty good right about now." He let out a good-sized wince even though his ankles, having no feeling to begin with, surely felt no pain, but discomfort was no doubt beginning to make its way from wrist to arm, from arm to shoulder, where nerves and muscles were in fine working order.

FYI, winces are as contagious as yawns when it comes to being chained upside down, so Marvin, bound by the same heavy chain as his fellow prisoner, joined in. The two then put great effort into their struggles against the chains, as if that would do any good. (Chain-securing being the first-order of Kilgorian starship training.) One last frustratingly fruitless struggle and they both went limp.

Seconds passed.

"I know what you're thinking," the administrator sighed. "You're thinking how in the world these Nor-Wayans ever got to be masters of space and time if they can't even stop one malcontented lunchroom cook."

Attempting to face Foggbottom, Marvin managed merely to swing in an arc. "Actually, I'm thinking" — fingers getting numb, blood settling in his head — "this, whadyacallit, Serubian Bog Oil? *Excellent* idea." He twisted to take another look at the vat, somehow stopping the swing. "Genius, in fact."

"Genius it isn't, my boy. It's merely the required atmospheric— Ah, oh I see, yes…" He looked below. "It *would* make a splendid plot device, wouldn't it? I certainly see that."

Marvin nodded in a way that said he wished *he'd* thought of it.

"But personally," Foggbottom put in, "I'd rather read about it than hang precariously above it." Then: "If it's plot device you want, my boy, the universe has an endless stockpile of odds and ends to keep those Winged Avengers of yours going. *Without* having to suffer the actual slings and arrows. Throw a dart at the cosmos and you'll come up with something perfectly do-able, plot-wise. 'Write what you know,' they say." He shot another glance below. "Trust me when I say it is far easier to write what you know *about*. Do you have to have been shackled to *write* about being shackled? I say no. Plenty of fodder in the *Encyclopedia Gargantua* to keep you busy for decades. For eons. No need to even get your lips chapped."

"I guess you're right," Marvin conceded, the bog gathering around his head like the rings of Gorff (an *actual* gas giant). "Good for plot, but not so good for, you know…" {*cough, cough*} "…breathing. The stuff does reek." He put more effort into his wriggling, then, in a bit of ill-timed luck, sneezed. Forward and back he went, during which time he could do nothing but watch the world go by in virtiginous arcs. He shut his eyes and prayed for it to end.

At this, little Pookie poked her pointy little nose from Foggbottom's jacket, took a few whiskered sniffs, saw their position above the tanks, and darted back into the safety of her master's chest.

"I do apologize for the accommodations," Foggbottom said as he twisted in the other direction. "But I had to make the place hospitable. There's an old joke: How many Serubians does it take to screw in a light bulb?" Pause. "Who cares? Nobody's going in there!"[86]

Foggbottom started to bring a finger to his lips in a don't-tell-that-in-mixed-i.e.-Serubian-company way, but, since his hands were unavailable for the maneuver, inadvertently put himself into a swing, pendulum-like, and now the two of them swung to and fro, fro and to, in a ballet of nauseatingly complementary arcs.

"I don't mean to be rude or anything," Marvin put forth, his swing finally slowing, "but I think we've gotten ourselves between a rock and a hard place. The hard place being those tanks down there. The rock being that gnarly dude outside the door. Plus, I hate to say this, but I gotta pee."

At this, the administrator, realizing he'd not written a single word about rocks *or* hard places in over a month, muttered the phrase repeatedly — "rock and hard place … rock and hard place" — trying to keep it in his head. And of course not being able to keep much of anything in there of late, once again spaced on the fact that his hands were tied and quite

---

86> Serubian jokes are well known throughout the galaxy. Here's another: How much is a Serubian worth? A thousand scents. And: What's stinkier than a Serubian? Two Serubians. And: What's the difference between a rotten fish and a Serubian? One smells to high heaven, the other one's a fish.

absent-mindedly reached for the notebook. Which, of course redux, put him into a full-blown spin. "Monkey balls!" he cried in a dizzying three-sixty. "Do I *never* learn?" And: "I swear I will never ever *ever* again hire a Kilgorian! Self-centered pustule-plaid *beasts,* every one of them!"

"Uh, seriously," Marvin said, reaching out an elbow to stop the poor guy. "What're we gonna do here? I really don't want to pee what with my head being below my groin."

The man thought for a moment. Then he thought for another moment. Then he said, "Here's an idea …" And that's when Reginald T. Foggbottom broke out in song.

• • •

BROK CRAGMAR stomped a scaly foot and swung his massive tail. "Stop it! Stop it at once!" he gurgle-screamed, shaking his fist at the prisoner. "You're ruining it!" He held his ears in tortured agony, spittle flinging from his gnarly lips. A leathery tail flicked and curled in fury-filled spasms like a slave master's whip. Clearly, this behavior is as far from happy nose-picking Kilgorian glee as you can get. It's also as close to the stereotype of an ill-tempered Kilgorian as you can get.[87]

87> Many people take offense at stereotypes, claiming they are unfair, oversimplified, patently untrue representations. But I say poo and peanut butter; stereotypes are stereotypes for a reason.

Consider, for example, the stereotype of a high school jock. This would be a person with an exceptionally thick neck and brain to match, who likes nothing better than to pummel less thick-necked peons while downing an entire pound of ground beef. Is this an unfair assessment? You bet. But is it based in truth? Let me put it this way: Show me a high school jock who would turn down a nice pound of ground beef and I will show you another high school jock who would jump on it.

Throughout history, stereotypes have been with us, from the Elizabethan Tights-Clad Panty-Waist to the Look-at-me-I'm-a-Loner Black-Clad Gunslinger. Stereotypes can be traced as far back as prehistoric times, when Neanderthals would get to laughing at Ogg, who'd once again fallen into a big pile of mammoth dung — Ogg being a stereotypical "oo-a-oonga" (dung-slipping clod).

Unfair? Sure. But as long as they're not stereotyping *us,* what do we care?

Twelve points if you can name anyone you know who is not a stereotypical something.

Foggbottom, hanging over the boiling vats of Serubian Bog Oil, was just beginning his fifth go at a hopelessly off-key rendition of the Gary Vaniloe version of "I'm Glad That You're Here"...

> *"I'm real glad that you're here,*
> *"So glad that you're here..."*

Below, the Kilgorian lieutenant stomped his massive feet across the Bog Chamber floor, fists clenched into tight meaty balls, eyes red with menacing rage. Which of course only encouraged the seersuckered Nor-Wayan, hanging precariously above, to raise his voice, the song echoing against the chamber walls ...

> *"One thing I've learned from a planet so wide,*
> *"It's great to have a pal by my side!"* [88]

"Stop it! Stop it!" the Kilgorian roared. "Stop it at once!"

"I dunno," Marvin called from on high. "I'm rather enjoying it." At which point he joined in, head bobbing (upside-down) in time ...

> *"It's definitely fine, you here with me,*
> *"I'm finding myself as glad as can be."*

---

[88]> "I'm Glad That You're Here" © Stanislaus and Zvezdan Smurd, 1975. The original verse: "I'm real glad you like beer / So glad you like beer," was originally written by the Smurd brothers for a Schnizzlepop Beer commercial but was unknowingly co-opted by Mr. Vaniloe as "I'm glad that you're here / So glad that you're here," for his debut 1978 album, *Starlight On My Mind*. The Smurds famously took the case to court as a violation of copyright, were offered a settlement in the form of co-authorship, turned down the deal, lost the case, then regretted the decision when "I'm Glad That You're Here" went platinum in 1982. Adding to their misfortune, the Schnizzlepop Beer Co. went belly up the following year after the unprecedented mass-coma of 18 members of Miskatonic University's *Omega-Omega-Mu-Mu* sorority due to high levels of formaldehyde in Schnizzlepop Lite.

What's in *your* beer?

"No!" Brok Cragmar cried, four fists clenched, teeth bared in outrage, his tail and other two arms hurling cutlery, linens and china at the prisoners. "It's blasphemy! It's sacrilege!"

Marvin and Foggbottom, seemingly oblivious to the display:

"It's not really true, what they say about you
"You're a helluva guy, true through and through!"

"I will break you into small pieces!" the Kilgorian lieutenant shouted, unable to contain himself. "I will pull your teeth through the back of your skull!" He stomped toward the vats, knocking over tables and chairs, his eyes ablaze with the reflection of the two brazen figures above…

"You know I'm real glad that you're here,
"So glad that you're here.
"Who would've bet, the two of us met,
"Not down the road, but light years from here!"

At this, the guard began to pull frantically on the chains, determined to lower the prisoners to his level, where he most undoubtedly intended to pummel them into worthless-for-pie condition. "You have made a mockery of timeless art!" he barked. "You have made a travesty of our sacred anthem!" (This last part because, unbeknownst to Marvin but certainly beknownst to Reginald T. Foggbottom, all of Kilgore had recently elevated, through royal decree, the entirety of Mr. Vaniloe's song list to great and prestigious preeminence. Proclamations were signed, statues were built, postal stamps were issued, commemorative plates were manufactured. In fact, whole celebrations were devoted to it, including the bi-annual Kilgorian Candypalooza Music Fest.)[89]

89> Don't ask me how young Marvin knew the words to a 30-year-old pop song, he just did. (Hey, if you're going to buy portable wormholes, surely you can buy this one, too.) Probably from watching a "mentoring" (read: shameless self-promotion) episode of "America's Got Idols." And just

Just when Foggbottom and Marvin got to the chorus again — *"I'm so glad that you're here,"* etc. — Pookie (remember Pookie?) came to the rescue. In the confusion of the Kilgorian's tantrum she had emerged from Foggbottom's seersucker suit, skittered up the chains, across the iron beam to which the chains were fastened, down the velvet curtains at the wall and, quite unobtrusively, up Brok Cragmar's massive leg. From there she climbed to the great brute's back, where she rode for a short while, unnoticed, masquerading as yet another unsightly growth. Now poised menacingly on the raging lieutenant's brawny neck, she was about to take a bite out of his broccoli-like ears.

Which she did.

Which, in turn, made Brok Cragmar grab his head in a most horror-struck way (or horror-stricken, depending on your preference), spin on his heels, pivot on his tail, and fall head-first into the closest, noxious, gahl-teeming vat of Serubian Bog Oil.

And from there he did not move.

Except for that melting into little globby chunks thing.

• • •

MARVIN AND FOGGBOTTOM looked into the vats below.

"That takes care of *that,*" Foggbottom declared. "Never let anyone tell you hanging out in karaoke bars is a waste of time."

"I stand corrected on that one," Marvin said as he watched bits of lieutenant float to the surface and vowed he'd never again enjoy a bowl

---

how would an American pop writer's works — clearly those of an Earthling — be allowed on Kilgore, much less revered with such fervor, especially given Kilgore's strictly enforced aforementioned import embargo?

Think about it. Mr. Vaniloe's record clearly singles out *starlight.* It's *on his mind.* And there's no mistaking that light years thing. I ask you: How many pop singers out there make reference to the distance light travels in a vacuum? (Other than Li'l Klaa2's 2009 R&B single, *That Ho Be Parallaxin' My Parsecs.*) Besides which: take a *look* at this guy and tell me he's from your planet. Who on Earth cuts their hair like that?

of soup.

They watched the vat for a second or two more, saw no signs of life, put on a range of stomach-turned expressions, and set about to wriggling again.

Foggbottom: "Remind me. How did your Yolando Plumadore get out of this?"

"Dude. It's a comic book," Marvin said, earnestly getting into the wriggling. "You can always get them out of things in comic books. You just make stuff up. Poof, it's there."

"Well anyway, I've had enough. It's time we got ourselves upright."

Marvin stopped wriggling just long enough for Foggbottom to see the expression on his face. "There's an idea."

It was here the Nor-Wayan called for Pookie, who, if you were worried about her, had leaped miraculously at the last second from Brok Cragmar's shoulders, skittered back up the curtains fifth-fastest-animal-in-the-known-galaxy style, across the beam and down into Foggbottom's waiting shirt pocket. At which point Foggbottom whispered into his lapel. Marvin watched as once again the little skerlish leaped up the chain, across the beam and, quite unexpectedly, through a heating vent and out of sight. He gave the administrator a look that asked how in the world that was going to help anything.

"The thing about seersucker," Foggbottom said, getting a gander at his suit, "it wrinkles something awful. What with the chains and all. Now I'll have to send it out."

Marvin, eyes on the vent: "I suppose Pookie's gone to get help."

Foggbottom, eyes on his suit: "She has."

"And," Marvin said, all-too aware he'd forgotten what it was like to have feeling in his feet, "it's going to be, like, soon, right?" In which was the implied notion that they were staking their lives on a four-ounce fuzzball to get them out of this. "*Right?* The pee issue's past important."

Foggbottom: "Look. Here's what's going to happen. Pookie's going to retrieve something for me, then I'm going to go take care of some business while you fetch Mr. Waddell, and then we shall meet at a designated time and place and continue with the mission at hand. I'm not worried in the least."

"And the bake-off …? No way I'm letting that monster cook up my friends. It's like a freakin' episode of 'StarQuest.' Without the laugh track."

"Do not fret, my friend. There will be no stargazy pie in *this* year's competition. And that Winston fellow? I assure you he has lost his position with *us*."

"So no worries."

"That's correct."

"The little fur-ball's gonna save the day."

"She is."

"And that'll happen …?"

Foggbottom gave him a look like he wasn't following.

"*When?*" Marvin pressed.

"When what?"

"When will Pookie save the day?"

"Ah, *when!* Why, in due course, of course."

"And that's …?"

Foggbottom: ???

"*When!?*"

Mr. Foggbottom had a look on his face that was completely taken aback. "I believe, if I'm not mistaken, 'in due course' means 'in due course.' I can't think of another way to say it without use of a thesaurus, and I don't seem to have one at the moment." He gave Marvin a look that this explanation should suffice and set back to trying to wriggle free.

"Well," Marvin said, eyeing once again the vat below and picturing what it would be like floating in it, Brok-Cragmar-style. "It sounds like you've got it all figured out."

"I do. In the meantime, allow me tell you a little story." He stopped wriggling and settled into Wait-for-Pookie Mode (albeit upside-down). "Years ago—"

"Look," Marvin sighed, completely sure his entire blood supply was now above (or, rather, below) his shoulders and really really *really* concerned about the combination of urine and gravity (vis-à-vis his nose), "how do we know—"

"Years ago," the administrator went on, "I was being held at the Maricopa County Jail for obstruction of … well obstruction of *something*. Doesn't matter. Suffice it to say I had to spend the night in the hoosegow for a minor offense. You know, I love that word, 'hoosegow.' Perhaps I should undertake a book of interesting vocabulary words. 'Flugelhorn.' I love that one, too. And 'molybdenum.' And 'onomatopoeia.' Excellent stuff. They're —"

Marvin stopped wriggling. "Mr., uh, Foggbottom? I'm pretty sure—"

"And 'kerfuffle.'

"—we ought to—"

"Hmmm? Oh yes, sorry. It was there in the Maricopa County Jail I met a chap by the name of Mook Sniggers. I'll never forget the name, Mook Sniggers. I've since wondered whether it was a *nom de guerre* — that's French for 'made up' … 'bogus,' if you will. Well anyway, after a couple of hours lying there on the bench, staring at the ceiling, which was in considerable disrepair I might add … many ceilings *are* … I posed a question. 'Whadya in for?' I asked, as is the custom.

"'Me?' Mook Sniggers says, looking at me like I was the last person on the planet he expected to address him. Me, of course, in white tie and tails, and he in leather, covered in tattoos.

"'Yes, you,' I say, thinking it obvious as there was no one else in the cell. "What brings you to these fine accommodations?'

"Mook Sniggers picked something from his teeth and shrugged.

"'Must have been *something*,' I say, trying to make conversation.

"Well Mr. Sniggers pauses a moment, then looks around to make sure no one is listening.

"'You really wanna know?' he asks.

"I nod that I do.

"'I figure it's on account of I come up with my own religion,' he says.

"'No kidding?' I say. I hadn't met anyone who'd started their own religion before, let alone get locked up for it. Not outside of Babylon anyway.

"'Dead serious,' he says."

Foggbottom jimmied himself a little, looking toward the heat vent. "'What's it called, this religion of yours?' I ask.

"Mr. Sniggers doesn't answer.

"'Ah,' I say. 'It's a *secret* religion.'

"'Ain't no secret,' he says. 'Just protectin' my flank.'

"Now assuming he wasn't actually in the military and had no flank except that related to his torso — I assumed he was alluding to the fact that further disclosure might get him into hotter water. [Looking below:] As it were. I say, 'What would *I* do with this information, Mr. Sniggers — arrest you? Looks like *that's* already been taken care of.'

"He thinks about this, then looks me right in the eye. He says, 'Okay, buddy. If you must know, it's called *Sons of the Pink Flamingo.* Happy?'

"'Sons of the Pink Flamingo,' I say, repeating what I'd heard and trying to avoid that eye patch. Did I mention Mr. Sniggers wore an eye-patch? This eye-to-eye business was most unnerving, given that eye patch.

"'Yup,' he says, looking at me with that one good eye. 'Sons of the Pink Flamingo.'

"So I ask him to tell me a little about it. Its tenets and such.

"'It's like this here,' he says as he leans forward in his bunk. 'Anybody can do whatever they want, whenever they want, however they want, *why*ever they want. Just because they've a mind to.' I wait for more, but clearly this is it. This is the extent of his beliefs. He looks quite proud.

"'Hmmm,'" I say, debating how I want to deal with this new information. I tap a finger to my lip several times. I ask, 'What if a fellow wants to, you know, shoot you in the privates?'

"Mr. Sniggers shrugs. 'He can,' he says, and he points to his eye patch, as if this very thing has already transpired some three feet higher than the area in question.

"So I say I felt this was—"

Marvin: "Lame."

"Exactly. Only I believe the word I used was 'foolhardy.' At which Mook Sniggers takes great offense. He looks at me the way a fellow looks at you the second before they head-butt you into a wall. At least I think so, relying solely on that one eye. Luckily, he doesn't. Head-butt me, that is. He does, however, roll over in his bunk, and face the other way. But not before he says, 'It's my *religion,* man. Have some respect.'"

And at this, Foggbottom winked at Marvin as if he had made some exceptionally profound point.

Marvin waited a moment, trying to fathom just what that point was. "That's it? That's the whole story? What's it supposed to mean?"

"I have absolutely no idea," Foggbottom shrugged. "I guess I just like it." Again he looked expectantly to the air vent. "Distracted you from your predicament, didn't it?"

Marvin felt his blood begin to congeal within the top inch of his skull. "Look, I'm beginning to think—"

Foggbottom did not wait for what Marvin was beginning to think. "Ah! There she is, my little angel!" he cried, his face taking on a hopeful rosy hue (which was not far from its previous unhopeful rosy hue, given the fact he'd been upside down for the better part of a chapter).

Pookie leapt through the ventilation screen, skittered down the chain and quickly into the folds of Foggbottom's seersucker suit. From whence came a few clicks and what sounded like the creak of rusty hardware. Foggbottom contorted his face in such a way it was difficult to notice that his torso was contorting in such another way, seeming, in fact, to almost completely unhinge. "Seeming" being a misstatement because, in a more accurate description of the moment, Foggbottom's torso *was* completely unhinging, and, to Marvin's complete and utter dismay, was in the throes of disengaging from Foggbottom's lower regions (or upper if you want to account for its current orientation). Meaning disconnecting. As in severing. As in separating therefrom.

The useless legs of Reginald T. Foggbottom hung by themselves from their shackles as the rest of the man, hands still tied, flipped upright, swung itself in a remarkable feat of acrobatic agility up and over the horizontal beam, shimmied like a reptile the few feet to the chains that held Marvin Plotnik, and now perched, legless, while proceeding to unlock the padlock that secured said chains. Which Foggbottom accomplished through the use of a nail clipper (source unknown) and tongue-and-lip dexterity.

All of which prompted Marvin to say, "I did not expect that."

Foggbottom: "Nobody does."

• • •

"I GOT THE IDEA thanks to your Yolando Plumadore," Foggbottom was saying once he'd helped Marvin to the floor. (Speaking of his acrobatics, not the removing his legs thing.) "I'm not usually the derring-do type, you understand, but it was getting old, that upside-down business. Plus, if it went on much further, it would totally upset the pacing of my chronicle of these events. And I was worried, quite frankly, about your *aim*." He nodded to Marvin's crotch. "*Something had to be done.*"

Marvin, not one for loss of words, nevertheless was. At the moment he could only come up with six of them: "Did you just remove your legs?" … "Did you just *remove* your legs?" … "Did you just remove your *legs?*" and so on in varying degrees of incredulity, which, I'm sure you'd be equally full of if you'd just witnessed the same. Also, he also no longer had to pee. The human bladder is a fascinating thing, yes?

Our young hero sat on the floor, leaning against an overturned table. He was having a hard time removing his gaze from the crossbeam from which Foggbottom's seersucker-clad legs dangled precariously — torso-less, armless, headless, the-rest-of-Foggbottom-less.

Foggbottom began work on Marvin's wrists. "Interchangeable parts," he explained matter-of-factly, speaking not of Marvin's wrists but of his own two legs. "Honestly, the set I was using was completely useless. Or is it 'were completely useless'? Whatever the verb tense, I hadn't gotten but two kilometers out of them when they went screwy on me. And I could not secure replacements until our return to Nor-Way. Of course, I tried to convince Mr. Waddell to swap — but he seemed quite attached to his." He examined Marvin face as if the lad might not be listening too closely. "That was a joke, my boy. *Attached.* Get it?"

Foggbottom's eyes followed Marvin's gaze, still glued to those dangling legs. "Now *that* is why I buy suits with two pair of trousers." He then proceeded to explain that Pookie had retrieved his nail clippers and BCD from his dressing room, further explaining that a BCD was a "bio-coupler/ decoupler," which, he added, he should have brought with him; he didn't know why he hadn't, he *always* had his BCD with him, he was just *mortified* he'd left his BCD behind, cannot apologize enough for the delay the oversight had caused, what *was* he thinking, at least they had time for the Mook Sniggers story which had been on his mind of late. "Now," he continued, "let us get some fresh air, shall we? Not too fresh, you understand, what with that bothersome vacuum outside the ship, but at least free of this insufferable bog. If you would be so kind as to fetch that wheelchair, we shall be on our way. *INGA, please apprise us of the whereabouts of Misters Waddell and Winston.*"

INGA did not reply.

"*INGA*," Foggbottom tried again, "*the whereabouts of Misters Waddell and Winston if you please.*"

Again, no reply.

Foggbottom's face went taut. "It seems our good friends the Kilgorians have switched off our navigation system."

"Maybe she's out to lunch," Marvin suggested, his feet tingling as he came to them. "Maybe she's, you know, on a break."

"An interesting concept, but I fear Pyrsnyki navigation systems do not take breaks. Even in the hands of a generous — *and* handsome — Nor-Wayan fetch-hauler. Unfortunately, we are dead in the water without her. This will have to be rectified." He took a moment, then apparently coming to a course of action said, "Since we have not heard from Waddell, I must assume he's still in my office sprawled in a dirty-shorts-like heap. He took a mean hit to the head, poor fellow. See if you can rouse him. Tell him the situation, and meet me back there in — let's see, I want to get the timing right — two hours and, say, twelve minutes ago. That should do it."

Marvin had been retrieving the wheelchair when Foggbottom said this, so it took a minute to sink in. Surely the blood had coagulated in the old codger's skull. "You mean two hours from *now*," Marvin said. "What are we supposed to *do* for two hours? Twiddle our thumbs?"

"Two hours *ago*, my boy. More precisely, two hours and" — checking his watch — "twelve minutes. *Ago*." He tapped his watch. "Make that thirteen minutes. That should be sufficient. I believe that was when the Kilgorian ship reared its ugly head. Or, rather, when" — shuddering at the mental picture — "Slag Udyedsu did. Go tell Waddell. The situation, that is, not the ugly-head-rearing bit. He'll be able to explain more I'm sure. I'm afraid you and I don't have time to discuss it. We've wasted enough already." He reached into his pocket. "You'll need this," he added, handing Marvin a small cylinder about the size of a D-battery. In fact, it looked remarkably like a D-battery, copper top and all; only this battery didn't have any writing on it. "Pookie could get you the key, but I'm afraid the poor dear has conked out on us." He lifted his jacket to show the sleeping skerlish had rolled herself into a snoring ball of fur inside his suit pocket.

"But what—"

Foggbottom did not delve into the what of anything and Marvin did not finish the question (which was going to be, "What is this, a D-battery?"), for the legless administrator had already wheeled himself halfway down the second-floor corridor and, after a fond *adieu*, was currently turning the corner and out of sight. Plus, Marvin really had to pee again.

Chapter TWENTY-SIX...

URNED OUT, Marvin didn't have to find Waddell. Waddell found Marvin. Or, rather, smacked into him — "smack" being a term that doesn't quite measure up to the force of the impact. It was on the way to the cafeteria; because naturally the first thing Marvin wanted to do was to throw Foggbottom's advice out the window. Finding his friends seemed much more agreeable than finding Waddell. So he'd headed straight to the cafeteria, where, some twenty feet short of his goal the great blue-satined countenance of Geraldine Fitzsimmons came barreling around the corner and the whole smacking thing ensued.

Stunned for a second, the two found themselves limbs skewampus, which isn't a word you see very often, but it is just the right one to see here because it means "all over the place" in a way no other word means "all over the place." Picture all the letters of "all over the place" *all over the place* — each letter in a different country for instance — and you'll have some idea of just how appropriate this word is. Needless to say, with all this skewampusing of limbs, it took a bit of cartoon-like head shaking on both their parts before either could come to his feet, but when they did, Geraldine Fitzsimmons pulled Marvin with commando-like dispatch into a nearby supply room.

More of a closet really. And if you've ever been enclosed in a small space with someone five times your size and an equal amount of toilet paper stacked about you, you'd have some idea of Marvin's feelings at the moment.

Geraldine Fitzsimmons nodded toward the cafeteria. "They're out cold," she said, her voice low (meaning not only low in volume, but also low to the point of it being the voice of Skylar Waddell). Skylar Waddell, then, was no longer bothering with the subterfuge, which, thankfully, allows me from this point to switch to simpler one-character-one-sex referents and make this whole thing a lot easier on the both of us.

"You'd think bulldozers came through," he said. "It's felled trees everywhere in there." At some point he'd lost the schoolmarm shoes that went with the dress (or had thrown them off for speed?) and his thick Geraldine Fitzsimmons makeup had begun to melt. The blue wig was disheveled, but not as disheveled as Marvin had seen it just before it succumbed to Winston's massive tail, which Marvin found slightly — but not enough to really care about it — curious.

Marvin thought it prudent to ask just what happened since he'd last seen Waddell — left out cold at the foot of the view-screen — but when he opened his mouth, Waddell brought a finger to his lips (Waddell's lips, not Marvin's lips), then cracked the door the width of an eye, his great blue derriere taking up the bulk of the storage room.

"The anomaly's fixed, right?" Marvin whispered.

"It is," Waddell whispered back.

"Then what's the holdup? Let's *go* already."

Waddell carefully and silently brought the door to. "Can't. Magbeam's too strong." He began to pace, which for a man his size in a "room" this size, was more like a weight shift than anything else. Thus, he began to stop pacing. "Magbeams haven't been used for thirty rotations," he pointed out, "not since the Klaad Campaign. Highly frowned upon in military circles these days. Basically, it's cheating. Then again, they're Kilgorians. They cheat. They *like* being frowned upon." Then: "Speaking of which: Where's the boss?"

"Foggbottom? Last I saw him he was wheeling his way to points unknown. *Legless*."

Waddell tilted his head and slammed his eyes shut, as if that somehow were going to help him come up with a way out of this. "Hmmm. If we could release the magbeam, we'd have a chance. Perhaps distract them."

"As in no legs."

"Wherever they're taking us, it isn't going to be good."

"You must have missed the part where I said Foggbottom had no legs. He removed them. You know, took them off."

"If only we knew—"

"He. Removed." Marvin, scanning Waddell's face for horror and shock. "His. Legs."

"—where they're taking us, we could plan for it."

Marvin forced a blast of air through his lips, the kind of air that said, "Oh for crap's sake, this guy needs a hearing aid," after which he related Winston's plans for the pie-baking competition at the Festival of Feasts. "With us as the secret ingredients." Again, he scanned Waddell's face for horror and shock. After all, these things happen in comic books and Saturday morning cartoons and drug-induced dreams, not in real life. "You did hear me about the leg thing, yes?"

Marvin didn't know it, but Waddell suddenly remembered Winston's requisition for new ovens, which was why the Nor-Wayan suddenly slapped his forehead. "'I can serve fifty easily,' he quoted in a mockingly Kilgorian accent. "Takes on a whole new meaning now, doesn't it?" He shook his head presumably at how stupid he and Foggbottom had been. "Where did you say the old goat was?" Again with the half-step pacing.

"I told you. Making his way to points unknown. He just said we were supposed to meet up. Two hours ago. *Ago*. The dude's gone batty."

Waddell turned to Marvin. "Two *hours* ago?" (Putting emphasis on an entirely different word). "What the hell's so important about two hours ago?"

"And sixteen minutes. Twenty-two minutes by now."

"How in the *hell* did he intend I accomplish *that*?"

"He wasn't very clear on that."

"And even if we were able to — well it's not like we've got a *Hel-IX* or anything. Because nobody *gave* me one. Like I *requested*. In *writing*. Seventeen *times*. Oh, ovens, sure, ovens they approve like *that*. But a Hel-IX for the only other Nor-Wayan on board?"

"What's a—"

"Twenty-four rotations without giving 'the new guy' the most important tool in the fetch-haul arsenal? Un-kerflarkin'-believable. Why have *two* of them if you're ..." He waved his hand to say he was *not* going there. "What exactly are we supposed to *do* two hours ago?"

Marvin: "He wasn't very clear on that either and hello? A) the leg thing and B) what the hell's a helix?"

Waddell swung around, his immense gut pressing Marvin into shelves of tissues and cleaners and sponges and bars of soap. "The Hel-IX SC, Helicoidinal Space-time Connibulator, ninth iteration," he explained, "*Hel-IX* for short and even if we had one — which we don't because no one ever ever *ever* listens to me — we'd also need the key. Which my esteemed colleague keeps hidden." He peered out the door again, closed it carefully then gave Marvin a big conciliatory sigh. "Look, we're running out of time here. Which is a shame if you ask me, considering we'd have *all the time in the world if we had a flarkin' Hel-IX.*" An exasperated breath later: "I'm going to explain this once, without the benefit of a light web, okay?" He looked Marvin in the eye. "Picture a book. There's a whole story in there, right? Beginning, middle, end. You open the book" — here, he opened his hands as if opening a book — "you're at a particular point in the story, a particular point in time. You close the book" — closing his invisible book — "and the whole thing squashes together. The whole story ... becomes one. Each page is now part of the whole, you see? It's all there, the whole story, past, present, future. Now put that together with Foggbottom's green light business and—" His eyes asked if Marvin was following.

Marvin's eyes, in turn, narrowed. "You're talking time travel? For real? Dude said 'masters of space and time,' said there was a portable wormhole on board, but I thought he was, you know, screwing with me. Giant rat-tailed bug-eyed monsters I'll buy, but time travel?..." He was shaking his head like he just wasn't going to fall for all of this.

Waddell scratched at Geraldine Fitzsimmons' blue satin dress. "Oh we are not screwing with you, young man. Screwing With You Time is over."

Marvin looked at him like he didn't know what to think anymore. One minute this guy's a short-tempered pointy-glassed old biddy and the next he's a no-nonsense tartar-sauced proctor; one minute he's an authoritative bully and the next a fellow recipe ingredient on the run. Which was the real Waddell?

"Look," Waddell whispered as if he could read Marvin's mind. "Forget Geraldine Fitzsimmons. Forget Higgenmeyer-Matheson. Forget Skylar Waddell. Forget Adelheid Pouncy and Erasmus Mintner and Zimicahr Soutani and a slew of other people you haven't yet met." Removing Geraldine Fitzsimmons' blue-gray wig, he turned to the lad. "See this, this right now? *This* is me." He pulled at his stubby red-haired scalp — clearly the latest look for Nor-Wayans — to show it was real. "Holsomback Mundy at your service."

"Holsom ..."

"The rest? It's play acting. It's a show. You know, a test. To separate the *brachk* from the *klakt,* the, uh, chaff from the wheat. We are *done* with screwing with you, my boy. The chaff has been separated." (Indicating Marvin.) "The wheat is lying face-first down that hall." (Indicating the cafeteria.) "This is no longer a test. We now return to our regularly-scheduled programming."

Marvin had no response to that. He stood there in the broom closet staring at the guy, not really knowing what to do.

"Look," Waddell whispered for the third time, sounding sympathetic. "I may be, as Mr. Foggbottom points out, a sanctimonious blowhard, but I'm a *dedicated* sanctimonious blowhard. To the job that is. I'm a firm believer in the Nor-Wayan fetch-haul program, always have been, always will be, and I do what needs to be done under whatever guise is necessary. I don't take my duties lightly. Which means I am sworn to protect those in my care. Meaning, of course — and you maybe surprised to hear me say this — you. Which includes your friends. Who are in no condition to help themselves. Bottom line? We've got to get the lot of you out of here. And by the way, I'm sorry I had to gas the dorm to get you and your friends to sleep. It was the anomaly, you understand."

Again with the half-pacing. He was working out a plan. "Winston's in there heating up the ovens, the Kilgorian ship's hauling us on magbeam, and that festival's a jump away. Trust me, you will not like that festival. Some of those guys will make the Kilgorians look like little old ladies out to tea. We need to get to Foggbottom's office, see if by some miracle he's left us a Hel-IX — and the key — and do what the man says. He says we're to go back two hours, we go back two hours."

Marvin: "And thirty-two minutes."

This unfortunately was the moment that Holsomback Mundy's eyes rolled back in his head. Which, in turn, began to loll and droop in a most disturbing neck-not-doing-its-job way, taking cleaning supplies, towels, a mop and a half-used box of latex gloves with it to the floor. Which was anything but quiet.

"You are not serious!" Marvin cried. "How're we going to … with you … like a pile of …" — grabbing and shaking of slumped and lifeless shoulders — "… *and what the hell does a Hel-IX DO?*"

He stood there for a good thirty-seven seconds replaying everything he'd seen and heard in the last twenty-four hours — which, if this were a movie would be presented as a montage of emotional clips in a rush of discordant violin chords and overlapping dream-like dialog — from his parents' high-five to Foggbottom's dangling legs. So please assume that this montage was going through Marvin's head (sans the violins; Marvin never thought in violins) when he realized something. You possibly could have realized it yourself, but most likely it was far more apparent to Marvin than you because when Marvin heard it two hours and thirty-seven minutes earlier, only Marvin could have recognized it. The casual reader, i.e., you, most likely would not have thought twice about the seemingly innocuous phrase, "hop, skip, jump" (which, you may recall, was uttered by Geraldine Fitzsimmons as she came into Foggbottom's office right before she was conked on the head). But Marvin would. Because it was a phrase he'd only last week decided to use. "Hop, Skip, Jump" was to be

the next chapter title in *Winged Avengers,* the chapter where Yolando
Plumadore would steal the time-capsule so he could go back sixty years to
the deathbed of the renowned Chinese Qi Gong master, Zhen-Li Chou,
and be told the Secret of the Spheres before the old master took it with
him to the Great Qi Gong Beyond.

Marvin hadn't even written it down yet. The title, that is. At this point,
"Hop, Skip, Jump" was only in his head.

Which meant the following: it wasn't Skylar Waddell (dressed as his
alter-ego, Geraldine Fitzsimmons) who'd come into Foggbottom's office
some two-hours-and-change ago. It wasn't Skylar Waddell who'd been
clunked on the head by the cook's tremendous tail. It wasn't Skylar Waddell
who was kicked around like a pile of dirty shorts.

It was Marvin.

Chapter TWENTY-SEVEN...

IT WAS THE STRAWBERRY TORTE that did it. Marvin found the Dastardly Dessert in Holsomback Mundy's pocket. What was left of it anyway (the torte, not the pocket), which wasn't much. He'd found it because he'd put his ear to the fallen Nor-Wayan's nose, which he didn't want to do *at* all — Geraldine Fitzsimmons' blue satin dress in all its disgusting corpulence was still just as disgusting as ever, even if it *was* a costume — but he had to see whether the dude was still breathing, didn't he? So he'd knelt at Mundy's side and listened. And what he got was the distinct air of strawberries and cream, and with *it* the realization that Mundy had eaten something he shouldn't have. (Not that Marvin could smell with his ear, just that he was close enough to get a whiff.) I'm not entirely sure why he checked Mundy's pocket, but he did, and there his hand met the gooey remains of toxic torte. (This, combined with that whole tartar sauce thing, explains a lot about Mr. Mundy — and why our dry cleaning bills have been so high. Don't get me going.)

Marvin's stomach rumbled. So he ate some of the strawberry torte himself, fainted dead away, woke up in the inferno of the humongous festival oven and died. The end.

Not really.

But he *was* on his own.

Marvin gave Holsomback Mundy one last look before taking to the hall, made sure he'd left him in a comfortable position (supply closet = pillow, natch), apologized to comatose ears for the "ten small sausages" bit and, upon carefully entering the hallway, wondered if Mundy/Waddell/Geraldine Fitzsimmons hadn't told everything he knew. Had Winston discovered the remains of Brok Cragmar floating in the Serubian Bog Oil? Had he discovered Foggbottom's dangling legs or even Foggbottom himself? Were there now more Kilgorians on board?

Marvin would have to assume all this was true.

So, armed with only a D-battery and the unsubstantiated hope a Hel-IX Helicoidinal Space-time Connibulator (whatever that was) was shaped like a D-battery, and that he'd figure what it did and how to use it, Marvin slinked down the hall and into the cafeteria where he found the metaphor of felled trees perfectly apt. Bodies everywhere. Each where they had fallen — on the floor, chairs and tables, in the dessert line, on top of one another, etc. If not for the low steady hum of vibrating adenoids and Winston's earlier bragging, Marvin might have thought the whole lot deceased rather than in a deep sleep. He therefore thanked his lucky stars Winston believed in super-fresh ingredients. There was still time to stop this.[90]

Marvin crept low, keeping an eye out for a blue fauxhawk, a Mets hat, braids, a whiff of grape Bubblectible gum — anything that was a sign of Dara and the rest. It did not take long before he'd settle for anyone *conscious,* fauxhawk or no, but still he searched, stepping carefully over each fallen comrade, looking for signs of life, and, finding none, making his way toward the kitchen door.

Beyond which: a clanking of pots, a banging of pans, an ominous wafting of Gary Vaniloe.

He was in there all right — not Gary Vaniloe, Slag Udyedsu's nephew,

---

90> FYI, the aboriginal tribes of eastern Tanganyika (not the one on Earth, the one on Zanticuli-8), do not count lucky stars, but, rather, count lucky bunions, as in "count your lucky bunions." Just, you know, in case you ever need the info.

feller of Waddells, preparer of pies. Marvin took a breath and tip-toed to the door. He inched it open and there, as before, sat the hulking figure of the despicable skerlish-eating Winston, pustule-encrusted back to Marvin, six arms cutting, dicing and various sundry things one does when concocting Certain Death for Creatures Down the Food Chain.

Marvin scanned the kitchen for something of use. And when he found it not three feet away — a large iron eggbeater the size of a baseball bat — he carefully reached for it. He crept toward the Kilgorian, the beater held high, and just as he was about to bring it crashing down on the brute just as he'd seen this very monster's tail come crashing down — dare he say it, on his future self … he — now how shall I put this delicately? — he farted. Blame it on hanging upside-down, breathing the fumes of Serubian Bog Oil. (Plus, trail mix + energy bars + Cola-Cola? Trouble.)

It was only the one, but it was enough. Winston swung around, rising from his hulking haunches with such ferocious fury the entire kitchen shuddered.

Grabbing Marvin by the throat with one hand and by a leg with the brawn of his powerful prehensile tail, the scaly beast lifted our young hero into the air as if he were made of cotton candy (our young hero, not the Kilgorian).

"What perfect timing!" Winston growled (with a disturbingly wet-and-fetid gurgle). "The oven just hit four-twenty-five!" Gnarly yellowed teeth formed a great satisfied grin as he seized the oven door, Marvin in hand. Bursts of tremendous heat came forth, blasting Marvin in the face as if from the fiery pit of the depths of hell, or some other overly-written super-hot place.

And just as Marvin was being forced into the dark and forbidding chamber (wondering, I might add, why the brute was dispensing with the other ingredients), Winston let out a cry. It was in Kilgorian, of course, sounding something like, *"Plakkel mon kongrek tu lakkel ka!"* but translating to something on the order of, "Yeow! Man that's smarts, where the heck did you two come from?"

Which is another way of telling you that Dara and Kit had turned up out of nowhere and had plunged not one, but two of Foggbottom's precious swords into the scaly beast — one into the monster's solar plexus and the other into his abdomen (courtesy Kit), while, in one swift movement, the front four inches of the beast's right toe-claw were hacked clear off by means of battle-axe (this one courtesy Dara).

Which of course made Winston drop Marvin Plotnik like a hot potato because it is difficult to hold onto prey while trying to choose between catching one's intestines or retrieving one's toes, and with just how many hands to do it.

Which gave Dara and Kit and Marvin plenty of time to push the slimeball into the freezer, where, freezer door at the ready, Bennie slammed the frickin' thing shut.

Which made everyone wipe their foreheads and get all wobbly-legged and post-altercation giddy.

• • •

SATISFIED WINSTON HAD BEEN secured (it took twenty minutes of Kilgorian barking and screeching and pounding of thick leathery blood-covered fists against the freezer door, wet hot breaths snorting into its thick window, before the bastard gave up), Marvin told his friends his tale to date — from the missing sketchbook pages to the green lights of Foggbottom's office to the unhinging of Nor-Wayan limbs to Waddell and the strawberry torte; and they in turn told him how they'd come to their senses way back in Higgenmeyer-Matheson's class when Marvin was taken from the room yelling about stars.

"From there," Dara said, "we just played dumb and followed what everyone else was doing. All we could do was wait for a chance to get out of there."

Bennie added, "It was like Zombieville, dude."

"Yeah, and when we got to the cafeteria there was this huge spread Winston had put out—"

"*Way* overboard," Kit put in.

"Right," said Dara. "Which was our first clue to leave it alone."

Kit: "I told 'em you ain't stuffin' *me* like no Thanksgiving turkey."

Bennie: "Zombie turkey."

Dara nodded. "We agreed not to touch the food. But it was too late for Flinn and Harlen. They'd gotten to the cafeteria before us. They already ate and were like—

"Zombie dudes."

Marvin, Dara, Bennie and Kit stood for a minute and digested all of this. Nobody actually said it, but it seemed they had but three choices:

(1) Stay put and wait for the Kilgorians to eat them.

(2) Go back to the cafeteria and wait for the Kilgorians to eat them.

(3) Go to the stairwell, or the dormitory, or Foggbottom's office, or the hidden anteroom or any other place on the ship ... and wait for the Kilgorians to eat them.

It wasn't like they knew how to fly a frickin' Nor-Wayan starship or anything.

Marvin produced the copper cylinder and studied it. "Whadya suppose we're to do with this?"

The three looked into Marvin's palm. "What is it?"

"Far as I can tell, it's a portable wormhole. It's called a Hel-IX ... I think." He passed it to Dara. "It's supposed to need a key."

"Looks like a D-battery to me."

"That's what *I* said." He took it back. "So say it's a *battery* to a portable wormhole. Whatever. Still doesn't mean we know how to use it. Or where the key is." He turned it in his fingers. On closer look, he now saw the cylinder had tiny reeded rings. Picture a stack of quarters until it's the size of a battery, with each of the quarters being a ring. It was not clear whether the rings rotated or allowed the device to separate, but no amount of pushing, squeezing or twisting seemed to make anything happen. "I guess," Marvin guessed, "that's what the key's for."

Chapter TWENTY-EIGHT…

DARA WAS THE FIRST through the door marked REGINALD T. FOGGBOTTOM, ADMINISTRATOR. "Good thing you explained the green lights," she said. "We wondered what that was all about when we came and got the swords."

Kit: "We thought it was some kind of trap."

Marvin put his finger to his lips. "Not a trap," he whispered, nodding toward the big window. "Camouflage." Having no idea how the window turned from a magnificent view of the cosmos into a view of Slag Udyedsu's ugly puss, he didn't want to find out. They ducked behind the webbing where empty places could be seen on the wall where his friends had removed the weapons. Now they made their way along the wall, hoping their luck would hold out. And, as no one so much as let out even a small hiccup, let alone another one of Marvin's audible emissions, they soon found themselves safely inside the Nor-Wayans' hidden anteroom.

Here they felt comfortable enough to raise their voices, but not by much. For all they knew, their every word was being broadcast throughout the ship … or worse, throughout the Kilgorian ship. Who knew, maybe if

Kilgorian guards don't check in, it sends off a distress signal … or when one is knocked into a vat of Serubian Bog Oil, each glob grows into a bona fide Kilgorian replicant … or Winston had been sprung from the freezer and the Death-by-Pie March had begun. Or all of the above.

"First thing's first," Marvin said, well aware of each scenario. "If I were a key, where would I be?"

Bennie: "Dude. You rhymed."

Dara gave Bennie's head a tweak of her finger. "If *I* were a key," she said, "I'd be on a keychain."

They all then began to rifle through the wardrobe a little more purposefully than the last time around, each grabbing a piece of clothing, a pair of trousers, a seersucker vest.

Kit was shaking his head as if the effort were stupid. We know this because he said, "This is stupid," as he rummaged through Flöckenheimer's pockets. "We don't even know what this key looks like."

"Or what it does," Dara added.

Bennie: "We don't even know if there *is* a key."

Marvin gave them all a look. "*There's a key.*"

Dara was shaking out the bus driver's scarf. "Even if we can find a key and figure out how to use that battery-looking thing," she said, "I still don't see what going back two hours is going to do anyway. What are we supposed to accomplish?"

Soon, every piece of clothing and every drawer had been gone through. Marvin had to admit he didn't know what they were looking for, either. "Well there's sure nothing in *here* that's going to help us," he finally announced. At which point he looked to the anteroom door and, tacitly, the room beyond. "It's not in the desk; I know that; I've already felt every inch of it. Crap, it could be anywhere. It'd take us hours to get through all those masks and books and—" He sat on the ottoman, turning the Hel-IX in his hand, noting the star-shaped hole that surely was for a star-shaped key. Once again he recalled his inventory of Foggbottom's inner sanctum. "What if … What if 'key' doesn't mean 'key' in the, you know, *key* sense, the kind that goes in a lock. What if—"

"Like a key on a keyboard, or typewriter," Kit said.

Bennie: "Yeah, or a key on a piano."

Dara: "Or a key to an exam."

Bennie: "Or a key to a code."

Kit: "Francis Scott Key."

There was a pause before Dara added, "Or a key to a map."

One of Marvin's eyebrows shot up. "There *is* a map. Not a *map* map, a globe. Foggbottom said he was particularly fond of that globe. Why would he make a point of that unless ..."

Marvin wasted not a second more. He crept back out to Foggbottom's office, his eyes set on the Old World globe. It was smack-dab in the middle of the green web. Hoping he'd have enough cover, halfway across the web he crouched to the floor, making his way to the globe, and, in a matter of seconds he was examining it. Under, around, on top and below. There were no drawers, no apparent openings, just the globe itself and the stand upon which it rested. It seemed like forever he rotated that globe — the thought with him all the while that he was, for the first time in his life, not standing on the world it represented — his fingers inching their way along the topographical relief of continents, mountains and oceans; the lines of longitude and latitude, inlaid in copper; the intricate calibrations on the semi-circle of the brass meridian, the smooth walnut of the horizon ring. But there was no opening, nothing that— And then he thought of another use of the word "key": An island, a part of an archipelago.

And in one swift movement he found the only archipelago he knew offhand, if only because he'd gone there one summer when he was nine. The Florida Keys. He closed his eyes and ran his fingertips to the southernmost point of the state ... and there it was.

Just south of the island chain, a tiny protrusion, like a snap buried into the ocean. He scratched at it with a fingernail. And out slid a few centimeters of brass.

"A key that wouldn't look like a key. Something in plain sight," he sniggered, fascinated that Foggbottom had used Marvin's own notes from *Winged Avengers* to hide the key for him. But how would Foggbottom ...

how would he have put it there on such short notice? Or was it possible — could it be? — the old goat hid the key before Marvin had even come to Sandy Rivers Hilltop Ranch for Wayward Youth, Juveniles, and Young Adults? Of course not, Marvin thought, that would be impossible. That would be—

And that's when Foggbottom's green web disappeared. Just like that. Gone. And Marvin stood exposed, out in the open, feeling very much — for want of a better simile — like a rabbit in a trap.

"What have we here?" came the gurgly bass of Slag Udyedsu. "Are my eyes deceiving me?" A thick yellowed nail, jutting out from the massive screen, seemed to stop just short of Marvin's nose. "Has one of Shar Winston's specimens escaped?" His voice dripped sarcasm and superiority and sadistic savagery and other S-words I can't begin to come up with — except, wait, maybe "scorn" now that I think about it — as if everything his bonehead nephew had ever done had failed and he was not surprised in the least.

Marvin answered by doing one of those "Who me?" chest point things that has no name, but certainly needs one.

The commander leaned into the screen, his face so close you could see every putrid pore. He looked down upon Marvin as if our hero were made of some sort of something Slag Udyedsu had scraped from between his crusty toes. "I thought you'd been taken care of," he snarled.

"Taken care of in what way?" our young hero asked innocently. "Were we supposed to have *better* service? Because personally I think the service so far has been excellent. Absolutely excellent."

Slag Udyedsu furrowed his gnarly brow. "*Service?*" he bellowed. "You've received no service."

"Well I don't know what else you'd call it," Marvin replied. "'Hospitality,' perhaps? Whatever you want to call it, we're all very appreciative. All of us. I mean that. It's been top-notch. A-one. First-rate. And a lot of other hyphenated stuff. We've been taken care of just terrifically. Is it you I should thank?"

Slag Udyedsu furrowed his brow even more. "The day a humanoid thanks a Kilgorian is a day that will never come."

"Well I don't know why," Marvin responded. "I'd think a thank-you is in perfect order. I've been quite satisfied with everything so far. More than that. *Extremely* satisfied. And I'm not one for compliments. Your wonderful nephew has been a *terrific* host. We all think so. The food, the entertainment, the hot towels. Aces all around. Why, he treated us to a sumptuous buffet only minutes ago." Marvin rubbed his belly as if he were sated past the point of ordinary contentment.

This evidently confused the commander because he closed one eye and studied the boy. "You enjoyed your meal, did you? No ill effects?"

"Ill effects? Of what kind? The only ill effect I had was that I wanted more. I tell you, if I spend more than my designated eight weeks here, I'm going to gain *another* ten pounds. They're calling that *first* ten 'The Sandy Rivers Sand Bag.' Not very clever, but that's what they're saying. My friend Bennie calls it his 'ol' spare tire.' Personally, I've named mine 'George.' That's a joke, you know. I mean whoever heard of giving their body fat a name? Then again, I call my little toe Lulabelle. Frankly, I'll be glad when George takes a hike if you know what I mean. Not that belly fat can walk. I mean, you know, that someday I can get back to a nice size and, you know, get a girlfriend or something." (Again with the belly patting.) "Why, we're all getting so fat we can't walk side by side in the hallways anymore!"

Slag Udyedsu sat back in his chair and interlaced three sets of fingers. "How is it you freed yourself from my lieutenant, boy? Were you not one of the pair hung by the rafters? You were to be the first in the ovens."

"*In* the ovens? Ha ha! Good one, your Slagship. I think Winston must've said 'into muffins.' That I am. That I truly am. I *adore* the muffins. Blueberry muffins, chocolate chip muffins, bran muffins, you name 'em, I'm into 'em. Dee-lish! He's in there right now making up another batch. Winston, I mean. Cragmar, too. We were headed into the gym when they announced it. '*Hot muffins at oh-three-hundred!*' You know, for the basketball game? Winston said he'd have them out by the end of the second quarter. Frankly, I don't think I'm going to have the space if you know what I mean. 'George' can't handle it!" This time Marvin grabbed a hunk of tummy fat and jiggled it. It was also the moment he carefully slipped the key to the Hel-IX into his pocket. (He didn't even need to point and say, "Look, a goat!")

"You're telling me Brok Cragmar did not hang you from the rafters? You're telling me Brok Cragmar has been shirking his duties?"

"Well, gee," Marvin said, trying to look like he'd just spilled some proverbial beans. "No, no, of course not. Mr. Cragmar has been terrif. Top-notch, A-one and more hyphenation! In fact, Mr. C — that's what we call him now — he told us he was going to help us with our studies. You know, tonight, after the sing-along? And I think someone said he's doing a scrapbooking class, too. Helluva guy. We all think so. Even my friend Kit likes him, and Kit doesn't like *anything*. Shirking his duties? Ha!"

Slag Udyedsu shot Marvin a cold and icy look, which of course is redundant, but I wouldn't go telling *him* that. The Kilgorian's eyes narrowed.

"Prepare," he seethed, "for reinforcements." And snapped his scaly fingers to make it so.

• • •

MARVIN BEE-LINED IT for the anteroom. "Um," he announced (with a small amount of embarrassment and a much greater amount of urgency). "I sorta, uh, just did something, uh, stupid." He slapped the panel closed then leaned his back against it.

"Sorta how stupid?" Dara wanted to know.

"Sorta real stupid. Sometimes I can't help but … well he caught me off guard! The green web went like … you know, poof!"

"And?"

"And … I think we're gonna have company … like soon."

Bennie: "They *are* gonna eat our brains, I know it."

Dara and Kit both looked at Marvin like Bennie was right. The Kilgorians *were* going to eat their brains, and their ears and spleens and elbows and kneecaps and those little hangy-downy things at the back of their throats. Glaring at Marvin, Kit snapped a tight Bubblectible bubble in a way that said, "Fix this."

Marvin nodded. "Good news is I got the key." Which he raised for all to see. He then produced the Hel-IX, and without even thinking about it, inserted the key into the made-to-order star-shaped slot.

There was a click. And the rings, previously unmovable, rotated and separated from each other. A pale blue light emanated from the spaces between them, revealing a series of characters silhouetted against the glow from within.

The four focused on the characters.

"That ain't English," Kit said.

"It ain't even Chinese," Bennie said.

They all gave him a look.

"I mean it's *not,* not even Chinese." Again with the look. "What?" he said. "I know Chinese when I see it." He pointed to his eyes. "Hello? It's all over my *house.*"

Dara squinted again at the markings. "I don't think it's even from Earth."

Marvin, turning the thing in his hand: "Okay. Let's assume each of these rings is a separate measurement of time. And each symbol is a place."

"Why would we do that?" Bennie wanted to know. "Why wouldn't they be, I dunno, each for a different purpose? One's like an address book or something. One's a GPS. One will, I dunno, program your DVR."

Dara: "For all you know that thing'll blow up the whole ship."

Kit was even more dismissive. "Can't be much of anything. It's only like two inches long."

Dara again: "An atom's a lot smaller than that and it can blow up half the planet. You can't just—"

"First ring for seconds," Marvin said, turning the Hel-IX in his hand. "Second ring for minutes, third for hours … then days, weeks, months, years. That's what I'm going with."

"But how do you *know?*" argued Dara. "Even if you're right, it could be the other way around. You go messing with that, you could end up in Timbuktu."

Bennie: "In 1937."

Dara: "Or dead."

Bennie: "In 1937."

Kit scoffed. "Aah, most he'll do is turn on a radio."

"Maybe," said Marvin. "But the alternative—"

The anteroom door suddenly reverberated with the pounding of fists and the eerie scraping of massive claws. "*Give yourselves up,*" came a deep and guttural and all-too-Kilgorian voice. "*There is no escape.*"

And with that, Marvin turned a couple of rings, clicking them into place. Then he gave the key another turn.

And nothing happened.

Chapter TWENTY-NINE...

"STUPID ALIEN TECHNOLOGY," Marvin sighed, seeing he was right where he started.

Although, ta da, the pounding *had* stopped.

And he *was* alone.

And all the things they'd pulled out of the wardrobe were out of sight, the wardrobe closed.

And there was another surprise: Marvin looked down to see he'd gained at least 100 pounds. Which sucked.

"It did work," he announced, as if there were someone to announce it to. To what else might he attribute this massive weight gain? Nothing, that's what. By the way, you don't usually see that in time travel stories, do you? Know why? Because they're stories. In truth, time travel requires approaching the speed of light (which somehow this little Hel-IX thing-a-ma-gizmo did), and the closer you get to the speed of light, the larger your mass. And the larger your mass, the less chance of a date on a Saturday night. Which meant, wherever — make that *whenever* — it was Marvin now found himself, two hours or two weeks from whence he came, he sure wasn't gonna get any. Not that he was going to get any anyway, but still —

being a hundred pounds heavier wasn't going to help.

He could only hope it would be short-lived.

Now at this point, which, luckily, really was two hours and fifty-five minutes before Marvin had turned the rings of the Hel-IX, Holsomback Mundy had already fixed the anomaly and, unbeknownst to Marvin, was busy accepting a piece of strawberry torte in the engine room from an oh-so-generous Winston, who most certainly was profusely expressing his heartfelt gratitude for the new ovens. Now at the time, since this was just a short while since he'd left Foggbottom's office, armed, you may recall, with only his trusty wrench (if only he'd used it), Holsomback Mundy was still dressed as Geraldine Fitzsimmons.

Fast-forward a few minutes to a familiar storage closet. Back then (two hours hence) when Marvin was making Holsomback Mundy all comfy cozy — he took it upon himself to remove Geraldine Fitzsimmons' blue satin dress from the comatose body thereof. Which was just as difficult and {~ugh, heave, gag~} creepy as you are now imagining. Which meant — yes, that's right — Marvin had already donned the whole Geraldine Fitzsimmons get-up before he'd inserted that key. (Your narrator just didn't know where to put that part.) Which meant that now, post-key-and-ring-turning, as Marvin was about to open the anteroom door and step into Foggbottom's office, he was already clad in Geraldine Fitzsimmons' dress and wig. Which, btw, thanks to that weight gain, fit. All of which adds up to Universal Life Lesson No. 78: "Time travel is complicated."

"Crap," Marvin said as he looked down at this abomination. "I am *so* never wearing blue again."

Opening the door, the first thing he heard was his own voice: "Now you're just making stuff up," he was saying. And there he was — "*Past* Marvin" let's call him — on the other side of the green webbing, standing at Foggbottom's side while the depth and breadth of the universe loomed lyrically at the window. Foggbottom then went into his spiel about the ill-advised hand-shaking habit of Marvin's fellow man. Presently, when the Kilgorian ship appeared on the view-screen and Foggbottom turned his wheelchair to say, "That's not good," Marvin — "*Present* Marvin" let's call him — recognized his cue.

He cleared his throat. He made his way along the wall of swords to the doorway where he'd earlier seen Geraldine Fitzsimmons, and took his position, as if he, Geraldine Fitzsimmons, had come from the hall. "Not necessary," he announced, trying his damnest to look like her, trying his damnest to remember exactly what she'd said the first time around, wondering if it even mattered. What if he were to say, "Peter Piper picked a peck of pickled peppers," or "I am a Son of the Pink Flamingo," or "twenty-three skidoo"? Would that instantly become what he remembered coming out of Geraldine Fitzsimmons' mouth? He hesitated for a second, debating whether to test it out. He didn't want to jump out there — "Hey, me! Look! It's Future Me!" — and later find out driver's licenses were no longer issued to anyone under 30 or Dick Cheney had made the cover of *People* magazine's "Sexiest Man Alive" issue or there wasn't any *Canada* anymore.

In the end, he opted not to take the chance; he concentrated on recreating the scene just as he remembered it. Until he understood more about time travel and the Hel-IX, he'd have to act it out, go through the motions. He'd have to make sure things happened just like they did or he might not be standing where he was. He might not be standing anywhere.

Past Marvin was not to recognize him but was to recognize the clue. That was a given. Why was it a given? Because he *hadn't* recognized himself and he *had* recognized the clue. Part of him said he couldn't screw it up, because obviously Past Marvin bought Geraldine Fitzsimmons — Bizarro Geraldine Fitzsimmons — as the real Geraldine Fitzsimmons. Why wouldn't he? Who *else* would she be?

"It's all fixed," he, Geraldine Fitzsimmons, finally came out with. "The, uh, anomaly I mean." He looked from one of them to the other, from Foggbottom to his two-hour-and-fifty-seven-minute past self. Were they — *he!* — buying it? Trying to capture Geraldine Fitzsimmons' superior tone, he went on: "Had to put in a new, you know, gamma thingamajiggie …" (Which he now recognized as something totally un-Geraldine-

Fitzsimmons-like to say. He wondered if Foggbottom had seen through it.) Still and all, by the time he got to "a hop-skip-jump and we're on our way" at least he felt like he had the voice down.

Thank goodness then for Marvin Plotnik's uncanny memory. Most people wouldn't remember exactly how the next line went — most people wouldn't remember what they had for lunch — but Marvin had no trouble with it. "You did hear me say 'hop-skip-jump,' yes?" he queried. "'Hop-skip-jump'?"

Expectantly, he looked over Geraldine Fitzsimmons' blue pointy glasses, thinking maybe another Foggbottom would appear out of nowhere — let's call him *"Present Foggbottom"* (or even *"Future Foggbottom"* depending on how all of this worked). You know, pop out of the woodwork and set things straight, somehow waylay Slag Udyedsu from appearing in the first place. (Where *had* Foggbottom gone anyway? Wasn't he supposed to be here by now, er, *then?*)

But that didn't happen. No Foggbottom. Just Past Foggbottom in his wheelchair by the window. So, coming to the last line Marvin remembered from Bizarro Geraldine Fitzsimmons (and now suddenly *immensely* sorry he hadn't thought of putting something more protective under that wig other than his skull), he took a breath. "We just put the ol' girl in gear ..." He said this with so much reluctance and resignation you'd think Geraldine Fitzsimmons was succumbing to a gastric situation. This of course because Marvin *was* succumbing to a gastric situation — because he knew what came next.

And it came with a *whump.*

A whump you no doubt recognize as the whump of Winston's tail as it came down on "Geraldine Fitzsimmons" before she was kicked to the corner like a pile of dirty shorts.

It is of course a tired trope to have one's protagonist (or "pile of shorts" as it were), hit on the head and left for dead, fall into a dream state, but since this is indeed what happened once Winston and his prisoners left the room, I'm not leaving it out just so some wonk at *Publishers Weekly* can deem the narrative "fresh and original," which is an industry term for

"I never saw this before." If this were a tale of fiction that might be a
different story, but it isn't so the dream stays in.

Which went like this {~*insert undulating image of our felled hero
here*~}:

Marvin finds himself in a great hall. The hall is full of people, certainly
more than should be allowed by the fire marshal, and they are dressed in
turn-of-the-century (i.e. 20th century) clothing — the women in hats and
shawls and bustles, the men in hats and vests and starched collars. Everyone
is enjoying a performance of some sort. An audience. They are shoulder-
to-shoulder (upon some of which children perch), some in the aisles,
some two to a seat because there isn't a spare in the house. They are almost
literally "packed to the rafters."

And they are laughing, slapping each other on the backs, slacking
their jaws in thorough amusement and generally displaying the sad state
of dental hygiene that is the hallmark of the times. Cigar smoke, rising
from the rabble, mixes with the smoke of the footlights, resulting in an
eerie glow that casts the performer in other-worldly light.

Marvin is at the back. He stands on tippy-toes, craning his neck,
trying to see over the crowd, trying to catch a glimpse of the performer. It
is someone Marvin really *really* wants to see, though he can't quite recall
the man's name. He is embarrassed about this but knows that as soon as he
sees the man, it will all come back to him and he will be immensely
pleased.

Someone moves and Marvin can see now not just a unicycle, but that
the man seated upon it is pedaling to and fro to keep his balance. He is
spinning a plate on a long pole that extends from his forehead into the air.
He keeps the plate going while juggling three red balls. With one hand, for
he is a one-armed acrobat. "Eggs," he says, answering an audience member's
question. "Scrambled."

Marvin laughs with everyone else. He hasn't heard the question, but
he knows what it is. A woman in the audience has asked what she'd had for
breakfast on a specific day. Six years prior.

Now a man stands and yells something at the man on the unicycle.

Again, Marvin doesn't catch what it is. But like in many dreams, where you understand a situation without being told, Marvin knows the man has yelled another very obscure question, a question nobody would know, not in a million years. Because the man on the unicycle is supposed to know all the answers, you see. To everything. That and juggling on a unicycle is the act.

Marvin feels like he's seen the man on the stage a dozen times and the man has never been stumped. Marvin feels his heart swell with great anticipation, like he is going to once again see his hero prove how clever he is. Marvin knows as well as he knows anything that the one-armed man on the unicycle will not only answer the question correctly, he will add information that is just as obscure; and he will not drop the plate nor any of the balls, either.

But his hero doesn't answer the question. Instead, the man stops juggling the balls and takes down the plate and hops off the unicycle.

"I can't say I have an answer to that," the man announces, looking truly embarrassed. "But I do know who does." And Marvin can feel his face turn red hot as everyone in the great hall turns to look at him.

And all at once the crowd recognizes him and applauds and begins to chant:

"Yolando!" "Yolando!" "Yolando!"

• • •

THE ROOM CAME slowly into view, like a rack focus, which is meant here as a filmmaker's term in which the lens is gradually focused, not as the term used by low-life barroom losers who think "rack" means something else.

Marvin lay there in the corner of Foggbottom's office, feeling somewhat angry (a) for being too stupid to put something more protective under that wig and (b) for standing by while his subconscious had the nerve to imply he was Yolando Plumadore. It felt, somehow, like turning your back on a friend (in an odd but-I-made-this-guy-up-in-the-first-place sort of way). Then again, his subconscious had a point. Maybe he wasn't Yolando

Plumadore *per se,* but he was definitely the guy everyone was depending on.

Okay, so now what? He'd done his duty, reenacted — or at least played out — Geraldine Fitzsimmons coming into the room. What else was he supposed to do? He looked down at the Hel-IX, still in his hand. He'd guessed correctly, interpreted the symbols without error, and appeared at just the right moment. What else could he do?

He thought for a good long while. He thought for a good long while more. Then, nervously, he turned the seventh ring.

Chapter THIRTY...

H ELLO! ME AGAIN! While Marvin was meeting with Holsomback Mundy in the supply closet, shoving Winston into the freezer, rifling through my personal belongings with his friends, and making like Geraldine Fitzsimmons, I was off preparing for a need some 22 paragraphs hence.

I'm sure you missed me, but suffice it to say I have been distracted For The Good of All and can now devote much more time to you, dear reader, and the chronicling of events. In the meantime, since you last saw me wheeling down the hall and out of sight, I'd left the narrative in the hands of my trusted assistant, Jean-Claude, and, now that I look it over, there is little I would change except for the notational comment about Tanganyikans counting their bunions, which, my dear Jean-Claude, is pure tish-tosh and monkey feathers. It is not the Tanganyikans who count their bunions, it is the French. And I'm talking about the ones right there on Earth. (Do not try to protect your brethren, J.C.; we only deal with the truth here.)

So. I will go over what happened next rather quickly, because it did happen rather quickly, especially if you were seeing it from the perspective of Dara, Bennie and/or Kit, whom, as you recall, were in the hidden anteroom at the back of Foggbottom's office, Kilgorians at the gate as it were, annoyingly pounding their grimy claws on the door with great abandon (the Kilgorians, not Dara, *et. al.*). The trio had just begun to pile everything they could at said door — the wardrobe, the ottoman, the divan, the hat-rack, the small table, the bags of Cheese Doodles — while mumbling variations of "They mean business," "We are so dead," "What the youknowwhat are we gonna do?" and "Oh crap I forgot to update my FaceSpace page."

The guards, in turn, had begun to use their weapons and were presently blasting away at the anteroom door, which was deafening to say the least.

Again with the "They mean businesses" and the "We are so deads" and the "What-the-youknowwhat-are-we-gonna-dos" — none of which was possible to hear with all that blasting going on — only this time they got their answer.

It came in the form of a heretofore unseen sliding door at the back of the anteroom just beyond where the wardrobe had stood. It slid open (the sliding door, not the wardrobe), and there stood Marvin Plotnik, outfitted not in Geraldine Fitzsimmons' oversized blue satin dress but in clothes the likes of which I'm sure they'd never seen before: a brightly colored purple cape, for instance, and dilapidated work boots and dark goggles and what appeared to be a battered top hat. And he also sported a rather dashing soul-patch on his bottom lip. Not only that, he appeared, quite frankly, fit. No longer Chubby Marvin the Dweeb, he was more like Marvin the Dashing Hunk.

"Hope I'm not too late," he announced, eyeing the barricade. He saw their confused looks at the sliding door. "Elevator," he pointed out. "I had it put in."

Then at what he was wearing.

Straightening his hat: "Don't ask."

The pounding continued, the wall between anteroom and Foggbottom's office pulsing from the force of the Kilgorian attack.

"Where have you *been*?" Dara cried, actually running to him and putting her arms around his neck.

"Oh, here and there," he replied, gladly returning the hug. It was with this simple act that Dara, Bennie and Kit undoubtedly noticed that Marvin had become, despite the unusual outfit, in some strange way older and, if you were to put a word to it, wiser. They were about to say just that when the wall began to show signs of wear and tear. Laser blast holes the size of baseballs began to make themselves apparent and with them glimpses of snake-like eyes and alligator-like claws, snorting leathery pig-snouts and other unsightly particulars of Kilgorian {~*gag, heave, ugh*~} anatomy.

"Good wall," Marvin noted, impressed with how it was holding out. He then suggested it was a good idea for everyone to move back a few feet and urged them toward the elevator wall. The three dutifully followed instructions, soon finding themselves with their backs against the wall, which is a phrase that means they were in a dire situation (in this case, both figuratively and literally). "It doesn't look good," Marvin said, completely unaware I had just basically said as much.

Again the elevator door slid open. "I totally agree," came a voice from within. This, of course, was Reginald T. Foggbottom, and he was not in a wheelchair, nor was he on a TransWay One-Man Vehicle. He was, in fact, standing on his own two feet, presumably replacements, along of course with the shins and thighs and buttocks that came with them, which makes the whole standing-on-his-own-two-feet thing a smoother operation. He looked around the elevator as if he were impressed. "Excellent idea," he said. "Wish I'd thought of it." Then: "Miss me?"

Marvin, raising his voice to be heard over the blasts: "Looks like we timed it pretty good. Stay against the wall, guys." And with that, he reached for a small panel to the right of the elevator, slid it open, revealing three buttons: a red one, a green one, and a yellow one.

All at once the door and wall to Foggbottom's office gave way, the wardrobe was pushed aside, and the Kilgorian guards came rushing in, weapons drawn and cocked, looking (and smelling) their angry, snarly best. Prompting, of course, the five figures against the far wall to reluctantly raise their hands in surrender.

During which ... Marvin pushed the red button.

And the Kilgorian troops were instantly encased in an elaborate dome of pulsating light. The dome, geodesic in structure, looked much like a force field, because in point of fact it was a force field. As it hummed in rhythmic waves, it not only held the Kilgorians in place, but completely silenced their annoyingly snarly wails. The Kilgorian guards then began shooting their weapons at our heroes, thankfully to no avail, as the force field merely gobbled up the energy like it was so much Rocky Road with sprinkles and whipped cream, the cherry on the top being it pissed them off like nobody's business.

Marvin felt the others' eyes upon him. "What?" he shrugged, removing the cape.

"How ... how did you *do* that?" Dara wanted to know.

"That? It was nothing really. After Winston conked me in the head and I came to, I simply turned the decades wheel three clicks, went back thirty years, retained a position in the Retcon Corporation's mail room on Pyrsnyk, worked my way up to lab assistant, then on to four years as head of R&D, where I spearheaded the development of defensive systems for the Pyrsnyki fleet, making sure each M100 starship, which the *Grace* happens to be, now has, as standard issue, reinforced titanium walls." He looked to the Kilgorian troops, spitting and snarling soundlessly inside the energy dome. "And an Anti-Invasive-Force Containment Unit." He acted as if it was an obvious solution. "Plus," he added, "that elevator thing."

They watched as the Kilgorians, increasingly irate, tried ripping at the field, arms and tails skewampus,[91] getting entangled not only in each other's limbs but ever more in the hungry grid — like bugs in a spider web, which would be a good metaphor had I not already used "web" for Foggbottom's expository green light beams; so let's just say "like bugs in a geodesic force field."

"This is very interesting," Foggbottom said, rubbing his chin, "because *I* went back thirty-*seven* years to *Gygaxia*, where as envoy with the Inter-

---

91> Two times in one book! Booyah!

Planetary Manufacturing League and Trading Consortium, I negotiated a trade agreement with the Pyrsnyki defense industry. It was through this trade agreement I spearheaded the development of *offensive* systems for our trade partners, including the Pyrsnykis, making sure each M100 starship, which of course *The Princess Grace* happens to be, has as standard issue a *Gygaxian Call-to-Arms System,* a panic button if you will, where every member of the Gygaxian fleet — currently numbering in the thousands I might add — will be instantly called upon to assist their Pyrsnyki trade partner should the system be deployed. Which, by the way, is initiated by means of a remote control GCAS device, issued only to the diplomatic — *how do you do* — corps. Thus." He opened his hand to reveal a small gold switch set in a not-quite-as-small velvet-lined box, the size in which you might find a very nice diamond ring, or, if you were mixed up with the mob, a severed toe. He flipped the switch.

"Interesting!" Marvin said. "Because I *also* developed— Did you say '*Princess*' Grace?" He glared.

Foggbottom: "It's a long story."

He felt Marvin's glare.

"Poker game." (As if that would explain it.) "Strip poker." (As if *that* would explain it.) "Well you can't very well expect me to go off for three decades without some R&R."

(Marvin's glare? Still there.)

"Okay so I sort of put the ship up for collateral and then … lost track of her and … I mean who knew the Bijoolians knew how to operate the homing device in the lining of my jacket? I mean, *c'mon!* They can't even balance a checkbook! *Nobody* would have seen that coming!"

Marvin glared at him in a way someone would glare at someone who could have very well screwed the pooch, or any number of synonymous metaphors listed under "screwed the pooch" in *Reginald T. Foggbottom's Dictionary of Peculiar Expressions, Adages, Idioms and Other Figures of Speech (English).*

"Look, I got her back didn't I?" Foggbottom said. "What can I say? Lesson learned. And INGA likes the new name better. And INGA's got *some* say in it."[92]

Marvin cleared his throat, put his hands on his hips just to drive home the screw-the-pooch-or-other-appropriately-chastising point, and took up where he left off: *"Because I also developed ...* an Anti-Invasive-Force Containment Unit *Tank,* thus." He pushed the green button. The floor of the anteroom, save the three feet upon which our quintet stood, gave way. And the geodesic dome / Kilgorian horde with it.

"Excellent!" Foggbottom declared. He peered over the side of the gaping trap door, fumes rising from below. "Serubian Bog Oil, I presume."

"Gorffugian Trag-acid," Marvin replied, still a little put out by the fact that Foggbottom could have lost the ship. "As you well know, Serubian Bog Oil's hard to get in these quantities. Seems *someone"* — another glare — "had cornered the market."

"Ah," Foggbottom nodded, looking down into the tank. "I do apologize. Excellent work then, considering."

You can well imagine what Gorffugian Trag-acid does when you have a five-meter-deep tank of it, since of course Gorffugian Trag-acid is to Serubian Bog Oil what Jim-Bob Jimmer's Hootin' Hollerin' Hotter'n Hell Jalapeño Sauce is to plain no-fat yogurt. Which means of course there was not much to see in the tank below, not even floating bits of not much to see. "Took care of *that,*" Marvin said, slapping his palms together in a manner that has no name.[93]

Marvin now pushed the yellow button, and the trap doors closed.

For six full seconds, Dara, Kit and Bennie digested this new informa-

---

92> The Poker Incident shall be expanded upon in a separate volume, *The Foggbottom Chronicles,* coming soon (budget permitting) to a dealer near you.

93> You know what? I'm just going to make up a word for it. Make that a hyphenated word: "Slap-clap." How's that? "Marvin slap-clapped his hands." Strike another one for Mr. Shakespeare, without whom we writers would be cranking out restaurant menus, technical manuals and insurance actuary tables. Go, "GB"!

tion, looked from blasted anteroom door to elevator to the now-apparent seam in the floor. I say a full six seconds because at the 6.1-second mark, Slag Udyesu's ugly puss showed on the view-screen out in Foggbottom's office. "Brok Goldfarn! Brok Ghazhik!" his creepy countenance barked. "Show yourselves! Report at once! We have arrived at the Festival of the Feasts!"

By way of proof, the screen switched to orbital view revealing they had indeed arrived above a much larger and much, well, crap-browner (pardon my Esperanto) world than Earth [Sol-7(3)], above which a great collection of ships had convened. Ships of all size, shape, color and design congregated at various orbital heights. At the fore of these ships hovered a humongous flashing sign: "SIXTEENTH ANNUAL GREATER KILGORIAN FESTIVAL OF FEASTS AND STARSHIP EXPOSITION. COME N GET IT!" (the N inexplicably backward).

"I'm afraid your lieutenants are busy at the moment," Foggbottom announced. He stepped through a blast hole to approach the screen.

Once again the screen switched to Slag Udyedsu's repulsive countenance. "*Another* escaped prisoner?" Then, clearly taken aback as he saw Marvin, Dara, Bennie and Kit make their way through the same blast hole from the anteroom, he bellowed, "I have had enough of this! Secure these prisoners! *Secure these prisoners!*" And: "I want two hundred men on that ship *this instant!*"

He snapped his fingers and alarms went off on the Kilgorian ship as dozens of troops in the background stormed out of view in the manner of highly-trained storm troopers, which is not an image George Lucas has rights to thank you very much, complete with clomping of feet and brandishing of weapons and they're-messin'-with-the-wrong-guys looks on their faces. [94]

Marvin counted to twenty before he told the commander, "I'm afraid you're wasting your time. You see, we have on our vessel not only an Anti-Invasive-Force Containment Unit—"

94> You can ask the people of Germany and Italy, c. 1942, about this one.

"And tank," Foggbottom added.

"*And* tank — which your lieutenants have so graciously volunteered to test out, but a further deterrent as well. I'm afraid your newly-deployed troops have been mis — er — appropriated. They have not boarded our ship. They have boarded a mere facsimile, or, to be more precise, a Doppelcraft, a newly patented proprietary creation of the Retcon Corporation, Ltd. Looks like the real thing from any angle. An illusion you see. I'm afraid your two hundred men, Commander Udyedsu, have boarded absolutely nothing at all." And he nodded to the screen to indicate there were now dozens of Kilgorian troops floating aimlessly about out there like so much cosmic flotsam and jetsam.

Foggbottom whispered out of the corner of his mouth, "However did you accomplish that?"

"Divergent Light Pattern Actuator," Marvin whispered back, then, seeing no recognition by Foggbottom: "Mirrors. Loads of 'em. Had them installed five months ago."

"Hmm …" Foggbottom hmmmed. "And I this." He tapped his lapel in a distinct pattern, and the ship lurched as if being untethered. "Magbeam Disengagement Module. Had *it* installed *four* months ago."

Marvin smiled. "Four months ago? If only we knew this afternoon."

For a few minutes they watched their handiwork come to fruition, as more alarms were sounded on the Kilgorian ship and scores of rescue pods appeared from its hull, dispatched hither and yon in a frantic attempt to retrieve the troops who'd been set adrift.

"Ah," Foggbottom beamed, "just in time." A quick nod to a league of approaching Gygaxian togships, responding to the call to arms. (Remember? The button in the velvet box?) "I see they've received our distress signal." And: "Should I give a heads-up to Commander Udyedsu?"

"Be my guest," Marvin said, inviting him with a wave of his arm.

Foggbottom opened his mouth to speak to the Kilgorian commander, thought better of it and turned to his young protégé. "*Naah,*" he said, a hint of mischief in his eye. "Let him find out himself."

Marvin then spotted another Kilgorian ship. It was coming full tilt. "Uh oh," he said. He straightened his hat. "Looks like Udyedsu has some help."

"No worries," said Foggbottom. "I sort of sent a message to his nemesis, Slag Perescu, this afternoon, in which *Slag Udyedsu*" — thumb to self — "was referring to him in a most unpleasant way. I can sound remarkably like the commander, you know."

"*How* unpleasant?"

They watched as Slag Perescu's ship took up position helm-to-helm with the commander's ship. "I might have mentioned a number of bodily orifices." Looking back, we now know Perescu was so focused on avenging his honor he failed to notice the entire Gygaxian fleet until both Kilgorian ships were surrounded.

"Well done," Marvin said, impressed. "Anything else?"

"Nothing I can think of. Oh, I did take the liberty of putting INGA back online. Simple matter, really. *INGA! If you would be so kind as to take us home?*"

"I'd be happy to," came that wonderful sultry voice. "There are hot towels in the washroom. Be sure to wash behind your ears."

Chapter THIRTY-ONE...

D UE TO THE unexpected delays of the time loop and the Kilgorian disturbance, *The Princess Grace* was the last ship to arrive, postponing welcoming ceremonies by two full weeks (Nor-Wayan time). Marvin and the others had spent that time on board, continuing their studies under the watchful eye of Skylar Waddell and the tutelage of Felix Flöckenheimer, Colonel Higgenmeyer-Matheson, and Geraldine Fitzsimmons. But only Marvin, Dara, Bennie and Kit were aware of the time loop and Winston's attempt at culinary carnage. The rest were blissfully ignorant, still thinking all the way up until they actually pulled into the spaceport that they were in the middle of Wyoming at a ranch for wayward teens. Which once again proves Marvin's Universal Life Lesson No. 42: "People see what they want to see."

Now, things were back on course: A crowd had already gathered in the atrium of the Nor-Wayan Institute of Cooperative Enterprises' Orientation Center. Sunlight streamed through four-story windows, giving the hall the feel of a new beginning, as scores of people — some human, some not — wandered about the black-and-white checkered floor, waiting to be told just what this was all about.

Marvin, Dara, Bennie and Kit were among the few standing on the catwalk that overlooked the crowd. They were soon joined by the unflappable Mr. Foggbottom and his trusted assistant, Holsomback Mundy, neither of whom was dressed as any of their previous personas. They now looked quite dapper in simple gray suits with simple gray ties, topped by a head of short-cropped red hair, and holding flutes of champagne. (The kids held glasses of delicious lime-green punch.)

"There's one thing I don't get," Dara said, as people in penultimate scenes often do. She turned to Foggbottom: "When did you hide the key in the globe?"

Marvin nodded. "Yeah. Thanks for that. We'd all be *pie* right now if you hadn't."

Foggbottom looked genuinely confused. "Key? What key?"

"To the Hel-IX."

"Key to the Hel-IX?"

"The Helicoidinal—"

"I know what it is, my boy, I just don't know what you mean by hiding its key. In a ... in a ... globe, you say? Just what kind of globe are we talking about?"

"The *globe*," Marvin pressed. "The old one ... in your—" He looked at Foggbottom like the old goat was one noodle short of a pancake.

"In the globe? The key was in the globe? Hadn't I handed it to you with the Hel-IX?"

Again with the one-noodle-short-of-a-pancake thing. "No," Marvin said, "you hadn't."

Foggbottom gave Holsomback Mundy a look.

"Wasn't *me*," Mundy said. He took a sip of champagne. "We're only allotted two Hel-IXes. And two keys. Neither of which was given to me. *In 24 rotations.*" He glared at Foggbottom.

"Wait a minute," Marvin said. "Don't tell me ..."

Foggbottom: "Let me see if I can help here." He reached into his pocket where he retrieved a small slip of paper, wrinkled, stained, and yellowed with age. He handed it to Marvin. "A receipt," he said somewhat unnecessarily, because, as Marvin examined it, it was clearly that:

Foggbottom patted him on the back then began to descend the great stairway to the atrium. "Do hurry back," he called over his shoulder. "Ceremonies are about to begin."

Marvin, frowned at the receipt. "You're not serious."

Foggbottom, mid-stairway: "Now that I think about it, that antiquities dealer *did* seem to know me somehow. Always felt a little odd, that. As a matter of fact, I now recall, when he handed me that receipt, he said something along the lines of, 'Happy now?' I thought it quite rude at the time. Of course *now*…" He smiled at Marvin before continuing his descent.

"Oh fer cryin' out loud," Marvin groaned, staring at the receipt. "Just when I thought I was done, I gotta learn *Spanish*?"

"And Italian," Foggbottom called. "Don't forget Belladini, the map-maker. You'll have to make sure he installs that button."

Marvin rolled his eyes. "Oh fer crap's sake …" And clicked the proper rings on the Hel-IX.

● ● ●

FIVE MINUTES LATER, Marvin reappeared in the atrium. His shirt was torn in a number of places, he had smudges about his face and shoulders, and under one arm he held an item about the size of a microwave. He looked tired and drawn.

He found Foggbottom at the stairs to the stage, upon which a woman stood at a podium addressing the crowd. Behind her, on the stage, a group of important-looking people sat in chairs.

"You didn't say anything about the riots," Marvin said through gritted teeth. He nodded at his condition. "You said nothing about the riots."

He decided to skip the full exposition — how he'd met the map maker, Giuseppe Belladini, in Rome, or how he'd arranged for the manufacture of the globe, or how Belladini had sold the globe to another party after already installing the only Hel-IX key Marvin had given him, or how Marvin then had to trace the damn thing to a Viennese nobleman in 1837, then the great Bulgarian Tsaritsa Alexandra Fyodorovna in 1911, and how, in 1957, he traced to one Lamont LeRouche, "Larcenist of Luxembourg," who claimed he had it in his apartment (he didn't), then had the audacity to leave Marvin with the check after clearly inviting *him* for a drink.

Ultimately, Marvin came upon the globe in the shop of an antiquities dealer in Barcelona, where, after spying it in the window, he hit the proprietor over the head with a fourteen-inch replica of the Eiffel Tower, posed as the fellow, and sold the globe to a silly looking little German man on whose bald head was a birthmark in the shape of Bhutan.

All during the preceding paragraph Foggbottom kept his eye on the stage as if waiting to be called to the podium. He then whispered, "Took care of it, did you?"

Marvin glared. "You know I did."

One hand on the handrail, still watching the proceedings, Foggbottom brushed a piece of lint from the sleeve of his jacket, nonchalantly adding, "Mr. Mundy has announced he is finished with the fetch-haul business. Says he wants to grow pineapples in the South Pacific, break in a hammock … some such nonsense."

"That so?"

"Indeed." He listened for a minute as the woman at the podium welcomed the new recruits. "I told him the cockroaches down there are the size of Buicks. Didn't phase him in the least. His mind is made up." Foggbottom shrugged. "Of course that means I'm in the market for a new assistant."

"And?"

"And I'm in the market, that's all." He listened a moment to the speaker. "I don't suppose you have any hidden discontent, do you? Seems, as I say, I'm always getting saddled with discontents."

Marvin felt the Hel-IX in his pocket. "I wasn't too keen on arranging for that globe, I can tell you that."

Just then, from the podium: "Without further ado, Bleektop Bladderhorn!"

There was great applause as Foggbottom stepped on the stair.

"You're kidding," Marvin said. "Bladderhorn?"

"Indeed," Foggbottom, er, Bladderhorn replied. Then, looking back at him: "By the way, were you ever going to mention *that*?" He'd pointed to the microwave-sized item under Marvin's arm.

"Oh!" Marvin said, trying to get his head around "Bleektop Bladderhorn," while shifting his burden to his other hand. "Almost forgot. I took a side trip." He revealed a familiar cage, once again full of active and playful skerlish. "Got there just in time, by the way — *this* time. Winston ended up using sardines." He scrunched up his nose at the foul thought of it. He poked a finger into the cage to pet a particularly adorable one: "I just couldn't let it happen to the little buggers."

• • •

REGINALD T. FOGGBOTTOM, administrator, Nor-Wayan fetch-hauler, bus driver, and collector of African masks, aka Felix W. Flöckenheimer, professor of torn paper, and now aka Bleektop Bladderhorn, mysterious figure who apparently garnered much admiration, welcomed the crowd to Nor-Way, asked if they'd had a good trip, waited for a reply, then described the Nor-Wayan Institute of Cooperative Enterprises as a "sort of inter-galactic think tank," which most of them already knew as they'd been there two weeks already. He then explained how each recruit had already been assigned a group leader, and invited them to seek them out. No one moved, of course, because no one thought they had enough information to go on.

"Let me give you a clue," Bladderhorn told the crowd, and surprised everyone by inviting Bennie Sterlati to the stage. With Bennie at his side, he then asked a wild-haired gentleman in a woolen vest — who'd been sitting among the group on the chairs, smoking a pipe — to join him as well. "Mr. Sterlati," Bladderhorn said as the man approached, "I'd like to introduce you to your group leader, Mr. Albert Einstein." Who, quite politely, removed his pipe with one hand and held out the other for that bewildering hand-shake business.

Immediately everyone from the Sandy Rivers Hilltop Ranch for Way-ward Youth, Juveniles, and Young Adults realized that before them now stood, in the flesh, someone they'd only seen in history books and PBS reenactments. Very much alive.

Brains began to work out how and why this was so.

"I'm sure Mr. Sterlati has realized by now," Bleektop Bladderhorn said into the microphone, "how his assigned name, Bennie Sterlati, relates to the name of his team leader." It was Dara who let out a little gasp. Followed by Flinn and Harlen. "How *stupid* of us!" Dara cried.

Bennie stood dumbfounded. "What?" He mouthed from the stage, still not getting it.

"It's an anagram, you dope," Kit called to him. "Bennie Sterlati. Albert Einstein. Same letters!"

Bladderhorn then asked the group of team leaders, mentors if you will, to join the recruits and watched as they filed, one by one, down the steps from the stage and into the crowd.

Dara stared at the last of them. A slender man with a crooked smile, he wore a "boater" which is what they call those straw hats you see in barbershop quartets, which, let's face it, you don't see anymore outside of "The Music Man" revivals. The hat was set at a rakish angle. That, combined with a carnation in his lapel, double-breasted jacket and two-tone shoes, gave him an air of "a man about town" (or, as they say nowadays, "Tommy Tune").

"Oh. My. God," Dara mouthed as she sheepishly walked his way. Standing not two feet away, she stammered, "Y-Y-Y F-F-F—" by which of course she meant "You're Fred Astaire!" This was her idol, right here, right in front of her, in Glorious Technicolor, which of course is something you will recognize from The Classic Movie Channel as movies that look like they were put together by the same folks who came up with Play Doh Brights. She finally came out with, "I'm very pleased to make your acquaintance," and even added a little curtsey. Luckily, Mr. Astaire took her hand and gave it a gentlemanly kiss because a man in a double-breasted suit and two-tone shoes would naturally think a curtsey quite charming.

And so it went, with Flinn Karneb discovering Ben Franklin and Harlen C. Skedics discovering Charles Dickens and Kit Warnam discovering Mark Twain (thank God for name-tags; Kit had a hard time telling him from Mr. Einstein). There of course were more — kids whose name-tags transposed to Pablo Picasso or H.G. Wells or Leonardo da Vinci or Thomas Edison or Groucho Marx, plus Bowie Steelestoyn and Flugilly Strongmeiser and others from other planets you've probably never heard of. (There were even some people of considerable accomplishment who are very much alive in your timeline whom, I'm sorry to say, I am not at liberty to divulge.)

And so, after everyone had found his or her (or "its" in the case of the Bijoolians) "mentor-to-be" and the small talk and chatter had calmed down, Bleektop Bladderhorn once again addressed the crowd.

"Well done!" he beamed. "And in record time, too. This is most encouraging." His voice echoed through the atrium, settling onto each mentor/mentorees group.

A sigh, then: "Now. This is how it works... Every five years, the Nor-Wayan Institute of Cooperative Enterprises will bring each of you to Nor-Way for as long as you like. Here you will be taught in an accelerated environment by the greatest minds in the universe, and we ask only one thing in return: that on each visit you bring us the products, inventions and concepts you feel will become the most ubiquitous on your home planets. We are of course interested in the ground-breakers, the game-changers and any other hyphenated contrivance you may come up with — just as a matter of keeping with the times you understand — but we are also interested in the basics: the duct tapes, the safety pins, the aluminum foils. Zippers. Ball-point pens.

"Fiber optics and MRI machines and cell phones and TV-remote finders come and go, but you'll always need good dental floss. And socks. And paper clips. My good friend Marvin Plotnik here once delivered a speech on the internal combustion engine claiming it pure folly. It is, indeed, that; it won't be around forever. But what *will* be around forever? This is what we're interested in. While your investors and venture capitalists throw unlimited cash at such a thing as the internal combustion engine (and the industries around it) we at the Nor-Wayan Institute of Cooperative Enterprises operate under the radar, reaping small but steadily profitable rewards one penny — peso, farthing, *paafakumolaka*[95] — at a time. Which, over the course of the ages, adds up." He gestured to their impressive surroundings. "Why, this great hall was built entirely on the proceeds from xanthum gum. In fact, the structural beams are *composed* of xanthum gum."

By now Marvin had moved to the foot of the stage. From here he could see the red-and-white emblem on the podium that read NOR-WAYAN INSTITUTE OF COOPERATIVE ENTERPRISES below which was the slogan: 'ANY TIME. ANY WHERE.' The center graphic — what once would have

---

95> The smallest denomination of currency on the planet Marff. Approximately 79¢.

passed for a fair likeness of an atom (tiny spheres orbiting a spherical center) — seemed, somehow, not like the insignia the Capt. Atomic Kosmic Space Blaster at the back of a 1956 issue of *Jet Pack Joe,* but, rather, given Marvin's new understanding of the Interconnectness of All Things, timeless. Which, yes, is a play on words.

Bladderhorn looked over the crowd. "Some of you, by the way, were not assigned an alternate name. This was not a mistake. As Mr. Plotnik has already discovered, we had other plans for you. Why, you may ask. Because we're NICE, the Nor-Wayan Institute of Cooperative Enterprises. And as masters of time and space, we have already *seen* your destiny. It is just, therefore, a matter of working our way backward.

"As you think back on your formative years, you may recall a few of our scouts. Perhaps you wondered why you'd been singled out for detention or extra work at school. Perhaps you wondered why your parents had, say, given one another a high-five when they sent you away. If there's one thing we want to instill in you, our future leaders, is that nothing is what it seems. … Wait. Except professional wrestling. That *is* what it seems.

"You'd be surprised how many things you've experienced in your lives that were not what you thought they were. For past graduates of NICE, always on the lookout for new recruits, a stint at detention might be a way to study you further; a high-five might be one of pride rather than relief; a roll of the eyes might just be a way of saying, 'We have found another candidate.' So from this point forward, do not assume derision is derision; do not assume ridicule is ridicule; do not assume jeers are jeers or sneers are sneers or taunts are taunts or Duluth is Duluth. Assume, under the surface, there is a purpose. Assume it's NICE.

"And when you graduate, you, too, will look for new recruits. And here is the neatest part: 'Every five years' — when you have at your disposal the means to bend space and time — is whenever you want it to be! Is Mr. Einstein here in the year you last left Earth, or in 1958? Frankly, I'm not certain myself. We'll have to get him up here to explain it.

"So. I now welcome you all to Nor-Way and to NICE, I wish you good studies, and I bid you *adieu.*"

(*Applause, applause*, some schmoozing with team leaders, a nice roast beef dinner and all-you-can-eat cream pie, and the release by Marvin of seven fluffy and playful skerlish, with whom little Pookie frolicked gaily outside on the lawn.)

• • •

WHAT HAPPENED during the three little dots above would require another twenty pages of description, and frankly we are out of space. Suffice it to say, Marvin Plotnik gave a heartfelt wave to the bus driver, watched as spindly fingers pulled the bus door closed and the rickety old thing (the bus, not the driver) coughed and sputtered its way into the distance. Up the walkway Marvin went, where, opening the front door, he announced his arrival in his standard "Honey, I'm home" fashion.

"Where have you been, young man?" he heard his mother say.

"Where *haven't* I been?" he replied, opening the refrigerator door. "After the Sandy Rivers Hilltop Ranch for Wayward Youth, Juveniles, and Young Adults took off into space and got stuck in a time loop, I was hung over a vat of Serubian Bog Oil, almost baked into a pie by a boil-faced six-armed lunatic from Kilgore, fired up a Helicoidinal Space-time Connibulator, masqueraded as a sanctimonious old biddy in a blue satin dress, went back in time where I developed an Anti-Invasion-Force Containment Unit for the Pyrsnyki star fleet, chased down a secret key in Rome, Russia, Bulgaria and Barcelona so I could plant it for my later self, then returned to the planet Nor-Way, where we all ate roast beef and had a nice laugh about it. Oh, plus they made me a junior fetch-hauler, so I'll be off to do more of *that*." Then, gazing into the fridge: "So what's for dinner?"

To which Marvin's mother replied, "How in the world did I raise such a smart-ass kid?"

A Completely Avoidable Addendum...

I WAS CERTAIN I'd tied up all the loose ends when this morning I found the following note in my inbox:

B.B.: You never explained the R.C. — J.C.

By this of course Jean-Claude meant I never explained just how the Nor-Wayan fetch-haul program managed to duplicate Marvin Plotnik's own design for a roller coaster. Fact is, I intended to deal with the matter in the text by pointing out that Mr. Plotnik had asked me this very question. To wit: "How'd you bastards manage to steal my coaster design anyway?" To which I replied, "That might be a good topic to bring up with yourself — the next time you run into you I mean." Meaning the whole pod interface was his idea in the first place, back when he was popping into the future and mucking about with the internal workings of *The Princess Grace*; i.e., he finally got a chance to finish it himself. We Nor-Wayans had nothing to do with it.

Same with the cross-over video games. All Marvin.

As it is, however, I don't recall where (or when) the exchange took place, and I didn't want to put something somewhere it didn't belong.

Which is what I told Jean-Claude in my reply. He said let's just put it anywhere, but I disagree: if I am anything, I am a stickler for accuracy. So I decided this addendum would suffice — and, seeing as I am relaxing on the beautiful black-sand beach of Kalapana, Hawai'i, at the moment, enjoying a refreshing piña colada (little umbrella, natch) while my compatriot is enjoying an equally refreshing root beer float (sans umbrella; he refuses to have one), frankly I have better things to do than even one more round of edits. Perhaps in another timeline.

Please do not write me letters about how the black-sand beach of Kalapana, Hawai'i, is no longer in existence as it was buried under the great Kilauea lava flow of 1990. Need I remind you I am in possession of a Helicoidinal Space-time Connibulator?

Hold a sec ... brb ...

I just turned to Mr. Plotnik and asked him his recollection of the exchange. His reply? "Whenev. Pass the sunscreen, yo."

THE TEST...

{ Think you're better than your friends? Only your scores will tell!
Unless otherwise noted, each correct answer receives 5 points.
Don't forget to add your points from footnote #36 to your final score. }

(1) What did Gopal Misra, the Indian cobbler, use to repair shoes?
   A. His teeth
   B. A crowbar
   C. Elves
   D. Popeil's Tummy Tucking AbCrunchBuster
   E. Joey's Shoe Repair down on 78th St.

   ANSWER: A.

(2) The Sons of the Pink Flamingo believe ...
   A. Anybody can do whatever they want
   B. Nobody can do whatever they want.
   C. Whatever nobody does, anybody wants.
   D. What can do, no can body want.
   E. Pink Flamingos are sorta creepy if you look at them up close.

   ANSWER: A. (D, of course, is correct if you are on the planet Lymel-7.)

(3) Knowing that large objects can affect your perceptions of time, which of the
   following would it be best to avoid if you have to make the bus:
   A. Another large bus
   B. Greenland
   C. Orca whale and or walrus
   D. Your lard-butt sister
   E. All of the above

   ANSWER: E

(4) The Pods of Angradorra … (circle all that apply)
   A. … are egg-shaped vessels encountered on the sixth level of *Styzzyx IV.*
   B. … emit a pulsating blue glow.
   C. … are so alluring, no player has yet been able to walk on by and get on with the game.
   D. … taunt you no end.
   E. … smell of broken dreams.

> ANSWER: All except E. (That's what comes from spending too much time playing Styzzyx IV.)

(5) Who designed *The Princess Grace?*
   A. Marvin Plotnik
   B. The Pyrsnykis
   C. Lockheed-Martin
   D. Andy Warhol
   E. Henry Hollingsworth Hathaway III
   F. That gay guy on that sitcom? The one who does the really gay things? Who's really funny? Not him.

> *ANSWER*: B and, technically, F.

(6) "Universal Life Lesson No. 42" states, "People see what they want to see." List five instances in the narrative where characters saw what they wanted to see. Five points each. Ten extra points if you can remember anything about Max Carboni.
   1. _____
   2. _____
   3. _____
   4. _____
   5. _____

(7) What does one find in a recipe for stargazy pie?
   A. Fish
   B. Stars
   C. 11 herbs and spices
   D. Secret sauce
   E. Gary Busey's loose screws
   F. All sorts of measurements

> *ANSWER:* A and F.

(8) Marvin was stuck with writer's block. Where was Yolando Plumadore stuck
before Marvin figured out a way for him to escape?
A. Detroit
B. In the Himalayas, hanging over a vat of boiling cream of wheat
C. In Lodi again
D. In a holding cell on the planet of Boojil
E. On Band-Aid brand 'cause Band-Aid's stuck on you.

ANSWER: B.

(9) Geraldine Fitzsimmons wore pointy blue glasses. Who else wore pointy glasses?
A. Professor Fingelheimer
B. Richard Nixon
C. The Laser X3000
D. Penelope Hastings
E. Nobody else, it's a trick question.

ANSWER: E. Not only that, there was no Professor Fingelheimer in this story.

(10) Which is funnier …
A. Bartholomew J. Finkensack
B. Felix W. Flöckenheimer
C. Buford T. Willicocks
D. Leonard R. Pipswaddle
E. Altoona

ANSWER: F. None of the above. "Monkey ball soup" is funnier than all of these.

(11) According to Professor Pipswaddle …
A. Television gives you cancer.
B. The Nielson ratings are the result of conspiratorial anti-government
anarchists.
C. The gap in David Letterman's teeth is a portal into another dimension.
D. Television is the opiate of the masses.
E. Paris Hilton's dog is a hand puppet.

ANSWER: B.

(12) What was the name of the first satellite in space?
A. O.R.B.I.T.
B. Sputnik
C. The LaserX3000
D. Uhny Uftz
E. "Steve"

ANSWER: B.

(13) In the Middle Ages, trebuchets were used to hurl things over castle walls.
Which of the following antiquities were *not* hurled over castle walls?
Circle as many as necessary.

DEAD COWS
BURNING BEE HIVES
BOULDERS
VICTIMS OF THE BLACK DEATH
PEANUT BUTTER COOKIES
PETRIFIED WOMBAT POO
BOILING OIL
PUPPIES ON SPIKES
1974 FORD PINTOS
ROCKS
PAPER
SCISSORS
WINDOWS 2000
BACK ISSUES OF "MAD" MAGAZINE

> *ANSWER:* Duh. (And if you said, Puppies on Spikes, shame on you.
> What are you, some kind of sick nut-job?)

(14) A major theme of this narrative is The Interconnectedness of All Things.
A good definition would be:
A. "Everything in the universe is interconnected."
B. "Everything is connected to everything else."
C. "All things, whether on the same dimensional space-time plane or not, are
separated by all other things, whether on the same dimensional space-time
plane or not, by infinitesimal increments."
D. "Possessing or displaying moral virtue."

> *ANSWER:* D.
> I did not say "a good definition of this concept," I merely said a "good" definition,
> and this is the one Oxford Dictionaries uses (© 2012 Oxford University Press).
> Get it? A "good" definition? Okay, okay, give yourself five points on this one just
> because it was stupid.

(15) Of the following, who use notational references in their work?
Circle all that apply.
A. Shakespeare
B. Marvin Plotnik
C. Writers on Glorfyndrak
D. Reginald T. Foggbottom

> *ANSWER:* All but A. (It is Shakespearean *scholars* who use notational references,
> not Shakespeare. He's dead.)

(16) What did the British call the American Colonists to make fun of them?
  A. "Buckle Boys"
  B. "Kettle Huggers"
  C. "Yankees"
  D. "Turkey-Lickin' Puritan Prisses"
  E. "Georgie Porgie Puddin' and Pie"
  F. "Here Boy!"

  ANSWER: C.

(17) What is written on all U.S. currency?
  A. *E Pluribus Unum*
  B. *Plur Bevius Eunum*
  C. *B Punius Evum*
  D. *E Plurinus Benum*
  E. *Nital ekil skool atros ti tub sdrawkcab si siht*
  F. *Spend at Will … We'll Make More.*

  ANSWER: A.

(17-1/2) Which means...?
  A. From many comes one
  B. From one comes many
  C. From Jersey comes people with low foreheads
  D. Latin rocks!
  E. Stacey Brillstein is still an idiot.

  ANSWER: A.

(18) What was Marvin's all-time favorite graphic novel?
  A. *Bug-Eyed Monsters Kick Ass*
  B. *Bug-Eyed Monsters, Inc.*
  C. *Bug Eyed Monsters, Go Home*
  D. *We Be Bug-Eyed Monsters, Yo*

  ANSWER: C.

(19) On what planet do they compare one's weight to that of salt?
  A. Mörflax
  B. Glorfyndrak
  C. Rogull
  D. Earth
  E. Marff

  ANSWER: D. (Another trick question. Had the question asked about granulontan, not salt, the answer would have been A.)

(20) The Kilgorians …
    A. … are a short-tempered lot.
    B. … are bent on death and destruction.
    C. … love Gary Vaniloe.
    D. … have six arms.
    E. … can dance a jig like nobody's business.
    F. … pick their noses when pleased.
    G. All of the above.
    H. None of the above
    I. Most of the above
    J. All except E

    ANSWER: G. They really can cut a rug, those Kilgorians. It's the tail.

(21) How many Boojilians does it take to screw in a light bulb?
    A. 43 (one to hold the light bulb, 42 to maneuver the starship on a counter-clockwise Y-axis trajectory)
    B. 2 (one to screw it in, one to write a poem about it)
    C. 12 (one to demonstrate the process, eleven to sign up for the Light Bulb Breakout Session at the Annual Boojilian Feel Good About Your Appendages Conference)
    D. 1,642 (two to ask how they could possibly get inside the light bulb; the other 1,640 to ask what a light bulb is. Wait, the light bulb *still* doesn't get screwed in, does it? Make this Zero.)

    ANSWER: All of the above.

(22) The rings of Saturn are composed of:
    A. Old Hulk Hogan shirts
    B. Booted-off reality show contestants
    C. Lost socks
    D. Cans of New Coke, 8-track tapes, Sony Beta machines, and floppy disks
    E. Donald Trump's exes

    ANSWER: C.

(23) INGA stands for
    A. International Navicular Gadgetry Association
    B. Integrated Navigational Guidance Assistant
    C. International Nanotechnology Guarantee Administration
    D. Integrated Navigational Grooming Assistant
    E. Intergalactic Noxious Gallbladder Aficionados
    F. Ignorant Neanderthals Going Ape

    ANSWER: B. (D would only be true if the question had been posed in past-tense. F is true if you happen to be at a soccer tournament.)

(24) Which of the following statements about Marvin's character Yolando Plumadore
are true?

A. Brought up by orangutans
B. Loves chocolate-covered macaroons
C. Spent his youth as a street urchin in Morocco
D. Has incredible intestinal fortitude (literally *and* figuratively)
E. Was rescued by Bhutanese monks

> *ANSWER:* All of the above. Just because I hadn't mentioned the macaroons
> doesn't make it not true.

(25) Which of the following is fictional? Circle all that apply:

Alexander the Great
Peter the Great
Catherine the Great
Olegstanislavitzki the Great
The Great Depression
The Great Famine
The Great Molasses Flood of 1919
The Great Dictator
The Great Gatsby
The Great Santini
The Great Gildersleeve
The Great Pacific Garbage Patch
The Great Pyramid of Giza
The Great Wall of China
The Great Barrier Reef
The Great Lakes
The Great Rogullian Way-Station of Earth
Great Caesar's Ghost
Great Balls of Fire
Stacey Brillstein

> *ANSWER:* Do your own work.

(26) Who is the most humorless person on the planet:

A. Ssgt. Gregory Humblecryer of Camp Pendleton, California
B. Dr. Fliegish Morgenstern, D.D.S., who evidently does not like to be paid in
pennies
C. Will Shortz, crossword editor of the *New York Times,* who thinks it's funny to
put *whole words in single squares.*
D. The guy who writes *"Whitney."*
E. Your mother!

> *ANSWER:* A (and maybe E; you tell me.)

(27) Pookie, Foggbottom's little skerlish, is from ...
A. Ping
B. Pong
C. Pog
D. Poughkeepsie

ANSWER: C.

(28) Essay question #1. In 25 words or less, refute the following statement, with references: *"Mark Twain and Albert Einstein were really the same person."* 50 points. Spelling counts.

_____
_____
_____
_____
_____
_____

(29) Essay question #2: In 50 words or less, refute the following statement, with references: *"Mark Twain and Albert Einstein WEREN'T really the same person."* 50 points. Spelling counts.

_____
_____
_____
_____
_____
_____

(30) Essay question #3: Your narrator pointed out that a single figure of speech — "It's what's under the hood that counts" — could be used to sell a Dodge Charger or hoochie skanks on the streets of Berlin. See how many figures of speech you can come up with to describe a hoochie skank. Conversely, see how many hoochie skanks you can come up with who can describe a figure of speech. 10 points for each of the former, 50 points for each of the latter. Spelling still counts.

_____
_____
_____
_____
_____
_____

(31) Essay question #4. Compare, contrast and elaborate upon the items described in Foggbottom's inner sanctum. The detailed curves and inlaid wood of Louis XIV furniture, for instance, often embellished with gold-leaf, which one usually associates with the courts of Baroque Europe, sharply contrasts with seersucker, which one usually associates with fried chicken. Do you see any symbolism here? What kind of symbol would a penned unicorn represent? What about African masks? What about the suit of armor? What about the sextant? Did you giggle when you read the word *sextant*? What does this tell us about the designer of such a room? What does this tell us about its occupant? What does this tell us about Louis XIV? What does it tell us about the fellow who came up with the word *sextant*? [Six extra points if you can get in a good stab at the French. Twelve if you can do it without compound adjectives. Fifteen if you can do it without the word "deodorant." (Okay, that one's just mean.)]

_____

_____

_____

_____

_____

_____

(32) List here as many words from your Mnemonic Device Recall List from Chapter Four. (Seriously? Yup.) 5 points each. The first has been filled in for you.

CUCUMBER   _____

_____   _____

_____   _____

_____   _____

(33) Marvin guessed at the purpose of the rings of the Hel-IX. Just for kicks, see if you can come up with what might have happened had he guessed wrong. Feel free to attach additional pieces of paper or to write your answer in code.

_____

_____

_____

_____

_____

_____

_____

(34) Use this space to draw a picture of Yolando Plumadore:

(35) Use this space to draw a picture of yourself:

(36) Use this space to draw a picture of yourself reading
Winged Avengers of the Apocalypse:

(37) Use this space to draw a puppy:

Aw. That's really cute. Can you draw a skeleton?

❏ Yes   ❏ No   ❏ Bite me

YOUR SCORE:

_____

About the Author...

BUSINESS OWNER, magazine art director, graphic designer, freelance editor, book designer. That's what D. S. THORNTON *used* to do ... before it drove her off-the-frickin'-charts insane. Today, she puts her own images to paper, writing and illustrating to her heart's content. Which is much much nicer indeed.

Ms. Thornton makes her home on the Big Island of Hawaii, where time is relative, gardening is serene, and there are way way *way* too many vowels. She lives with her husband, Donald, and their little dog, Paco. You can find her in the jungle amid the ohias and palms, often wielding a stylus or paint brush, or, sometimes, giggling at the keyboard.

An admitted television addict (ask her Robert Petrie's middle name), she is an avid gardener, a pretty good cook, a fan of the (very) occasional dirty martini (gin, natch; don't get her going), and really did attend Harmony Hills Elementary School and Zadok Magruder High. She couldn't have thought up funnier names.

Makin' like an artist.

Find her online at:
www.thorntonarts.com
Twitter: @D_S_Thornton
Facebook: www.facebook.com/DSThorntonIllustwriter

Acknowledgments...

I COULD NOT HAVE PRODUCED this book without the help of so many, and by "many" I mean: "I don't know who you people are, you Wikipedia contributors, but I wouldn't know a rod from a cone without visiting your pages on the human eye ... or Machu Picchu, killer whales, the Moon, Spanish conquistadors, Bhutan, and the rest." I thank you.

Others, I can name: first off, many thanks to my husband, Donald, for leaving me the eff alone while I was struggling with plot lines and forgetting to make dinner; to my son, Mark, for reminding me that retroactive continuity totally rocks; to Bambi Nicklen, who do that voodoo that she do so well; to my small-but-trusty cadre of editor friends including the good folks at *Stanford* magazine for steering me toward better sentences; thanks to early readers for their kind encouragement, with special shout-outs to Doreen Peri, Mary Larenas, Kathy Watts, Jill Vanderweit, and Robert Schiff for their thoughtful and critical eye; to all my sisters for their support; and to Stephen Prosapio, whose e-publishing workshop convinced me the world had changed. A Big-Ass-Love-Hug goes to Reader Extraordinaire Bahia Simons-Lane, whose feedback and counsel was always beyond the call of duty.

Last but not least, a final word of gratitude goes to the baffling world of "humor" literary agents who routinely turn down anything that's not that elusive needle-in-a-haystack they're evidently waiting for; if it weren't for those ever-so-nonchalant punches in the stomach, I wouldn't have taken the plunge. I am grateful for the control I secretly wanted anyway.

Muchos mahalos, all.

— D. S. Thornton, September 2012, Kea'au, HI

19684129R00179

Made in the USA
Charleston, SC
06 June 2013